Praise for

'*The Final Party* is the best kind of psychological thriller – compelling, accomplished and atmospheric. Superbly paced and plotted, I raced through it. A. A. Chaudhuri has rapidly established herself as a crime writer to watch. Recommended.'

M.W. Craven

'A dark and twisty read full of secrets set against a stunning Amalfi Coast background where everyone has secrets and no one can be trusted.'

Catherine Cooper

'A. A. Chaudhuri is one of the best writers of crime fiction around. You will keep turning the pages of this book late into the night. *The Final Party* has intriguing characters in a riveting story, full of secrets, lies and betrayal. I thoroughly recommend!'

Howard Linskey

'*The Secret History* meets *The Holiday*, only darker, sexier and absolutely crammed full of twists and suspense. It's a big, fat 5 stars from me.'

Lisa Hall

'A dark and addictive thriller set amidst a gorgeous Italian backdrop, it's well deserving of 5 sparkling stars. I loved it!'

Jane Isaac

'Thrilling twists, terrific characters and a settling to die for. *The Final Party* is a thoroughly gripping ride!'

B P Walter

'A dark, captivating, and sumptuous thriller. Completely addictive and utterly atmospheric. Chaudhuri pulls you in and doesn't let you go until the final page.'

Julie-Ann Corrigan

'A compelling page turner with a gasp around every corner. If you're looking for a holiday read, then this is the perfect unravelling of a friendship built on secrets and lies.'

Lauren North

'A tortuous web of secrets and lies – I could not put it down.'

Marion Todd

'*The Final Party* is a perfect "just-one-more-page" summer holiday read. A gorgeous location. Dark and deadly secrets. And a brewing storm that – when it hits – leaves no one unscathed. I absolutely loved it.'

Derek Farrell

'The most well plotted and expertly told thriller I've read in years … a masterpiece of deception, betrayal and murder that will astound you till the very last page.'

Graham Bartlett

'Draws you into a dark web of secrets and lies that unravel with exquisite timing in a beautiful setting.'

Sarah Clarke

The Final Party

A. A. Chaudhuri is a former City lawyer. After gaining a degree in History at University College London, she later trained as a solicitor and worked for several major London law firms before leaving law to pursue her passion for writing. She lives in Surrey with her family, and loves films, all things Italian and a good margarita!

Also by A. A. Chaudhuri

She's Mine
The Loyal Friend
The Final Party

A.A. CHAUDHURI

The Final Party

hera

First published in the United Kingdom in 2023 by

Hera Books
Unit 9 (Canelo), 5th Floor
Cargo Works, 1-2 Hatfields
London SE1 9PG
United Kingdom

A CIP catalogue record for this book is available from the British Library.

Print ISBN 978 1 80436 364 5
Ebook ISBN 978 1 80436 363 8

Look for more great books at www.herabooks.com

Printed and bound in Great Britain by Clays Ltd, Elcograf S.p.A.

I

For Dad, thank you for booking our first holiday to Sorrento all those years ago. I will always treasure the wonderful memories you, Mum and I made. Love you so much, always. xx

Every guilty person is his own hangman.

Lucius Annaeus Seneca, Roman Stoic Philosopher,
4BC–65AD

Prologue

The storm has finally abated. The trees no longer being punched from every angle, the rain less fierce. More of a sedate spitting than a persistent pinballing of hailstones. The wind has died down too. For much of the night, until around 3 a.m., it had howled like an animal in pain. Now there is more of a soft whisper travelling through the air, causing a faint rustling of leaves, the chirping of birds and tittering of insects just about audible having previously been drowned out by the thunderous elements. But the sky remains a grim fossil grey, a hue that sits ill with the usually heavenly scenery. Bleak and ominous but scarily fitting for what awaits them.

The poolside area is soaked. Mammoth-sized puddles of water have gathered in certain patches, causing the officers recently called to the scene to tread cautiously for fear of slipping underfoot, while a carpet of sodden leaves and stray twigs has layered the normally spotless swimming pool.

But there's something else in the water. Something that catches their attention as they venture further.

A body, floating face down. Swimming in its own blood.

They eye the rest of the villa's inhabitants suspiciously.

Six friends had started the week on seemingly good terms, here for a rest and the perfect birthday celebration.

But the perfect week in paradise has turned into the holiday from hell.

Because one of them is dead.

One of them is a killer.

But which of them here is *guilty?*

Chapter One

Padma

Three Days Ago
Surrey, England, Monday, 5th August 2019

No turning back now. This is it. Let the holiday commence.

I say this to myself as the taxi pulls away from our three-bed semi in Walton, situated at the end of a quiet cul-de-sac. It's 5 a.m. and, predictably, there's no one about. Not that I can see much in the dead of night, particularly when it's sheeting down with rain. Who knows what creep might be lurking in the shadows, even though it's true to say we live in one of the safer neighbourhoods in the area. Something I made sure of before we bought the place. I know it's no way to exist – forever on edge, fearing the worst – but old habits die hard, and the reality is I'll never be able to shed a suspicion that's been ingrained in me for nearly twenty years. It's who I am, who I'll always be since that night. The night that changed my life. Everything about me, really. Including the course of my future, and who I chose to spend it with.

The cab turns onto the main road, and I check my handbag once again, making sure I have Nick's and my passports. I'm a stickler for being organised, prepared. One of those people who turns up at least half an hour early for any kind of engagement, gets stressed if I'm running even a few minutes late. It's not like I suffer from OCD or anything, I just don't like surprises, or being put under pressure. So different to how I was in my teens, when I revelled in spontaneity, taking risks, seeing where life took me. Happy carefree days.

I'm a shadow of my twenty-year-old self, intent on taking the world by storm and letting nothing and no one get in my way. My friends and family would tell me this in the immediate aftermath of what happened. Not to hurt me; at least, I don't think so. But because it saddened them to see me so altered. And so, when they mentioned the change they had seen in me, it was in a head-cocked-to-the-side sympathetic, almost pitiful tone of voice they hoped would comfort me, but only ended up doing the opposite because it actually made me feel like some kind of charity case who needed to be soothed to sleep to stop the nightmares from returning. The fact is, I didn't need them to confirm who or what I had become since the darkest time of my life; I knew it in my gut to be true. I still do. And it's the reason I've battled depression on and off. Why I'm so anal about triple-checking that I've locked all the doors before I go to bed. Why I can never seem to shed this cloak of melancholy that weighs me down like a black cloud that refuses to lift even when pierced with chinks of sunlight. The truth is, my changed personality isn't the cause of my depression. The reason I sometimes feel unable to get out of bed. Why I sporadically take anti-depressants and reach for the wine a little too often.

It's the not knowing *how* and *why* it happened that's driven me near crazy over time. Not to mention *who* is responsible for turning me into a nervous wreck.

Relieved to see the passports are there, I tuck them back in the middle fold of my handbag, zip it up then rest my head against the back of the leather seat and momentarily close my eyes.

We're headed for Gatwick, taking the 8.30 a.m. flight to Naples, Italy, and from there a hire car to Sorrento on the Neapolitan Riviera where we'll be celebrating an old friend's birthday. It's somewhere I've long wanted to visit, but until now have never had the chance. Or perhaps the motivation to organise. Holidays abroad take so much effort, and Nick and I have tended to stay in the UK, enjoying coastal summer breaks in Devon or cosy winter weekends up in Scotland. I say I've not had the motivation, but my fear of flying doesn't help. Any jolt or tremor has my heart going like the clappers, plus all those funny noises make me nervous. Despite Nick always being at pains to point out that they're perfectly normal. 'It's just the flaps opening, darling,' 'just the plane levelling off, it's not dropping, I promise.' Having said that, we've been to Spain a few times over the years – it suits our budget better – and so that's been nice. Time alone with Nick always is, and with both of us having demanding jobs – being a social worker I always feel guilty about abandoning my clients to swan off on holiday – we don't get nearly enough quality time together when we can unwind and switch off. But this week will be different. Spent with four of our closest friends – Vanessa and her husband Marcus, and Lana and her husband, Johnny. Despite our closeness, we don't make a habit of vacationing together. In fact, it's rare we gather as a group anymore, despite having known each other for the best part of twenty years. Except for Marcus, that is, who came on the scene later. The last time we were all together was for Lana and Johnny's youngest's confirmation ceremony. None of the Harker family are regular churchgoers, but it was the 'done' thing to do, making the back pages of *Tatler*, and poor young George didn't get a say. Neither did Lana. Hard to believe their eldest, Josh, is fifteen now; I'm not sure where the time has gone. In all honesty, I never thought her and Johnny would last that long. I don't think any of us did.

As is always the way, despite me, Johnny, Nick and Vanessa being firm friends at Oxford, over the years we've drifted apart, what with the pressures of work, kids, life in general, although I've often wondered if that's something we all say to avoid what's really going on here. The fact that there are too many cobwebs in our pasts, too many secrets, resentments and unspoken jealousies that rise to the surface and threaten to spill over whenever we are together and too much alcohol has been consumed. It's why I was slightly surprised when Vanessa, who turns forty on Wednesday, suggested this week. She must have new friends she'd want to celebrate with? Easy, uncomplicated friends. History can never be erased, no matter how many boundaries you erect. Or however many years go by. Certainly, since what happened to me in our final year at Oxford, I've never felt as relaxed in our group as I once did. I couldn't wait to graduate so I could escape the place. Escape the people associated with it. Our reunions only serve to bring back memories of that time: the fear, the pain, the uncertainty. The sense of betrayal. Nick says I need to let bygones be bygones, but it's easy for him to say – he didn't go through hell like I did. He wasn't let down by the one person I'd expected to be there for me, come what may.

Vanessa is the first of us from uni to hit the big four-zero. Only Marcus, who she met eight years after we graduated, can trump that at forty-two. Although I have to say he looks like he's pushing fifty. Perhaps that's what quitting law to become a stay-at-home dad does to you. I'm only speculating based on what I've heard, from other couples who have kids. The hardest job in the world, apparently. Although I wouldn't be able to comment on that, as much as it saddens me. As much as it fires the guilt in me. Then again, I'm pretty sure his premature lines and salt-and-pepper hair aren't solely the result of having two full-on kids to fuss over. I'm betting they stem from deeper, darker issues. Issues Marcus hides well, but I can tell grate at his soul. Takes one to know one I suppose.

I open my eyes and turn to look at my husband who's busy checking BBC Sport on his phone. Why are men so obsessed with that website? It's like a compulsion. 'Are you looking forward to this week, babe?' I hear the tone of my voice. A sense of dread pervading its inflection rather than eager anticipation. Something Nick picks up on instantly. He always reads me so well. Right from the first, he had this uncanny knack for seeing into my soul. It's why I was so drawn to him.

'Yes, sure, aren't you?' He puts his phone away, looks up to meet my gaze while pushing his glasses to the bridge of his nose and giving my hand a little squeeze. The way he often does when we take a cab and find ourselves sharing the backseat. He does it inside a plane too, particularly at take-off and landing, when I'm at my most nervous. I smile gratefully at him, give a little squeeze back. He's as attentive as the day we married in front of thirty friends and family at Islington registry office, followed by a low-key do at the Islington Arms. Not the big Hindu ceremony my father had wanted, but what with him being a bit of a rebel in his youth and Mum being English, it's not like he ever enforced his religion on me or my brother as children, so I wasn't about to start as an adult. Particularly as I don't really believe in anything. Nick's C of E but in name only, so wasn't much bothered about having a religious ceremony either. Said all that mattered was me becoming his wife, and all the pomp and ceremony was immaterial. I was so relieved, I couldn't have coped with the stress of organising a big white wedding, or the six-day ordeal of a Hindu one. That's just not me, and it's not Nick either. It's what I love about him. He may not have the gift of the gab or debonair charm of his best friend, my ex, Johnny, but he was there for me when I needed a steady pair of hands. A comfort blanket who made me feel safe and secure when the world around me no longer made sense.

Which is why I hate myself for lying to him all this time. Why I feel that I don't deserve his love. In fact, sometimes it's hard to look him in the eye because the guilt is so breathtakingly acute. Twisting at my guts. Causing me sleepless nights. He of all people deserves my honesty. But I'm just not sure he'd understand if I were to tell him the truth.

'Sort of,' I say as the rain continues to batter the windows like a volley of machine gun pellets. Good old English summer weather. Never fails us. 'It's just, well, Johnny can get so mouthy when he's had a few, and you know how things can become a bit tense between him and Marcus. Marcus hates how close he and Ness are, it's obvious.'

Nick frowns, pushing his glasses against his face once more. I think it's become a bit of a habit, but I daren't pull him up on it. There're a lot worse faults a man could have. I should know. 'Johnny and Ness are childhood friends. Practically grew up together with their dads being as thick as thieves. You know that.'

'It's always felt like a bit more than that, though, hasn't it?' I say. God, I'm so bloody tired. I stifle a yawn, having barely slept last night, not that I was ever going to get a proper night's rest with an early start on the cards. Unlike Nick, who can fall asleep at the drop of a hat, I always take time to drift off, my mind beset by the same dream that plays on a loop night after night. Although lately that dream has evolved into something far worse. A nightmare that haunts my waking hours, consuming my thoughts and threatening my sanity. And last night I kept thinking about the week ahead, worrying how it was all going to pan out. 'A sort of us-against-the-world thing,' I explain further. 'Even when Johnny and I were dating I felt it. Not that he and Ness ever excluded me, there was just something in the way they behaved around each other. A closeness that seemed as natural as the stars in the sky.'

Nick sighs. 'I guess that's true. But look at their fathers – a high-profile Tory MP beset by scandal in the case of Johnny, and a wanker banker CEO who never gave poor Ness the time of day. Not to mention a couple of pretentious plastic mothers who preferred the company of wine, the gym and Botox to their only children. It's no surprise they found solace in each other with no siblings to confide in. That they're both a bit screwed up in their own ways.' Nick gives a chuckle, but it feels inappropriate to me, and I sense it does to him too. But it's the kind of reaction men often give in such situations, simply because they're generally not so good at emotional stuff. 'Makes me grateful for my humble upbringing in Pompey,' he goes on. 'Unlike Johnny, I never had to worry about the tabloids poking their noses into my life. And Mum and Dad couldn't have been more supportive parents.' He smiles at me. 'Bit like yours.'

I smile back, thinking how right he is. There's a pause as the taxi turns onto twisty backroads — a short cut presumably — the rain still battering its shell from every angle before it eventually hits the M25. After a minute or two, Nick says with a chuckle, 'Forget Marcus, I'm more worried about the laser beams Lana fires at Johnny. All's not well in paradise, judging by the last time we saw them.'

He's right there. Only, I'm not sure they were ever in paradise. Certainly not on Johnny's part, at least. But Nick said Johnny had come to love Lana in his own way, didn't feel he could abandon her after what she went through. It's typical Nick — seeing the good in people. Especially his best mate. But it had always felt odd to me, and I sensed there was perhaps something else that bound them together. Something bigger. Darker. And although she never said as much, I could tell when we watched Johnny place that ring on Lana's finger on their wedding day at The Hurlingham Club sixteen years ago that Ness was thinking the same.

'Oh well, at least it'll be nice to leave this grim weather behind and get some sunshine,' I say more cheerily. 'And it'll be good for Ness to chill out for a bit. Let her hair down. I swear to God that law firm will be the death of her. She seems to spend day and night there. When we spoke on the phone the other evening, she sounded worn out.'

'I dunno, I think she gets a kick out of it,' Nick says. 'It's just the way she's built. She's always been a go-getter, you know that. No one worked harder for their finals than her.'

He's right there. I, on the other hand, could barely focus on mine. I'd been predicted a first in English Literature but ended up with a 2:1. Luckily, my marks had been consistently high in the first two years, leaving me with a respectable overall grade. Not to mention the college taking my unfortunate circumstances into account. 'Yeah, maybe,' I say. 'Or maybe she just doesn't want to go home. You must have noticed the tension between her and Marcus.'

Nick gives me an incredulous look. 'She adores Marcus and the kids! Doesn't see enough of them, granted, but it's just the nature of her job. It's why I never wanted to work in the City, despite Johnny offering to put in a good word. Sure, it pays double my salary, but I wanted a life.' He squeezes my hand again. 'To spend quality time with you.'

I smile. Relieved that Nick never got sucked into that cutthroat world. Even so, despite the excuses he's making for Ness, there's just something about the way she behaves around Marcus that feels off to me. And I'm sensing that's why Marcus looks so distracted half the time. Because he feels it too.

'Then why does she avoid spending time with them?' I ask. 'That's what Marcus implied the last time we met up.'

'You don't think she's having an affair?' Nick looks genuinely shocked, as if the idea hadn't even crossed his mind.

I shrug my shoulders. 'Who knows. I mean, no, I don't think so. I don't think she's the cheating type. But I do think there's something else she's not telling us. Maybe we'll find out this week. I'll try and get her alone. Girls' heart-to-heart over a cocktail or two. Only I'll make sure Lana's otherwise engaged. Ness will never open up to me in front of her. You know as well as I do – she's never been Ness's favourite person.'

Chapter Two

Before

Oxford, England, mid-October 2001

Dear Luke,

How are you? How's the land of Oz? I know I promised to write since we last spoke on the phone, so here I am. You'll be pleased to hear I'm settling in OK after a bit of a shaky start. You know me, I'm such a homebody and I miss Mum and Dad like mad. Mum especially. I'm sure you could hear it in my voice, even though the line was a bit crap. Mum's always been my best friend — you know that better than anyone — and when I first got here, I wasn't sure if I'd made the right decision. Everyone seems so posh, so confident. OK, well, not everyone. But a lot of them are and I feel like a bit of an outsider, even though my grades suggest I deserve to be here. I don't know if it's the college I chose, but all the students seem like they're rolling in cash, which we never were, and I'm not sure I can compete. One of the girls on my floor is the daughter of a frigging Lord can you believe it? All her clothes are designer, and she looks and sounds like Tamara Beckwith or something. She also has a Porsche. And there's this other bloke whose dad is the CEO of some giant US investment bank. He's a bit of a dick but I guess he thinks he can get away with doing what the hell he pleases because his old man helped fund a new science block. It's a bit intimidating but

I'm trying my best to fit in. A few of the girls are normal like me, thank God. I tend to hang around with them. We've been out to the uni bar most nights – and don't worry, I'm not going mad, not getting shit-faced every night, having learnt my lesson the first week – also hung out in the junior common room and in our rooms together, just generally spent time getting to know one another. So I think I'll probably stick with them for the most part. One of them, Jenna, is reading History like me, and I'm hoping we'll be in the same tutor group. The College Master is a bit of a tyrant, although the second and third years claim he's a softie deep down. That he just likes to impose his authority on newbies from the start – you know, lay down the ground rules – but that once you get to know him and break through his surly exterior, he's OK. Not sure if they were winding us up, I know quite a bit of that goes on with freshers – playing pranks, doing dares, debauched drinking games just to embarrass the hell out of us etc, no doubt you had the same at Warwick – but somehow, I think they were being serious, and in any case, he's been fine with me, so I'm keeping my fingers crossed. I just need to stay out of trouble.

Freshers' week was good, although I got a bit pissed and threw up all over the bathroom floor the second night. It was a bit scary, actually, I thought I might have alcohol poisoning at one stage. I know you told me to take it easy, and generally I have been. You hear about students going too far and nearly dying and that scares the hell out of me. But I was just trying to fit in like I said and went a bit mad. Drinking's big here, you're almost made to feel like a wuss, a bit of a loser, if you don't drink loads, and I don't want to be the lonely dork, twiddling my thumbs in my room at night. But I've learnt my lesson and I promise to take it easy from now on. I've joined the debating society, as well as film club and the choir. Hopefully that way I'll get to make more friends. Might even join the Dramatic Society if I'm feeling brave enough. Who knows, I could be the next Emma Thompson even though she obviously went to Cambridge. You know how much I enjoyed drama at school, although things were obviously not quite on the same scale at Bankside Primary!

Tomorrow there's a big party for us freshers. Not everyone's invited so it's top secret, and Rachel, another of the 'normal' ones who I'm friendly with and who's also on the select guest list, said we should go because it's quite a privilege to be asked. Rach said the guys organising it are super popular and uber cool, so it'll be good to show my face and get in with the crowd that matters, and who can make your life easier. She said I just need to go with the flow and have fun. So, I think I will, having ummed and ahhed about it. Also, because there's this guy I've seen out and about who I quite fancy, and who I'm hoping will be there. I've only seen him a few times, in formal hall and the library, but he always smiles at me, like he might fancy me too. He's so cute, seems popular, and part of the cool crowd I mentioned which is why I'm hopeful he'll be there. I know you'll warn me to be careful, that guys are only after one thing, but I'm not stupid, I know how to take care of myself. I have done ever since that horrific episode. Anyway, let's see.

I hope you're getting on OK, and the trip is going well. I know you feel a bit guilty for not being around to take me to uni with Mum and Dad, but don't be. You've always been there for me, and of course I miss you, but you need to live your life, and I suppose it's good I try and stand on my own two feet. I can't rely on you forever, as much as I know you'll always look out for me. Something I'm grateful for. I hope you know that.

Take care, and make sure you write with all your news.

Hopefully you can come visit once you're back in the UK. There's something I need to tell you. A secret I've been keeping from you these past few months, just because I swore I'd keep it to myself. But it doesn't feel right hiding something so huge

*from you, there should be no secrets between us. It's so exciting,
life-changing really, and I hope you'll be as happy as me when I
tell you what it is.*

*But for now, don't worry, no harm's going to come to me. I'm
as safe as houses here.*

Love,

Leia

Chapter Three

Vanessa

Sorrento, Italy, Monday, 5th August 2019

Peace at last.

I open my eyes and savour the quiet; the rare ability to just lie here and do nothing. Usually, my day starts at 6 a.m. following a rude awakening by my alarm clock. No time to gather my thoughts, adjust my eyes to natural daylight. I'm up like a shot, straight in the shower, dressing in the spare room so as not to wake Marcus or the children, then it's a quick cup of black coffee thrust down my throat before I'm out the door and headed for Wimbledon Tube station, ready to battle the crowds onto the equally packed, stuffy Tube. *Bang, bang, bang.* And that's pretty much the speed at which I go about my entire day at the law firm where I'm a partner in the Corporate Department, until my head hits the pillow far later than is healthy in preparation for the same rat race routine the next day.

Marcus and I arrived at the villa yesterday morning. I thought it would be nice for us to have a day alone together before the others arrive. As much as I love Johnny to bits, he does tend to take over, and when that happens it's hard to get a quiet moment to ourselves. I think Marcus was surprised at my suggestion, just because I haven't been the most attentive of wives these past few years. I've had a lot on my mind, not just work, but other stuff too. Although he's not to know that. He must sense something's not right, though. There are only so many excuses one can give – ranging from work, to tiredness, to hormones – before it becomes tired. Suspicious, even.

The villa is positioned in the quaint hill town of Sant'Agata sui Due Golfi, which roughly means Saint Agatha on the Two Gulfs. I know from my research that Sant'Agata is the capital of the Sorrentine Peninsula which marks the division between the Gulf of Naples and the Gulf of Salerno. Less well known than the neighbouring glamourous hotpots of Amalfi and Positano, both of which I've no doubt Lana would have preferred to stay in, just because over the years she's become imbued with the traditional Harker snobbery, I like the fact that it's less commercialised, has more of a rustic feel to it that I find calming. Reached via a winding, craggy road leading up from the main town of Sorrento, the amazing panoramic views more than make up for the challenging route and need for a cab to get out and about. So tranquil, in contrast to the hustle and bustle of Sorrento with its relentless stream of traffic and tourists, it almost feels like I've been transported back in time, the perfect place for me to reassess my life. To make peace with my mistakes.

Having unpacked and familiarised ourselves with the villa, we'd ordered a cab back down to Sorrento around 6, and found the most glorious fish restaurant in the smaller of the two marinas – rather ironically named Marina Grande – where we dined on the freshest Dover sole washed down with some chilled white wine. It was like being back in the early stages of dating – chatting and laughing, getting to know one another again. No kids, no work. I'd never felt more alive, more free. We'd held hands trudging back up the path to Piazza Tasso, the central square and main hub of the town, having stopped off at a supermarket for some groceries, stumbling every so often as we were a bit tipsy by then. We got a cab from there to the villa and then, no sooner had we stepped inside the hallway, I threw my arms around Marcus's neck and kissed him long and hard, the heat of the balmy evening air having made me feel more sensual than I'd felt in a long time. I'm not sure he expected that. OK, so we were a tad drunk, and it's not like there haven't been occasions over the past few years when we've both had one too many. But last night was one of the rare times in that period that we'd properly *made love*. Lost in each other, like we had wanted it to last forever. I can't say I blame Marcus for being taken aback. I've been withdrawn from our marriage for so long now, my uncharacteristic desire to spend some quality time with him, but more so to get naked with him, must have come as quite a shock. Albeit a welcome one, I hope. It certainly felt like he was there in the moment with me as we'd ripped each other's clothes off before we'd even entered the bedroom, unable to contain our longing for one another. And it assured me that his love for me hasn't waned, despite my aloofness. Although, to be honest, even before last night, I guess I knew in my heart that Marcus still loves me deeply. I can feel it in his gaze, in the way he kisses my cheek before turning out the light, in the little things he does for me that shows me he cares. Not to mention the fact that he's obviously been saddened by my distant behaviour. Something that tears at my soul, but which has not been in my power to rectify.

Until now.

I'm not sure he's convinced I still love him as much as the day we said our vows nine years ago, though. And that also pains me. Because in truth, I love him more. The way he's taken a backseat from his career to raise Kitty and Owen while I forge ahead with mine at the firm makes him a hero in my eyes. There never was a kinder, more selfless man and our kids are so lucky to have him fully present in their lives. One of us should be. We decided that even before I got pregnant with Kitty eight years ago, eleven months after we married at The Dorchester. The best day of my life, aside from the births of our children. My childhood was so lacking in love, in parents who genuinely loved one another, I'd never imagined that one day I'd stand up and say my vows with a man who looked at me like I was the most beautiful woman he'd ever seen. Even though I'm not beautiful. Well, not in the classic sense of the word. I'm not blessed with delicate features, long lustrous hair or shapely curves that catch a man's eye off the street the way Padma is. It's not me and I've come to accept that. But the way Marcus looked at me on our wedding day made me feel like a catwalk model. And the same was true yesterday at the marina, as his gaze met mine across the table, a look that made me blush and sent a thrill of excitement through me as it had done on our first date. I was the happiest I'd been in a long time, and I hadn't wanted it to end.

When I first met Marcus, who'd joined my firm as a partner, eight years after I left Oxford and was a year off partnership myself, I knew I'd met 'the One'. Until then no man had sparked my interest the way he did. I've never been one for being with someone for the sake of it. Some people need the company of another human being to feel whole, secure, but that's never been me. I'd rather be alone than with someone who doesn't fulfil me in all the ways I want and need them to. There's always been something 'real' about Marcus, a vulnerability that drew me to him. Not only that, he's smart, warm and funny. The opposite of my father, I suppose. The father who never loved me in the way I had secretly prayed that he would. There was no point in me trying to convince him otherwise. Such love should never be forced. That's not how it's meant to work.

When our kids were born, I vowed they'd never grow up feeling that way. Dumped with the childminder, whose face they knew better than their own parents. Not feeling they could talk to us about their worries or fears, because we were far too wrapped up in our own lives and, anyway, that's what the childminder was for. It's no wonder Johnny's such an attention seeker, as am I to a lesser extent. We both crave the love we never got from our parents as kids, both determined to make our marks on this world to give us that sense of self-worth, of being valued.

I guess that's partly why I excuse Johnny's behaviour, why I have such a soft spot for him. I get what he went through, why he is the way he is. Really, underneath that swagger, he's just a little boy wanting to be loved. And that's also why he did what he did. Why, when push came to shove, he needed an out. Even though that's by no means the full story.

Anyway, I hope after last night, Marcus realises I'd do anything for him. Despite me fearing that before this week is through his love for me will swiftly turn to hate. I don't deserve a man as decent as him. He should have chosen someone better. But for some reason he chose me. Perhaps because he thought I needed saving from my fucked-up parents. Or because he thought me to be a better person than I am. I'd like to think that I am, even though the guilt that weighs me down like a ball and chain suggests otherwise.

I stretch out my arms like a caged bird set free, spreading its wings for the first time in what seems like forever, unencumbered by the shackles of my hectic life, then rub the sleep from my eyes, gradually becoming more conscious of my surroundings. And as I do, I realise I am alone. I turn my head to Marcus's side of the bed, note his absence and assume he is perhaps downstairs making us some breakfast. I smile to myself as I again think back to pouncing on him in the hallway last night and him nearly dropping the grocery bags in shock. Now that would have been a messy affair. Smashed eggs all over the pristine parquet floor. The thought makes me giggle out loud.

My husband has always been a dab hand in the kitchen. He has a natural flair and artistic eye in the way he presents whatever he's rustled up that makes it appear so appetising. He says he gets it from his mother who always put a homecooked meal on the table. I can't recall either of my parents ever cooking anything from scratch in the entire time I lived under their roof. We had a housekeeper who did that for us. Dad was always out the door by 7 a.m., and chucking cereal into a bowl was about as much as my mother could manage. The kids love it when Marcus makes pancakes or French toast on the weekends. They'll come tearing into our room, tugging at the duvet, begging their father to wake up and get started on breakfast. And he'll pretend to groan and act all grumpy but really, he loves it, is just winding them up and then suddenly he'll come alive and bear hug the both of them, causing them to giggle uncontrollably. Precious moments I never had as a child but which I treasure for my children.

I yawn for the third time since waking up. One of those loud, unflattering yawns I'd never dare show in public, but somehow feels so satisfying in private. Despite getting eight hours overnight, I still feel exhausted. I'd like to think it's my body winding down, unused to this slower pace of life. Or perhaps down to the frantic, heady sex of last night. But I know different.

I almost don't want to move, but our friends will be here by 2-ish, and I need to ensure everything's perfect. Also, capitalise on the remaining time Marcus and I have alone together before the madness kicks in. In some ways, it'll be good to see their familiar faces, Johnny's especially. I think you reach a stage in life when you hanker after the proverbial. There's something comforting about it, experiencing that sense of nostalgia, slotting back into the group and almost feeling like we've never been apart because we know each other so well.

But I'm also dreading it.

The fact is, we all have our dark secrets, things we'd change in an instant if presented with a magic wand. Padma's about the only innocent one amongst us, but that's precisely why it's never easy seeing her. Her face is just a constant reminder of what we did. They say time's a healer, but it hasn't been for us, because we've not had the guts to face up to our pasts. We've been walking a tightrope ever since Oxford, never quite managing to relax even though, with every year that goes by, we should feel more secure in our freedom.

I unwrap myself from the safe cocoon of my duvet and force myself off the bed. Then pad barefoot to the French doors, before opening them up as wide as they go and stepping out onto the vast balcony where I soak in the view of the stunning Sorrentine coastline; a sight that makes me feel like I must have died and gone to heaven. Not that I believe in a heaven, or a hell, despite often thinking the latter is where I belong. It's only 9 a.m. but already the temperature must be pushing thirty, not a cloud in the powder blue sky. It's like the balcony tiles have underfloor heating, while the blast of warm air that envelops me like a second skin is a stark contrast to the ice-cool air conditioning of the bedroom.

The villa we're staying in belongs to a client of mine. The billionaire founder and CEO of an Italian car manu-facturer. When I happened to mention a few months ago that I had a big birthday coming up and wanted to get away, treat myself and my friends, he offered it to me free of charge. Said it was testament to the fabulous job I'd done for his company over the years and that he wouldn't take no for an answer. I said I couldn't possibly, just because it was the polite thing to say, although inside I was jumping for joy and hoping he'd insist. Which he did. Somewhat treacherously built into the cliffside with its own private lift down to the sea, the villa has four levels including a basement gym, and is more beautiful than I could ever have imagined. The photos on the website don't do it justice and I can't wait to see the looks on the others' faces when they get here. It's as if it's been built for royalty and when Marcus and I first arrived he'd joked about our being like imposters who would surely be kicked out as soon as we were discovered. We're no royalty, granted, but I couldn't help pointing out that we could probably afford to stay here off our own backs. A truth I know he often struggles with.

The exterior is equally stunning – a veritable oasis of verdant gardens and fragrant citrus groves, with sliding doors opening out from the largest sitting room onto a paved terrace offering outside dining, and just beyond that to the left a rectangular swimming pool flanked by sprawling palm trees beneath which Marcus and I had indulged in a nightcap of the local speciality – limoncello – after making love. A bottle had been left for us as a welcome gift on the kitchen sideboard, and so we sneaked downstairs – me in a flimsy satin chemise, Marcus in his pyjama bottoms – and drank it al fresco to the soothing sound of chattering cicadas and gently lapping ornamental fountains, not the faintest hint of a chill in the mild evening air. There's nothing overlooking us here, so it's very private, and we could pretty much run around the place naked, or commit murder, and no one would know.

Despite only being here a day, I feel like I never want to go back to London. To grey high rises and even murkier weather. To reality. This place couldn't be more perfect really. It's just a shame it's not going to end perfectly. Well, not in the usual sense of the word. But at least my mind will be free.

I'm just so relieved everyone could make it. We six all need to be here together, as one. That's the only way this week is going to end as it should.

The way I want and need it to.

It is time for a wrong to be righted.

For the truth to come out.

And then, before the year is over, I can die peacefully.

Chapter Four

Before

Oxford, England, mid-October 2001

They're coming for her. Gaining on her. The prey of feral beings she cannot outrun. It doesn't matter how smart she is. Sheer numbers are against her. It's only a matter of time.

She doesn't know these streets the way they do. She is an outsider amongst a city of natives – too smart, too fast, too driven. She knows nothing of choice hiding spots, untrodden paths or covert alleyways, perfect for concealment. She imagines their nostrils flared at the scent of unsullied blood, their lips salivating and greedy for the taste of victory – to them as sweet as ripe cherries grown under the glare of the Turkish sun; their appetites whetted and ravenous for fresh meat.

She is no match for them. Her capture is inevitable. She'd resigned herself to that even before she'd started to run. It's a rite of passage. And when she thinks on this it makes her feel a little nauseous. Just because of what happened before.

A multitude of voices, breathless with anticipation, draws closer with every second, as her own breathing becomes shallower, her gait slower, and yet her heartbeat gallops that much faster. Faster than she can ever remember it beating. The temperature is uncommonly warm, the air sultry, so close it almost chokes the air out of her, so still the leaves in the trees appear to be painted into the sky. No longer summer, the light is fading fast, although the unseasonable heat remains intense. She feels the sweat coating her brow, her top lip, smothering her back, her breasts, her underarms, like transparent lacquer. They won't care; if anything the spectacle will only arouse them more. She can just picture the excitement on their faces. In some warped way, she's kind of excited too. Just because she hopes it might lead her closer to the object of her affections. The one she'd told *her* about the other night on the phone. The one she hopes will capture her. Fall in love with her. Be the boyfriend she had always wanted. Although, admittedly, she might be getting a little ahead of herself. But she's also scared, and perhaps a little ashamed. After all, she had a choice to be involved.

Didn't she?

Closer still, and she fears she might faint with the sheer intensity of the adrenaline coursing through her veins.

This feels so real. But what calms her is that she knows it isn't. That she is living in a phony world. Not like what happened before. She remembers this, clings to it.

As the inevitable happens, and finally, she is caught.

But the worst isn't over.

The worst is yet to come.

And that isn't phony.

That is all too frighteningly real.

She just doesn't know it yet.

Chapter Five

Lana

Sorrento, Italy, Monday, 5th August 2019

We've just emerged onto steep roads set into a sheer limestone cliff-face dominating the other side of Naples, having left the airport and mad bullring of Italian drivers around thirty minutes ago, while safely bypassing the less-than-salubrious shipping town of Castellammare di Stabia via a long dark tunnel en route. I finally feel a little cooler having got very overheated in the short space of time we were standing outside the terminal building waiting for the dishy taxi driver who met us in the Arrivals area to bring the car round. He took one look at my scarlet face and wasted no time in turning the air con up full blast. It was so chaotic at Naples airport, much more so than at Gatwick, despite the terminal building being half its size, and having been up at an ungodly hour I didn't have much patience for loitering in the heat, a cacophony of horns and heated conversations ringing through the air, even though I benefited from valet parking at Gatwick then business class all the way. Here in Italy, it's termed 'organised chaos', things never happening in a hurry or in an orderly fashion the way we Brits tend to favour, but which get done eventually. One of Italy's many charms apparently, although I don't find it particularly endearing. Just goes to show how pampered I've become I suppose. How the smallest of things bothers me. It's appalling really, especially when I think about Nick and Padma just about managing their mortgage, not to mention my cousin, Jess, the only relative I'm close to, scrimping and saving her way through life. Camping in Wales is living it up for Jess and her family. In fact, I'm not sure her kids have ever been abroad. But sixteen years of being a member of the Harker clan has instilled the spoilt child in me, I guess. Once you get a taste of the good life, of having a husband, a family, a nice house, financial stability – something I always craved coming from a low-income single parent household – it's hard to give it up, and that's perhaps why I can't bring myself to leave Johnny. That, amongst other reasons. One of them being that I've simply sacrificed too much, including my own conscience, to throw it all away.

I really need to set a better example for my children, but I suppose I consider myself entitled to make the most of the few perks of being married to an arsehole. Being able to afford whatever I want being the main one.

I should feel free as we continue to drive, watching the bright blue expanse of the Mediterranean stretch out as far as the naked eye can see, the sunlight sparkling like tiny jewels on the crystal-clear calm water, yachts and speedboats dancing along it and making tiny waves in the process, jet skis speeding across making bigger ones, swimmers savouring the ocean's cool refreshment over their sun-kissed skins. It's a world away from the dismal conditions we left behind at Gatwick. Chilly, bleak and unseasonal for the time of year. It's also a break from my kids and the mundane nature of daily life. But I don't feel liberated. Instead, I feel like I'm swapping one prison cell for another. The sun may be shining here, the temperature fifteen degrees warmer, but really, it's not much different to the home I've left behind. Frosty and unforgiving. Just because I've not escaped the one person who makes it so. Or the guilt that eats away at me.

I've never been to this part of the world, and the sheer natural beauty of the area takes my breath away as we curve our way around the picturesque, yet hazardous coastal road. I gaze in wonder at the dramatic scenery, not just the astonishing views of the Gulf of Naples, Mount Vesuvius and the Isle of Capri, but the orange, lemon and olive groves descending the slopes down towards the sea, lush vineyards offering the ripest olives and sweetest grapes abounding on either side. It's heaven on earth. A place that exudes hope, life, and vitality. Every couple in love's paradise. So why do I feel like I am headed for hell? Who am I kidding, I know exactly why – it's the thought of being stuck in one place with the five people who make me feel the most ill at ease, my husband being top of the list. At least in London I only have to see him in the evenings or on weekends, and even then, he's often out with clients, or if he is at home, I can escape to another room in our vast six-bedroom house in Barnes, or use the kids as a distraction. Alternatively, he's up in the sodding gym, honing his perfect body, while I secretly stuff my face with crisps. But there's no escaping each other here. It feels weird being child-free. Any normal happily married woman my age with children would be lapping up a week away without the kids, the chance to feel like a desirable woman again, looking forward to a week of uninterrupted sex, dusting off her sexy lingerie, fully waxed and raring to go, excited about the idea of rediscovering her husband, of fucking his brains out and being fucked senseless right back. But that's not the case for us, it never has been, and it makes me sad, brings home to me just how messed up we are. Instead of revelling in a child-free week, I wish more than anything the kids were here to act as a buffer. An excuse not to have to make conversation with each other or reflect on our regrettable pasts.

Johnny's nodded off as usual. Missing all this stunning scenery as the taxi winds its way around one bend after the other, making me feel slightly queasy, a persistent stream of noisy Vespers mounted by aspiring Lewis Hamiltons fearlessly overtaking us on either side, a string of tiny beaches passing beneath us, strewn with sunworshippers shaded by parasols or with their faces exposed to the sun's fierce rays. Jesus Christ, he pretends to be such a culture vulture but really, he's all mouth and no trousers. Just like his pig of a father. All part of his showman façade and innate arrogance. An arrogance I once found so hot, so irresistible, but which over the years has found me loathing him more and more. Although, and rather vexingly, whenever I catch sight of him naked, or in nothing but his boxers, I still fancy him. Still feel the urge to run my hands all over his body and imagine him screwing me. Because I can't deny that he's good at that. He always has been. Even though the first time we had sex, it wasn't all candles and roses the way I had hoped it would be. It's the only time I let my guard down, though – when I find myself turned on by his naked body. I'm still human after all, still have my needs, my desires, like any red-blooded woman. But when he opens his mouth, when he spouts his venom at me, gives me a look that tells me he wishes we'd never crossed paths, that's when I find myself wanting to chop his balls off. Guess it's to be expected. That I deserve it. After all, if you lie and cheat and scheme

31

your way into someone's affections, and at the expense of others, why the hell should you expect anything better in return? I never believed in Karma before. You don't when you're young, because you consider yourself untouchable; you have no idea how your actions can come back to bite you. But now I do. If only I could turn back time, make different choices. With the benefit of hindsight, I'm certain that I would have followed a different path. Owned up to what I knew, then gone on to marry someone average like me. A man who might actually have loved me, respected me, not made me feel like a poor second best. But I can't expect applause for wanting to change the past. That doesn't suddenly make me a good person – my regretting the decisions I made, failing to act when I knew someone close to me was in trouble because it suited my own ends. The fact is, I made a choice back then, a choice I knew in my heart was wrong, and it's cost me dearly. I have no option but to live with it, make the best of things, for my children's sakes, if not for mine. But as I contemplate the week ahead, it almost feels like my past is catching up with me. Toying with me. Wanting to elevate my awkwardness, my regret, to heights that make me dizzy with lack of oxygen. I can't and I mustn't spend too much time around them. It's the only way to get through this week alive and with my secrets intact. That, and making sure no one else takes it upon themselves to spill them. That's always been a worry at the back of my mind. I trust myself to keep my mouth shout, but do I trust the others? Especially when too much alcohol's been consumed, as it inevitably will be this week when the six of us get together.

I look at my watch. Just after midday. Eleven a.m. in the UK. I wonder what Erin and George are up to. I know Josh will be out with Jess's eldest, Lyle, perhaps kicking a ball around or at the skate park. I'm already missing their faces, even though they inevitably drive me up the wall half the time. Josh especially, now that he's a mouthy teenager and neither Johnny nor I can ever say anything right. I try not to take offence, try not to feel hurt by my child, the one who I grew inside me, but it's hard. Although, after losing our first child at sixteen weeks gone, I've since made a point of berating myself whenever I feel like I'm taking them for granted or not being as patient as I should be. My children are a gift from God, not to be taken lightly. They're also the only three human beings in this world who love me unconditionally. As I do them. They're the best thing I've done with my life, a thought I cling to whenever I have the urge to run away or worse, end it all. They, and they alone, keep me going through the darkest times, and that's why although we could afford it, I shun childminders and nannies. The last thing I want is them turning into their father. And I'm so glad they have each other. For me, growing up as an only child was lonely, and that's why I always wanted Josh to have siblings, as did Johnny. One thing we agreed on at least.

No doubt Erin and George are having a blast with my cousin's younger kids, running amok around her tiny house in Dorset. Or monopolising the PlayStation if the weather is bad. Jess is so chilled compared to me. So content and together, both in her work as a midwife and in her life with boring, yet reliable mechanic husband, Tim. Despite not having our wealth, living the simple life. What I wouldn't give to trade places with Jess and experience what it feels like to be adored by the man you're married to. I bet the kids pick up on the difference between our house and theirs whenever they visit. And I don't mean the fact that theirs is half the size. Rather, that it's full of laughter and hugs, silly pranks and playful jibes rather than clipped conversation and malicious snipes. Johnny and I try our best not to argue in front of them, but they're bright little things, they know all's not right between their parents, even though they never say anything. Especially when he comes home drunk and gets vindictive with me. Then again, perhaps they're not bothered, purely because they've never known any different. But that in itself is pretty fucked up, isn't it? That's not the way children of ten, twelve and fifteen should exist.

As always, the person I'm dreading seeing the most this week is Padma. And not purely because of the way Johnny's gaze always falls upon her like she's the most exquisite thing he's ever seen. He thinks he's being discreet, that I don't see the lust in his eyes. But I do. Everyone does. Even Nick. God knows why he tolerates it, but then again, he's always been a bit of a wet blanket. Although that's better than being a selfish, womanising prick I suppose. But really, my husband's hard-on for his ex is the least of my worries. In truth, it's seeing her tortured expression that makes my guts seize up. And that's why I'm so abrupt with her, can barely look her in the eye, even though she doesn't deserve the cold shoulder.

Marcus is the only one I can be normal around. I wonder if he notices the friction between me and Ness. He must do, but I'm certain Ness tells him it's all in his imagination. She's always been good at acting like everything's fine, taking charge. Directing Johnny on how to behave. Telling him that so long as he follows her lead to the tee all will be well. But I often wonder how she feels deep down. Surely there must come a stage when it all gets a bit too much?

The radio is tuned to some local Italian pop station. I've no idea what the singer is going on about, but I find myself drumming my fingers along with the music all the same. As I do I catch the eye of the cab driver and he gives me a smile. I'm in awe of his relaxed style, the way his elbow casually rests on the open window while he navigates the perilous bends as if it's child's play. He's bloody gorgeous, must be in his mid-twenties with jet-black hair and that classic Italian olive skin. I fleetingly imagine him stopping the car, pulling Johnny from the backseat, and hurling him over the cliff before taking me on the bonnet and driving me to unbearable heights of ecstasy. *Stop it!* I scold myself. *Don't go there! It's never going to happen, and besides, he'd never want you so why torture yourself?* I pinch my sides, feel the love handles that have never shifted post-pregnancy, not that I've ever tried that hard, what incentive did I have? There just seemed little point and anyway, besides my kids, I like the company of cake and wine way too much to give them up for the gym or some fad diet. I could ask Johnny for a divorce, I suppose, it's not like I want him so bad it hurts the way I used to, but it would feel like giving in, and I can't bear to give him the satisfaction of being free of me. Neither do I want my children being raised in two different homes. He'll never grant me sole custody, so they'd be constantly turfed from one to the other. I can't stand for them to bear the brunt of such instability. And, like I said, it would make everything I did back then feel so pointless.

The cab continues to swerve its way around the cliff-face and, as it does, I watch Johnny's head loll from side to side. I wonder what he's dreaming about? Maybe he's fantasising about having sex with Padma this week. That she'll magically forget about Nick and fall back into his arms and they'll skip off into the sunset together. I feel a surge of envy just thinking about it despite the disdain I have for my husband. He's never looked at me the way he looks at her, and that's what I resent the most. Not being desired by a man the way she was and continues to be. By Johnny, by Nick, by God-only-knows who else. She doesn't know how lucky she is.

Once we were best friends – at primary school you couldn't tear us apart, we did everything together, and I loved her like a sister. I remember her being a little shyer back then; she'd get picked on by the playground bullies who'd mock her for being a 'half-breed'. I'd defend her, make it all right, and she'd been grateful, almost worshipped me for making the bullies stop. But then puberty hit and changed us. Me for the worse, her for the better. Blossoming from a skinny little brown girl to a curvy, raven-haired beauty who had all the boys hitting on her. And that in turn had elevated her confidence while undermining mine. Boyish, flat-chested, I was the classic plain Jane to whom no one gave a second glance. And even though we continued to be friends, through senior school and into our university days, I found my resentment growing, particularly when she'd proffer 'helpful' hair and fashion advice, back when she had her sights on being a women's fashion magazine editor, patronising me in front of her smart Oxford friends as if I belonged in a different class going to Leeds and didn't fit in amongst her elitist crowd. That's how I took it, anyway. She only grew up in a row of three-bed semis like me, for God's sake. Attended the local state comp, which had some pretty rough kids, and even rougher parents. But her dad had

I am alone. An empty chair to my left, several vases of brightly coloured flowers on the table to my right. I wonder to myself who they are from.

It's obvious where I am, and now I feel really scared. Dizzy with fright, in fact, making me want to vomit. I'm in a hospital, but why am I here? Am I ill, did I suffer some terrible accident? What happened to me?

And most importantly, *why can't I remember who the hell I am?*

Chapter Seven

Nick

Sorrento, Italy, Monday, 5th August 2019

The baby at the front of the plane has quite the pair of lungs on it. Who knew something that small could produce a noise that loud? It sounds like it's being tortured or something. I'm reliably told by Johnny that the same comparison can be made when it comes to infants' poos. 'It's like it came out of a fucking dinosaur,' I distinctly recall him commenting at Josh's first birthday party nearly fourteen years ago now; not exactly what I wanted to hear as I'd bitten into one of the sausages off the BBQ he'd been manning in his usual expert way. But as usual Johnny didn't notice my discomfort. Too busy being the centre of attention, swigging his beer and playing to the crowd. I remember that party being a massive affair, more of an excuse for a piss up for the adults than for Josh's sake who, let's be fair, wouldn't have known a birthday from a bar mitzvah. But that's just Johnny all over. Always the showman, got to make a splash and prove he's bigger and better than anyone. I admired that once, wished I could be more like him. Have that kind of innate confidence and charisma that draws people to you like moths to a flame. I thought that's the only way I'd ever land the girl of my dreams. But I was wrong. And so was he.

After we left uni and Lana and Johnny got married the following year, they always seemed to be busy, either jetting off somewhere, or entertaining Johnny's clients with lavish dinner parties, and then later, visiting Johnny's parents who craved time with Josh in a way they never did with their own son. It was never a good time to visit, and I thought perhaps they were avoiding us. And with good reason, I suppose. To be honest, I was relieved, even though it was hard for Padma. She and Lana were close once, and although Lana was hugely supportive in the immediate aftermath of what happened, once she fell pregnant with Johnny's child, to Padma it had felt like she'd abandoned her. As if all those years of friendship counted for nothing. I'm in no way suggesting Padma secretly gloated when Lana miscarried – she's not that sort of person, and she certainly never said as much to me. Besides, she and I were together by then. But I wouldn't blame her for not being cut up about it. She's only human after all. Just like the rest of us.

Unlike Lana and Johnny, since getting hitched, Padma and I have lived a relatively quiet life, which is how we both like it. Occasionally we go out with friends we've made locally, see our families on the weekends, catch a movie or fork out on dinner in town, but that's about it. It doesn't bother me at all as I've never been much of a partygoer and, to be honest, I prefer it if her and Johnny don't see too much of each other. The last thing I want are any old feelings resurfacing, even though I feel sure Padma no longer sees Johnny that way. Still, he's so bloody handsome, and they used to look so good together, 'the golden couple' of our year at Oxford, I can't help feeling a poor second best. That one day the dream scenario I've found myself in will evaporate, and she'll go running back to him.

The quiet life suits me fine. All I want is to be with Padma, plus kids of course. I'm fifty per cent there, but I'm starting to lose hope of making our life complete. Not that it's anyone's fault. Plus, knowing how fragile Padma can be, the last thing I want is to put pressure on her, even though time is ticking. I know her parents are desperate for their first grandchild, and the look that her father sometimes gives me – like there must be something wrong with me, while a good fertile Indian boy would most certainly have given him at least two grandkids by now – makes me a little hot under the collar. But everyone knows that kind of pressure isn't the way to make a human life. The doctors have assured us that we're perfectly healthy, that sometimes these things just take time. But time isn't something we have a lot of with both of us pushing forty, and so I'm thinking now might be the right moment to bring up the idea of adoption even though Padma has never been that keen on the idea.

I'm on the aisle, Padma to my left, Arnold Schwarzenegger's twin brother to hers. The typical economy squashed sandwich. It feels stuffy, airless, while there's a strong whiff of body odour hanging in the air almost making me want to puke.

No doubt Padma and I will be the only ones out of the group to have travelled economy. It makes me laugh when Johnny and Ness comment on how they can't understand why anyone would travel cattle class. How the other half live, eh? I know for a fact that Johnny's never experienced economy in his life. Never had to mix with the riffraff or struggle to put pennies together to be able to afford an airfare. It's sad in some ways, that he and Lana are so far removed from reality, but it also stokes an anger in me. I saw enough of that snobbery at Oxford, and it appalled me. Truth is, I always felt a bit of a misfit there, and sometimes, looking back, I wish I'd never applied. Thinking I would have been better off somewhere more down-to-earth. But I was smart, and I had the best maths teacher at school who encouraged me to aim high. As did my parents, neither of whom went to uni, let alone Oxford. And secretly, although I've never told anyone, not even Padma, my father was a bit of a bully. He'd slate me for not being great at sport, for not being the kind of son he had hoped for. But I was smarter than him, and excelling at my studies was my way of sticking two fingers up at the old duffer. Anyway, I suppose the fact that I was offered a scholarship proved me and my teacher right. That I deserved to be at Oxford. With the rich kids. Like Johnny and Ness.

After a bit of a tense start to the flight with some 'unexpected yet perfectly normal' turbulence as the experts like to say but which is of no comfort to Padma, she's rather miraculously managed to fall asleep on my shoulder. Even more amazing considering the wailing baby. She never sleeps easy at the best of times and so I'm glad of it. Although, when I gaze at her beautiful face, it still has that same disturbed look about it, as though her biggest fears plague her dreams. I yearn to make her pain go away. But I can't.

I catch our fellow passengers' looks of disgust and irritation as the baby continues to make its presence known. My ears hurt as the plane bobs up and down so I can't even imagine the level of pain the little mite is in. I'm tempted to point out that they were that size once, no doubt inciting similar looks of derision from intolerant jerks like them. But I manage to hold my tongue. It's not worth the trouble, plus I don't want to risk waking Padma. Just then, an attractive blonde flight attendant passes by with the drinks trolley. She asks if I'd like anything, for a charge of course. The price we paid for our tickets doesn't warrant a free tea or packet of crisps. Even though it was by no means cheap. Shocking when you think about it. I imagine Johnny living it up on Champagne and God-knows-what else in business class. I ask for a black coffee, aware that I'm driving at the other end, then hand the attendant a fiver. We've hired a car to get to and from the airport, also in case we need it during the week, a prospect I'm slightly nervous about. I've visited Italy before and am aware how crazy the driving can be. Still, I don't like being beholden to taxis, especially as I know the villa Ness has rented is stuck up in the hills. I just need to have my wits about me until we get there and I can finally allow myself to unwind. That's the hope, anyway. Because, when the six of us get together, I can never be sure things won't go terribly wrong. There's always this unmistakeable air of unease that seems to underline every laugh, every smile, every cheery word or gesture of affection. Not to mention the knowing looks that pass between Ness and Johnny. Looks that unnerve me. That tell me they'll never rest easy because things could change in the blink of an eye. Maybe I'm wrong, maybe I'm just being overly suspicious. I hope I am. Because rightly or wrongly, they'd do best to leave the past in the past.

It's the safer option. For all our sakes.

Chapter Eight

Padma

Before
Oxford, England, mid-October 2001

It's been two days since I was rushed to John Radcliffe Hospital, and since coming round, I've made friends with one of the nurses. Her name is Rani. She only works nights, but it means she's able to keep me company when visiting hours are over. I told her how I feel too afraid to be left alone. It's hard enough being in hospital with your memory intact, but to exist in isolation when you have no idea who you are or the circumstances that brought you there is scary beyond belief.

Although Rani is Indian in origin, she has a broad Brummie accent, with a pretty face and kind eyes. She feels familiar; there's just something about her that resonates with me, but obviously I don't know why because my mind remains a blank canvas. I keep getting flashes of something in my head, but no more, and it's driving me insane. What if nothing ever comes back? The very thought terrifies me. A possibility I can't stop from turning over in my mind, despite urging myself not to think so negatively. Instinct telling me I'm a strong person, capable of fighting back. A gut feeling endorsed by everyone who's been to visit me. My parents included, who look like they're battling an avalanche of tears every time they walk through the door.

I have something called Focal Retrograde Amnesia, which affects memories that were formed before my brain injury, but not my ability to conceive new ones. It's apparently caused by damage to the memory-storage areas of my brain and, amongst other factors, can result from a traumatic injury. It can be temporary, permanent or, and what scares me the most, get progressively worse over time. It also means that my most recent memories are likely to be affected. Of course, I've had all the tests. And they can try various treatments. But there's no magic quick-fix solution. Even though the doctors are confident of my memory returning, albeit perhaps not in full or as quickly as I'd like it to. They said there may yet be blanks in time, which can be normal in a head trauma such as the one I have suffered. Particularly if the events leading up to my fall were especially harrowing. That it's imperative I stay calm, remain positive. But it's easy for them to say. They're not the ones to have lost two decades of their lives.

Someone called Nick, who's apparently a good friend of mine at Oxford, rode in the ambulance with me, after another friend – Jacob, a guy in my tutor group – found me and called 999. Jacob had come round to the student house I share with my boyfriend, Johnny, who I don't remember either, to return a book he had borrowed. He had found me lying on the living room floor unconscious, blood oozing from the back of my head. Nick seems nice, caring. He has a studious look, along with a soothing voice that relaxes me. This morning I woke up and he was sitting by my bedside watching over me. He asked how I was feeling, whether there was anything he could get me. I told him I'd like some water and then, after taking a few sips from the glass he had handed to me, he enquired whether I was beginning to remember anything. His face was steeped in concern, and that touched my heart, although it had also made me wonder why Johnny wasn't by my side asking the same question, if he was meant to be my boyfriend. I didn't respond, there was nothing to say. All I found myself doing was shaking my head and turning to face the other wall so that Nick couldn't see the tears streaming down my cheeks. I just feel so utterly alone. Vulnerable, tense and unsure of everyone around me, despite their best intentions.

Apparently, Johnny is Nick's best mate. Johnny and I moved from halls into a two-bedroom student house in our second year to have more privacy. My mother told me he and I are besotted with one another and have been dating for two years. He's drop-dead handsome, and when he first came to visit after I'd woken up and he explained who he was, I couldn't help thinking I'd done well for myself bagging a boyfriend like him. Even so, something feels off. Just the way he behaves around me, I guess. Unlike Nick who's stayed for an hour at a time, Johnny's visits have been brief. Maximum ten minutes. And in all that time he just looks at me nervously, almost like he doesn't want to be here, but feels obliged to show up out of duty. So different to my parents who dropped everything to rush to Oxford when the college notified them of what had happened and have barely left my bedside.

Two young women about my age – Lana and Vanessa – have also been to visit me. Both are good friends of mine, so my father told me the first time they appeared at the door. Lana and I go way back, while Vanessa is a childhood friend of Johnny's. She introduced us in our first week, apparently. They both seemed very cut up about my condition. Said they wanted to help in any way they could, eager to know if I remembered anything at all. Lana urged me not to stress about it. Said it was crucial I focus on taking one day at a time, on healing physically, rather than fixating on remembering every little detail which could slow my recovery. Again, it's easy for her to say, she's not the one who's lost her memory. When I questioned Nick on why Johnny always seems in such a hurry to get away, he explained that my boyfriend's never been good in these types of situations, but that he was sure in his heart he was worried for me. He told me I shouldn't mention that to him as it will only make him feel bad. Still, it makes me wonder why I'm with Johnny. Why I would choose a boyfriend who doesn't know how to be comforting in my time of need. Was I really OK with that all this time? Or has something happened since to make him behave so coldly towards me? Something just doesn't ring true, but with my mind so muddled and my memory drawing a blank there's no way I'll get the answers I need.

The police were here today. They're pretty sure I was attacked. There are painful, livid bruises on my forearms, suggestive of a struggle during which I fell and hit my head on the sharp glass edge of our coffee table, causing a severe gash to the back of my head, so deep it needed stitches. There was no alcohol in my system, while I have no history of fainting or any other medical condition that can cause me to pass out at a whim.

All the evidence points to me being pushed – violently. A notion that terrifies me. Johnny had been over at Nick and Vanessa's place at the time. They aren't together, but like me and Johnny, had wanted to get out of halls to have more privacy. Vanessa said that Johnny blames himself for not being around when my attacker made his move, and that's why he's been acting so off. They're assuming it's a 'he', but they can't be sure, of course. It could just as easily have been a woman. The house has been swept for prints, DNA, but loads of people come and go through our place, apparently, including me and Johnny of course, so I'm not sure what good that's going to do. I was meant to have followed Johnny on to Vanessa and Nick's that night, Vanessa having offered to cook, but as I hadn't turned up and Johnny's dad had phoned unexpectedly, Nick had offered to pop over to see what was keeping me. He said he'd been shocked to see Jacob hunched over me, trying to shake me awake. Jacob told the police that the front door hadn't been shut properly when he turned up, which the police said might be indicative of someone having made a quick getaway.

I'm sick of being in this hospital bed. But I'm also frightened of leaving it before I remember who I am. It would be like going into the wilderness blindfolded.

But even more than not remembering who I am, my biggest fear on leaving this place is not knowing who put me in here.

Chapter Nine

Johnny

Sorrento, Italy, Monday, 5th August 2019

'*Grazie mille, Signor.*' The taxi driver grins widely as I hand him a twenty-euro tip on top of the 100 euros that's already been charged to my account for the drive to Sorrento from Naples airport. He looks like he belongs on a Martin Scorsese film set rather than behind the wheel of a cab. Everything about him emanates effortless style. Perfectly groomed hair, Versace sunglasses, crisp white linen shirt open at the neck, dark blue jeans complete with a D&G belt. I feel wholly inadequate, even though I know I still attract my fair share of female attention. Or perhaps that's what I like to believe. Mistaking the flattering comments and sheep's eyes I receive from my female clients and secretaries for attraction rather than sucking up to get what they want. Like that multi-million-pound deal or hefty pay rise. Whatever the case, the fact that this guy must be nearly half my age and seemingly full of youthful optimism while I'm on the brink of hitting forty and can't help thinking it's all downhill from now, hasn't helped my sense of inadequacy. OK, so I'm a director at one of the UK's largest investment banks. But so what? It's not that special. Nothing to write home about. It's not as if I'm a movie producer or an Olympic athlete. There are tons of people in my position, and it's not as if we're admired as a profession. Not the way top footballers or doctors are. The public see us as money-grabbing sharks. What we do doesn't make a difference to their lives, doesn't bring them joy or fulfilment. Well, newsflash – it doesn't bring me joy or fulfilment either. But it's what my father expected of me. It was either that or follow him into politics. So really, it was the lesser of two evils I suppose. At least I've lived up to the knob-head's expectations where my job's concerned. Unlike my marriage. He never understood why I'd chosen to be with Lana, and for that, I can't exactly blame him. But it's a question I can never answer truthfully. Not to him, nor to anyone. In all honesty, a part of me had felt like giving my old man the finger and joining the sodding army after I left Oxford. Or perhaps the circus would have been more appropriate; I know I'm nothing but the consummate performer. It's not like I hadn't considered running away from it all. The timing couldn't have been more perfect. Not that it would have made much difference in hindsight. The fact is, no matter how much distance I try to put between myself and what happened at uni, my guilt will always follow me. I could travel 10,000 miles and it would still stalk me like my own shadow.

I notice the unashamed wink the cabbie gives Lana, and the coy smile she gives him in return, flicking her shoulder-length auburn hair behind her ear the way women do when they're being flirted with and feel the desire to flirt back. I should be consumed with jealousy, but I'm not. I couldn't give a fuck who she flirts with to be honest. If it wasn't for the kids and the other thing keeping us together, she could run off into the sunset with

Robert de Niro here on the spot and I'd be as happy as Larry. Free at last!

De Niro speeds off, leaving a trail of dust in his wake. I pull down my shades as the grit and glare of the sun stings my eyes. Then I wipe the sweat that's spread across my forehead in the two minutes we've been standing here. It's just on 1 p.m. and the heat is intense, saturating my back and underarms. Despite the perks of travelling business class, I still feel like shit – it's just how travelling is – and I realise I need a shower badly. And a drink. In fact, I'm going to need a lot of that this week. Then again, what's new? Booze is the only way I keep my nerves in check.

'He was nice,' Lana comments, a wistful look in her eyes as she watches the car disappear from view. I know what she's thinking. She's wishing she could have driven off with him. Not just to avoid me, but the next five days. Like me, she's been dreading it. But it's Vanessa's fortieth and I can't let her down. She's everything to me, and I owe her. All of us do.

'Hello, welcome!' a cheery voice calls out from behind me. Speak of the Devil. Ness's voice is unmistakable – full of authority, yet warm and reassuring – and it brings an instant smile to my face. I catch Lana rolling her eyes and will myself to keep calm rather than give her an earful. How dare she be so rude about my closest friend. She's lucky Ness is civil to her, all things considered. If only she was half the woman Ness is. If only she knew the sacrifices she's made for me. I fight down the persistent urge to put my hands around my wife's neck and strangle the air out of her. And not for the first time think how much easier my life would be without her around. Always reminding me. Always having a dig. She really has no idea what she's talking about. But I can't tell her that. And it's something that niggles me like a sore that won't heal but instead grows more and more septic by the day.

'Hey, gorgeous,' I swivel round and scoop Ness up in my arms, spinning her full circle, the way I used to when we were kids and life was so much simpler. It's like hugging home. Although it strikes me how much lighter she feels. Her face looks a bit drawn too. Perhaps she's been on a diet or working too much as usual. Burning the candle at both ends. Mind you, I'm not one to talk. About work that is, not the diet. I eat like a horse but exercising for an hour a day in the gym keeps the weight off. I brush my fleeting concerns for her health aside and catch Lana's sour puss expression, her eyes turning green with envy. She can go to hell. It's just how she's always been. Jealous of Padma, jealous of Ness. Never content in her own skin, always thirsting over something bigger and better. Just like her mother. Kathy's such a cow, I can't say I blame Lana's father for leaving them. Still, it's pretty low he cut himself off completely from his own daughter. Small wonder Lana's got such a gigantic chip on her shoulder. I only wish I could meet the fucker, tell him what a twisted, manipulative daughter she's turned out to be because of him.

Despite Lana's obvious disdain for my and Ness's warm embrace, once we break free, she gives Ness one of her classic fake hugs. She's not stupid. She knows it would be a mistake to rub Ness up the wrong way. Ness is a formidable woman, tougher than the rest of us put together, and that scares Lana. Because deep down, and with the limited knowledge she has, she can never be certain of what Ness is truly capable of.

'Hi, Ness, how's it going?' Lana says cheerfully. 'So lovely to be here. The villa looks incredible.'

I can't disagree with her there. I knew it would be from the photos Ness shared in our WhatsApp group, but it's even more stunning in the flesh. Seeing the photos convinced me that maybe this week wasn't such a bad idea after all, having secretly quizzed Ness on the phone as to whether the six of us spending five nights abroad together was such a good idea. She knew exactly where I was coming from, but reassured me that it would be fine. *It's been OK this long, why would anything change this week,* she'd said. And when I'd thought about it, I realised she was probably right; it was simply my own paranoia getting to me.

Just then, Marcus appears. I feel a tug of irritation, or is it jealousy? That someone can live their life freely, without being weighed down by guilt or regret. Even though he sometimes has this distracted look about him, as if there's a little part of him that's not quite with us. He looks well now though I have to say. Somehow younger. Less preoccupied. It must be the Italian air, getting away from it all. The kids especially. I could never be a full-time dad like him, as much as I love my three. I'm too selfish, and I swear I'd go bonkers. I need time away from our house. From the stuff that's always lying around everywhere, no matter how many times Lana or our twice-weekly cleaner tidies up. From the constant noise, washing and sound of CITV going on in the background. From the incessant bickering and fighting over the Xbox or PlayStation. I'm not sure how Marcus does it while still managing to keep sane. On the flip side, I suppose I should be grateful for the noise, for the three kids that between them monopolise all of my and Lana's spare time so we don't feel the need to talk to each other. Lana's a good mum, I'll give her that.

It's why I was OK with having more children. I knew I was stuck with her, and I wanted my kids to have each other for support when Lana and I are gone. Still, I'd rather someone else was the mother of my kids. But I blew that long ago.

'Hey, you two, welcome.' Marcus gives me a firm handshake, then goes to hug Lana, planting a kiss on each of her freckled cheeks. I notice how tender their embrace is, in contrast to her and Ness's. Then I catch Ness's eye and can tell she's thinking the same. But that she's also not much bothered. Unlike Marcus, she knows what a devious woman my wife is. I think Lana sees Marcus as a kindred spirit of sorts, with him being the other 'outsider' of the group. The one who has no choice but to socialise with the 'uni gang' courtesy of marriage. But she's kidding herself if she thinks her and Marcus are the same. Things couldn't be further from the truth.

I've always sensed that Marcus views me as a threat, which is absurd. Ness and I are best friends, pure and simple. We virtually lived next door to one another as kids, attending the same co-ed prep school before we both got carted off to respective boys' and girls' boarding houses. Even then, and although I made some good mates, as well as some diehard enemies, we'd write to one another. I missed her like crazy; she was the one person who seemed to really get me, to understand what I was feeling and going through. And I think that's how she saw me too. I couldn't wait for the holidays when we'd catch up and go on family vacations together, to the Caribbean or somewhere similarly exotic. Sneaking off to the beach, plotting our escape from our lousy parents, me usually wanting to pull some stupid prank to make their lives hell, her setting me on the straight and narrow and stopping the both of us from getting into serious trouble.

Like I said, she's always had my back.

It was expected of us both that we'd go to Oxford just as our fathers had done. There was no choice in the matter, not if we wanted our dads to foot the bill for uni. It was a lot to live up to, but neither of us could bear the stigma of failing to meet their expectations. And even though it bugged me that I never knew if I got in on merit or because of who my father was – there were boys at school ten times brighter than me who didn't make the cut – I was glad I went there purely because Ness was there too. I couldn't have got through my final year without her. Anyway, point is I resent the way Marcus's jealousy makes our platonic love for each other feel like something sordid. It's so not like that, but I have no way of convincing him otherwise. Short of reliving a memory I've tried so hard to suppress.

Finally, they break away and Ness beckons for us to come inside. She takes the lead, linking her arm in Lana's, telling her what a great few days we're going to have, chattering away about the villa and how marvellous it is, how later we'll have a swim and then dinner down by the marina, while Marcus and I trail behind with the luggage, which somehow feels like it's gained two kilos since leaving Gatwick. Looking around – the setting really couldn't be more idyllic – I can almost feel myself relaxing, warming to the idea of five days away from it all. But it's at this point that I contemplate the text message that popped up on my phone this morning just as we were about to board the plane at Heathrow. A message from an unknown number that made my insides turn and caused me to shut my eyes and pretend to be asleep throughout the drive here because I didn't want Lana seeing the fear on my face.

> I know what you did. How can you live with yourself?

Chapter Ten

Padma

Before
Oxford, England, November 2001

It's been three weeks since they brought me here, and over the last few days I've slowly started to regain my memory: details about my childhood, the people who are special in my life, the small things that make me *me*.

I'd already learned such details from my friends and family. But it's not the same as remembering them for yourself, is it? Because it's their version of my life, not mine. The latter being the version I know to be unequivocally true. And now that my memories are returning, I can't help reciting them over and over in my head, just because I am utterly petrified of losing them once more.

I know that my name is Padma. That I just turned twenty-two. That I'm from Reading and had a very happy childhood growing up with my parents and older brother, Kris. That my father came over from Bombay in the late Sixties, moving around the UK as a trainee dentist, before meeting and marrying my mother and forming his own practice. I also realise why Nurse Rani feels so familiar to me. It's because she reminds me of my father's younger sister who, coincidentally, was also called Rani. Tragically, she died of breast cancer six months ago. Something that had devastated me. Still does, in fact. Although she showered us with love and would undoubtedly have made the most wonderful mother, she couldn't cope with the responsibility of bringing a child into this world, having been raped on the eve of her arranged marriage. The shame had been too great, and she'd followed Dad to England, becoming a social worker in a bid to help victims of abuse like her. She was my hero, and I miss her terribly, wish I could have talked to her about my own ordeal. She would have been the perfect person to understand what I'm going through. Still, I'm so grateful to Nurse Rani for taking the time to sit by my bed and let me talk through the night. Just having her near has been a great comfort to me, and I'll miss her when I leave. She hasn't come round this evening, so I hope she's not unwell. Hopefully I'll see her before I'm discharged.

I've told Rani everything I remember. That Lana is my best friend from primary school. That she'd defended me against the racist bullies there, after which we became like sisters, attending the same secondary comprehensive before going our separate ways at university – her at Leeds, me at Oxford – but that she still comes to visit me here as I sometimes visit her. That I was nuts about my boyfriend, Johnny, from the moment Ness introduced us. That his father's a bit of a pompous twat, his mother a self-centred sort, neither of them initially keen on their only child's choice of girlfriend. Not because I'm mixed race, more so because my parents aren't mega rich like them. If Dad had been an Indian steel magnate rather than a dentist that would no doubt have made all the difference. But thankfully they seem to have warmed to me, which makes life easier. I know it's not easy for Johnny constantly living in his father's shadow, being forced to meet his exacting standards. And that he's terrified of doing anything to upset or embarrass him, with Ed being in the public eye. I told Ness I love Johnny with all my heart, that he had seemed head-over-heels in love with me before I was attacked, which is why I am confused and upset by his cold behaviour towards me since I was brought here. I told her it makes no sense, that I couldn't understand why he wasn't skipping for joy when I told him the memories were returning. She urged me to be patient, said it had been hard on him seeing me in such a state, and that with time, now that I've regained most of my memories, things will go back to normal. I'm trying to give him the benefit of the doubt, to take heart from Ness's words, but I still find his behaviour upsetting.

I remember other tiny details about myself: the fact that my favourite meal is my dad's chicken biryani, my biggest indulgence Häagen-Dazs ice cream following a plate of deep-fried samosas. The fact that I can roll my tongue, ice skate, do a wicked impersonation of Edina from *Ab Fab*. I know that I hate rollercoasters, adore romantic films, loathe horror movies and watching rugby, except when Johnny is playing.

There's other stuff too, a list that's too long to recite.

But there's still one big gaping hole in my memory. And it's the reason I can't be content with the memories I do have. Why I can't rest easy at night. Why I toss and turn and regard everything and everyone with suspicion. Why I can only seem to sleep with the aid of Diazepam.

And it's the fact that I don't remember how I ended up here. A week of my life is missing. I have no idea what happened in the days leading up to Jacob finding me lying unconscious on my and Johnny's living room floor.

Was it an accident or was I pushed? And if it's the latter, which the bruising on my arms would suggest, why did someone want to attack me?

What did we argue about, what did I know?

And the two biggest questions of all:

Who was it and will they try to harm me again?

Chapter Eleven

Marcus

Sorrento, Italy, Monday, 5th August 2019

Johnny and Lana have scarcely been here five minutes and I already feel wound up. I'm trying my best not to show it, but as usual, the minute he and Ness caught sight of one another I was made to feel like the gooseberry in the room. And I'm pretty sure Lana felt the same way.

I know they practically grew up together, but there's something about their relationship I've never quite been able to put my finger on. An intensity bordering on the sexual. Or perhaps I'm letting my imagination run wild? Mainly because I've always felt slightly intimidated by Johnny's film-star looks. I suppose it's just that they seem to have this innate understanding. This almost inexplicable bond. I see it in their eyes, in the way they seem to fuss over each other. Causing me to wonder why they didn't become husband and wife – they just seem so secure in each other's company. Plus, I always get the feeling they're party to some secret information that eludes the rest of us. I daren't ask Ness about it because I know she hates the clingy, paranoid type. She told me so on our first date, and from then on I vowed that she would never see the insecure side of me. All that changed, of course, after the children were born and I felt I could no longer keep my real self and the demons that plagued me a secret. But for a long time, I kept that side of me well and truly hidden. Just because I didn't want to scare her off.

To be fair, looks-wise, Ness isn't Johnny's type. She's too tall, with sharp, aristocratic features, rather than being quintessentially feminine, which I've noticed is how Johnny likes his women. Padma being the perfect example. He tries not to show it, but it's so obvious. His eyes follow her like tracking beams. I know the look of a man in lust, just because it's how I was with Ness at the beginning. It's laughable the way he tries to keep it at bay, but he may as well have a flashing neon sign stuck to his face saying: *I fancy the pants off Padma and would like nothing more than to screw her brains out.*

It can't be easy for Lana, knowing her husband is still hung up on another woman. I think that's why we don't get together that often as a group. It's mainly the four of us who hang out, only seeing Padma and Nick on special occasions like this week. Ness tries to deny it whenever I broach the subject. But really, I think it's too difficult for Johnny seeing Padma with Nick, while Lana can't bear to see the look of longing on Johnny's face. Nick, bless him, is a little better than Lana at hiding his irritation. But it's clear it gets his back up. And who would blame him? Seeing your best friend – your very good-looking best friend who used to date your wife – virtually drool at the sight of her must be galling. If I were Nick, I'd pull Johnny up on it, but he just keeps quiet. Something I find odd. I mean, why let him get away with it?

I was surprised when Ness suggested this week. I know it's her fortieth and that she'd want to mark the occasion in a big way, but I was thinking maybe a party was more her style. An excuse to invite lots of clients and drum up more business for the firm. Call me a bit of a grouch and perhaps it's my middle age talking, but when she told me she wanted to be able to celebrate with the five people she was closest to in this world, my heart sank. Obviously, she didn't mean Lana when she said this; there's always been this underlying frostiness between them even though they both try to act otherwise. It was really all about Nick, Johnny and Padma, plus me because I'm her husband. Although, at the time I had wondered whether she'd be happy to leave me behind so they could celebrate old times without feeling guilty. Last night put paid to those doubts, though. Having dinner together, just the two of us, making love, it felt like we'd reconnected, and I'm suddenly feeling more positive about our marriage. If only it was just the two of us here all week; now that would be bliss. No chance of the others spoiling things.

I watch Johnny as we settle down to drinks on the terrace. How does he manage to look that bloody good? It's infuriating, given the way he abuses his body. I mean, I know he works out a lot – it's evident from his washboard stomach and defined arms, which he's showing off to perfection right now in a fitted blue t-shirt. Plus, he's still retained the chiselled jawline and full head of hair he had when I first met him nine years ago, and which I suspect is dyed because there's not a fleck of grey in it. In contrast to my receding hairline and middle-aged spread, the latter not helped by the fact that I eat too much junk while the children are at school and can't be bothered to use the family gym membership we pay a fortune for. But it's no secret how much Johnny drinks. Granted, drinking is par for the course in his industry, but even so, I've never been to a social event with him where he's not ended up plastered. I also know from Ness he smokes weed on and off and dabbles in coke. She said he did a lot of drugs at uni, much to Padma's disapproval. It's so bloody irresponsible of him. For Christ's sake, he's a dad now, what kind of example does that set his kids? Especially with Josh being at an impressionable age. He acts like he's still in his early twenties at Oxford, rather than a man of thirty-nine who should know better. The way he abuses his body upsets Ness and she's constantly on at him to tone it down, but he won't listen. It's like he's got a death wish or something, and it makes me wonder why. Surely not everything can be put down to his childhood. Or to him being miserable over losing Padma and being married to Lana. I mean, Ness's upbringing wasn't a bed of roses, but she's always had her head screwed on. And I'm sure she had her wild days at uni – didn't we all? But you have to grow up, don't you? Especially when you bring kids into this world. They become your priority, but I'm not sure that's the case where Johnny's concerned. It seems to me he's always looking out for number one. Perhaps that's another reason why Lana always looks so ticked off. Perhaps she realises what a selfish bloke she married. But then why stay with him? That I don't get, besides the kids of course, but it's not like she wouldn't be able to survive on the sizeable alimony she'd get from him were they to split. Whenever I raise the subject with Ness, she always gives a fudged response, says every marriage goes through ups and downs, then manages to shift the conversation to another topic.

Having given them a guided tour of the villa, we'd left Johnny and Lana to sort out their room and freshen up, before reconvening outside for a round of ice-cold beers and a light lunch Ness whipped up in the villa's charming rustic-style kitchen. Of course, Johnny was game for the booze, said it was the perfect way to kick-start the holiday. But in truth, I felt we needed some Dutch courage to offset the palpable tension that simmers at the surface, even though, as usual, we're all doing well to hide it behind a veil of pleasantries, false smiles, and overinflated laughter. Once I thought it was just me feeling like the outsider, but now I'm not so sure.

We're seated around an L-shaped wicker sofa with plush cream cushions overlooking the sprawling Mediterranean, the tiled roof above us providing a welcome shield from the blazing sun. The view and setting really couldn't be more perfect, and it's hard to believe that only twenty-four hours ago Ness and I had got drenched in the short walk from the taxi drop off at Gatwick to the terminal building. I love this part of the world. The food, the culture, the people and their genuine joy and love of life is somewhat contagious. It's something we English could learn from – at least, those of us who live in big cities and go about life like it's a race to the death. I mean, why do we do it to ourselves? It's what I ask Ness all the time, but she never listens. Says we have two young kids to put through private school and can't afford to let up. I guess she's right, and with Kitty and Owen only being eight and six – Ness and I didn't meet until after she turned thirty – there's a long and considerable financial burden to meet. But then again, would it really be so bad if the kids went to our local comp? The last thing I want is Owen turning out like Johnny. I want him to know that business class and five-star holidays aren't the norm – they certainly weren't for me at his age – and that there's a huge social divide in this world that people like us who are fortunate enough to have pot loads of money need to be aware of and help make right. Still, there's no reason why my boy shouldn't be socially aware. I'm always around to keep him on the straight and narrow, whereas Johnny didn't have that kind of attention or guidance from Ed. It's silly to compare, really. I want to be there for our kids, which is why I quit my high-flying job as a banking partner and let Ness earn the money. A choice I don't regret making one bit, even though I sometimes find myself going a tad barmy at home. I'll always be grateful for the time, love and attention Mum gave me when I was small, despite me secretly resenting her for leaving Dad. Back when I believed her to be indestructible, cosseted by the innocence of my youth. When time ran slower, and my days were filled with joy and laughter. How I long for that time again.

'*Saluti!*' Johnny's booming voice brings me back to reality as he raises his beer bottle and gestures for the rest of us to follow suit. The way he always expects us to blindly follow him. He was the same at Oxford, apparently. Like the Pied Piper leading the other students astray.

I notice Ness eyeing me with concern.

'You OK, darling?'

Lost in my thoughts, I'm guessing Ness can tell from my expression that I was daydreaming about my child-hood just then, even if the others won't have a clue.

I smile, try to make light of it, even though there's no fooling my wife. It's one of the things that attracted me to her – her intuition and empathy. 'Yes, just a little too relaxed I guess.' I give her another reassuring smile, hoping she'll accept my explanation and move on. 'Perhaps a swim is in order. To wake me up. How about you guys? You up for that? We didn't get a chance to test the water yesterday, and it looks so inviting.'

My gaze falls on Lana and Johnny, although I'm not entirely sure why I'm encouraging this, knowing the sight of Johnny's chiselled abs and toned thighs in his trunks is going to make me feel like a walking lump of lard. But we're on holiday, with a pool on site. It's not like I'm going to be able to avoid it, so I might as well get the humiliation over and done with.

'Great idea, mate,' Johnny says before popping a grape into his mouth. Even the way he does that is cool, effortless. Like some Roman senator. I could see him posing for one of those men's aftershave adverts. *Acqua di Gio for Men* or something. 'You'd be up for that sweetheart, wouldn't you?' His eyes focus on Lana, not in an affectionate way, it's more of a menacing stare, like he's telling her not to be a party pooper and sulk in the corner like a child the way she often does. I have to say, his condescending tone riles me, even though it's not my place to interfere. Suddenly the tension feels more stifling than the heat.

Lana takes a sip of her beer, then replies flatly, 'Yes, absolutely, I could do with cooling off, this weather is murder on my Irish skin.' Lana has Irish blood on her mother's side, resulting in a milky white complexion that doesn't respond well to the southern Italian heat. She gives a nervous smile, then reaches for a plate and helps herself to some bread and cheese.

'I have factor fifty in case you need it,' Ness offers.

'Thanks, Ness,' Johnny butts in, 'but we have plenty of sunscreen. Truth is, the excess pounds Lana's not managed to shift since having Erin, despite the fact that it's been four years, don't help with her ability to tolerate the heat. Do they, sweetheart?' He looks at Lana, then at me and Ness, as if expecting us to agree and laugh at his 'witty' remark. *Bastard*. What gives him the right to behave like such an arse towards her? I badly want to teach him a lesson. Make him feel small and vulnerable the way he makes others feel.

I watch Lana's face turn scarlet. She looks down at her plate, seemingly too ashamed to eat following her husband's insult. 'Too many afternoon teas with the mums and scoffing crisps in front of daytime TV, and not enough gym time,' Johnny carries on. 'Isn't that right, darling?'

'Johnny, that's enough,' Ness says with a cross look, as if she's reprimanding a naughty child, before glancing at Lana who's now necking her beer like water. I wriggle in my seat, feeling more and more uncomfortable by the second, hoping to God this isn't how it's going to be for the entire five days. 'You try having a baby and see what it does to your body,' Ness adds. 'You men, you really do have no idea.' She smiles at Lana, who gives her a grudging half smile in return.

There's a lingering silence before Johnny swigs his beer, then says with a laugh, 'Yeah, course, sorry, totally uncalled for. You forgive me, don't you, sweetheart?' He looks at Lana with pleading eyes that scream insincerity.

'Sure,' comes the abrupt response. Before she adds, 'I know how much you're in need of forgiveness.'

It's Johnny's turn to go a shade of crimson, and I'm just wondering what the hell she meant by that, when the doorbell rings.

Johnny is up like a shot. 'Allow me. Hopefully that'll be Nick and Padma.'

'Yes, hopefully,' Lana mumbles sarcastically.

Saved by the bell, Johnny disappears back into the villa and as he does, I can't help noticing the look of triumph in Lana's eyes as she starts munching on her bread and cheese.

Chapter Twelve

Padma

Sorrento, Italy, Monday, 5th August 2019

'Hey, Padma, Nick!'

Johnny is there to greet us at the front door of the villa after a somewhat nerve-racking drive from the airport. Looking at Nick's intense expression as he cautiously circumnavigated the death-defying bends to get us here in one piece, his hands gripping the steering wheel so tightly I could see the whites of his knuckles, I got the impression he was regretting hiring a car and wished we'd just got a taxi like the rest of the group. Safe to say, I'm not sure he'll be driving it again before Saturday when we head back to Naples. Which is fine with me.

On first impressions, the villa looks amazing with its stately cream facade; a world away from Walton that's for sure. Having reached the front entrance via imposing wrought iron gates opening out onto a curved driveway, immaculate areas of lawn and exquisite flower beds lining either side, I'm expecting the inside to be equally stunning. All the same I can't help feeling guilty for being here. The world is full of starving, homeless people – I see it all the time at work – and here we are, about to live like kings and queens for a week. Still, I try not to beat myself up about it. After all, it's not my birthday, and this week is not my choice. Plus, if it wasn't for Ness's client footing the bill, there's no way Nick and I would be able to afford to stay here. All we had to pay for were our EasyJet flights, plus whatever we spend out and about by way of food and drink, token gifts and the like. That aside, after a tiring journey, I'm glad to finally be here. It was only a two-and-a-half-hour flight, but the combination of an early start, a bumpy plane ride and the sudden hike in temperature has somewhat drained me. Despite my Indian heritage, I've never really liked the heat. Then again, I think that's true of most Asians. Dad says it's always the white people who lay out in the midday sun burning themselves to a crisp while people of our culture seek shade wherever they can. Mad dogs and English men and all that jazz.

Johnny is all smiles as he cheerfully ushers Nick and I into the welcome cool. He hugs us in turn. Me first. I notice how he pulls me to his chest a little too tightly, so much so I can feel the tautness of his abs pressing into me, the combination of his aftershave and natural scent invading my nostrils, his hands wandering to the small of my back rather unnecessarily. It's a touch I know all too well, but which now makes me flinch. When we first got together at uni, having finally succumbed to the mutual attraction we'd felt from the outset, I'd happily spend whole weekends in bed with him. In fact, I couldn't get enough of him, and he of me. He was good between the sheets, I'll give him that. Back then I was so wild and free, lapping up the sex like a bitch in heat. God knows what my parents would have thought if they knew. My dad especially. I'd never felt so turned on by a boy, not that I'd had many boyfriends before him. My parents met Johnny numerous times back then of course, on the rare weekends when they came up to visit, and during the holidays. But I know Dad never really liked him. It's not that he'd have preferred me to date a good, well-behaved Indian boy who studied hard – he knew better than to think that was ever going to happen – it's just that he found Johnny too full of himself and the entitled world he came from. 'Untrustworthy' and 'insincere' are the words I remember him using. While Mum also feared he'd break my heart. And she was right. There was no telling me, though, and they had to let fate take its course. Which it did. In a far more extreme form than they or anyone could ever have imagined.

I'm pretty sure Johnny is oblivious to my antipathy. In fact, he probably thinks I enjoy his displays of affection. It's funny how he's gradually become more demonstrative over time since we split up, having given me the cold shoulder for so long. For years we barely saw him and Lana. Admittedly, they were busy with the kids, and their hectic social lives. But it had almost felt like they were avoiding us, and whenever I raised the subject with Nick, he'd tell me I was reading too much into things, that they lived in a different world and so it was inevitable we'd see less of each other.

I catch the flicker of irritation in Nick's eyes as I break away from Johnny's embrace. Poor thing, he must know by now he has nothing to fear. Even so, I give him a look as if to say *it's OK, it's just Johnny, let it go, I love you, and only you*. He gives me a reluctant half smile in return, seemingly pacified, whereupon he and Johnny share a somewhat briefer man hug. 'Mate, how you doing? Long time, no see. How was your trip? This place is incredible, the others are out on the terrace. You have some catching up to do on the beers.'

As usual, it's hard to get a word in edgeways with Johnny. I take a moment to study him. Hoping Nick doesn't notice. There's no arguing he's a beautiful specimen. Tall, slim, broad-chested, come-hither eyes that undress you with the merest glance. I briefly consider how many affairs he's had behind Lana's back. No doubt too many to count. I also wonder if, had we stayed together, he would have remained faithful to me. I guess the way he behaved towards me at the end should answer my question. But the funny thing is, I never caught him eyeing up another girl while we were dating. And I remember Ness's words as clear as day: 'He's never going to let you go, not in a million years.'

'Not too bad, glad to have escaped the crap British summer,' Nick responds, pulling out a hankie and wiping his brow. Poor thing, like Lana his pale skin doesn't fare well in the heat, whereas my olive complexion takes it much better despite my aversion to the sun. As does Johnny's, judging by his bronzed forearms. 'Drive here was a bit hair-raising. Plane journey was OK,' Nick goes on. 'No decent grub on offer, though, starved.'

'Well, what can you expect in economy?' Johnny looks at me as he says this, as if seeking my endorsement, clearly forgetting that he and I operate in very different worlds. 'I managed a full two hours' kip on the flight over, after a top-notch breakfast of smoked salmon and scrambled eggs washed down with a drop of bubbly. It was a bit early, but it seemed rude not to make the most of what was on offer. And it passed the time. I mean, I run up enough air miles flying business with the bank, I've earned it!'

I think I can see the beads of sweat lining Nick's forehead multiplying by the second, the veins running either side of his neck suddenly more pronounced. He pushes back his glasses which are gradually slipping down his nose and I feel the urge to hug him. Instead, we lock eyes again and I give him a 'keep calm' look, even though inside I'm not feeling so calm myself. I could really do with a shower and a lie-down.

'Afraid us high street accountants can't afford business class, Johnny, you know that. Plus, I wasn't born into money like you. It's why I worked two jobs in the summer holidays, not to mention helped run the student bar. I've reminded you of that, like, a million times.' Nick says this in a jokey fashion, but I know my husband. Inside he's ticked off at having to repeat the same old thing, and rightly so. Either Johnny has a memory like a sieve, or he just doesn't listen, or perhaps he doesn't care. Or maybe there's a fourth option. Perhaps he delights in lording his financial superiority over Nick in front of me. Making me see what I'm missing out on, even though it's his fault we aren't together anymore. How the hell did I fail to see what he was really like back then? The naivety and capriciousness of my youth never fails to astound me. I didn't come from the privileged upbringing Johnny and Ness did. Mum and Dad weren't poor by any means, but neither were they rich. We were comfortable. Took three-star holidays to Spain and Portugal, ate out once a month, and they scrimped and saved to ensure Kris and I had the best they could afford. So, I guess, when I first met Johnny – rich, handsome, popular, sporty – who knew exactly what to say to a girl, and whose eyes drank me in like I was the only woman alive, I was instantly smitten. We were like the Prom Queen and King of Oxford, the glamorous couple everyone admired and aspired to be, and I'm ashamed to say I enjoyed the attention. Revelled in it, even. Truth is, I believed myself to be indestructible back then. Nothing bad had ever happened to me to knock my confidence, to make me question what it was I was doing with my life, what truly mattered. But then it did, and I woke up from the dreamworld I was living in.

Nick never loses his temper when Johnny tries to show him up. He knows how much I dislike confrontation, and I love him for biting his tongue when he must be itching to have a crack at him.

'Anyway, where are the others, Johnny?' I attempt to lighten the mood. 'I'm dying to see everyone. Lead the way!'

Nick and I follow Johnny through the elegant entrance hall lined with white marble columns along with several Roman statues, and into what he describes as the largest of the villa's three sitting rooms boasting a white marble floor, stucco walls, and several more antique statues and sculptures. Its frescoed high ceilings and immaculately painted walls are adorned with several impressive pieces of art which further enhance the feeling of spacious-ness and elegance. The furniture looks equally grand and expensive, including luxurious chenille off-white corner sofas complimented by matching armchairs, a sleek sliding top inlaid coffee table and a stunning blue-cushioned panelled bar, while a white baby grand piano sits proudly in the corner. As we walk, a stream of sunlight fills the room, and I make wide eyes at Nick. He grins as if to say *yeah, I know, it's bloody insane.*

The room opens out through French doors onto an impressive terrace. Lana, Marcus and Ness are seated on a sofa, several bottles of Peroni resting on the glass-topped table in front of them. The view from here is phenom-enal, one of the most beautiful panoramas I've ever seen, and it's as if I'm on some glamorous film set, rather than on holiday with my university friends. They immediately turn their heads in our direction, but before I can get to her, Ness is up like a shot. She rushes over, hugs both of us in turn. 'Ooh, I'm so glad you made it,' she squeals. More like the nineteen-year-old Ness I met on my first day at Raziel College, than the high-powered tough-talking lawyer she's since become. I feel a touch of nostalgia at the thought; the memory of happier, less complicated days.

Marcus gives me a bear hug, before shaking hands with Nick. He's genuinely one of the nicest guys I know, and I often wonder if he regrets marrying Ness and falling into our complex fold. I know they see a lot of Lana and Johnny, living that much nearer to one another in south-west London, and mixing in similar social circles, but given the way Johnny and Ness are around each other, it must sometimes feel like there are three of them in the marriage.

Maybe it's a good thing Marcus never experienced the Oxford scene. Unlike Lana. Sometimes I think it's my fault she became the way she is. Obsessing after a life she wasn't born into, constantly coveting more. If she'd never visited me at uni, she'd never have met Johnny, never have got sucked into our crowd, and perhaps we'd still be close, and she wouldn't always look so miserable.

'Hey, Lana,' I say. I notice she's gained some weight since I last saw her six months ago. I suspect she's been comfort eating again, like she used to at senior school. Back then she'd chalk it up to her mum who never made her feel pretty or smart enough. And I'm ashamed to say that Kathy would compare her to me, who was both those things in her eyes. She'd tell Lana that losing weight was the only way she'd attract boys and get a place on the netball team. But I guess Lana's father taking off before she was born didn't help matters. Food made Lana feel better, that fleeting sensation of having something delicious in her stomach, a silent friend who filled a gaping hole that should have been filled with love. And she's probably right, her mum no doubt was to blame for her overeating back then. But now? Now I'm not so sure Lana has anyone to blame but herself.

'Hi, Padma, how's it going? It's been ages, so nice to see you.'

She gives me a stilted hug and then we air kiss on both cheeks.

I'd like to think she means what she says, but I'm almost certain she doesn't, and it makes me sad. I know she's been jealous of me since puberty hit. But it's not my fault I look the way I do. I always included her, always invited her up to Oxford, bent over backwards to make her feel welcome. But it was never enough for her.

We all sit down and before long Marcus has handed Nick and I a couple of beers. Beer's not normally my thing, but right now I'll take anything cold with alcohol in it. I momentarily rest the frosted glass against my cheek, savouring its chilliness against my skin. As I do I catch Johnny staring at me. His eyes linger on me a little too intensely, so much so I can feel the heat of his gaze burning through me. It's unsettling, angers me even, but in a strange way, and rather shamefully, it also excites me. Knowing I still have this power over him, and that it must be agony for him to see me with his best friend. I quickly look away, having felt a brief stirring between my thighs, then give Nick a broad smile, wanting to show Johnny how Nick is my everything now.

'Get that down you,' Ness says, 'then I'll show you guys to your room.'

'Thanks, Ness,' I smile. 'This place is phenomenal. Must be worth millions.'

'Six point five to be exact.'

'Shut the fuck up,' Nick gasps. 'And your client didn't want any rent for the week?'

Ness shakes her head. 'I've worked my arse off for him. All-nighters, back-breaking negotiations, ugly phone calls, the lot. I guess he thinks I've earned it.'

'You have, my darling.' Marcus reaches for Ness's hand with a smile. She takes it without hesitation. They seem different, closer than the last time we saw them. Not the way I'd described to Nick this morning in the taxi. Ness seems noticeably less tense, a warmth radiating off her I've not witnessed in ages. It makes me wonder what's caused the change. It can't just be that she's away from the office, can it?

'So, how have you guys been?' Johnny focuses his gaze on Nick and me after we've all clinked bottles. I notice he's already halfway through his second Peroni. Same old story. I can't work out if it's nerves, or if he uses alcohol to fill an emptiness inside him.

'Ah, not too bad,' Nick replies. He swigs his beer, then lets it rest on his knee. 'Work's been a bit hectic, so I'm glad for the break.' He stretches his arms wide, then looks out towards the horizon. 'Jeez, I could look at this view all day.'

'Yeah, I know, it's bloody awesome,' Johnny says. 'The Italians really do have it all in my opinion. And I'm totally with you where work's concerned, it's been unusually busy for August. Thought it was the one month the clients were meant to fuck off and leave us in peace.' He looks straight at me, his smouldering dark eyes almost twinkling. 'And you, Padma? How's life in social care?'

I catch the appalled look on Lana's face, her back stiffening. She reaches for her bottle, but doesn't drink from it, just holds the base of it in her right hand, while twirling the neck with her left. I don't think Johnny meant to sound condescending, but it certainly came across like that. I'm convinced neither he nor Lana have a clue about what being a social worker entails. It's a world away from their mollycoddled lifestyles, and there's just no way they'd be able to comprehend the heart-breaking things I deal with day in, day out. My job is tough, there's no denying that, and sometimes I wonder if I'm up to the task, just because I can't even deal with my own issues. Then again, that's exactly the reason I went into social care. Because I know all about feeling helpless.

'It's challenging, but hugely rewarding,' I say. 'I can't imagine doing anything else. And I'd like to think I've made my Aunt Rani proud.'

I glance at Nick, his eyes filling with love. 'Without a doubt. She was a wonderful woman from what you've told me; I'm just sad I never met her.'

'Yes, that's a shame you didn't,' Johnny chips in. 'I did, of course, *several* times.' He glances at Nick, as if to make a point. 'Brilliant woman, and she adored you, Padma.'

I wouldn't say this to Nick, or to anyone for that matter, but Aunt Rani told me she liked Johnny very much. Didn't agree with my parents' low estimation of him. She said she believed underneath all the big talk and superficial arrogance he had a good heart and was clearly mad about me. It had given me confidence at the time, convinced me that my parents were wrong on this occasion, just because I'd always considered my aunt to be a good judge of character. But it just goes to show how even she could be wrong at times, as much as I valued her opinion.

'It's very commendable what you do,' Ness says. 'I can't imagine being in your shoes, I wouldn't have the strength. Or the patience. Or the mindset for that matter. I just help my clients make money – I couldn't give a fig about their personal lives if I'm being honest. Half of them aren't particularly nice people anyway, and they couldn't give a fig about me. They'd sell their own grandmothers to make another million. You're really amazing, Padma, you know that?' She gives me a tender smile and I feel my eyes moisten, remembering how close we were at uni. She was the first friend I made. We clicked from day one.

'Yes, it's hard to imagine that once upon a time, back when we were doing our A-Levels, you wanted to be editor of *Vogue*. I remember you'd watch *The Devil Wears Prada* on repeat. *Quite* the about-turn.'

I swallow down Lana's catty remark, her tone riddled with condescension. She's just bitter. Unfulfilled. Jealous I'm doing something worthwhile with my life. I don't know why she doesn't go back to teaching – she worked at a prep school up until Josh was born – but maybe she thinks it's beneath her now. Or perhaps a certain someone won't let her. I left uni a changed person, and the world of glossy fashion magazines was no longer for me. I realised I wanted to be like my aunt, do some good in this messed up world. To this day the police have never found out who attacked me, never been able to set my mind at ease, and so I guess going into social care was my way of dealing with that, by throwing my body and soul into a career that helped victims like myself.

'Padma's the type who, once she puts her mind to it, can do anything,' Johnny says. 'Unlike us one-trick ponies.' It's a comment seemingly meant for everyone, but his eyes rest on Lana, who looks fit to burst. He takes another slug of beer. 'Still wondering when we're going to hear the pitter-patter of tiny feet, though.' His gaze flits between me and Nick, and I feel my stress levels rise.

'Kids aren't for everyone, Johnny,' Marcus says, giving me a reassuring smile.

'That's true,' Johnny laughs. 'They drain your time and your bank balance. And from what you said, Nick, you don't appear to have much of either.'

I watch Nick's face redden. He looks on the verge of erupting but manages to hold it in by seeking solace in his near-empty beer bottle.

'Right, I think we all need a swim to cool off.' Marcus breaks the tension. 'Meet you all back down here in half an hour?'

'That's a good idea,' Ness says. 'But Nick, Padma, you must be starving. Come and grab a bite to eat in the kitchen first, then we'll go upstairs.'

Chapter Thirteen

Padma

Before
Oxford, England, December 2001

'I think we should take a break.'

I heard the words. But surely, I heard them wrong?

It's been nearly a month since I left hospital, so still early days since I regained my memory – well, most of it anyway – and my boyfriend, the supposed love of my life who previously said he could never imagine being with anyone else, is dumping me?

Am I dreaming? Locked in a nightmare? Is Johnny playing some sick joke on me? And if he is, how could he at a time like this? What the hell has got into him? He can barely stand to look at me. It's as if I disgust him in some way. He's just not the same person I knew.

We're upstairs in Nick's bedroom, in the student house he shares with Ness. I couldn't bring myself to go back to my and Johnny's place after being discharged from the hospital. The thought of returning to where I was attacked terrifies me. But there's something else. Two things, in fact, that have elevated my fears, meaning I can barely walk a hundred yards without looking over my shoulder. Firstly, the police searched our house and found a wireless mini spy camera installed in our bedroom. It was discreetly positioned on top of the wardrobe opposite our double bed, giving it a bird's eye view of the room. It freaked the hell out of me. Knowing someone's been in our most intimate space, placed a camera in there with the intention of spying on us. That they will have seen me undress, seen me and Johnny having sex, heard our private conversations meant for no one else's ears but our own. Unfortunately, the police couldn't trace the source, because whoever put it there appears to have disconnected it from whatever device it had been linked to. Of course, the minute we found out I had to question Johnny as to whether he knew anything about it, having fleetingly wondered if he'd been secretly filming us having sex, me going about the room naked, watching it in his own time for his own pleasure. Or worse, sharing it with his drinking buddies. The very thought had sickened me, that my boyfriend might be a closet pervert of the highest order, bragging about his sexual prowess to his mates. But he'd flatly denied it, had looked offended when I asked him, angry even, and to be honest the genuine shock on his face when the police told us what they had found reassured me he knew nothing about it. The officer in charge said it's very possible that whoever planted the device in our room was the same person who attacked me, but that there's also every chance they're unrelated, and so I couldn't go jumping to conclusions. This gave me little comfort. It just means I may have two creeps to freak out about rather than one. And now I have the added worry of whether, whoever this person is, they might have made some sort of sex tape they intend to share. I mean, what if they try and blackmail me into handing over extortionate sums of money in exchange for their secrecy? Especially with Johnny being the son of a politician. Or worse, share the tape just for the hell of it, to humiliate me and Johnny? I can't imagine ever being able to look my parents in the eye again.

The other thing that's set me on edge is learning that a female fresher at Johnny and Nick's college has gone missing. I only found out about it the week I was discharged because people had thought it best not to worry me, my nerves having taken too much of a beating to be given another shock. Apparently, she was last seen at a party in Baron College's student bar two nights before I was knocked unconscious and she seems to have disappeared into thin air, despite a widespread police investigation having taken place. I've seen her photo in the press; she's a dainty thing with blonde tousled hair and striking blue eyes. I can't imagine what her parents must be going through. I've seen her father on television, appealing to the public at a press conference given by Oxford police. He looked like his world had come to an end, his head hung low, his face gaunt and unshaven, like he hadn't eaten or slept in weeks. According to newspaper reports, his daughter had had no problems with drink or drugs in the past or any prior history of depression or running away from home. So the fact that she's disappeared without a trace is alarming to say the least. And I can't help wondering if her disappearance and my attack are linked. It just seems like too much of a coincidence. Anyway, all this means that I can't face staying in my old place right now, so I've taken refuge in Nick's room while he sleeps on the sofa bed in his and Ness's tiny living room. Having offered, he said he wouldn't take no for an answer, while Ness was also lovely about it, said I could even bunk in her room if I wanted to. But I prefer having complete privacy. Both have been pillars of support since all this happened. Lana too, when she's been down to visit, sleeping in Nick's room with me. I feel bad, just because she was used to having a bit more space staying in my and Johnny's spare room in the past. But she doesn't seem put out. She calls me regularly from Leeds to see how I'm doing. All that being said, it cuts me up that the one person I had expected to be there in my time of need has been avoiding me like the plague. In fact, Johnny had been the first to encourage me to move in with Ness and Nick. Perhaps naively, I thought he was being understanding of my feelings. But now, based on the bombshell he's just dropped, I realise otherwise. That really, he just wanted me out.

Is it me? The fact that what happened to me has changed me? That I don't feel the desire to go out partying with him, have sex, that I'm no longer acting like the confident ambitious go-getter he fell in love with. That all I feel most of the time is tired, scared and depressed. Worn out by my ordeal, struggling to get out of bed because I can't help thinking *what if my attacker is still out there?* Christ, I can barely get undressed, have a bath, without wondering if I'm being watched. Funny, I had never considered Johnny to be *that* shallow. Underneath the roguish smile and cocky banter, I'd seen a deeper side to him. A side he only showed me. And possibly Ness. Which is why hearing his words right now breaks my heart.

'You're abandoning me?' I say in disbelief.

I watch him fiddle with his Omega, the one his father bought him for his twenty-first, then ruffle the back of his hair. He's so jittery and it makes me wonder if he's high. He does have a bit of a coke habit, despite me trying countless times to make him stop.

'I'm from a fucked-up family, you know that. I just don't think I'm the right person to help you through this, I'm not built like that. I don't know how to help you, it's too hard for me.'

I didn't think I could get any angrier, but I was wrong. 'Oh, I'm sorry, sorry that it's too *hard* for *you*, you poor thing.' I hear my tone. Mocking. Resentful. 'Being here would be a start! Rather than avoiding me at all costs, the way you have done since all this happened! I thought you loved me, that you cared about me. I'd never turn my back on you, how can you do this to me?'

I study his face, will him to respond, but he remains eerily mute, his expression hard to read. 'I just look at you, and I feel powerless. Like I'm more of a hindrance than a help. Plus, I've got my finals coming up. I can't be distracted. Dad put in a good word for me at that investment bank I told you about, and I can't let him down.'

'Distracted! You fucking piece of shit! Get out! Get out now!'

He doesn't even hesitate, making me feel that much worse. I hear him mumble a pathetic 'sorry', and then he's gone. For a moment I am still, and then I start to cry, my entire body shaking, while a mountain of pressure builds on my chest, almost crushing the air out of me. I know it's just panic but I feel like I'm having a heart attack.

I hear a knock on the door. And then it opens. I momentarily think it might be Johnny come back to apologise, having realised that he's been acting like a total shit and has now come to his senses. But it's not. It's Nick. He sits down beside me on the bed, wraps his arm around my shoulder, and I soon find myself sobbing hysterically into his chest.

Chapter Fourteen

Nick

Sorrento, Italy, Monday, 5th August 2019

Padma and I are in our bedroom unpacking, having first grabbed some food in the cool of the kitchen. Thank God Marcus chimed in when he did because I think I might have taken a swing at Johnny after he made that dig about our childlessness and me not earning as much as him, despite knowing how my actions would have upset Padma.

We've not been here two hours and yet he's already trying to make me look like a loser. That I'm not good enough for Padma. It drives me mental how he feels he has the right to show me up like that. Almost as if he delights in my humiliation. But what's worse is knowing that there's absolutely nothing I can do about it – just because of the history we share – short of pushing him off the cliff this place is balanced on. I can't say I'm not tempted. I mean, it's his fault entirely that we've been walking on eggshells these last eighteen years. If he hadn't been such a show off none of this would have happened. And yet he has the nerve to treat *me* like shit! You'd think he'd have learnt his lesson.

I try to focus on the positives. It's a fantastic villa, I can't deny that. And this bedroom we're in is like something out of *Global Living Magazine*. Not that I expected anything less having seen the photos Ness sent round. It's got a whopping super king bed and a black and white marble ensuite bathroom, not to mention a spacious balcony looking out across the ocean. I don't think I've stayed anywhere this swanky since our honeymoon when we splashed out on a five-star all-inclusive in the Maldives. Two weeks of unadulterated bliss, being waited on hand and foot. It's the freest I remember seeing Padma since before that fateful night. She was almost back to her old self – happy, untroubled, uninhibited in bed. We had sex twice, sometimes three times a day; crazy, passionate, all-consuming sex, sometimes on the sand in front of our villa – sex I didn't think could be that good. It's a wonder we didn't make a baby then and there, we were just so alive and into one another. And in between our lovemaking, we'd swim, dive, eat and drink, beholden to nothing and no one. Johnny was a lot to live up to, and so it had made me so happy that I satisfied her in the bedroom. Reassured me we were destined to be together, even though for so long we had only ever regarded each other as friends.

But then we came back to reality and no sooner had we touched down at Heathrow, the old memories resurfaced. Or more like the nightmares. For her. And for me.

I close my now empty suitcase and store it under the bed. Then I glance over at Padma, who's just hanging up the last of her clothes in the wardrobe, having gone in search of more hangers while I was in the bathroom. Apparently, that's the one thing this place is lacking although, being a typical man, and having packed the bare minimum, it's not a problem for me. I come up behind her and wrap my arms around her waist, as slender as the day we married. It should feed my ego, knowing the woman I'm with is the best-looking one here, having retained her toned, youthful figure, more like a twenty-year-old than one pushing forty. But all I feel is a sense of sadness, of something missing from my life, wanting more than ever for her belly to be swollen, for our child to be growing inside her. And that's why Johnny's behaviour just now got to me. It wasn't so much the money issue that needled me, it was him drawing attention to our lack of children. I know ending up with Lana has been a colossal disappointment to him, but at least he has kids. Kids who adore him, who will carry on his family name when he is dead and buried. He needs to appreciate that more, focus on the good in his life instead of pining for the past and what could have been.

Still, I mustn't let my melancholy spoil our time away. Sooner or later his cockiness will catch up with him. I'd almost bet on it.

'It's not bad here, is it?' I say perkily. 'I mean, I could get used to this life. You realise this bedroom is practically the same size as our living room.' I give a light chuckle.

Padma turns her head and presses her lips against the light stubble peppering my cheek, which has not seen a shaver in twelve hours. 'Well, it would be perfect if it were just us. Are you sure we can't just stay in here the whole week? There must be a butler or someone who can bring us room service?'

She smiles that smile of hers I don't see often enough, and I have the urge to push her down on the bed and take her right now. 'I'm just hoping the conversation isn't all going to be as uncomfortable as it was just now,' she carries on. 'Johnny was bang out of order and I'm proud of you for not hitting back.' My insides go all warm and fuzzy as she says this. All I've ever wanted was her approval, and so knowing I make her proud tells me again that we were meant to be together, even though I often wonder to myself – if that night hadn't happened, would she and Johnny be married with kids, living the glamorous high-flying lifestyle Padma was once set for? And perhaps deserved? There's no denying how crazy they were for each other. It's why Johnny's cold behaviour hit her so hard. To her, it had seemed so out of character, but to me, it was inevitable. I pinch myself back to reality as Padma continues. 'As for Lana, I get that she's unhappy, but that doesn't give her the right to have a go at me. Constantly making spiteful comments. The way she goes on, anyone would think it's my fault I got attacked that night, and my career didn't go the way I'd planned. Not that I regret my choice now, because I love my work. Wouldn't trade it for the world.'

It's reassuring to hear her say that. Even so, I see the tears collect in her eyes and it breaks my heart, while I almost want to break Lana's neck. First Johnny, now Lana. I need to stop visualising them both meeting a nasty end at my hands. Life would be so much simpler if they weren't around, though. I keep listening.

'But I guess she's entitled to think like that because none of us know what happened. Least of all me. Maybe she thinks I brought it on myself. Maybe I did. I only wish I bloody well knew the truth. And that's what gets me. She knows that every day since has been torture. Not knowing who attacked me, or why they did it; whether it was some random nutter or someone I knew. Not knowing whether they're still out there. Whether it's the same person responsible for that female fresher going missing. More than anything I want to remember, doesn't Lana think that I do?!'

I swivel Padma round, see the tears trickling down her face, and can't help feeling rotten inside. Just because I do, and yet don't, want her pain to go away. I bring her towards me, cradle her head against my chest then place my index finger under her chin and tilt it upwards so that I am staring into her big brown eyes. And then I kiss her tenderly on the lips.

'Johnny can go to hell. And who cares what Lana thinks?' I say. 'She's always been jealous of you, you know that, everyone does. Jealous of the fact that despite what happened to you, despite her being married to your former boyfriend who she fancied the pants off from day one, you remain as popular as ever. Think on that. Take comfort from the fact that the rest of us love you. Even Johnny, in his own selfish way.'

She smiles, nestles her head against my chest once more. 'I just want to remember, Nick. Just want that missing week of my life to come back. It's been eighteen sodding years.'

'I understand,' I say, 'but you also know what the doctors said. It's common for patients who've suffered amnesia arising from a traumatic event to subconsciously block it out. It can take years for the memories to return, if at all. And I worry that if you do remember, it will only make things worse.'

Padma cuts free from my embrace, shooting me an angry look. 'How can you say that? The not knowing all these years has been torture. It goes round and round in my head like a carousel. Sends me crazy imagining all the possible scenarios. I thought you understood that, that you'd want to know too, so you could punch the bastard's lights out!'

She continues to glare at me, her voice replete with pain and frustration, and I feel like the worst husband in the world. She's right, I would want to know if I were her, and I should have foreseen her reaction to my tactless comment. I feel the guilt pulling at my guts again. The last thing I want is to push her away. Make her stressed. Not when I still yearn to make our family complete. Fuck Johnny again for bringing that up. It's as if he's asking for trouble.

I'm about to reach out and beg for her forgiveness when I'm stopped short.

By a piercing scream that nearly shatters my eardrums.

Chapter Fifteen

Marcus

Sorrento, Italy, Monday, 5th August 2019

It's approaching 3.30 p.m. and Ness and I are just on our way down to the pool when a scream stops us in our tracks. One of those ear-splitting Hitchcockian screams that makes the hairs on the back of your neck stand up. We eye each other in alarm, then do a sharp about-turn, clambering back up the stairs, weighed down by our oversized swim towels and sliders which make a clattering sound on the marble stairs underfoot. Just as we reach the landing Padma and Nick dart out of their room. Telling me the scream must have come from Lana and Johnny's room – by process of elimination. And then comes a loud banging, causing my stomach to lurch. I wonder if Johnny has finally lost the plot and lashed out at Lana. He was a bit tipsy when we all left the terrace, and perhaps seeing Nick and Padma for the first time in ages sparked something in him.

'What the hell's going on!' Padma yells, looking panic-stricken as I take the lead and hammer on Lana and Johnny's door, Ness hovering anxiously at my side. Ness told me that Padma still suffers from anxiety, remains fearful of strange noises, the possibility of violent intruders. It's hardly surprising given her ordeal.

'Talk to us, guys,' Nick says.

After a few seconds the door opens, Johnny standing there with a big grin on his face. It throws me a little, but at the same time reassures me that Lana must be OK. He's in his swim trunks, and I can't help noticing the way Padma's gaze is immediately drawn to his six pack. Along with the irritated look on Nick's face having spotted the same. I can't exactly blame Padma, it's the first thing I noticed, although perhaps not in the same way as her. My wife, however, seems totally oblivious, which pleases me no end.

'What the hell happened?' Ness demands.

'Guys, chill out,' Johnny says, pressing the palms of his hands down as if we've all gone crazy and are making a fuss over nothing. He runs his fingers through his perfect hair, adjusts the waistband of his trunks drawing attention to the V of his washboard stomach. I bet his dick is as massive as his ego, just to make matters worse. 'Lana found a gecko in her drawer, that's all,' he says in a blasé fashion. 'A pretty lively one. Was a bit of a shock. I mean, we all know she's not too keen on them.'

Not too keen on them. That's the understatement of the year. He grins again and I almost want to deck him. How can he make light of something like that? Typical Johnny. Sometimes I think he's got a sadistic streak to him. We go inside to find Lana sitting on the edge of the bed, her head bowed, her shoulders trembling ever so slightly.

'It's not funny, mate,' Nick fires Johnny a hard look. 'You know Lana's got a phobia of reptiles.'

It's true. I learned this from Ness not long after we met. Apparently, Lana was bitten by a non-poisonous adder when she was a child and has been scared of reptiles ever since. Maybe that's why Johnny found it so hilarious.

Delighting in her distress. Given how he taunted her earlier on the terrace, it's not unthinkable. I watch Padma go over and sit down next to Lana before putting an arm around her shoulder. Lana doesn't brush her off, but neither does she warm to Padma's attempts at affection. Rather, her eyes remain focussed on the floor beneath her feet.

'You OK, Lana?' Padma asks.

'I'm fine,' Lana says stiffly, still not looking up.

'How the hell did it end up in the drawer?' Ness asks. She looks at me as if I'm an expert on the subject and therefore have all the answers.

'Don't look at me,' I shrug my shoulders, 'I haven't a clue, darling. It's a hot country, lizards are everywhere, and like any kind of bug they're no doubt sneaky blighters that can slip in through the smallest crack. That's why it's important to keep your balcony doors shut, even when you're outside admiring the view.' I pause, letting my gaze work the room. 'It's the only explanation, isn't it? Open to other thoughts though?'

My question seems to hang in the air as everyone just stares at each other in silence. Bar Lana, of course, her eyeline still directed at the floor. Finally, Johnny breaks the awkward hush. 'Well, it's dead now. I used the back of my shoe to give it a good beating. Crushed it to a pulp.' That explains the loud thumping. His eyes are gleaming, almost triumphant, as if he expects a medal for his cruelty.

'Was that necessary?' Padma looks up, her brow creasing. 'You could have pulled out the drawer, tipped the creature out onto the balcony. It's harmless enough.'

'For Christ's sake, it was a spur of the moment reaction,' Johnny says indignantly. 'You heard her scream, why's everyone getting onto me?'

'It's fine, it's done now,' Ness says, 'and like Johnny said, he was just acting on instinct. Let's go have that swim. We're all a bit tired and cranky and could do with cooling off.'

As usual, my wife is the first to defend Johnny. It irritates me. The last thing he needs is to feel any more cocksure of himself. What he did was hideous, unnecessary, like Padma said. I catch the anxious look on her face. Clearly, she's terrified of violence in any shape or form.

Ness kneels by the side of the bed where Lana and Padma are perched. 'Must have been an awful shock, but I'm sure it was a one-off. Let's go downstairs. A swim will relax you.'

Padma gently smooths the back of Lana's hair. 'Ness is right, you need to get out of here.'

Reluctantly, Lana forces herself up. 'OK, but I need to get changed first.' She looks over at Johnny, says, 'You go ahead,' then turns to make eye contact with Padma for the first time since Padma sat down beside her. 'Will you stay, while I get dressed? I don't want to be alone right now.'

I don't think I've ever seen Lana show Padma any genuine warmth since I became a part of this group, let alone ask for her help. And as I catch the others' eyes, Padma's included, I can tell they're as amazed as me. As unsettling as this unfortunate incident must have been for Lana, perhaps our little lizard friend was the icebreaker they needed?

Padma smiles, beams in fact. Says, 'Yes, of course.' Then she looks up at the rest of us. 'You guys go ahead. We'll be down in a sec.'

I'm so relieved Lana's OK, but at the same time I notice the somewhat nervous look on Johnny's face as we make our way out.

Making me wonder why he's so afraid of leaving his wife alone with Padma.

Chapter Sixteen

Lana

Sorrento, Italy, Monday, 5th August 2019

Padma is being so lovely, and it feels like old times, back at primary school, before the hormones and the grudges set in. Before boys and superficial appearances got in the way of genuine friendship. Whenever one of us was upset or had a problem, we'd be there for each other. I miss those days. We were both so innocent then, so oblivious to how shit and twisted life could be. Because of the people who make it such. Like my loser of a dad and cow of a mother. Both of whom reek of selfishness.

I emerge from the bathroom, having splashed my face with cold water and changed into my swimsuit. It's an all-in-one number, cut low at the hips. Black, because everyone says black is slimming, even though, let's face it, it's never going to hide the fact that I'm at least a stone overweight, the tops of my thighs rubbing together like a wobbly blancmange, the excess flesh either side of my breasts hanging over the sides of the suit which cuts into my skin and leaves unsightly marks. I breast-fed all three of my children. Loved the whole experience. I felt such a bond with them, knowing it was my milk that nourished and helped them grow into healthy little human beings.

It's the only pure thing I've done in my life. But it's played havoc with my boobs. I had quite nice breasts before. But now they sag like balloons that have had all the air taken out of them, a bit like the rest of my body. The stretch marks aren't too bad though, because I was quite good at rubbing in the Bio-Oil. Even so, my mother would be appalled if she saw me right now. I hate wearing a swimsuit. It's like going out in public in your underwear and who the hell would do that? I bet Padma will look like a bloody model in hers, even though I can tell from the colourful sarong secured tightly around her tiny waist that she's not wearing a bikini. Thank God for small mercies. Johnny wouldn't have been able to hide his erection if she had been. Even Vanessa looks slimmer, I've noticed. All over, in fact. Must have found time to fit in a workout during her busy schedule. Probably at some ungodly hour. I know her firm has a swanky gym their employees get to use for free because their lives aren't their own. Oh well, I shall just have to resign myself to being the fatty of the group. The gym always feels like too much of a chore. And besides, I like my food too much. It's the only thing in my life that gives me pleasure apart from my children. And my vibrator.

'How are you feeling?' Padma asks. She's moved from the bed to a red crushed velvet chaise longue positioned in the corner of the room, so I take a seat beside her.

'Better,' I say with a heavy sigh. 'Sorry to have caused such a fuss. I feel like a bit of a fool.'

'Don't worry about it,' Padma says soothingly. 'It would have shocked anyone. I think I would have bloody screamed finding a lizard scurrying around in my drawer! And I'm not even that fazed by them.'

It's kind of her to say, but I bet I know what else she's thinking. She's wondering how on earth it got in there. Whether it was just chance, as Marcus suggested, or whether someone might have put it there to scare me. Like my darling husband. It doesn't take a genius to work out he gets off on my discomfort. I asked him this very question after watching him smash it to smithereens. That was disturbing enough in itself. Bordering on the psychotic. The thing had started to crawl up and over the lid of the drawer, but he hadn't given it a chance to escape as I'd stood there, petrified. Instead, he'd grabbed his shoe off the floor and smashed its skull. As much as I dislike reptiles, it was barbaric. Made me wonder what else he might be capable of. As if he was using the poor creature to expel a pent-up anger he was finding hard to contain. And it had me thinking – was he pretending the lizard's skull was my skull he was pulverising?

Or was it something else entirely he was trying to smash out of his system?

Like the guilt that refuses to dissipate despite the passage of time?

Padma smiles and I smile back. It feels good chatting to her, like we're best friends again. I've missed having a female companion to talk to, share my problems with. The school mums I sometimes socialise with don't count, largely because I don't really have anything in common with them, but we hang out all the same because our children seem to get on. And when we do meet for coffee or a glass of wine we inevitably spend most of the time complaining about the school, or the teachers, or the fact that our children don't get as much attention as they should do in comparison with so and so. And don't get me started on the WhatsApp messages. Always some idiot who never reads the school's emails and so expects everyone else to act as her school admin PA. Always someone who complains about having to contribute to the class kitty, but then expects their child's name to be in the teachers' Christmas cards. It gets on my nerves, bores me to tears sometimes, but I also can't bear to be left out. It's been the story of my life. Wanting to be part of the 'it' crowd.

'I'm just glad you're OK,' Padma goes on.

'Thanks. So, enough about me, how have you been?'

She smiles. 'Not too bad. Work's constantly busy for the both of us, but I can't complain, I enjoy it for the most part.'

I wasn't really talking about work. And I think she knows that.

Johnny's reference to the 'pitter-patter of tiny feet' or lack thereof in her and Nick's case was so uncalled for. Him being his usual tactless self. Although, to be fair, my husband isn't stupid. It makes me wonder if he knew exactly what he was doing. Drawing attention to their childlessness to make Nick feel inferior. I know he's jealous of how happy Padma and Nick are, but even so, he needn't be such a bastard to his best mate; it's not fair on Nick, who takes it on the chin every time. Sometimes, I'm sure I see the fuse being lit in him, that little flex of the jaw that tells me he's trying his utmost to contain his anger. Which he does well to do. Presumably he knows Johnny's never got over Padma and feels the need to cut him some slack. Despite it being Johnny's fault that things didn't work out for them. Still, it's always felt like there's more to it than that. That I don't know the full story there.

Nick and Padma's childlessness has long been the elephant in the room. Principally because, with the rest of the group having five children between us, their failure to start a family stands out like a sore thumb. Kids aren't for everyone, and no one should feel obliged to have them if they're not truly wanted. That's a crime in itself. My mother being a prime offender because, quite frankly, she doesn't have a maternal bone in her body. But the thing is, I know that Padma's always wanted a baby. She was broody in her late teens, while I had no desire to be a mother back then. My dad clearly saw me as a curse to have taken off before I was even born, so it had felt like the dumbest idea in the world to have a child of my own. But I remember Padma saying how one day she'd like at least four, two of each preferably, despite also wanting a career and the financial independence that went with it. It's obvious how badly Nick wants a family. He's so good with Erin and George, a real natural. I see the envy in his eyes whenever Johnny hoists one of our younger ones up onto his shoulders, or they cuddle him adoringly. George hero-worships his father, while Erin is Daddy's princess. Johnny may be a shit husband, but I can't fault him as a father. He's the best version of himself with them. And I guess it's another reason I can't bear to leave him. I want our kids to have that precious time with their dad, to benefit from what only a father can offer them. Stuff that I missed out on.

Truth is, none of us have had the guts to ask Padma and Nick what the story is behind their childlessness. Until now. It just feels like the right time, with us being here in this room alone together. And with Padma having just been so kind to me, like we're finally reconnecting after years of polite but restrained conversation. It's unexpected, but that's life, sometimes the unexpected happens. To hell with the past, it's been so long now, I need to move forward. Have faith that everything will be OK. 'Padma, I know I've not been a great friend since we left uni, but I feel like perhaps this week is our chance to reconnect.'

Her face instantly lights up, and it warms my heart. 'I'm so happy to hear you say that. I thought you hated me.'

'No,' I almost choke up. 'I don't hate you, how could anyone ever hate you? I guess deep down I've always felt guilty for stealing Johnny away from you, especially after what happened to you at Oxford. It became hard to look you in the eye.'

For more reasons than you could ever imagine.

She shakes her head. 'You didn't steal him away from me. He did that all by himself. It was his choice to end things. And after we split, he was a free man, could see whoever he wanted.'

'Yes, but it can't have been easy for you seeing your best friend swoop in. I should have been more considerate. Should have waited. In truth, I should have steered clear of him. Realised that anyone who could dump the love of his life when she was at her most fragile, wasn't to be touched with a ten-foot barge pole.'

And that's the least of it. Doesn't even compare to the other stuff I know that should have warned me off him. Stuff I don't have solid proof of, but which I've always had my suspicions about, yet turned a blind eye to. Because I was blinded by love. Or more like obsession. God, how I feel so stupid, so selfish, looking back.

She smiles. 'Well, that's what love does to a person. It was no secret how mad you were about Johnny, everyone could see it.' I feel myself blush, appalled by my behaviour, embarrassed by my naivety in thinking I had managed to keep my infatuation with Johnny under wraps. Back then he was all I could think about, and I had been so jealous of Padma, who seemed to have it all – good looks, an adoring father, a doting boyfriend, brains, popularity. How I wanted her to fail at something. 'We all do things we regret when we're young. God knows I have,' she goes on. 'And to be honest, ending up with Nick was the best thing that happened to me.'

She's right there; while I got the Devil, she got a saint.

'Which kind of brings me onto something I've wanted to ask for a while,' I then say, my eyes penetrating hers, which are suddenly wary. I don't blame her, but I have to plough on all the same.

'What's that?'

'Are you OK? Health-wise, I mean. It's just that, we'd all expected you to have kids by now. It's obvious what great parents you and Nick would make, plus you always said you wanted them. So, if there's anything you feel like talking about, or need some advice on, I'm here.' I take her hand, give it a gentle squeeze, my chest burning, hoping to God she's not going to slap me across the face or tell me to mind my own bloody business.

But she doesn't. Instead, she smiles, seemingly grateful for my concern. Although there's a sadness in her expression that tells me she has a lot on her mind.

'Thank you, but I'm fine. It just hasn't happened for us. There's nothing physically wrong with me or Nick. The doctors say it's not uncommon for perfectly healthy couples to have trouble conceiving. We just need to relax, try not to dwell on it, let nature take its course and hope that one day it will happen.' She pauses, then adds, 'I suspect it's me, though. You know what a stress bunny I am, how the slightest thing sets me off these days. I expect it's my body in permanent defence mechanism rejecting any chance of making a baby.' She looks away and I see the tears gather in her eyes. 'It's all my fault,' she carries on. 'Nick wants kids so desperately, and I just can't seem to give them to him. I feel like such a failure, like I've let him down.'

I'm suddenly overwhelmed by guilt. Feel heartbroken for her. It must be torture still having that blank patch of time. I know it would drive me crazy. No wonder she's stressed. I wish I could make it all go away for her, especially if that's what's stopping her and Nick from conceiving. But I can't. Not without a lot of collateral damage being done. All I can do is be here for her. Trust that it's safe to get close to my friend again.

'Come here.' I stretch out my arms and pull her towards me, stroking her hair and telling her it will all be OK.

Even though I am far from certain if it will be.

Chapter Seventeen

Johnny

Sorrento, Italy, Monday, 5th August 2019

I'm lying on one of several sun loungers scattered around the pool. There are a few more in the surrounding garden area, all shaded by lofty palm trees gently swaying in the breeze, but I guess, with it being our first day, and us being typically English, we're all keen to work on our tans even though it's roasting. There's a parasol shielding the sun from my head, but the heat still feels intense through the cloth. I've saved a lounger for Lana next to mine, spread out her towel along the length of it, placed the factor fifty and a bottle of water I grabbed from the kitchen on a side table between us, as a gesture of goodwill. I've decided I don't want to spend the entire week arguing, it's too draining, and so from now on I intend to try and be civil towards her, not just for my sake, but for everyone here, Ness especially. This is her week not ours, and she deserves to have fun. I don't want to be the arsehole who spoils it for her. I just hope Lana can find it in herself to be civil back.

Nick's bagged a couple of loungers directly across the pool from us. He too has laid out Padma's towel for her, put both parasols up, but I expect she'll want to move into the garden area. I remember how even back at Oxford she'd avoid putting her face in the sun. Said it was the quickest way to age the skin, and I guess she was right because her face looks as unlined and blemish-free as it was twenty years ago. Breaking up with her is the hardest thing I've ever done, and it kills me that she doesn't know this. But staying together would have been impossible. For so many reasons. Doubtless she still believes me to be a shallow, lying piece of scum who was using her for sex, who didn't have the emotional capacity to deal with what she was going through. But she's wrong. So wrong. More than anything I wanted to be able to tell her that. To hold her, support her. But I couldn't. And then when Nick dived in to take my place and fulfil that role, it sent me off the rails: booze, drugs, women. Lana included. The second biggest mistake of my life.

I'm just contemplating a swim when my phone pings. I pick it up on instinct, thinking it might be Lana asking if I need anything from the room. It worries me that she and Padma still haven't appeared.

> How can you swan off to Italy and pretend it's all OK? Have you no shame? One missing piece of the puzzle is all it takes, then you can kiss your charmed life goodbye.

Fuck. Not another one. Panic floods my insides. I've no idea what this person's endgame is, but it's frightening the crap out of me. Making me feel claustrophobic, that my every move is being watched. But by who? That's the question. Right now, Ness and Marcus are in the pool, while Padma's busy comforting Lana upstairs. Clearly the sender knows where I am, but aside from us lot here, the only other people with that information are my PA, my boss and my parents. When I'm on holiday I always make a point of telling my whereabouts to a minimum number of people. Sure, anyone can email or phone me, but they don't need to know where I am. Which brings me back to the question – who on earth can it be? After eighteen sodding years, why has this person, whoever it is, decided to make noise now? It had been dark, and we'd been careful, but based on these messages it's apparent that someone had been watching us closely back then, hiding in the shadows, tracking our every move. Either that, or they've been talking to someone else who was. One of *her* friends, perhaps? And by *her*, I mean Carys, the missing fresher. I guess it could be the girl who told the police about what went on that night. Rachel, I think her name was. Having said that, maybe I'm barking up the wrong tree. Because it's not exactly clear what this person is alluding to. It could be one of two things, or both, I just don't know and the not knowing is driving me bonkers. As is the fact that I haven't a clue what their intentions are. I mean, what if they appear here, challenge me in front of Padma? What if they go to the police? It doesn't bear thinking about. My life as I know it will be at an end. I will myself to stay calm, but it's not easy, especially as I find myself getting increasingly worked up about what the hell's keeping Padma and Lana.

It's been ages, for Christ's sake. At least forty minutes. It can't take that long for Lana to change. And she can't still be worked up about the blasted lizard. I'm really not sure what came over me. I just suddenly felt this rage, like I'd had enough and needed to thrash out at something or someone and it was either Lana or the gecko. It doesn't help that I'm knackered – from work, the kids, my dad's constant criticisms, my utterly miserable marriage, the wearisome weight of worry and guilt that presses down upon my shoulders and never eases up. Not to mention seeing Padma in this beautiful place, stirring all sorts of feelings in me. And now this latest message is threatening to tip me over the edge.

'Hey, you coming in? It's so refreshing!' Ness giggles as Marcus grabs her from behind then swirls her around to face him. After swimming a few lengths, they're now mucking around like carefree teenagers. She locks her arms around his neck and kisses him softly on the mouth, her eyes animated and smiley, her hair already wet through. It's lovely to see her enjoying herself. Especially when I think how she used to hate the water as a child. In fact, I can't remember seeing her look this relaxed in a long time. Or the two of them being so easy in each other's company.

I'm sure I've not imagined the tension between them in recent years, but Ness always insists it's nothing, just life, the kids, getting in the way, making it hard for them to work on their relationship. It seemed like a bit of an excuse to me. Chiefly because it's the same one I give whenever anyone asks me about my relationship with Lana. My mum being a classic example. 'Why don't you take Lana out on the town, your father and I will babysit.' She says it all the time. To think, when I was a kid, she'd hardly give me the time of day, but with her grandchildren she's so different. I don't begrudge my kids that. But I do resent her for not being the hands-on mum I'd craved when I was their age. Of course, my parents have no clue that time alone with my wife is the last thing I desire, despite our putting on a good show for them at the start of our marriage. They just think we've grown apart, like so many couples do after having kids. But the truth is, it's impossible to mend something that was broken to start with.

Still no sign of Lana and Padma. What the fuck can they be talking about? No way would Lana risk the life she's bagged for herself with any loose talk, so perhaps it's Padma who's confiding in Lana? There was no mistaking the affection between them just now in our bedroom. An affection I've not witnessed in a long time. If only I could somehow find out. I'm pretty sure Lana won't tell me. If Padma did say anything to her, my devious wife will delight in keeping it from me. She's always revelled in having the upper hand.

It's how she trapped me in the first place.

Chapter Eighteen

Lana

Before
Oxford, England, mid-April 2002

This is your chance. Don't blow it.

Ness and I have just turned up to a party kick-starting Trinity term at one of the larger Oxford colleges. Famous for its alcohol-fuelled bashes, and where Johnny has a lot of mates. Padma suggested I come down from Leeds for it. Thought it might cheer me up, after having yet another massive row with Mum the other week while I was at home for the Easter break. Despite me losing weight, the cow still finds fault in me. Grudgingly acknowledging that I've lost it from my thighs, but at the expense of my boobs which are looking smaller, and which perhaps explains why men never look at me the way they look at Padma. When she says stuff like that, sometimes I don't blame my father for leaving her, God knows she must have made his life hell. But I still can't forgive him for abandoning me. He could have stayed in my life, even if he chose not to be in hers.

I suppose I get why Mum's been more of a bitch than usual lately. I know exactly what's been bothering her even though she thinks I'm clueless. But the fact that she's deliberately concealed something so important from me, only makes being around her that much more unbearable.

I've been playing it smart since Padma's attack. Still visiting her, offering up my help with her recovery, but grabbing any opportunity I get to cross paths with Johnny, even though that's proved a bit harder to do with them no longer living together. For months I've been holding onto the one piece of dynamite I have at my disposal. Waiting for the right moment to ignite it; to launch a plan of action that might actually work now it's clear that Padma's memories of that week aren't coming back, and that her and Johnny's love story is well and truly over. Especially as she's with Nick now. I know I'm unhealthily obsessed with Johnny, but I just can't help myself. And when they split, it was hard to conceal my delight. This was my chance to muscle my way in, making me glad I never told the police what else I know about the events of that week, even though I fear keeping such a secret will torment me until my dying day.

I know Johnny's been sleeping around. Something that both upsets and pleases me. It bothers me that he's having sex with other women, but it's also comforting to know that he doesn't like any of them enough to form a steady relationship. There's only a short time to go before he finishes at Oxford, after which I might never see him again, so it's now or never.

I was so relieved when Padma said she wasn't going to the party, leaving me free to go for it with Johnny. Though it still feels a bit weird going without her, just because I've only got to know everyone through being her friend. Ness said I could tag along with her. Granted, she hadn't looked that enamoured with the idea, which made me feel like a bit of a desperate hanger on, but I knew I had to swallow my pride if I wanted my chance with Johnny.

As we enter the main room, the music is loud and grating, everyone wasted, downing pints of lethal cocktails, some of the crowd dancing, some snogging each other at tables or up against the wall. Loads of the girls are wearing next to nothing, some have even stripped down to their bras, the particularly gorgeous ones making me feel fat and frumpy. I scan the room for Johnny, am dismayed to see him chatting up some skinny blonde in the corner as Ness abandons me to go find a couple of friends on her course. At least I can now breathe easy with her gone. To my delight, the blonde suddenly stomps off in a huff – clearly Johnny's said something to piss her off – so I tell myself this is my moment.

He's drinking neat vodka from the bottle, a cigarette dangling nonchalantly from the fingers of his free hand. He looks so hot, and I try to pep myself up, thinking I look pretty hot myself. For me at least. I've lost more than a stone, got highlights in my hair especially for the occasion, and I'm wearing a strappy mini dress that doesn't leave much to the imagination. Padma had looked somewhat shocked when I appeared earlier, while Ness gave me the once-over with her typical wordless death stare. As usual, Padma was her kind, diplomatic self, told me I looked stunning, even though she probably thought I looked like a slut and was asking for trouble.

My heart feels like it might burst from my chest as I make my way through the mass of sweaty gyrating bodies, music blaring in my ears. I walk directly up to Johnny, my legs shaking with fear and excitement, and say, 'Hey, how are you?'

And that's when he looks at me – really looks at me – in a way he's never done before. And it's the best feeling in the world. Gives me hope that I can make him love me without using what I know.

'I'm sorry about you and Padma,' I go on as he casually flicks his cigarette to the floor, then stubs it out with his shoe. 'I know it can't be easy, but really, she's never been the same since her attack. If there's anything I can do to help, just say the word. I hate seeing you look so sad.'

God I'm such a suck up. I wait for his response. Half expect him to call me a bitch, question how I could be so disloyal to my friend. But he doesn't. Simply says, 'Fancy a dance?'

I feel myself blush, thinking that all my Christmases have come at once. 'I'd love that.'

He sets down the vodka then takes my hand, presses his body up against mine, slow and sensual, our lips almost brushing. I tell myself to play it cool, even though I feel like I must have died and gone to heaven. I don't question why this is happening, how he can possibly want to be with me having rejected so many girls since Padma. All I can think about is being in this moment with the boy I have worshipped from afar for so long. Just then, I spy Ness over Johnny's shoulder. She catches my eye and I see the look of surprise in hers. And perhaps a little disgust. I tell myself not to let it bother me. She acts all holier-than-thou, but I know for a fact she's no angel, has no right to judge me, or anyone else for that matter. Even so, I avoid her gaze, look straight into Johnny's dark pools, willing him to want me as much as I have wanted him for so long.

'Let's get out of here,' he says with a roguish grin as the song fades out.

Those five words are like music to my ears, and for a second, I think I must be dreaming. But then he takes my hand, sending a rush of electricity through me, before whisking me up the stairs and outside. Out into what's fast becoming the most magical evening of my life, my pulse rocketing, the sweet anticipation of spending a night with my crush almost too much to bear.

'Where are we going?' I say breathlessly.

He grins. 'Back to mine. Ness will be a while, so we'll have the place to ourselves.'

A sliver of guilt shoots through me as he says this. I think back to the numerous times I stayed there as his and Padma's guest. But I quickly brush it off – this is no time for compunction or hesitation. Instead, I focus on getting naked with him. Imagining him slowly undressing me, kissing every inch of my body. Sexy yet romantic movie-style love. How I've always fantasised it would be, all those nights I've lain awake dreaming about him. Padma's told me what a tender lover he can be; not that I need her to tell me that, because I know it in my heart to be true. I can't wait to experience the same tenderness for myself. Just can't believe this is finally happening for me. But instead, no sooner have we stepped inside the hallway, he asks me if I am on the pill and I find myself lying and saying yes, only because I don't want to put him off, and then before I have time to think or say another word he's shoving me hard up against the wall, hitching up my dress and yanking down my knickers, then unzipping his flies before roughly spreading my legs and entering me with a force that makes me gasp out loud, so hard I can't help but flinch. I've never had sex like this before. And for a moment I feel exhilarated, knowing that he wants me so badly, like a scene from a porn movie. But then, as it happens, him grunting like an animal as he thrusts himself into me, me worrying about Ness walking in, while at the same time catching sight of my face in the hall mirror as his chin rests on my shoulder, lipstick smeared around my cheeks, I feel sick, cheap, dirty. Humiliated. No better than a prostitute. I want to cry, want this not to be happening, just because it's so far removed from how I'd envisioned this moment to be. He climaxes, while I feel nothing. Nothing but heartache and humiliation. And relief that it's over.

'You'd better get back to Padma and Nick's,' he says, having buttoned his flies up. 'Ness will be home soon.'

That's it? I want to vomit. It's as if he's commanding a child or a dog that needs to be kept in its place. So cold. So matter of fact. I'd imagined us cuddling up in bed after making love, him showering me with kisses and gestures of affection. His excuse about Ness walking in on us is utter crap. We could easily sneak into his room, and she'd never know the difference. I want to suggest this, but I also can't bear to suffer further humiliation with some cruel knockback. It's obvious that having 'serviced' his needs, now all he wants is to be rid of me so he can crash out on his bed.

I pick up my knickers, quickly pull them on. And all the time he says nothing.

It's so awkward, so utterly mortifying, and I want to scream, I feel so hurt, so wronged.

'Bye then,' I say feebly.

'Bye.' He barely glances my way as he says this. Not so much as a peck on the cheek goodbye. I think he's too drunk, too stoned to care. Then again, if I were Padma, I bet he'd be all over me.

I slink away and out the front door. Do the walk of shame back to Nick and Padma's. Luckily, they're in bed when I slip in quietly, grabbing some water en route to the spare room. As I undress, I feel slightly sore where he penetrated me so hard. I crawl under the covers, not even bothering to wash my face or brush my teeth, despite feeling so dirty, so utterly worthless. In truth, I'm desperate to shower, to wash the humiliation off me. But I can't chance waking Padma and Nick. The last thing I need is Padma coming out and asking me questions; not when I lack the strength to pretend that everything's OK.

Once again, I can't help resenting her, lying in the arms of another man who adores her, worships her, no doubt makes love to her with sweet affection the way Johnny once did.

How dare he treat me like that? I could make his life hell if I wanted to.

He has no idea I have information at my fingertips that could send his pampered world crashing down around him.

Chapter Nineteen

Vanessa

Sorrento, Italy, Monday, 5th August 2019

There's Padma and Lana. Thank goodness. It's about time. I'm still in the pool with Marcus and Johnny. It's so refreshing, feeling the soothing cool of the water on my skin as the sun fires its rays on us. It's been fun mucking about with my two favourite men. They even seem to be getting along, and that makes me happy. I noticed some friction between them when Johnny and Lana first turned up, but seeing them laughing and joking just now I'm hoping that perhaps being here in this beautiful place, relaxing, having fun, will stop them from behaving like a couple of childish schoolboys. Surely, after last night, Marcus knows he has nothing to fear from Johnny. He never has, if truth be told, but I can understand how he must feel a bit intimidated. I mean, Johnny does have the body and face of an Adonis. He could have gone into modelling, I've often thought, but Ed would have laughed in his face at the suggestion. And then, having realised Johnny wasn't kidding, blown a gasket. I can just picture his irate ruddy expression now, telling his son to *stop acting like a frigging faggot and concentrate on doing a man's job!* Anyway, it's true that a lot of women fancy Johnny.

But I've never looked at him in that way. Not before, when we were in our early teens and started having those kinds of feelings, and certainly not now. We've known each other since we were babies. For Christ's sake, I've seen him whip out his penis as a five-year-old and pee in the paddling pool the nanny used to set up in the garden for us. Even then, he was something of an exhibitionist. I chuckle to myself at the thought. Anyway, point is, thank God he and my husband seem to be getting on. I at least want to enjoy the first few days of this holiday, before it all goes to pot at my own instigation.

Am I being selfish? The question keeps turning over in my mind. Selfish in being focussed on appeasing my own conscience to the detriment of others? In failing to acknowledge the consequences of my coming clean not just for us, but for our children. I guess, the thing is, when I look at Johnny and Lana, when I see how miserable they are, how their children suffer because of it, it makes me question where keeping silent all these years has got us.

I have to say, Padma and Lana are looking more relaxed in each other's company than I've seen them in years. There's a spring in their step as they approach the pool, locked in conversation, arms linked. I wonder what they talked about up in Lana and Johnny's bedroom. Seeing the distracted look on Johnny's face just now as he spots them approaching, while absentmindedly passing an inflatable ball back and forth with Marcus, I expect he's thinking the same. And with good reason, given Lana's track record. Nick appears to have fallen asleep on the sunbed, his earbuds in, head turned to one side as he lies there fully reclined on his back. I wonder what's going through his mind too. A mind I feel sure can never have peace. Just like the rest of us.

'Hey, you two, wondered if you'd taken a wrong turn to Narnia or something,' I joke.

They both laugh. 'Well, the wardrobe is frigging massive,' Lana replies. 'Like just about everything else in this place.'

'We were just having a catch-up,' Padma says. She's wearing sunglasses – square black Audrey Hepburn frames – along with a wide-brimmed straw hat, so I can't read her expression. Whether her gaze is fixed on anyone in particular. 'Talking about the good old days back at uni.'

'Oh yeah,' Johnny says somewhat nervously. 'Care to share with us?' He looks at Marcus. 'For Marcus's benefit, I mean.'

Marcus smiles, although inside he's probably thinking *you lot harping on about your Oxford days is the last thing I bloody well want to hear.*

'No, sorry,' Lana says. 'We'll just keep that between us girls.' She gives Padma a mischievous wink before trotting over to her sunbed. Call me paranoid but it felt like she was trying to make a point with that comment: that any *girls'* chat between them is out of bounds for me. I try not to let it bother me. She's always been the same, adopting an air of self-importance, when a lot of what she says is literally hot air. It maddens me, but as ever, I bite my tongue for the sake of appearances.

The remainder of the afternoon passes without incident, and we finally seem to be relaxing in each other's company. Even Johnny and Lana seem to be making an effort with each other, while Padma appears the most chilled I've seen her in ages. I can't imagine how stressful her job is so it can only be good for her to get away, as much as I suspect she feels guilty for taking such an extravagant vacation. We talk about old times, the various fashion and make-up faux pas we made back then, about work, our parents, the kids, that new restaurant that's opened up in London, movies, books and so on. Normal stuff we always find ourselves chatting about, while patently avoiding the one glaringly obvious subject that's always lurking at the back of everyone's minds – what happened to Padma that night.

It's just hit 5.30 p.m., and I realise I've not eaten much to speak of all day. Not by mistake but out of choice. I'm hoping that, what with the commotion of everyone arriving earlier, Marcus didn't notice me hardly partaking in the spread I laid out for us on the terrace. Unlike at home, where my excuses for not eating range from being too stressed with work and the kids to being late for that meeting, or saying that I ate earlier. My hunger comes and goes. Last night, I enjoyed the fish as it was light and so tasty, while the wine helped stimulate my appetite. But sometimes the nausea and pain are so acute, food is the last thing I crave, while when I do feel the urge to eat something I often pay for it later in the most distressing way. Right now, I'm suddenly overcome with fatigue, my exertions in the pool, along with the heat, having exhausted me.

'Guys, I think I'm going to take a late half-hour siesta,' I announce as chirpily as possible, hoisting myself off the sunbed. I glance at Marcus and hope he doesn't read this as code for sex.

'Good idea,' Nick says, 'do as the locals do, and why not, you work bloody hard enough.'

'My thoughts exactly,' I say, shoving my book, sunscreen and phone into my cloth beach bag. 'So, see you guys later? I've booked a table down by the marina for eight, so shall we reconvene for a pre-dinner drink around 7.15?'

'Great idea,' Johnny says, rubbing more cream onto his arms, which have already gone a dirty shade of brown. I notice his eyes wander to Padma in the pool as she grabs the handles of the steps, pausing to tilt her head backwards and allow the water to suffuse her hairline before climbing the rungs and raising herself out. Her suit clings to every inch of her slender physique like a second skin as she does so. Lana catches Johnny staring too, but tries to look unfazed.

Everyone endorses my plan for later. 'Shall I come up with you?' Marcus asks. There's a touch of concern shrouding his face, so I don't think he's after sex. Hopefully he just thinks I'm finally unwinding and taking the opportunity to recharge my batteries before the evening's frivolities.

'Only when you're ready.' I smile. 'It's been a tough month at work, as you know. And I think the adrenaline drop has finally hit me.'

He smiles back, appears to accept my explanation.

Ten minutes later, having changed out of my swimsuit and into a bathrobe, I crash down on the bed.

Then cry myself to sleep, thinking about everything I'm going to miss.

But most of all, the fact that once again I've failed to be honest with the man who worships the ground I walk on.

Chapter Twenty

Marcus

Sorrento, Italy, Monday, 5th August 2019

I try not to let the worry take hold of me. But there was something in Ness's expression as she stood up and announced she was off for a lie down that makes me nervous. It's true she seems to be enjoying herself, a blitheness about her I've not seen in years, and we had so much fun in the pool earlier. But I still can't help thinking she's hiding something. Perhaps it's a work issue? Some trouble with a client, or her senior partner with whom I know she often clashes. I don't want to spoil things by putting her on the spot. After all, she's here to celebrate a milestone birthday, forget about work, real life. But while the fretfulness in her gaze perhaps bypassed the others, I'm sure I wasn't imagining it because I know my wife. And it's a look that's hard to shake. I might wait until after her birthday on Wednesday before saying anything. Get the big day over with then ask her if something's up. Speaking of the big day, with Ness out of earshot now's my opportunity to fill the others in on the plan.

I sit up on my lounger, my pasty white legs straddling either side, my face fully exposed in the gaze of the late afternoon sun. The heat is more bearable at this time of the day, having lost that ferocity that makes you feel like your skin is being lasered. I throw on my Oakleys, then say rather loudly, 'Guys,' in an attempt to grab everyone's attention.

Lana and Padma are both engrossed in books, Nick's swimming lengths in the pool while Johnny's lying on his stomach browning his smooth hairless back. Those perfect buttocks of his are just about concealed by the tight trunks he's wearing. I expect he gets everything waxed, there's no way at nearly forty he wouldn't have hair growing in all kinds of unwelcome places. I'm thinking of my own unsightly stomach fluff, the straggly black hairs sprouting from the backs of my pink-tinged shoulders, not to mention my nose and ears. As opposed to the top of my head which is where I'd like it to grow, but instead is getting sparser by the day. I should make more of an effort I guess, but I've never been one for male grooming. It all seems like too much of a faff, a bit effeminate. Using Nivea for Men facial wash is about my limit, but I'm guessing Johnny's at the spa more often than Lana.

The women put down their books, Johnny swivels over onto his back, while Nick front crawls to the edge of the pool nearest to me and rests his arms over the side, all four of them giving me their full attention. I launch into my spiel. 'As you know, Ness's birthday is the day after tomorrow, and I want to do something really special.'

Johnny grins, 'Great idea, I was thinking—'

'Shut up, let the man speak,' Lana growls while cutting Johnny a fierce look.

I give her a grateful smile whereupon Johnny raises his hand. 'Oh, yeah, course, sorry Marcus, go ahead.'

I take a deep breath. 'Thank you. So, I've hired a local chef and a couple of staff from one of the best

Michelin-starred restaurants in the area to come in and make us a special Champagne breakfast that morning. I'll delay Ness, but if you guys can be up for 7.15 to let them in, show them the kitchen, help them get started, lay the table and so on, that would be marvellous. I know it's early for a holiday, but you'd really be helping me out.'

Padma claps her hands, displaying an uncharacteristic show of excitement. 'Ooh, Marcus, how wonderful, definitely fine with me.' She looks at the others who all eagerly nod their agreement.

'Let me foot the Champagne, Marcus,' Johnny says, 'least I can do. Not sure if you know but her favourite bubbles is—'

'Bollinger, yes I know,' I say. 'She is my wife.' I point this out in a flippant fashion, give a light chuckle, but in truth it gets on my wick. It's like he has this compulsion to score points. Arrogant like his father. I mean, she's my bloody wife, obviously I know what her favourite Champagne is.

'Of course, mate, just trying to be helpful,' Johnny says somewhat graciously, making me feel a bit shabby for thinking ill of him.

'Anything else you need us to do, just say the word,' Nick offers up.

'Thanks,' I say. 'As for the rest of the day, I've hired a boat to take us all out. Bit of a cruise around the islands, Capri, Ischia and the like. Ness especially loves Capri so I thought we could stop off there, do a spot of shopping, have some lunch, before heading back to the villa late afternoon.'

'Sounds fabulous, Marcus,' Padma says. I grin at her seal of approval. Just envisioning the look on Ness's face when

I surprise her on Wednesday ignites a spark of excitement in me.

'And last, but not least,' I go on.

'There's more?' Lana remarks. 'All I can say is that your wife is one lucky woman.' I can tell Lana's made a special effort to be civil with Johnny all afternoon but there's no mistaking the glare she gives him with this comment. He sees it too, and I will him to remain silent rather than come back with some juvenile retort, but sadly he can't resist.

'Well, she's one special woman. One in a million, in fact.' He doesn't look at Lana as he says this, just grins knowingly at me.

'Anyway,' I go on. 'I'm thinking we have two options for the evening. We can either have a chilled one – dine in al fresco on the terrace – or I've provisionally booked a restaurant up here in Sant'Agata with the most magical views. We'll let Ness decide. See how tired we're all feeling after a day out in the sun. What do you say?'

'I think that's a good plan,' Padma says with a smile. 'Hope we're walking down to the marina from the main square later, because with all this food we're going to end up the size of houses.'

I catch Johnny's eye, can see he's almost tempted to make some snide comment about Lana's weight, but manages to restrain himself.

'Yes, I think that's the idea. And that way you get to experience Piazza Tasso at night. It's got such an electric vibe about it. Right, well on that note, I'm going to see how the birthday girl's doing. It's nearly six and we need to be making tracks for the restaurant by 7.30.'

Chapter Twenty-One

Lana

Sorrento, Italy, Monday, 5th August 2019

I've just emerged from the shower, a towel wrapped around me and tucked securely under my arms, to find Johnny sitting upright on our bed, the back of his skull resting against the cream and red trimmed headboard as he stares intently at his phone. We've barely said two words to one another since coming upstairs, but I know what's going round in his head. He's desperate to ask me what Padma and I chatted about. Stressing about what I might have said to her. It's killing him not knowing. And it bothers him that she and I seem to be getting on better than we have done in years. I can't deny what a sweet sense of satisfaction it gives me to feel like I've regained a semblance of power over him. Power I'd had at the start of our relationship, forcing him to be nice to me, to marry me. But which, over the years has dwindled. It's not like I'm ever going to tell Padma what I know – I can't risk losing all that I've striven so hard to acquire, even though the shame is becoming harder to live with. But I can perhaps lead my husband to believe that I'm thinking about it. Just to make him suffer. The way he's made me suffer. He's forever telling me I know nothing;

that I think I've figured out the truth when in fact I'm a long way off. But how do I know he's not just messing with my head, like the gaslighting shit that he is? Maybe I'm spot on with my hunches – even though I don't want to be because the very thought makes me shiver – and the truth of which he claims to know is a load of crap. After all, he's always had a way with words, it's one of his fortes. Cajoling people into his way of thinking, getting them on side. And anyway, I know stuff he doesn't. Stuff I should have spoken up about years ago, but chose not to because at the time it didn't suit me to do so.

'How's the shower?' he asks without looking up.

'Good. Powerful,' I say. 'Not one of those drippy contraptions you sometimes get abroad. But then again, we're practically living in a palace so I wouldn't expect any less. What are you looking at?'

'Just work stuff.'

Even on holiday, he never switches off. I know it's normal for people who work in the City, but it gets on my nerves sometimes. It's not like he doesn't have people at the office to cover for him. Seeing his expression just now, though, I'm not so sure it was work that was occupying his thoughts. He looked worried, rather than frustrated, which is his usual reaction to a work email.

'You'd better get a move on,' I say. 'We need to be downstairs in forty-five minutes.' I go over to the dressing table, squirt some detangling spray on my wet hair, throw my head upside down, then start to comb through it.

I slyly glance at him through the damp strands as I do. Finally, he lays down his phone and looks up at me. 'Are you going to tell me how it is that you and Padma suddenly seem to be getting on like a house on fire? What did you talk about? You took ages to join us by the pool.'

And there it is. Bingo!

I straighten, wet hair sticking to my back as I shrug my shoulders. 'What can I say? She was nice to me after I found that creature in my drawer. Knowing how much I hate them. How shaken I was after watching my husband pulverise it to kingdom come.'

A flashback, a memory of a face I've tried so hard to erase. Don't go there.

'I already told you, I have no idea how that thing got in there.'

'Yeah, whatever.' I shrug again.

He starts to say something, but I purposefully turn on the hairdryer, blocking him out. 'Sorry, can't hear you,' I say loudly. It's childish of me. But somehow, I can't resist.

Before I know it, he's leapt off the bed, wrenched the dryer from me and switched it off.

It gives me a fright, although I try not to show the alarm in my voice. I say angrily, 'What the hell are you doing?! Are you crazy? How dare you!'

He presses his face up close to mine, so our noses are almost touching. Once I found the sensation of his skin against mine so erotic. Now it repulses me.

I see the face again. Haunting me, fuelling my guilt.

'Don't toy with me, Lana. Don't try and play your nasty little mind games. You know as well as I do that if she finds out what you've kept from her all these years, you'll be in as deep water as me.'

He's right, I know he is. But I can't let him think that. Can't let him see my fear.

'What I did is nothing compared to you. Even though you claim I know nothing. And that's why I've been calling the shots all these years. Controlling you. Dictating your every move. You can't harm me, you can't leave me.

129

You can't fucking touch me. You know that, and it kills you!'

He pulls away, his chest heaving, his nostrils flaring, and I can see that it's torture for him to give in. That he's itching to respond. To possibly even strike me. But he doesn't. He's too smart for that. He wouldn't do such a thing with our four closest friends nearby. He makes for the bathroom. Then turns to make eye contact with me once more, his hand resting on the door frame. 'Let's just get a divorce, Lana,' he says, his voice gentler, more conciliatory. It throws me. 'Why live like this? I know you were mad for me back then, which is why you did what you did. But I also know the way I've been all these years has soured that love. Understandably. So, what do you say? What good is it doing us being miserable? How can you live like this?'

Everything he says makes sense, there's no denying that. But I cannot bring myself to give in. 'There's no way I'm sharing joint custody of the kids with you. They need to be with me, their mother. I can't have them repeating your mistakes.'

'And you think us being like this around them is doing them good? You think that's healthy?'

Again, he has a point. Still, I can't bear to admit defeat. Because if I do that, it would somehow feel like keeping the secrets I've kept for the last eighteen years would all have been for nothing.

I make it clear the conversation is over. 'Go shower, Johnny, else we'll be late.'

Chapter Twenty-Two

Vanessa

Sorrento, Italy, Monday, 5th August 2019

It's 7 p.m. and I've just told Marcus to go downstairs and have a beer with the boys while I put the finishing touches to my make-up. After a thirty-minute nap, followed by a tepid shower, I'm feeling somewhat refreshed and looking forward to the evening ahead. I tell myself not to think about how things will be between the six of us in a few days' time. That there's no point dwelling on it now, because it won't change anything. Over the years I've become good at compartmentalising things. Blocking out the bad, focusing on the moment – which mainly involves throwing myself into my work, albeit to the detriment of my marriage and spending time with my children. It's the only way I've felt able to survive.

As I sit at the small but tasteful Baroque-style dressing table, as decadent as just about everything else in this place, I study my face, the lines smoothed over with foundation which also, more importantly, disguises the yellowish tinge to my skin. My hazel eyes are enhanced with mascara, my cheekbones accentuated with a touch of blusher. My face is markedly thinner. I've always had quite a long face, but now it looks practically oblong. Marcus hasn't said anything but I'm beginning to think he suspects all's not well – it's just a feeling I have. Something in his gaze, in the way he fussed over me before leaving the room, that told me so. I was dreading him asking me what's wrong. Because I'm not ready to tell him yet. If I do, the tears will come and before I know it, everything else will come out too. And it can't. Not yet. Not before I've cleared my intentions with Johnny, and had one last birthday that will stay with me until I take my last breath.

When I first started having pains in my stomach, I thought perhaps I had an ulcer. That the long working hours combined with excessive alcohol, the wrong foods and lack of sleep had finally caught up with me. But then, when I saw blood in the toilet, I knew what I had was far worse than an ulcer. That something was terribly wrong.

I can't help thinking this is my penance for what I did all those years ago. My sins catching up with me. I've never been a religious person, but now, with death chasing me far quicker than I would have dared to believe six months ago, I find my beliefs changing. I don't want to die without confessing my sins, asking for forgiveness. If I stay silent, I'll never have peace, and I can almost imagine myself haunting this earth, tormented by my guilt and deceit. Looking back, we should have come clean. Should have realised that telling the truth wouldn't have been the end of the world. But we were young and scared, and our priorities were all wrong.

Having applied some rose-pink lipstick to brighten up my face, I'm about ready to go when there's a knock on the door. It can't be Marcus, he'd never knock, plus he's only just left me in peace to get ready, so I figure it must be one of the girls.

I'm dressed so I don't hesitate to call out, 'Come in.'

It's Padma. She's wearing an eye-catching flowing red chiffon dress with thin spaghetti straps which shows off her golden skin tone to perfection. It strikes me how she's revealing more flesh than she has done in years, and I wonder what's brought this on. Her long dark hair is straight and sleek, while she's accentuated her eyes with black kohl liner, her lips with a frosted nude gloss. As ever, she looks beautiful, and I can't help thinking how hard it will be for Johnny seeing her like this.

'Padma, come in, everything OK?'

She closes the door and comes up by my side, taking my hands in hers. My heart skips a beat as I wonder what she's going to say, although I take comfort from the fact that her mannerisms are warm rather than hostile. 'I just wanted a moment alone with you to say thank you for arranging this week. I had my doubts, I won't lie, and it still feels a bit indulgent, but I think it's what we all needed. Connecting with Lana again this afternoon, it's been so lovely. Since what happened to me at Oxford and her getting together with Johnny, you know things have never been the same between us. Truth is, our friendship meant the world to me, but the way she behaved after they became a couple – it was as if it meant nothing to her. And that hurt, more so than her being with Johnny if I'm being honest. I think she recognises that now. So, I suppose what I'm saying, is that time is mellowing us, making us see that we need to put the past behind us. Because really, life's too short, isn't it?'

It's wonderful to see Padma looking and sounding so content and relaxed, but at the same time I can't help feeling a pang of guilt knowing I'm on the verge of shattering her newfound happiness.

'I'm so glad,' I say, just about managing to hold it together, while keeping my contempt for Lana to myself. 'It was so nice to see you two getting along. There's something to be said for getting older, I agree. I think we're all a lot wiser than we were back at uni. We know what matters and what doesn't. You look lovely, by the way. Nick had better watch out, you know what Italian men can be like. I saw some real Romeos strutting their stuff last night, eyeing up the ladies. They really are quite incorrigible.'

She giggles, a sound I've not heard from Padma's lips in the longest time. But then, just like that, her expression grows sombre. 'Ness, are you OK?' She reaches out, touches my arm. 'It's just that I get the feeling something's troubling you. Call it women's intuition or the fact that we've known each other the best part of twenty years.'

My heart kicks again. Does she know? Her eyes drill through me, like they're delving deep into my soul, reading my every thought. 'It's just that Nick and I, well, we've noticed that things have been a bit tense between you and Marcus the last few times we've seen you. I mean, you two seem great here, so perhaps we were worrying for nothing? Sorry, I don't mean to pry, we're just concerned for you.'

I'm suddenly desperate to unload all my problems on Padma. To tell her I'm sick, just because for six months now I've been carrying that burden alone. The doctors have said I could extend my life by up to a year with chemo and radiotherapy. But I couldn't face spending what little time I have left in hospitals, suffering the side effects of the treatment, Marcus and the kids seeing me like that. I want to work, to be at home, to be here in Italy enjoying the last birthday I'll have to the full. To live life to the max before the cancer takes it from me. I look into her eyes and it's there on the tip of my tongue, itching to come out, but then I stop myself. I don't want to spoil Padma's evening, or mine, by dwelling on something so grim. She's just reconnected with her best friend, she doesn't need to lose another close friend so soon. Besides, I don't want her feeling sorry for me before I tell her the truth about what happened that night. I don't deserve her pity. I deserve the full force of her wrath.

'Thank you for your concern,' I say. 'But I'm fine. It really is just life – too much work, not enough time for each other. And yes, you're right, things are better here, because we've been able to leave all that behind. It's reassuring, tells me Marcus still loves me.'

'That was never in doubt.' Padma smiles. 'You only have to look at his face whenever you walk into the room. It lights up like a Christmas tree.'

'That's kind of you to say,' I reply, willing myself to hold back the tears. 'Don't know what I did to deserve a man like him.'

'Don't be so modest! You're one of the kindest women I know. I mean, sure, you can be bloody scary' – she gives me a playful dig in my side, making me smile – 'but the way you've always looked out for Johnny, it's amazing. He's been so lucky to have you in his life.'

You don't know the half of it, I sigh inside. I badly want to tell her I'm no saint, that a good person wouldn't have done what I did, wouldn't have lied all these years. But I can't go there now, it's too soon. I need to block it out. Even so, I feel the urge to defend Johnny. A habit that's never going to change.

'Thank you, he's not all bad you know. He puts on a show, but really, underneath all that bluster, he has a heart of gold. And I think, if he could go back in time, he'd do things differently.'

In so many ways, I think to myself.

I'm not sure why I say this to Padma. I mean what good will it do? But it just tumbled out, which is so unlike me, because usually I'm good at thinking before I speak. It's my job for God's sake. She doesn't say anything – what can she say? Johnny dumped her at the lowest point of her life. Why would she want to see any good in him? And the fact that she abstains from commenting perhaps confirms this.

'Come on,' I say, standing up. 'The others will wonder where we are.'

But Padma doesn't move or speak, her gaze vacant, seemingly lost in thought. 'Padma, are you coming?' I say, somewhat unnerved by her silence.

'Do you ever wonder about that girl, Carys?' she finally says. 'About what happened to her?'

My shoulders tense. This is the perfect moment to tell her. But I can't, not yet, for the reasons I've already gone over in my head. But neither can I not answer her. And so, I do. Tentatively. 'The fresher who went missing? Yes, of course. It's not something that's easy to forget. Why are you asking that now?'

'I don't know, you were talking about going back in time, doing things differently, and I guess it triggered memories of Oxford. I still can't help wondering if my being attacked and her going missing are linked.' She holds my gaze, and I'm contemplating how best to respond when the door opens and Marcus walks in, catching us both off guard. 'Oh, Padma, you're here too. We're all downstairs, wondering where the both of you had got to.

136

No time for a drink now, I'm afraid. Not if we plan on walking down to the marina from Piazza Tasso.'

I've never felt more relieved to see my husband. 'Right, yes, we were just having a catch-up,' I say. 'Also comparing outfits, what do you think?'

I give a twirl, and as I do I catch the circumspect look on Padma's face. I've always prided myself on my ability to adopt a deadpan expression, but now I'm wondering if it's failed me.

'You look incredible, darling,' Marcus says, giving me a peck on the cheek. He smiles at Padma. 'And you look ravishing too. Nick and I had better keep a close eye on you both this evening, you know what the Italian men can be like.'

'That's what I said,' I chuckle.

Finally, Padma gets up. 'Thanks, Marcus, let's get going. I'm absolutely famished.'

Chapter Twenty-Three

Padma

Before
Oxford, England, early June 2002

'It happened that weekend in April. When I came to visit. We were drunk. Like, *really* pissed.'

I'm in the house I now share with Nick. The one he used to share with Ness, who's been living with Johnny since he and I split up. Nick and I are together now. We have been since early January. Lana now stays with us when she comes down from Leeds to visit. Like she is this weekend. There're only a few weeks left before I leave this place for good. And as far as I'm concerned, it couldn't come sooner.

I look at her, hear her words, but can't quite take them in.

Because she's just told me that she's pregnant. With Johnny's baby.

I don't speak, sensing she has more to say.

'I went to that party with Ness,' she carries on. 'You and Nick didn't want to come, remember?'

I do. These days I hate parties. All those people. All that smoke, noise, booze. Drugs. Plastered students talking rubbish and acting like morons. I can't be doing with it anymore. It's all so senseless. And the worst of it is, I can't help thinking that any one of those morons could be my attacker. Could be behind the missing fresher's disappearance, for which the police still don't have any leads, eight months on. It's like she's dropped off the face of the earth. They did discover something, though, just after Christmas. Something those who had been in the know had been too afraid to speak up about. The night before the girl, Carys, went missing, she'd taken part in some debauched female fresher 'hunt' organised by the male drinking society Johnny and another third year called Richard head up. Rather than having attended a bog-standard party in the college bar as the police had originally been told. Another fresher, a girl called Rachel, eventually owned up to the police about it, having initially been scared she'd get into trouble with the teachers and her parents. I couldn't believe it when I found out Johnny had helped organise something so demeaning, and it made me wonder if this was why he had gone all funny and ended things with me. Perhaps because he was ashamed and felt he might be indirectly responsible for her disappearance. Of course, he denied it was the reason when I asked him, but I couldn't be sure he was telling me the truth. To be honest, I'm so over him now, I couldn't be bothered to pursue the issue. I was upset, however, when Nick also admitted to being there that night. Both he and Johnny, along with everyone else who participated, were questioned. But as Carys was last seen leaving the bar alone, this new information sadly doesn't appear to have made any material difference to the investigation. Apparently, she was spotted talking to a lot of students that night, both male and female, something the police already knew. I was angry with Nick initially for keeping it a secret. But

Johnny told me not to be. Said he'd forced Nick into it, made him promise to keep his mouth shut and that, being the loyal friend he was, Nick had agreed. As much as it had pained Nick to lie to me. I asked Johnny if I'd known about the hunt at the time and he'd told me that I hadn't because he'd been afraid of my reaction. And he'd be right there. I never liked the idea of him belonging to an all-male drinking society. It reeked of chauvinism. But I'd let it go because I knew his father had been a member and it was expected of Johnny to follow in his footsteps. Like some outdated male Harker tradition. I know how much pressure Ed puts on him to 'be a man' and all that rubbish. But what Johnny did is a step too far and quite frankly makes my stomach turn. If he's capable of something like that now, at university, God only knows what he'll be like when he starts working in the City, surrounded by clones of his father. And now, more than ever, I feel so relieved we aren't together anymore. Ness, as usual, tried to defend him, saying it was just a bit of harmless fun, but it seems fishy to me that this girl went missing the day after the hunt took place. Despite her having been seen leaving the bar alone. I can't help thinking someone knows more than they're letting on. Her bed wasn't even slept in that night, according to friends who live in the same halls. So where did she go after leaving the bar? And why does it feel like there's some sort of cover-up going on? The College Master claims to know nothing, but I know how cliquey things are here. It wouldn't surprise me if Johnny asked his father to have a word in the ears of the people who matter so the whole thing could be hushed up. Particularly as the hunt seems to have been downplayed in the newspapers, no mention of any names who took part.

'Yes, I remember,' I say to Lana, having been lost in my thoughts. I don't know why I'm suddenly feeling so rattled by her having slept with Johnny. After all, I'm with Nick now. It was perhaps a bit precipitous of me to jump into another relationship so soon. But Nick has been my rock since that night, and I've gradually fallen in love with him. It's different to how things were with Johnny. With Johnny, there was this insatiable physical attraction between us, so hot, at times it took my breath away. That butterflies in your stomach all-consuming feeling, when you know you have to be with this person come hell or high water, and that you can't rest until that happens. Things were wild with Johnny, wild and exciting. Whereas with Nick, it's a calm, steady sort of love. He makes me feel safe and so I can't bear to lose him. He also knows something I've been too ashamed to admit to anyone else: that I imagined Nurse Rani. I found this out the day before being discharged. I'd asked the nurse on the morning shift what had happened to her, and although she tried to be as tactful as possible, it was clear I'd been hallucinating, clinging to the idea of someone who reminded me so much of my beloved aunt being in the room to comfort me. I felt so ashamed, like I'd gone crazy or something, but she assured me it was nothing to feel embarrassed about. That it's quite normal for patients suffering from post-traumatic amnesia to hallucinate, with neurons firing incorrectly, and that as I'd stopped seeing Nurse Rani, this only proved that I was on the road to recovery.

Nick had said the same, but I made him swear not to tell a soul, just because I know how judgmental people can be. I don't want anyone thinking I've gone insane, least of all Johnny who might have felt justified in breaking up with me. But it just demonstrates what a strain this whole thing has been on my mental health, and because of this, I can't help hating the person who did this to me with every fibre of my being.

Nick and I got together one night when we found ourselves alone in the house. My head had been resting on his shoulder as we sat watching some soppy romcom, and then we turned to look at one another and in that fleeting moment kissed. And it felt so right. And I guess, having been ditched so coldly by Johnny, it was a boost to my low self-esteem to be wanted by a man. And not just any man, but his best friend. It was a chance to get my own back, I suppose. As petty as that might sound. Being vindictive has never been my style, but on this occasion, I couldn't help myself.

But Lana and Johnny? They're having a baby together? It just seems so inconceivable. Mad, even. I mean, I know Lana's secretly worshipped Johnny from the moment I introduced them. And I think that's partly why things had started to change between us. She was jealous. Jealous that her skinny half-Indian friend who used to get picked on at primary school was now at Oxford mixing with the upper crust, but not only that, dating the sexiest guy she'd ever set eyes on. And rich to boot. She's always had a thing about money. Perhaps because growing up she and her mum were always short on it. Thinking about it, if I were Lana, I'd probably feel envious. She's only human. But now? Now she has nothing to feel jealous of. Because look at me? I'm a mess. I hallucinated my dead aunt, I get scared when anyone knocks on my bedroom door, I'm too afraid to walk home alone at night, I have no urge to study for my finals and I was dumped by the supposed love of my life, because he couldn't 'hack' being with damaged goods like me.

Even so, I can't help thinking about all the unkind remarks Johnny's made about Lana in the past when we were alone in our house, sometimes after making love and cuddling up in bed. I can't imagine her reaction if she knew. All I can think was that Johnny was off his face when they had sex – Nick told me he's been sleeping around a lot since we split up – that his ego needed massaging, his penis a release, and Lana was clearly ready and willing to fulfil both requirements. I remember the look on her face when I told her Johnny had dumped me. She'd tried her best to console me, but I could tell from the glint in her eye that inside she was jumping for joy. Telling me I was better off without him, that I could do a lot worse than Nick who'd been so supportive since my attack.

'Say something, for God's sake.' Lana's shrill voice brings me back to reality.

'What are you going to do?' I ask.

I'd been so taken aback when she made her announcement, I hadn't fully grasped the implications of what she'd said. But now, as reality dawns, with the difficult choice that's facing Lana, because there's no way in hell Johnny's going to want this baby, I feel overwhelmed with concern for my friend.

I take her hand in mine. Pull her close. 'I'm here for you, babe. If you need me to come along to the clinic, just say the word. I know you won't want your mother knowing, so I won't tell a soul. I presume you've not told anyone but me?'

She pulls away, at which point a sly sort of smirk spreads across her face, her eyes glistening like stars. 'I think you're mistaken. I'm not getting rid of it,' she says.

Once again, I'm gobsmacked. 'Lana, you've got no money and you've not even graduated. Your mother will disown you, I'm sorry to say that but I know how heartless she can be and it's the truth. You can't manage a baby by yourself, that's insane. What about your plans to become a teacher?'

She's practically beaming now. Has she lost the plot?

'But I won't have to, silly.'

'How do you mean?'

'Johnny's going to help me raise it. We're together now. Please be happy for me. He says he wants me to be his wife. For us to be a proper family.'

Chapter Twenty-Four

Johnny

Sorrento, Italy, Monday, 5th August 2019

The blood-orange sun has almost retired for the night as we all troop out of the villa, Marcus being sure to set the alarm before we clamber into the six-seater cab he ordered earlier. It's still warm, but pleasantly so, a whisper of a breeze filtering through the air, along with the sweet aroma of rhododendrons and the incessant chatter of insects; that unique special sound you always hear abroad somewhere hot. It's as if they're sensing the night is about to begin in earnest now that the temperature is more tolerable.

I barely have time to buckle up before the driver speeds off like he's competing at Silverstone, navigating his way around the area's famous bends downhill towards Sorrento with easy aplomb. We reach Piazza Tasso in less than twenty minutes. It's heaving, but in a different way to earlier when our taxi from the airport had passed through and taken a left turn off Corso Italia, the main street running through town. Then, it had been a frenzied hubbub of motorists and pedestrians: impatient locals rushing to get to their destinations via scooters and cars hooting their way through brave yet terrified tourists trying desperately to cross the road without being mown down. But by night, it's a different story, a parading ground for tourists and locals alike, scarcely a car in sight. I climb out of the cab and take in the scene, assimilate the more relaxed, carefree buzz in the air that was missing earlier, no cars allowed apart from the taxis permitted to pull up at their rank. They make a curious contrast to the traditional horse-drawn carriages parked opposite offering tourists a more refined, romantic way to explore the town. I see families ambling along with babies and toddlers in pushchairs, loved-up couples walking hand in hand, beautiful young men and women dressed to kill, strutting their stuff and perhaps hoping to get lucky. The bars and restaurants either side are already packed to the brim with clientele enjoying good food, wine and each other's company, prime spots for soaking in the atmosphere and people-watching. Nick, Marcus and I are dressed in half-sleeved shirts and chinos, the girls in flowing summer dresses. Even Lana looks nice — she's actually made an effort for once, wearing a blue Bardot-style skater dress and having highlighted her eyes with matching eyeshadow — although neither she nor Ness are a patch on Padma, who literally took my breath away when she and Ness had appeared at the top of the stairs as the rest of us waited for them in the hallway. For a moment it had felt like someone up there was taunting me, throwing this vision of beauty I had given up in my face, but also making me paranoid over what Ness and Padma might have been discussing, the same way I had been paranoid only a few hours ago when Padma had been alone with Lana. Even though, unlike my wife, I've never had cause to doubt Ness's loyalty. I know she'd never say anything deliberately provoking to Padma purely to spite me. Perhaps it's being here away from home, so close to Padma after such a long time, along with the threatening messages I've been receiving, that's making me so distrustful. Suspicious of everyone and everything. I had tried to hide my feelings on seeing Padma, but clearly did a bad job of it because I then caught Nick glancing at me from the corner of his eye, an irritated look on his face. I know it pisses him off the way I can't seem to stop myself from gazing at his wife. It would piss me off if I were in his shoes. But what does he expect? She was mine once, long before he became her knight in shining armour. He swears he never set out to fall in love with her and that, if anything, he was trying to protect me. And I believe him. I do. After all, he's not to blame for me and her splitting up. Well, not entirely. I dug most of my own grave. But the thing is, and what's most galling, is that I know deep in my soul that if it wasn't for what happened, Padma and I would still be together. We clicked from the outset, both physically and intellectually, so it maddens me the way he adopts this indignant air, as if I have no right to feel jealous, to feel pain and regret. He knows as well as I do that the story behind our break-up is far from simple. And I guess that's why I couldn't resist having a dig earlier, despite it being pretty low of me to refer to their childlessness. I just couldn't help it. And the best part was, I knew he wouldn't dare retaliate.

We make our way through the crowds, almost brushing shoulders as we do, crossing the main square and then down one of the many cobbled side streets. Being the continent, all the shops are open – jewellers, lacemakers, leather stalls and so on – with tourists browsing inside them, looking for a bargain or souvenir to take home, while the various cafés and trattorias are bustling with diners enjoying an aperitivo or early evening meal.

As we follow Marcus and Ness's lead, a mixture of envy and pleasure surges through me seeing them stroll hand in hand. I feel jealous of Marcus for having a wife as wonderful as Ness, for being in love with her, and yet, at the same time, I want more than anything for my darling Ness to be happy after the sacrifices she's made for me and for others. I sometimes resent myself for letting her take control that day. For not being more of a man about it and taking responsibility for my own actions. But it's force of habit, I guess. She's always been there for me, and I've always been shit-scared of my father. Taken together, it's really a no-brainer that she was the one I called. Even so, I can't help thinking how her life could have been so much simpler had I not forced her to become a part of the whole sorry affair. It's a wonder she doesn't resent me, that she has remained so forgiving of my mistakes. Then again, maybe it isn't…

'Hey, you two, stop browsing, we've got a booking!' Ness looks back over her shoulder, having spotted Padma and Lana peering in the window of a jewellers. They are seemingly enchanted by the rows of coral, cameo and pearl pieces, all typical of the area, as well as other dazzling brightly coloured gems that are just too tempting to pass by.

'Sorry,' Lana apologises. 'It's so hard not to look though, isn't it, Padma?'

'Torture.' Padma grins. 'I don't have the money to splash around,' she says, glancing at Nick, 'but I feel I must get something with lapis lazuli for Mum. I know it's a speciality of the region and some of the pieces are just so beautiful. Blue's her favourite colour too.'

Nick smiles adoringly at her. Goes up and puts his arm around her shoulder, then lovingly kisses her cheek. 'Of course, but you should get something for yourself as well. You deserve it, hon.'

Lucky bastard. Fuck, how I long to be in his place, feeling the touch of her skin. If she was with me, she could have anything she desired, money wouldn't be an issue. Not having to scrimp and save the way she does with Nick. I catch Lana giving me a cold look. 'What about me, darling,' she mocks, her eyes narrowing deviously. 'Can I have something?'

I don't wish to get into a slanging match. 'Of course,' I say. 'But maybe later, else we'll miss our booking like Ness said.'

Lana almost looks annoyed I didn't rise to the bait. I catch Ness's eye, and can tell she's proud of me for acting like a grown up for once.

'Come on,' Marcus says, 'I'm starving!'

We keep going, following the pathway round, past the main viewing point in town and the best place to marvel at the Bay of Naples and Mount Vesuvius looming large across the water, until we come to a long-walled stretch which winds its way round to the right and down some chunky paved steps towards the smaller of Sorrento's two marinas. As we venture nearer to the ocean I can hear the call of birds, the odd plane flying overhead, while the rev of scooters and tinkling of piano music is never far behind. There's something so revitalising about the place, and for a moment I catch myself daring to be hopeful, to believe that life can be better. But then I look at Nick and Padma, not to mention my wife, and the grim reality of the situation hits home once more.

Finally, we reach Marina Grande, all of us by now somewhat hot and sweaty from our exertions, despite it being gone 8 p.m. It's a tiny but charming part of town, almost like a mini village in itself. There are several restaurants and cafés, along with a lacemakers and a standard *tabacchi* selling everything from cigarettes to bus tickets to token souvenirs. A rather potent smell of seaweed fills my nostrils as I inhale the fresh sea air. I see a few locals still paddling in the low waves lapping at the black volcanic sand, a jet ski whooshing across the calm ocean in the distance, the sun having not quite gone down yet, although very soon it will disappear for good. The restaurant Ness booked for us is called La Cambusa, and we're greeted warmly by the maître d' before he shows us to a table positioned on a wooden walkway that stretches out onto the water. Despite the frenetic activity going on around us, you can still hear the gentle swishing of the ocean, although, with the light fading fast by the time we've all sat down, it's hard to make out what or who is out there.

We order some still water and two large carafes of white wine, and soon after that our food.

'Ahh,' Nick sighs, leaning back in his chair and clasping his hands behind his head. 'This is the life.' A waiter stops by our table and places a basket of bread, olive oil and balsamic vinegar in the centre. I'm famished, so immediately grab a piece, my hunger intensified by the divine aroma of food that hit me the moment we entered the restaurant.

'Don't get used to it,' Padma jokes, before taking a sip of her wine, a simple yet elegant Frascati. 'We won't be able to afford to come back before retirement.'

Everyone laughs. Bar Nick. 'We're not that badly off,' he says. 'It's just that *you* think it's extravagant. I mean, it's not like we have children to pay for. We could afford to return whenever you like.' No one says anything as

Nick's remark lingers in the air like a bad smell. His tone was light-hearted enough, but it also felt like he was trying to make a point. Perhaps wanting to get back at me for my earlier crack, making it clear he's just as capable of providing for Padma. I see the wounded look on Padma's face and feel angry with Nick for upsetting her like that. Even though I know I'm such a hypocrite for even thinking it.

Thankfully, Padma manages to compose herself. 'How did you find this place?' she asks Ness.

'The client recommended it,' Ness replies, looking as relieved as the rest of us that the conversation didn't turn into an argument. 'He told me it's long been a favourite of the locals and produces the most amazing seafood. But that it's also reasonably priced.' She glances at Lana, raises her glass. 'But I did check it has other things on the menu before booking, I know you're not terribly fond of fish.'

'Ness, really, it's fine,' Lana assures her with a smile. 'There was plenty to choose from. This is your week, and you needn't worry about me. I'm just happy to be sitting in this beautiful spot.' She says this so genuinely, I feel an unexpected rush of affection for my wife, even though I'm not wholly convinced she means it with there being no love lost between her and Ness. The only other time I've felt any sort of warmth for Lana was following the births of our children. For all her faults, she went through hell in childbirth, something I couldn't help but have huge admiration for. And that's why I could never do anything to harm her, as much as I sometimes want to.

Before long, our starters have arrived, and we're onto the second carafe of wine. The conversation has veered from work to kids to parents and places in the world we'd still like to visit before we die. Interspersed with laughter, people watching and general commentary on our idyllic surroundings. But it's telling that the one topic we all seem to be avoiding is university.

'How's your dad, Marcus?' I ask. Marcus is an only child. I know from Ness that he's always been exceptionally close to Eric, his father, even though his parents divorced when he was six and Marcus went to live with his mother and stepdad in Glasgow. Following his mother's passing, they grew even closer, sharing the kind of unconditional father-son bond I can only dream of. None of us ever met Marcus's mum, because she died before he and Ness started dating, but it's clear from the conversations we've had over the years that her death hit Marcus hard. She'd suffered from depression for years, and her suicide therefore hadn't come as a huge surprise to the family, according to Ness. Even so, to lose a mother is never easy, no matter the circumstances. Marcus blamed his stepfather for her death. Hasn't spoken to him since the funeral, calling him too wrapped up in himself to spot the warning signs. He never talks about him, and we've never even seen a photo. I get the feeling Marcus wouldn't give a damn if he was six feet under, which may well be the case.

I know he sees Eric as often as he can, and that Kitty and Owen are extremely fond of him. Having lost his mum before she'd had a chance to become a grandmother, Marcus had been keen from the outset to ensure they forged a strong relationship with their grandad who, unlike Ness's parents, dotes on the pair of them. Dominic and Karen aren't too fussed, much to Ness's dismay, limiting their visits to birthdays and other 'special' occasions, while content to send expensive gifts in the interim as a means of appeasing their grandchildren and their own consciences. In that respect, for once I can say that my parents have come through for me, in that they can't seem to get enough of Josh, Erin and George.

'He's good, thanks,' Marcus says. 'Found himself a lady friend, in fact.'

'Woo-hoo,' I say, grinning at the others, 'way to go Eric. Younger, older? Fit?'

'Johnny, do you have to be so nosey, not to mention vulgar, it's none of your business,' Lana scolds. She picks up her wine, chucks it back like lemonade.

'It's fine,' Marcus says. 'About the same age, I think. They met on the golf course.'

'How lovely,' Padma says.

'Yeah, it's nice. I met her last time I went down to Truro. Lovely woman, pretty for her age I suppose you could say. Quite lively, always been sporty like Dad. Think that's why they get on so well. Mum was never into sports. She preferred a book or listening to music. It's partly why things didn't work out between them, I guess. I know they say opposites attract, but they were too different. Not just in their interests, but in their personalities. Dad's always been an optimist, while Mum, well, she was...'

Marcus looks away, and suddenly I regret asking after his father. It was just a polite enquiry, but even now, after all these years, it's clear that his mother is never too far away in his thoughts. I can't imagine still missing my mother after sixteen years. Christ, whenever we see Mum and Dad, I can't wait to get away from her, she irritates me so much.

'Sorry, Marcus, I didn't mean to upset you.' I swig my wine, glance at the others, then mouth an apology to Ness who's eyeing her husband with concern. She doesn't seem upset with me, thank goodness, more of a distracted look on her face, as if her mind is occupied by other thoughts. I can't help wondering what they are.

'*Ecco qua.*' The waiter arrives with our starters, and I breathe a sigh of relief. Hopefully someone can think of a more cheerful topic to help dispel the darkness that's suddenly masking our table. But just as he's setting down the dishes, I notice Padma pull out her phone from her handbag. I didn't hear it ring, but then we're surrounded by noise and kerfuffle plus I'm sitting opposite her. She appears to enter her pin. It's not ringing now so perhaps it's a text. I watch Nick lean over, ask her if everything's OK. She says yes, but then I see her alarmed expression when she reads whatever the text says.

'Padma, what's wrong?' I ask. But she doesn't respond. Just gets up and excuses herself to the Ladies', the rest of us left staring at our food.

Left to wonder what the hell she just read on her phone.

Chapter Twenty-Five

Lana

Before
Oxford, England, early June 2002

God, I'm such a wicked person. Seeing the astonishment on Padma's face just now when I told her Johnny wanted us to be a proper family made my insides tingle with triumph. I don't know why I resent her so deeply. It's not like she's ever done anything nasty to me. It's just that I've been jealous of her for so long now it gave me such a thrill winning for once. Even though I know she won't see it as a competition. She's too nice for that. To think that I, plain old Lana with average grades, am having Johnny Harker's baby. It's unthinkable. Hence her shock. The same reaction I expect most people to have. Including Ness. And my darling mother although, being the spiteful bitch she is, she'll no doubt suspect I've got something over him. Well, she can think all she wants but my lips are sealed. I'll not do anything to jeopardise my future. Least of all tell her. I know how she gossips after a few.

Obviously, I didn't tell Padma that those weren't Johnny's exact words, and that my one-night stand with her ex wasn't all I had dreamed it would be. Just as I'll never divulge the real reason he agreed to marry me.

The day after we had sex, I returned to Leeds earlier than planned, faking the excuse of needing to get back to study for a Monday test. Like the trusting soul she is, Padma bought my lie, had no idea I was desperate to get as far away as possible from her ex-boyfriend.

For the next few weeks, I tried to shelve the whole episode to the back of my mind. Throwing myself into my studies, finding any excuse to go out, to occupy my mind, even with the most banal of tasks. The nights were the hardest though. Alone in my bed, reliving the degradation over and over in my mind, seeing my face in Johnny's hall mirror, hearing the coldness of his voice when he'd ordered me to leave. But then, I started feeling sick – really off my food, which is unlike me – and I knew something was up. And when I missed my period last month, I realised I was pregnant, just because my cycle usually runs like clockwork. At first, I'd cried. I felt so angry with myself for pretending to be on the pill, just so he wouldn't change his mind, knowing the moment would be spoiled by him looking for a condom. I'd told myself it was what I deserved after throwing myself at him. For acting so cheap. But then, thinking about how the hell I was going to explain this to my mother, how I couldn't bear the thought of proving myself to be a disappointment to her yet again, an idea hit me. I realised this was my chance to use what I knew to my advantage. I had so wanted to make him love me without having to resort to such measures, but now, with his baby growing inside me, this was my opportunity to snare him and get the life I had always dreamed of.

I told him about the baby last night. After I'd tried to give him one last chance by asking him how he was and whether we might repeat the night we'd had. As if it had been all hearts and roses.

He'd almost laughed in my face, and that had hurt like a bitch. 'Lana, you and me, that's never going to happen,' he'd said. 'I'm flattered, but we're from two very different worlds, and that night was a one-off. We were both very drunk and looking for a release. At least, I was. I'm sorry if I gave you the wrong impression. Go find yourself someone who's looking for a girlfriend because I'm not. I'm done with long-term relationships, they're overrated.'

And that's when I dropped the bombshell. 'I'm pregnant with your baby.' My voice was calm, my gaze unblinking. My heart juddering.

At first, he looked at me like I was playing a joke on him. Started chuckling like some inane schoolboy. But then, when I remained poker-faced, the chuckling stopped, because he'd realised I was serious. And that's when he got angry.

'I thought you were on the pill!' he'd growled, running his hands through his thick head of hair.

'I am.' I shrugged my shoulders, hoping he wouldn't see that I was lying through my teeth. 'But these things happen. Nothing is foolproof.'

He'd darted right up to me. Thrust his finger in my face. 'You need to get rid of it. Whatever it takes, I'll pay. Just get rid of it.'

I should have stopped then, seeing the hostility in his eyes. But I'd come this far, and I needed to follow through. Needed to make him sweat, feel helpless, the way he had made me feel helpless that night. What's more, and as much as I hate myself for it, the fact is – I still love him. Can't help loving him, despite the pain he's caused me.

'I'm not getting rid of it. And unless you do the decent thing and stand by me, I'm going to tell Padma your vile secret. In fact, I might tell the world, and then what will your daddy say? Where will that leave him, leave the precious Harker name?' As I said this, I'd pushed down the guilt gnawing at my insides.

The shock on his face was priceless. 'What are you talking about?' he said.

'I think you know. And I think Ness does too.'

The fear in his eyes told me I was right and at that point I proceeded to tell him everything I knew about that week, the week he'd been trying so hard to blot out – with the girls and the drink and the drugs – but which still stalked his every waking thought no matter how hard he tried to repress it. I told him about another suspicion I had about what he might have done, something I have no conclusive proof of, but which makes perfect sense to me.

As I stood there, my gaze penetrating his, I thought he might strangle me. But I stood my ground.

'Be with me, support me and our child, and I won't tell a soul. Abandon me, and the whole world will know what you did, and you won't be able to live under the weight of shame brought down upon you and your family.'

I didn't know I had it in me, but the power I felt at that moment was nothing short of exhilarating. Despite knowing in the back of my mind that in keeping his secret I was potentially depriving others of the answers they craved. And selling my soul to the Devil.

Put to him like that – the entire world he'd been born into threatening to implode – he'd had no choice but to agree. It was either that or kill me. And I suspected he knew he already had enough blood on his hands. He couldn't risk shedding more.

I just pray to God that Padma never remembers that night. Because if she does, Johnny's world won't be the only one that founders.

Chapter Twenty-Six

Lana

Sorrento, Italy, Monday, 5th August 2019

'I'll go see what's up.'

It's evident that none of us are going to be able to relax and enjoy our food until we know what's upset Padma. Nick said he should be the one to check on her but as he can't exactly follow her into the Ladies', I've just offered. I hope nothing bad's happened to her parents or her brother. She's exceptionally close to them, particularly her father. I remember he barely left her bedside the first week she spent in hospital, holding her hand for hours on end, willing her to remember who she was, who did this to her. I can still picture the tears streaming down his face as his daughter stared back blankly at both him and his wife, Jennifer. I can't comprehend how heart-breaking it must have been for Jen – not to be recognised by the child she gave birth to. Now that I am a mother, I can only imagine the pain and terror I would feel. Feelings of utter helplessness and despair. Along with the urge to bring the person responsible for harming my child to justice.

To want to kill them.

The message could have been about work, I suppose. Padma cares deeply about her clients, and in her field

I expect there's the possibility of bad news every day. Hopefully, now that things feel easier between us, she'll tell me what's wrong. Because I genuinely want to help. Despite knowing that's exactly what I should have done eighteen years ago.

I make my way along the walkway lined on either side with lively diners merrily chatting away, then inside the restaurant where there's another sizeable dining area with air con, until I find the Ladies' toilets. I go inside. There are four cubicles but only one appears to be occupied. 'Padma,' I say, 'you in there?'

I hear a sniffle.

'Padma, it's Lana, what's up? Please come out. Talk to me.'

It gives me a warm feeling, being there for my friend again. And I don't mean that in a smug way. Like I'm giving myself a pat on the back for doing my good deed for the day. It just feels nice, pure. Human. Emotions I've not experienced in such a long time.

I hear the lock being turned and then Padma appears. I can tell she's been crying, her eyeliner slightly smudged in the corners, her foundation streaky, but more worrying is the frightened look in her eyes. It's the same look I saw the first time I came to visit her in hospital.

'What's happened? It's something you read on your phone, isn't it? It upset you.'

She gives a faint nod. Then washes her hands at the sink, before drying them with a paper towel.

'Who was it from? What did it say? You can tell me.' I place my hand on her shoulder, as if to reassure her that she can trust me.

She still doesn't speak. Simply slips her hand inside her bag and pulls out her phone, types in the passcode then goes to her text messages. 'That's just it,' she finally replies, 'I have no idea who it was from. But the sender clearly knows who I am.'

Feeling puzzled, I watch her open the relevant text before she passes the phone to me.

'Read it,' she says.

I'm full of trepidation as I take the phone from her, not knowing what to expect. And then, when I read the text, I realise that it's worse than I could ever have imagined.

> Johnny knows what happened to you that night. And he is guilty of so much more. Don't trust him. He is poison. Soon the whole world will know what he did and then a wrong will be righted.

Chapter Twenty-Seven

Vanessa

Sorrento, Italy, Monday, 5th August 2019

It's 11 p.m. and we've just got back to the villa, having taken a cab in relative silence from the main square. When Lana and Padma returned to the table, it was obvious from their quiet manner that something was very wrong. 'Are you OK?' I'd asked Padma. She'd sat down, laid her napkin across her lap, insisted she was fine, her voice clear but terse. Said she'd heard some bad news about one of her clients, that was all, and didn't want to talk about it. So, we left it at that. It was evident from Lana's face that she knew otherwise, though, and that Padma had been lying. And it put a dampener on the rest of the evening. Like a bad taste in the mouth that couldn't be washed away by the delectable food and wine before us. Padma barely engaged in conversation, while Nick played with his food, clearly concerned for his wife. Even Johnny wasn't his usual exuberant self. Conversation was polite but strained, almost as though we were strangers to each other, having met for the first time today. No one was in the mood for dessert after the waiter enquired if we'd like to see the menu again, while all thoughts of a post-dinner digestive in the square, which we'd previously thought we might treat ourselves to, were ditched. In no time at all we had paid the bill and were trudging back up to Piazza Tasso.

'What the hell's happened, I wonder?' Marcus whispered into my ear as I linked my arm in his. I felt exhausted, and needed the support, even though he took it as a gesture of affection and me having had too much wine. At least the air was cooler by then, the black sky dotted with the brightest of stars that resembled perfectly cut diamonds. Something you never see in the smog of London.

'I've no idea,' I whispered back, an uneasy sensation kneading my gut, just because of the way I had noticed Padma eyeing Johnny across the table every so often. A guarded look, as if she didn't trust him. As if whatever she'd read on her phone concerned him, even though I can't believe that after all this time it could have done. And I had watched Johnny's expression too, his gaze switching between Lana and Padma, no doubt wondering what Lana had discovered, while very much alive to Padma's wary glances. The way one can't help being when under scrutiny from the person you love.

There's a stirring in the air, something feels off, but do I approach Padma and ask her outright what's wrong, or let things be and proceed with my original plan? It's unsettled me. I just hadn't anticipated this complication.

'Nightcap, anyone?' Johnny asks as Marcus double-locks the front door. I notice Padma slyly watch him do this, her eyes apprehensive, almost as if she's worried about being trapped in the villa with us. It's quite a half-hearted offer of Johnny's, as if he knows what the response will be and is asking just for the hell of it.

'I'm going to bed,' Padma announces abruptly. Before any of us can respond, she kicks off her mules, picks them up and starts making her way up the winding stairs.

'Not for me either,' Nick says, before following her lead. 'Good night, all.'

The remaining four of us linger for a moment in awkward silence, waiting for Padma and Nick to disappear from view.

Then, once they have, Marcus is the first to speak. 'Lana, what's up with Padma?' he whispers. 'It seems like more than a work thing. She barely made eye contact with any of us once you got back from the Ladies'.'

Lana's mouth twitches, the way it does when she's nervous, her fingers fiddling with the clasp of her clutch bag, a sure sign she knows something but is sworn to secrecy.

'Maybe we can help?' I offer. 'If you tell us what's upset Padma?'

'I don't think so,' Lana mumbles, while giving Johnny a brief but stern glance.

It's a clear warning sign. I watch Johnny swallow hard.

'Like she said, it's a work thing and she doesn't want to talk about it,' Lana goes on. 'It would be wrong of me to betray her confidence. Anyway, I'm bushed, it's been a long day, and I'm off to bed too. See you in the morning.'

As Lana trots away and up the stairs, Johnny catches my eye. I can tell he's desperate to get me alone, but now is not the time. It would only arouse Marcus's suspicions. I'll text him from the bedroom, suggest a time tomorrow when we can meet in private. I need to talk to him anyway. It's only right I tell him what I have planned. I can't just spring it on him. This will be life-changing for all of us. And anyway, perhaps by the morning he'll know more about what's upset Padma, because although I'm not usually one for gambling, I'd bet my last pound coin on him interrogating Lana the minute he's alone with her.

Chapter Twenty-Eight

Johnny

Before
London, England, August 2002

Last week, Lana told me she'd lost our baby. It should have been music to my ears; I'd prayed in the early days of her pregnancy that she'd miscarry. I know it sounds callous, but in my defence, she trapped me. Blackmailed me into going along with her plan, because it was that or risk bringing disgrace on our family name, not to mention jeopardising my freedom and the job Dad's lined up for me. Ness knows all about her scheming of course. She was livid when I told her. But she also acknowledged there was nothing we could do about it, short of seeing to it that Lana met a nasty end. Despite all that, I couldn't bring myself to rejoice at the loss of our baby. As much as I resent Lana for being a conniving bitch, that child growing inside her was a part of me, and having reluctantly gone along to the scan, seen my flesh and blood in black and white, I couldn't help but love it, had even felt my heart softening, as much as being tethered to Lana for life had filled me with dismay. In any case, now that I've lost Padma for good, what does it matter who I marry? I'll never love anyone like I loved her – still love, in fact. No one can ever compare.

Seeing the distraught look on Lana's face, I had even felt some level of sympathy for her. I told her I was sorry, that I realised how hard losing the child she'd been carrying must be for her, and that I would help with any counselling she needed to get her through the worst. Also, that I was sure this wouldn't stop her from conceiving more children in the future.

I had expected tears, some kind of breakdown perhaps, but what I hadn't foreseen was a reaction that made my blood run cold.

'This doesn't let you off the hook,' she said, her eyes bloodshot from all the crying she'd done, steely. 'You know, the funny thing is, if the way our baby had been made had been from a place of love – ha, not even that, the remotest hint of affection would have sufficed – if you had actually treated me with an ounce of respect, I might have walked away, told you it's OK, we'll go our separate ways, it wasn't meant to be and I'll keep your despicable secret. But you made me feel no better than a whore that night, and for that, you deserve to suffer. I have loved you from the first, have done nothing but sympathise with and console you since you and Padma split up. But you don't see that. You're so selfish, so utterly ignorant of what's staring you in the face. And yet, despite you treating me like shit, I still want to be with you, that's how much I love you, Johnny Harker, although I won't deny at the same time it gives me pleasure to make you sweat. So, if you don't want your horrid little secret coming out, you'll know what's good for you and stick with me.'

At that I flew into a rage, placed my hands around her neck and told her I'd murder her right there on the spot.

But she hadn't flinched. She simply stared back into my eyes, her own gleaming like spotlights. And it scared the fuck out of me.

'You don't have the balls,' she said. 'You know you won't get away with it, not now we've been together for a few months, and having just lost a baby. The press would be over my death in a shot. There's nowhere to hide. I *will* talk, I have a lot less to lose than you. So, what will it be? Stay with me, give me the life I always desired, the life I deserve, or ditch me and bring shame on your family's name?'

I couldn't believe how stupid I'd been. How I'd found myself in such an intractable position. But I also knew she was right. I had no choice, not if I wanted to keep the truth buried. Plus, it wasn't just about my freedom and future, there were others to think of. Others whose lives would be ruined if I didn't do her bidding. I saw that this had become a sort of vengeance for Lana, my fault for treating her so coldly that night. And seeing her resolute expression, there was no doubt in my mind that she'd go to the police if I didn't abide by her wishes.

And so, last night, I agreed to marry her.

This is my prison sentence for what I did.

My life sentence.

Chapter Twenty-Nine

Nick

Sorrento, Italy, Monday, 5th August 2019

'Darling, are you going to tell me what's wrong? Talk to me, maybe I can help?'

No sooner had we stepped inside our bedroom, than Padma had tossed her mules on the floor, removed her jewellery, then started undressing with a manic urgency that set my nerves jangling. As did her failure to speak or make eye contact. It was like she was lost in her own little world, and I dared not say anything to upset her further. I'd let her use the bathroom first, before I quickly peed and brushed my teeth. And now, as I inch myself under the duvet of our massive bed, my wife's back facing me, the covers pulled up to her neck, which is so unlike her, I bite the bullet and gently enquire what's wrong. She doesn't respond immediately, and for a moment I think she's going to give me the silent treatment all night. Either that or she's on the brink of erupting, and if I ask her once more what's up she's going to tell me to leave her the fuck alone. But then finally, to my relief, she rolls over, fat tears filling her eyes.

'What's the matter, my darling?' I ask again. Of course, I hadn't failed to notice the daggers she occasionally shot

Johnny across the table after returning with Lana. And that's partly why I'm feeling scared. Scared she knows something. Something we've all been at pains to keep buried.

'Johnny's been hiding something from us all these years, I know it.'

'What makes you say that?' I say as casually as possible, my stomach heaving.

She hoists herself up, then reaches for her phone on the bedside table, goes to her messages. 'Because of this.' She thrusts the screen in my face at which point my pulse accelerates at a rate of knots on reading what's written.

'Who the hell sent that?' I ask, unable to contain the alarm in my voice.

'I've no idea.' She shrugs. 'That's not the point.'

'Of course it's the point,' I say, trying not to lose it. 'It could be some scam artist or hacker, trying it on.'

'Don't be ridiculous,' she retorts sharply. 'The words, the meaning, it's all too specific. *That night*. We all know what that's referring to.'

'OK, so perhaps it's someone with a grudge against Johnny, trying to paint him in a bad light. Lots of people know you were attacked that night, many of them at Oxford at the same time as us and quite possibly aware of how he ended things with you. I mean, you two were quite the famous couple. A number of them doubtless work in the City, mixing in the same circles as Johnny. You know what a big mouth he has, how tactless he can be. Maybe he rubbed someone the wrong way and now they're out to make trouble for him. Plus, you know how it is for Johnny being Ed's son. Ed's got so many haters, and so has his son by association. It can't be easy for Johnny.'

Christ, stop talking. You're going over the top.

Padma frowns, her eyes narrowing. 'Why are you always so quick to defend him? He constantly puts you down. I mean, look how he was with you earlier. Flinging insults. About our lack of money, kids. How can you stand for it?' Another cross look. 'It's like he has you wrapped around his little finger, and I can't for the life of me understand why.'

Fuck, keep calm, Nick, think fast. 'Don't be daft, I just know how much you dislike confrontation, and I don't want to upset you. I have you and he doesn't. That's enough of a victory for me, I don't need to get into some childish slanging match with him.'

'Victory? Is that what I am to you? Sport? Like one of those "foxes" you caught in that disgusting hunt the pair of you took part in at Oxford?'

I flinch at the mention of that night.

'Padma, that's not what I meant, and you know it.'

'Do I?' she glares.

'Look, why the hell are you getting at me?' I say, feeling my blood pressure rise. 'I didn't send the bloody text, but we need to focus on who did, and what their intentions are. I assume you don't recognise the number?'

'No.' She shakes her head. 'If this person wants to remain anonymous, they're bound to have covered their tracks. This isn't some generic swipe at Johnny because of who his father is, however much you try to convince me otherwise. Clearly, they know him, and they know me. But, more importantly, they believe he's been lying to me all these years.'

I can't argue with her there, as much as I try to. The words, like she said, are clear.

Johnny knows what happened to you that night. And he is guilty of so much more. Don't trust him.

'Don't trust him,' Padma enunciates each word. Then looks at me guardedly. 'To be honest, I've not trusted Johnny since the day he ended things with me. But the question is, can I trust you, Nick?'

I try not to swallow, despite the lump that's developed in my throat making it hard to breathe normally. I thought this week would be our chance to get away from it all, relax, have fun, possibly make a baby, but it's rapidly turning into the vacation from hell. Who is this person, and why are they meddling in our lives all of a sudden? What's the angle? And just how much do they know? So many questions are spinning around in my head, making me dizzy, because I'm terrified of losing everything I've worked so hard to build these past eighteen years.

'Of course, you can, darling,' I say, kissing her forehead. 'I'm so sorry this has happened. I understand how upsetting it must be. Do you want me to talk to Johnny tomorrow, see what he has to say?'

'No.' Padma's tone is firm. 'Leave it for now. I don't want to upset Ness before Wednesday. I'll be OK. I can hold it together until then. Fob it off as a work problem. That's what I told Lana.'

'You showed Lana the text?' I'm flabbergasted. Having seen the message, I'd assumed Lana had been telling the truth, and that Padma had told her it was a work thing after all. Purely because of what it's insinuating about her husband.

'Yes.'

'Do you think that's wise? I mean, it accuses her husband of lying to you, of having done something bad. What did she say? Surely, she won't keep it a secret from him?'

'She was shocked. Swore she knew nothing about it. Promised me she'd say nothing to him for now.'

'And you believed her?'

'I think so, I mean she seemed genuinely taken aback, and we all know she hates his guts. But now, thinking about it...'

'Yes?' I say, a bit too urgently.

'Now I wonder if she was shocked because her husband was being accused of something she had no knowledge of. Or because she's terrified of the truth coming out. I mean, I've always wondered why they stayed together after she miscarried. Granted, they weren't at loggerheads back then the way they are now. But it's never been the romance of the century, has it? Lana got pregnant by mistake and Johnny did the right thing, and I guess I bought into that eventually. But to stay together after they lost their unplanned child, that never rang true for me.'

My wife is smart, small wonder the pieces of the puzzle don't fit for her. That bit never washed with me either. I've just been too afraid to ask Johnny the real story there.

But then, having realised my wife might be onto something, I panic and say something I immediately regret: 'Are you sure this isn't about you feeling resentful of him wanting to be with her and not you?'

Before I have time to react, she slaps me hard across the face, then darts off the bed in a rage. I should have expected that. God knows I deserved it. It's the first time either of us have displayed even the merest hint of violence against the other, and I hate it. But I can't have her fishing. I had to put the thought into her head. The way I've been putting such thoughts into her head for pretty much the last eighteen years. That's how Johnny came to terms with our relationship. I'd assured him I could keep tabs on her, that if there was ever any hint of her starting to remember that week, but more so that night, I'd let him know, try to put the brakes on it. What we'd then do if she did remember, we never actually discussed, just because we'd hoped it would never come to that. The thought was too horrifying. Simply because I love her too much. Can't even contemplate the idea of any harm coming to her.

'I'm sorry, that was uncalled for.' I leap out of bed chasing after her. Her expression a mixture of hurt and hostility. I hate seeing her like this. And I realise it's the third time I've upset her since we got here. 'Please, forgive me. I guess it was my own insecurity talking.'

She frowns. 'What do you mean?'

'I see the way you look at him sometimes. Especially when he's got his shirt off.'

'Nick, come on—'

'Stop, let me finish.' I hold up my palm, and she lets me continue. 'I don't blame you, his body is incredible and you're only human, plus you have all that history together, I get that. It's only natural you'd still have feelings for him.'

'But that's just it, I don't have feelings for him. Well, I do, but they're not nice ones like you think.'

'Are you telling me your eyes don't linger on his body a little longer than necessary sometimes? I saw it earlier, when he opened the bedroom door to us, after we'd all heard Lana's scream. Tell me I'm wrong?' I hold her gaze. Would love for her answer to be no, but unlike the rest of us, the one thing Padma isn't is a liar. She may hate

Johnny for ending things with her when she needed him, but you can't stop basic human desire. Especially between two insanely attractive people who were once besotted with each another.

'OK, so I looked at his body. But so did you, so did Marcus. It's natural because yes, sure, he has a fit body. But I can assure you the last thing I'd ever want to do again is get naked with Johnny. I feel nothing for him, nothing but regret I was ever involved with him in the first place.' Her tone has softened, and I think I am off the hook. Relief washes through me as she comes up and places her palms against my chest, looks into my eyes.

'You were there for me when Johnny wasn't. I'd never have got through that time otherwise. And that's why I fell in love with you. You are sexier to me than he could ever be, because you are a kind and decent man. Please never doubt that. Nothing could ever change the way I feel about you. Nothing.'

Just hearing her say this should fill me with joy, make me feel like the luckiest man alive. And the latter is true. I am the luckiest man alive, to have someone as wonderful as Padma to love me. But instead of being filled with joy, all that consumes me is regret. Knowing I am a liar and a fraudster, undeserving of her love.

I pull her to me. 'I love you so much, you know that.'

'Yes, I know.' She keeps her head buried in my chest a while, then pulls away and looks at me with a determined expression. 'So, promise me you'll say nothing to Johnny, or anyone for that matter?'

I want to say I promise and mean it, but I can't. And so, I lie once more. It's become second nature, I guess. 'I promise.'

'Thank you,' she smiles, before the steely look returns. 'But just so you know, come Thursday, after Ness's big day, I'm showing him that text. And I'm asking him point blank if he knows what this person is talking about.'

Chapter Thirty

Johnny

Sorrento, Italy, Tuesday, 6th August 2019

It's 3 a.m. and I've not slept a wink since Lana and I finally switched off the light an hour ago. No sooner had we come upstairs and locked our bedroom door, I demanded to know what had happened with Padma earlier at the restaurant after she'd followed her to the Ladies'. Keeping my voice low, of course. Walls have ears and the last thing I needed was to be overheard by the wrong person. At first, I thought she'd dig her heels in and refuse to tell me, just because she had that all too familiar self-righteous look about her, as if she was revelling in my torture. It's been the story of our relationship, and I suppose I can't blame her for gloating. After all, I've been a complete bastard towards her over the years since she trapped me, and maybe she felt she'd regained the upper hand in our relationship. I should never have got physical with her the night she told me about her miscarriage. Because it put other ideas into her head. Ideas about the kind of person I am and what I've done. It's a wonder she's felt safe with me all things considered. Even so, it's not as if she's without fault here. She knew I didn't love her, had no desire to be with her, and yet she persisted with her threats and left me with no choice but to tie myself to her and her deceit. We're both miserable, but it's a misery of our own making, and in that sense, I guess we deserve one another.

'Say please,' she'd mocked. 'Then I might tell you.'

I wanted to tell her to fuck off and die with that comment, but she knew she had me in a corner and if I wanted the truth, I had to play nice.

'Please, Lana, I implore you,' I said. 'I saw the way Padma was looking at me when you came back from the Ladies'. Her eyes were cold and full of suspicion. This could affect you as well as me, you know.'

'I'm not so sure about that,' she said with a smirk. 'There was no mention of me, or anyone else for that matter. Not even your beloved Ness. Besides, you made your opinion very clear all those years ago; that I don't know anything. You were pretty high and mighty about it, in fact. Said the less I knew, the better.'

'Yes, I did. Because it's safer if you don't know. Just tell me what the text said for God's sake! You realise this sort of thing might trigger something in her brain. And if she remembers what happened that day, you won't be so sure of yourself then. She'll despise you in fact. And the friendship you're suddenly so keen to rekindle will be lost for good.'

I could tell from her expression that this possibility had crossed Lana's mind, but that she'd been so intent on enjoying my misery, she'd told herself not to dwell on it. Even so, having made it clear that none of our secrets will be safe if this anonymous messenger continues to push and knows more than he or she has so far let on, her face swiftly lost its smugness and she caved, telling me the gist of what the text had said. After she'd finished, I wanted to be sick, thinking about the messages I've been receiving. It has to be the same person. But who? Who was watching us that night? Could it have been someone at the bar that evening? One of the members of the club, or perhaps even one of the female freshers? A friend, perhaps, of Carys's? That girl, Rachel, who occurred to me before? Or perhaps Carys's family have since discovered something? I remember watching the father on TV, appealing to the public for any information they might have regarding his daughter's disappearance. Although he was clearly grief-stricken, I can still see his eyes – hard and menacing – telling you he wasn't the type you'd want to cross. Even so, why start making threats all these years later? That bit just doesn't add up for me.

'What aren't you telling me?' Lana then demanded to know. 'What is it this person knows that I don't? I've always had my suspicions – I mean, the fact that you agreed to marry me is a sure sign you did something bad. Even so, I've known you for too long now, and my heart tells me there are some things you're not capable of. If we're to keep this thing buried, it's important we're all on the same page. She'll tell Nick, you know that, don't you? She tells him everything, and when he sees that message, he'll go berserk, because I'm assuming he knows nothing about what went on that week either?'

'That's right, he knows nothing,' I lied a bit too quickly, while having no clue if the person sending these messages knew different.

Despite being tempted to tell Lana everything at that point, if only because it would have felt good to offload, I knew I couldn't. Simply because I don't trust her. And because all this may come to nothing. Thus far, keeping it between the three of us has worked.

'Did Padma ask you if you had any idea what the sender was talking about?' I then asked.

'Yes. I told her I hadn't a clue and that I was shocked. Pointed out that it could be some scam artist, or someone from university who has it in for you and therefore anything he or she says should perhaps be taken with a pinch of salt.'

'Thank you,' I said.

'Don't thank me. I did it for me and the kids. What happens to you affects us, don't ever forget that. What are you going to do, Johnny? What if she confronts you? She said she wouldn't before Ness's birthday. But Thursday is only two days away. You need to be prepared. You need to get your story sorted.'

Her warning echoes through my mind as I continue to lie here in the grip of insomnia. Tomorrow is going to be nothing short of torture. I just need to stay calm and act like I have nothing to hide. It shouldn't be that hard. After all, I've had enough practice. Even so, it's vital I get Ness alone tomorrow. We need to talk this through; she's the only one I can trust. I lean over and grab my phone, send her a text.

As ever, I'm depending on her for a solution, but in my heart of hearts I worry this is one problem she won't be able to fix.

Chapter Thirty-One

Vanessa

Sorrento, Italy, Tuesday, 6th August 2019

Nick and Padma are already having breakfast on the terrace when Marcus and I make an appearance just after 9. They've laid out granola and chopped fruit, a plate of sliced wholemeal bread, three varieties of cheese and two types of jam, while there's also a pot of tea on offer as well as a cafetiere of real coffee that permeates the air like an inviting scented candle.

'Morning both, this all looks fabulous. You must have been down quite a while already. Sorry for not being up in time to help out.'

'Don't be silly,' Padma smiles at me, 'we're on holiday, and there are no rules. Especially for the birthday girl. Nick and I just happened to wake up early, didn't we, babe?'

Nick smiles. 'Yeah, that's right,' before going back to spreading some raspberry jam on a thick slice of bread. I'm relieved to see Padma smiling again, her tone more buoyant, but there was something in the way Nick's eyes lingered on mine as he spoke that worried me. Almost as if he was trying to tell me that things are far from OK.

'Well, anyway, thank you, both,' Marcus says equally cheerily, oblivious to our exchange. 'After that mammoth-sized plate of spaghetti vongole at the restaurant I didn't think I'd ever feel hungry again, but blow me, I'm famished. Must have been that trek back up to the square, not to mention the heat, that burned off all the calories.' He chuckles and we all laugh with him. I only wish I could say the same. I'm feeling particularly nauseous this morning, having been up half the night with abdominal pains, something I realise I only have myself to blame for by indulging in alcohol. In fact, my belly feels more bloated than usual, but I manage to nibble on some bread while drinking my tea, hoping no one will notice my poor appetite.

Last night, when we got back to our room, I was too tired to make love, despite having planned this in my head before we'd set out for the evening, knowing that my days are numbered and that I need to take advantage of the time I have left with my husband. On the bright side, I think Marcus was shattered too, the escalating tension between the others – Padma and Johnny especially – having caused our stress levels to rise just when we'd finally started to relax. The fact that sleep eluded me meant I was still awake when a text from Johnny came through a little after 3 a.m. saying that we needed to speak urgently. I'm guessing he got something out of Lana, and whatever it is, can't be good. Marcus asked me again this morning if I had any idea what could have upset Padma, and I said it was probably work like Lana mentioned, and he'd seemed content with that. Once again, I had lied to my poor unsuspecting husband, my guilt swelling to new heights.

'Plans for today?' Marcus asks, before helping himself to coffee. The air is still, and it already feels like a sauna out here. I wipe the sweat from my forehead with a napkin, then use it to fan myself as a dragonfly skims past my line of vision.

'I promised Lana I'd go back with her to that jewellery shop we looked in the window of last night,' Padma says. 'These five days are going to whizz by and I don't want to leave it to the last minute to buy Mum something. I saw the perfect lapis necklace for her.'

'Sounds good,' Marcus says.

'You're welcome to join us, Ness?' Padma offers.

The last thing I feel like doing is trekking around town in this heat. I'll probably pass out and I can't bear the thought of any fuss being made over me. Besides, there's no point in me buying anything. I can't take it where I'm going. 'No, I'm fine, you guys go ahead. I think I'll just have a lazy morning. Marcus thinks I have way too much jewellery anyway, don't you, darling?' I smile teasingly at Marcus and he doesn't deny it. Just gives me a wry grin in return. 'Besides, we need to call the rug rats,' I carry on, 'make sure they're OK.'

'Sure, no problem,' Padma says. 'Need us to pick anything up from the supermarket while we're there?'

'Actually, that's not a bad idea,' I say. 'Mind if I write you a list once we're done here?'

'Yes of course.'

'And what about you, Nick?' Marcus distracts Nick from covering his second slice of bread with a layer of jam. 'What are you going to do while the ladies are out indulging in some retail therapy?'

Nick puts down the knife. 'Thought I might go for a run, actually.'

We all look at him like he's gone mad.

'A run? In this heat?' Marcus raises his eyebrows. 'You know it's going to be 36 degrees today? Doesn't sound like much fun to me.'

Nick pinches the sides of his waist. 'The middle-aged spread is starting to set in. Can't get away with stuffing my face like I used to. And with all this Italian food I'm indulging in, I feel like I have to do something to stop the weight from creeping up. The pool's not quite big enough to get any decent lengths in.'

'Fair enough.' Marcus puts up his hand as if to acknowledge this is one argument he's not going to win.

'Sounds like far too much hard work,' Padma shakes her head. She looks up and I watch her gaze travel over my shoulder, her expression darkening.

'Morning all.'

Johnny.

'Good morning.' To my surprise, Padma returns the greeting, albeit curtly. I notice the hurt in Johnny's eyes. It must kill him to suffer her laser looks, remembering the adoring way she used to gaze at him. How I wish more than anything that I had the power to turn back time and change what happened. I know they would have been happy together. They were *meant* to be together.

'Hi, everyone.' Lana's not too far behind, and before long they've joined us around the table, helping themselves to breakfast. I notice Johnny toying with his, unusually quiet, as if preoccupied, or perhaps too afraid to speak. We repeat our plans for the day. All except for him.

'Think I'll just stick around here,' he responds when Marcus asks him. 'Use the gym, then go by the pool.'

'You don't fancy running with me?' Nick says.

Johnny considers this for a second, then shakes his head. 'Nah, I think I'll stick to the air con. Not as tough as you, mate.'

I can't tell if this was a dig or said in harmless jest, but Nick doesn't seem to care. 'Each to their own,' he shrugs his shoulders.

I see this as my chance to get some time alone with Johnny, even though the last thing I feel capable of doing is exercise. 'I'll join you,' I say.

'Great,' Johnny smiles.

With the others occupied, we'll be able to talk freely, even though Johnny's not going to like what I have to say.

Chapter Thirty-Two

Nick

Sorrento, Italy, Tuesday, 6th August 2019

I'm in the bedroom, having just kissed Padma goodbye before she wanders into town with Lana. Although I had hoped to be spending lots of time with her here in Italy, I couldn't help feeling relieved that she decided to go shopping. The text she'd received last night was all I could think about over breakfast. The gist of which I had relayed to Johnny first thing this morning via a text of my own, his quick response being that he'd already got the truth from Lana. It was almost as if I couldn't breathe, my appetite non-existent, though I forced down two slices of bread in a bid to appear normal, my head splitting with too much wine and lack of sleep, but more so from anxiety. I could tell it was occupying everyone else's thoughts too, despite our attempts at small talk, and I'd been dying for Padma to finish her food so we could make tracks.

I'm all set for my run, kitted out in shorts and a t-shirt, my Nike trainers and iPod. Vanessa's right, I am a bit mad to go running in this heat, but I feel like I need it, mainly to temper my rising stress levels. I make sure I have everything I need then head for the door, but just as I do, I decide to take something for my headache because it only seems to be getting worse. I know Padma brought a load of painkillers in the medicine bag she always packs for us when we go away, bearing in mind booze always features heavily in our reunions.

Usually, she keeps the stash of pills in her suitcase or in the wardrobe for easy access. I check first in the latter but with no luck. Then fish under the bed for her case lying adjacent to mine. I slide it out, open the zip and locate the little black bag stuffed with various packs of paracetamol and Nurofen, upset stomach remedies, anti-histamines, and indigestion tablets. I open it, grab the first pack of ibuprofen I see and take two tablets from the blister tab. But then, just as I'm zipping the bag back up, I catch sight of another tab peeping up over the right inside pocket. Curious to know what it is, and thinking it must somehow have found its way out of the black bag with all the other medicines, I pull it out.

It takes me a few seconds to fully grasp what I'm holding. But then, once I do, I feel a crushing sense of betrayal by the one person I thought I could count on to be honest with me.

My wife.

Chapter Thirty-Three

Johnny

Sorrento, Italy, Tuesday, 6th August 2019

The air con's on in the gym, but the sweat still pours off me, making puddles either side of the rowing machine as I pull the handle with every ounce of muscle I have. Desperate to blot out the suspicion I saw in Padma's eyes when I appeared at breakfast this morning, if only briefly. Faster and faster I row, my arms and legs working in sync and at full capacity, my fitness levels being tested to the max, my breathing increasingly laboured. The steady whir of the machine buzzes through my ears despite the fact I have my buds in. I'm listening to The Prodigy, still one of my favourite bands to work out to, reminiscent of drunken university raves, even though my eldest, Josh, tells me I'm lame and should be listening to Stormzy or Drake, who are both so much *cooler*. I smile to myself thinking back to when I was his age, considering my father to be lame too, never for a second believing that one day I'd be called the same by my own son. Oh well, at least I'm a better father than Ed ever was. I'd like to think that Josh would feel able to come to me should he ever find himself in trouble. That he wouldn't worry about disappointing me or prefer to live a life looking over his shoulder the way I have the best part of two decades. Waking up every day wondering if it might be my last one as a free man.

I could never in a million years have gone to my father telling him the full extent of the trouble I was in. He'd only have feared for his own reputation, and the first thing he would have done was work out how much damage limitation could be done in terms of his own career, rather than worry about me. He didn't want me to succeed because he felt I deserved it, or because he wanted to feel proud of me. He did it to serve his own best interests – having a son who would carry on the family name and ideally be another mouthpiece for the Tory party and his political ambitions. Little wonder I couldn't go to him when I needed a father more than ever. That I couldn't be honest with him. What I did would have been the stuff of nightmares for him. And that's why I only told him the bare minimum. Glossing over the grisly details. Because I needed him to speak to the College Master on my behalf. Which he did. And it had helped all of us, kept our names out of the papers, for which I am eternally grateful. But at the same time, it's something that fills me with shame.

My arms and legs are really aching now, the lactic acid building up, my muscles increasingly tight. I reach my goal of 5,000 metres, then start to slow down, gradually grinding to a halt, before I ease the bar back into its resting position and loosen the stirrups around my feet.

Music still blares in my ears, though, and that's why I almost jump out of my skin in response to the tap on my shoulder from behind. I whip out my ear buds, turn my head sharply to see Ness standing there. 'Shit, Ness, you scared me.'

'Sorry, I didn't mean to, hadn't noticed you had your buds in.'

I get up, my legs burning, go over to the water fountain and grab a paper cup, fill it to the brim then gulp it down before getting a refill.

'Good workout?'

I wipe the sweat from my brow and the back of my neck with the towel I brought down from the room. 'Yeah, it was good. Needed it.'

Ness lowers her voice, even though we're alone. 'You said you needed to talk. And I'm guessing I know what about.'

There's nowhere to sit, apart from on the gym equipment. I'm tempted to go elsewhere, but at least there's no chance of anyone overhearing us here in the basement. We perch next to one another on the chest press bench.

'So, what did Lana say?' Ness asks. 'I presume you quizzed her last night, hence your text?'

'Yes, I did.' I run through my conversation with Lana, adding that Padma confided in Nick about the text, too.

'Christ,' Ness says. 'We don't know for sure if this person knows anything significant, though. They could just be trying their luck, with no actual clue as to what they're talking about.'

I adore her for trying to ease my mind, the way she always does, and I'd love to think that's what's happening here. But my gut tells me otherwise, just because the text felt too close to the bone. I tell her this and she nods reluctantly.

'You could be right, and we therefore have to assume the worst.'

'What are we going to do?' I say. 'What if they know exactly what happened? What if they call the police, the press? Our lives will be over.'

'Listen, Johnny, before you say anything more, I need to tell you something.'

'What?' Her ominous tone worries me, as do the tears collecting in her eyes.

She pauses, then says, 'I think we should own up. And it has nothing to do with the text Padma received.'

Is she joking? I know she can only be referring to one thing, but even so I find myself saying: 'To what?'

'You know what. To what happened that night. We can't live like this. It's no way to exist. It's slowly killing us all.'

I feel my chest tighten, my legs already wobbly from the rowing now like jelly. 'Have you gone mad? Why? We've done OK for eighteen years. If she was going to remember, she would have done so by now. We're safe, in the clear.'

'But we're not free, are we? We've lived that time treading on thin ice, not knowing when or if our secret might be outed. How can you go to your grave with a clear conscience, knowing what we did?'

I frown. 'My grave?' Then I chuckle uneasily. 'I know we're getting on a bit, but forty isn't that old. With any luck, we're not even halfway through our lives. There's so much more to live for, and think of our kids, what it would do to them.'

She takes my hands, and it strikes me that her own are freezing. The air con isn't up that high, so how can they be that cold? 'I get that, but if we tell Padma the truth, she may understand.'

Is she serious? I cannot believe what I'm hearing. Maybe the sunshine's gone to her head. I get up, start pacing the room. 'Did you see Padma's reaction last night? Do you really think she'd be understanding?'

192

'That's only because she doesn't have the full story. This person, whoever they are, they're making it sound sordid, twisted. But we can put Padma right on that. Make her see we only did what we thought was best, that we were young and reckless, had no one to guide us.'

'And you think she'll just accept that? Accept the fact that we've been lying to her face all these years? I'm not doing it, Ness, I'm just not.'

She starts to cry, and I want to go over and console her, but right now I'm too mad, too confused by her bizarre behaviour. The whole point of our meeting in secret was to determine how we were going to find and silence this person, not ease their path to blowing up our lives. Not to mention work out how I'd explain myself to Padma when she confronts me on Thursday. As Lana indicated to me that she would.

I go over to the fountain once more, pour another cup of water, start to drink it, my back facing Ness.

'I'm dying, Johnny.'

The words hit me like a bullet. I feel myself go rigid, and then I slowly turn around. She's looking straight at me. Her face unsmiling. 'I've got stage four bowel cancer which has spread to my liver. I'll be dead by Christmas.'

At this point, I think my legs might actually give way, and it's a struggle to walk the few steps to reach Ness's side. I collapse to my knees on the floor in front of her, gaze into her eyes and see that she's deadly serious.

'No.' I say the word in a whisper, taking her limp cold hands in mine once more. It's the only word I'm capable of getting out, because I'm too much in shock to say anything more. Now it all makes sense. The weight loss, the drawn, pasty look about her. The fatigue. I thought it was work — if only.

'It's true. It's why I wanted this week to be special. My last birthday spent with my best friends. Away from London, from the stress and the strains. But also, the perfect time to confess, so I can depart this world with a clear conscience, knowing I did the right thing.'

I'm still smarting from her revelation that she has cancer. She's only forty, only halfway through her life, how can this be happening?

'Why didn't you tell me?' I ask. I'm suddenly filled with hurt and rage. 'You're my best friend, and I thought I was yours. I could have helped you.' At that, I realise I've not asked the one question that should have sprung to mind the moment she told me the ghastly news. 'Does Marcus know? I'm assuming not? There's no way he'd have been able to conceal his grief. He seems way too happy.'

She shakes her head. 'No. I couldn't bear for him to see me suffer. If it had been caught early, if there was a chance that I could live a few more years, I would have told him. But there isn't.'

'There's always a chance, miracles happen,' I say, squeezing her hands, tears spilling over my eyelids and down my cheeks.

'No.' She shakes her head again. 'Not in this case. I know you both would have persuaded me to do the chemo if I told you, but I didn't want my last few months to be spent in and out of hospital, Marcus and the kids seeing me hooked up to some drip, at the mercy of the doctors and drugs that aren't a match for this disease that's ravaging my body at breakneck speed.'

'How am I going to manage without you?' I say. It's typical of me, such a selfish thing to say, thinking of myself, instead of Ness, the one who's dying here. But it's the truth. She's my best friend. My go-to if I ever need a sounding board. My soulmate.

'You will,' she says with a sad smile.

Just then I remember how this conversation started. I understand her need to confess her sins, but what about those she leaves behind? What about our kids? I make this point and she bows her head.

'We can't tell, don't you see?' I say. 'It will unleash a storm. Scar the kids for life. Blacken their names before they've had a chance to make their way in the world. Surely you don't want that?' I look at her imploringly. 'Please, Ness, say you won't do it.'

'I have to, Johnny.'

'Why?'

'Because there's something else. Something I should have told you a long time ago.'

I can tell from Ness's tortured expression how hard it's been, keeping whatever it is a secret from me.

'What? What is it?' I cradle her face in my hands, kiss her forehead tenderly, tell her it's OK, that she can tell me, yet at the same time dreading what it is she's been hiding.

She takes a lungful of air, as if summoning up the nerve to unburden the load she's been carrying. And then, after a few seconds, but which feels like forever, she tells me.

And at this point, I think I might pass out with shock.

Chapter Thirty-Four

Marcus

Sorrento, Italy, Tuesday, 6th August 2019

I can't believe what a fool I've been. Ness and I have been getting on so well since we got here, I was beginning to think I'd been imagining stuff about her and Johnny. Mistaking their affection for one another for something more than friendship. My own insecurities talking.

But it seems that I was wrong. I saw the way he caressed her face just then, as I peered through the window of the gym, the heartfelt way they gazed into each other's eyes, the tenderness with which he kissed her forehead. They're in love with one another, always have been. That's why he broke up with Padma, because he was in love with Ness. Why he always looks so bloody miserable whenever we see him and Lana, why he resents his wife so much, why he insists on spending so much time with us, wanting to pay for the bloody Bollinger tomorrow. It all makes sense now, and it makes me wonder, all those nights Ness has been working late in the office – *was she with him?*

I feel shaky, broken. How the hell am I going to carry on this week pretending everything's fine, going ahead with my surprise plans for Ness's birthday tomorrow, without exploding at Ness and punching Johnny in the face? I tell myself that maybe I'm exaggerating, that it's not what it seems, but judging by the way they looked at each other just then, the affection that passed between them, there can be no other explanation.

I wonder to myself what they were talking about? Frustratingly I couldn't hear a word of what was being said through the soundproof doors. Perhaps they were professing their love for one another, working out how they'd be able to leave me and Lana and be together. I pound my head with the knuckles of my clenched fist, as if to pummel the thought from my brain, wanting more than anything to believe I am wrong. Particularly when I think about the way Johnny gazes at Padma. But perhaps that's just lust, whereas with Ness it's true love? I think back to Sunday night when Ness and I kissed like randy teenagers, made love like porn stars, and wonder – was she faking? Was she imagining it was Johnny making love to her? It had felt so real, that we were so in sync with each other. But all I can see is Johnny's washboard stomach, my wife running her hands all over it. Him making her grunt and groan and cry out for more.

And yet I can't think what's stopped them from being together all this time. If he broke up with Padma because he loves Ness, why didn't they take their chance then? Was it their parents? Did they not approve? That's what I don't understand. All I know is that I feel like I want to kill someone right now, I'm so full of fury and humiliation.

I need to talk to someone. Someone who might be able to shed light on this.

Nick.

Chapter Thirty-Five

Johnny

Sorrento, Italy, Tuesday, 6th August 2019

I feel numb. Dizzy with shock and disbelief, having been dealt two blows in quick succession. My burden has been heavy all these years, but it's nothing compared to the load Ness has been shouldering. I can still scarcely believe it.

After she'd told me, we left the gym in haste, thinking our protracted absence might make Nick and Marcus suspicious, but just before we did, I told her about the messages I've been receiving. She agreed it had to be the same person who'd texted Padma. It was too much of a coincidence that two different people could be sending them, unless, of course, they were in it together. She tried to persuade me how it's important we get in there first and tell Padma the truth. That it's clear this person intends to make trouble for us all, and therefore only a matter of time before he or she talked. First to Padma, and then, presumably, the police.

'It's better we tell her now, before this person does their worst, don't you think?'

What she said made sense, and so I'm slowly resigning myself to coming clean. It's too risky keeping quiet. Plus, it's the right thing to do. But it doesn't stop me thinking about the ramifications of doing so, not just for me, but for our families. Padma will never speak to me again, and all our lives, our futures, will be ruined. The fact is, we should have owned up when it happened, but we were young and scared. Wanting to protect those who had even more to lose than ourselves.

Just thinking about certain people's reactions when the truth is revealed makes my stomach turn, and I'm not sure how I'm going to get through the next two days before that happens. How I can possibly act normally, pretend like nothing's up. Every second is torture, wondering if the person tormenting us with their messages will strike again.

I'm in the shower. The sweat comes off me instantly; how I wish I could wash off the guilt that easily. I almost feel like ending it all, but that would be cowardly and an insult to Ness and the courage with which she's faced the last six months alone. Plus, I can't do that to my kids, innocents in all of this. I turn off the shower, grab a towel, wipe myself dry, wrap it around my waist, before unlocking the bathroom door. The air con hits me like an Arctic wind as I step into the room. I wonder if Lana and Padma are back, and decide to check my phone for messages. I pick it up from the dressing table, see that I have a text. Hesitantly I open it up, can't help fearing the worst. And with good reason it seems.

> Unless you come clean by the end of the week, I'm telling her the truth. Don't delay the inevitable. Do the right thing for once.

Chapter Thirty-Six

Nick

Sorrento, Italy, Tuesday, 6th August 2019

I've just returned to the villa, having jogged for thirty minutes before the heat got the better of me. I feel wilted, like I'm going to pass out, my head muzzy with dehydration, my legs like lead. Locals I'd passed had looked at me like I was insane, and for that I can't blame them. It's pushing thirty-seven degrees Celsius, several degrees hotter than yesterday, and while I trekked around the mountainous pathway, I noticed them sensibly keeping to the shaded side of the road rather than frying themselves in the full glare of the sun like me. Really, I should have waited until late afternoon to venture out, but after last night, and then finding what I did in Padma's case, I felt like I needed it. Needed to release the anger piercing my veins through pools of sweat that dampened the arid ground around me.

I've decided not to confront Padma just yet, even though it's going to be hard keeping my cool around her. I'm going to suggest to her that we do our own thing later – head into town for an early dinner, and then, at some point, I'll raise it.

I make a beeline for the kitchen, grab the filtered jug of water from the fridge and pour myself a tall glass. The water races through my bloodstream, but it takes another glass to cool me down significantly. I rinse it out at the sink, my pulse gradually slowing, and at the same time can vaguely make out female voices coming from the hallway. I realise that Lana and Padma must be back. Before they left this morning, I was willing them to have a good time, hoping that Padma would allow herself to relax a little, forget about the text, if only for a few hours. But the way I'm feeling right now, I don't much care. I just feel so wronged. Lied to. Even though I suppose that's a bit rich coming from me.

I can't face her right now, so I decide to sneak upstairs for a shower, but when I swing around to leave I see Marcus standing there. Looking as mad as I feel.

'Marcus, what's up? Everything OK?' It's hard pretending to care for someone else right now, when all I can think about is Padma's betrayal.

He doesn't answer immediately, but starts pacing the room manically. It unnerves me. I can't think what could have happened to cause his change in mood. This morning Padma and I had left him at the breakfast table laughing and joking. What the hell is happening to us all? It's like we're all slowly going crazy.

He comes back over to where I am standing on the tiled floor, scratches his head so hard I'm sure I spy blood, then says, 'Johnny and Ness are having an affair, I'm certain of it.'

For a moment I think he must be having me on. I laugh out loud. 'Good one, Marcus, you had me there.'

But he doesn't see the funny side, his expression sober. 'I'm not bloody joking, Nick. I saw them in the gym.'

I frown. 'Saw what exactly?'

'Johnny had his hands clasped around Ness's face, he kissed her forehead, and it was pretty clear they were having some sort of deep and meaningful conversation.'

I'm almost sure I know what they were talking about. Johnny and Ness have always been close, but I've never suspected anything sexual in their relationship. I try to reassure Marcus of this.

He shakes his head, as if he doesn't believe me. 'I know what I saw. There was tenderness, a look of love.'

'They do love each other, as childhood best friends would.'

Marcus shakes his head. 'I've always had my suspicions. I mean, look at him, he's like a bloody god.'

'So what? Like I said, they've known each other since they were kids. There's nothing sexual going on. I lived in their pockets for pretty much three years, I think I would know!' I hear the agitation in my voice. I shouldn't get so wound up; it's not Marcus's fault, he doesn't know I'm angry with Padma, but even so, I'm having a tough time staying calm.

I look at Marcus earnestly, hold his gaze as if to reassure him of my unflinching belief that nothing untoward is going on between his wife and Johnny, and then finally his expression softens, like he might believe me. 'Trust me, you're letting your imagination take over,' I say more gently. 'Ness loves you, only you. It's obvious.'

A grunt. 'Still, what was it they were talking about? It was clearly something important. Something must have happened.'

I shrug my shoulders as if I haven't a clue. 'Who knows?'

'Well, I've got no choice but to ask Ness, it'll eat me up otherwise.'

My heart judders. 'Is that wise?' I say. 'She'll think you were spying on her.'

'I have to, Nick. Like I said, if I don't, it'll fester. I can't have it hanging over me, over Ness's special day tomorrow. I'm doing it now.'

He walks off and I immediately pull out my phone, go to my messages and type a new text:

> Ness, Marcus saw you and Johnny talking in the gym. He thinks you're having an affair. You need to think up something quick. I'm begging you, Ness, don't sell me out now. Not after all these years.

Chapter Thirty-Seven

Johnny

Before
Oxford, England, mid-October 2001

'Nick, what's wrong?'

It's Sunday, 6 a.m., and I'm whispering because Padma's lying fast asleep next to me in our bed. When I got home from the bar last night, she was sitting on the sofa in our living room, waiting for me. Her face like thunder. She'd repeated what she'd told me on the phone earlier, having ordered me to get home quick sharp if I didn't want to find my belongings flung out on the street. That she'd found out about the 'female fresher hunt' organised by the exclusive male drinking society I help run with my mate Richard, and I had five minutes to explain myself. She was meant to be away for the weekend, visiting Lana in Leeds, but had come back early, having heard rumours about the hunt from a friend at her college, although I later discovered that she and Lana hadn't been getting on all weekend, so really, it was a good excuse to leave. I begged for her forgiveness, blamed it all on Richard, told her that he had egged me on, reminded me that it was something our fathers had done back in the day and so I'd felt the need to prove I was as 'cool' as him by carrying on the tradition. But that now, in hindsight, I regretted my actions, realised how wrong it had been. I promised her it was a one-off, that I'd never again partake in something so degrading towards women. And I assured her I hadn't laid a finger on any of the girls, let alone slept with one of them. That there was only one woman for me. Her. The love of my life.

Eventually she had calmed down after I told her again and again how much I loved her, wanted to be with her forever. We kissed, had the best make-up sex we've ever had, before drifting off to sleep in each other's arms around 3 a.m. Which is why, having been locked in a blissful slumber, I'm not quite with it when my mobile starts to vibrate on the bedside table to my left and I see from the caller ID that it's Nick.

His voice is frail, barely audible. 'Johnny, you need to come. I don't know what the fuck to do.'

Gently, I remove myself from the duvet, checking Padma's not stirred as I do so, then creep downstairs to the kitchen where I can speak more freely.

'Johnny, you there?' Nick says.

'Yeah, sorry, mate, had to shift to the kitchen, Padma's fast asleep.'

'She's dead.'

I'm certain I misheard. 'What?'

'The girl I slept with from the hunt. Carys. She's fucking dead, mate.'

A wave of nausea grips me. Is he high? Still off his face? I only gave him coke, not ecstasy, so he can't be hallucinating. It's not like he's a regular user. Even so, why is he saying this? It can't be true.

'Dead? You must be mistaken. Are you stoned?'

'No, I'm not fucking stoned, right now I couldn't be more sober. Jesus, Johnny, how is this happening to me?! She took some of the coke you gave me – I, I didn't feel like it, but she was pretty keen, so I let her go ahead. You know what freshers can be like, they're keen to try everything. She became really hyper, then was on me like a wild animal. We had sex, then we both fell asleep in my bed. Ten minutes or so ago, when I got up to get some water, I noticed her face was unusually pale, and she just seemed too still. It fucking freaked me out! I put my ear to her chest but couldn't hear anything. Couldn't see the faintest rise and fall of her chest. I, I tried to wake her, tried to feel for a pulse but there was none. I think she must have taken something else, or had a reaction to the coke, who the fuck knows?! I mean, who knows what's in that stuff? Assume you got it from your usual supplier? She'd drunk a lot of booze too. She's dead, mate, fucking dead, and I, I don't know what the fuck to do!'

I slump down on one of the kitchen chairs. My insides churning, like I'm going to puke at any second. This can't be happening.

All kinds of questions start pinballing around my head. *It can't be the drugs, can it?* Nothing like this has ever happened before, plus I paid top dollar for them. Having said that, I didn't get them from my usual guy. It was a contact of Richard's, but I'm certain Richard wouldn't have put me in touch with someone dodgy. *Would he?* For fuck's sake, if Nick tells the Master he woke up with a dead fresher in his bed, he'll ask him how he came to be with her last night and before long they'll find out about the hunt *I* organised, along with the drugs she took which *I* supplied, and then there'll be an inquiry, my parents will be called in and before I know it the press will be all over it like the vultures they are and label her death as *yet another* 'Oxford scandal,' caused by *yet another* immoral misogynistic male drinking club headed up by the son of none other than womanising Tory MP Edward Harker whose son gave her the illegal drugs that killed her. And no one will be able to correct them otherwise because they'll be printing the truth! Fact is, she might be lying dead in Nick's bed, but I'm the one with blood on my hands if it was the coke she reacted to. Or at least, that's what the press will say.

This cannot get out. I've got a job in the City lined up, and my father will never forgive me. And then there's my future with Padma. We'll be finished.

I try to think quickly, rationally, but I've never been good in stressful situations. All my life, but more so since I became a teenager, whenever I've found myself needing a quick fix it's Ness who I've turned to. I don't trust myself to make the right decision, I need her to guide me, to tell me what to do. But she's not in Oxford right now. She's visiting a friend up in Durham. I have no choice but to call her, bring her in on this. She'll fix things, the way she always does.

'Stay put, I'm phoning Ness,' I say.

I hear the alarm in Nick's voice. 'Ness? No, we can't tell her. It's too risky. Besides, we need to do something now. I've got a dead girl's body in my bed for Christ's sake!'

'Nick, calm the fuck down, will you? What the hell do you expect me to do about it at six in the morning?'

'Please, you have to help me. My parents will be distraught if this comes out. It'll break Mum – Dad will never speak to me again. I can't lose my scholarship, it's all I have!'

Nick's almost hyperventilating, and I worry he's on the verge of having some gigantic panic attack. 'Look, just stay put for now. I know it's not easy but try to remain calm. It's still early. And it's a Sunday. You're not expecting anyone are you? Don't have to be anywhere?'

'No.'

'There you are then. Just thank God it's not Monday, and that she won't be missed in lectures. I assume she's in halls?'

'Yeah, she said she was.'

'So it's not like she's got a flatmate who's going to miss her either.'

'But she may have had something planned for today.'

'Yes, that's a possibility, but we can't dwell on that. Did anyone see you leave with her last night?'

There's a pause. 'No, I don't think so. It was dark, and I didn't see anyone about. Anyway, I followed you out first, remember? She came outside to see where I'd got to. And before that, when we were all gathered in the bar, Giles and Tom were with us. Plus a few of the girls, who left before you and I did. It's not like I was alone with her the whole time.'

Of course I remember Nick following me outside. It was me who'd asked him to, having just got off the phone with an irate Padma. I had panicked, told Nick I needed his advice, her ultimatum having put the fear of God into me, just because I can't bear the thought of losing her. As ever, he'd been a good mate, advising me to shift the blame onto Richard, to tell Padma he'd forced me into it. And thankfully, she'd believed me. Forgiven me.

Which is why I owe him.

'Good, hopefully any witnesses will think she left of her own accord,' I say. 'It's good you weren't just talking to her the whole night. I saw Mark and David chatting with you both at one point too.'

'Yes, that's true, but we were alone for some of the time, and it was me who caught her in the hunt.'

'Doesn't matter. Fact is, it wasn't just you and her alone together the entire evening and, more importantly, you left the bar at least twenty minutes before she did.' But just as I say this another worrying thought occurs to me. 'Did she have a mobile phone on her?'

A pause, then, 'Christ, I don't know.'

'Check her bag, pockets. If you find one, see if you can get into it. Work out if she messaged anyone to say who she was with.'

I wait with bated breath while Nick does as I ask. Thankfully, not everyone uses a PIN on their phone like I do with the expensive phone my parents bought me. So I'm praying that's the case with this girl.

'Found the phone,' Nick's voice comes back on the line.

'What is it?'

'A pretty basic looking Nokia.'

'OK, good, nothing too fancy then. So, press and hold down the hash key. Hopefully that'll get you in.' I wait on tenterhooks once again, my heart racing. As I do, I take a quick peek outside the kitchen door. No sign of Padma. She must still be sound asleep.

'I'm in.'

'OK, first check the last call she made and when.'

More anxious waiting. I drum my fingers on the kitchen table, fearful of what Nick might find. 'Shit.' *Oh fuck.* 'She made a call at 1 a.m. To someone called Sis. Presumably her sister? Jesus, Johnny, I think I'd gone to the bathroom then – why the fuck did she call her sister? What if she mentioned my name?'

This isn't good, but I tell myself to stay calm. 'I don't know, maybe she was excited to tell her sister what a great time she'd had. It was obvious she had a crush on you, and you know how girls like to gossip. They tell each other everything. It doesn't mean she told her your name, plus you're not the only Nick at Oxford.'

I hear Nick breathing hard, can tell he's trying to process what I'm saying.

'OK, yes, I suppose you're right, it's unlikely she'd mention my surname.'

'I agree, it's unlikely. Even so, check her recent texts.'

After maybe a minute, Nick says, 'Her last text was sent at four p.m. yesterday afternoon. Telling someone called Luke she was off to a party that evening, and that she'd speak to him soon.' I hear the relief in Nick's voice, and I thank heavens for small mercies that she doesn't appear to have mentioned the hunt to anyone. Casually referring to it as a party. The invite had specified it as being top secret, strict invite only. One less thing to worry about, although this Luke guy is bound to tell the police about the party, so Nick and I will need to get our stories straight ASAP in case we're questioned.

'OK, that's all good then,' I say, feeling a touch calmer. 'You still need to get rid of the phone. Take out the SIM, smash it to kingdom come, then dump it in a refuse bin in town. I'm going to call Ness now, she'll know what to do. I guarantee she won't talk. Trust me. Everything will be OK, just sit tight and don't do anything stupid.'

I hang up, then take a few seconds to summon the courage to make the call. I hate bringing Ness into this nightmare, but neither can I handle it alone. Nick's in too much of a state to think clearly, and I can't risk him falling apart. I also couldn't bear to see the look of disappointment and disgust on my father's face should this girl's death be pinned on me. There's no way his career would recover from the scandal, while mine could quite possibly be finished before it's even begun. And the thought of Nick losing his scholarship all because I forced him to take part in some stupid sexist hunt makes me feel physically ill. It's my fault he's in this scrape, so it's my job to get him out of it.

After five rings Ness picks up and I don't hesitate to tell her what's wrong. 'Ness, you need to come back to Oxford now. Something really bad's happened, and I need your help. My whole future could be in jeopardy.'

Chapter Thirty-Eight

Vanessa

Sorrento, Italy, Tuesday, 6th August 2019

I'm sitting in a secluded area of the villa's extensive gardens, a tall glass of Limonata resting on the table next to me. After my earlier conversation with Johnny in the gym, I felt like I needed some quiet time alone to think, to settle my nerves, having finally confessed my secret to him. Unloading the additional burden I've been carrying was liberating. Even if it's done nothing to assuage the guilt that's tormented me for so long now. To finally share it with someone, and not just anyone, but my closest friend, was a huge relief. And yet I cannot forget the shock on his face, hit with two successive blows. But despite what I told him, I'm still not sure it convinced him that telling the truth about that night is the only way forward for us. And in many ways, who could blame him? It's easier for me to fess up. After all, I won't be here for much longer, won't have to endure the aftermath of our confession, or watch our kids suffer for something we did back when we were effectively still kids ourselves. But when I look at Johnny, when I see how unhappy he is, the pain he's carrying, I can't help thinking that ultimately, it's for the best. Particularly given the messages he's been receiving.

It's almost like a higher force is telling us to own up. Still, he didn't agree or disagree, he simply left me alone after that, said he needed time to absorb it all, get things straight in his own head. I hate to hurt him, hate to leave him to fend for himself in this complicated, sometimes hugely unfair world we live in, but I don't have a choice. Not on this occasion.

I decide to give it five more minutes before going to find the others. Padma and Lana must be back by now, and Nick won't have lasted too long running in this heat. I saw him jog off earlier. He'd looked cross, his face drawn and sullen, as if he'd received bad news or was cheesed off about something. Perhaps he's just worried about the text Padma received. Understandably so, although he has nothing to fear there. I'll make sure of that.

I'm sitting on a padded chair beneath a sprawling maple tree that blocks the sun's vicious rays from beating down on top of my head. As I lean back, close my eyes and inhale deeply, I let the sweet smell of flora and fauna infuse my nostrils and for a moment it's almost like I am imbued with a new lease of life.

If only.

You wouldn't believe that this part of Italy is blessed with an average ten hours of sunshine a day for months on the trot; the grass is such a lush green, as soft as silk underfoot, an assortment of vibrant flowers and towering trees lining the garden's parameters in colourful abundance. Now that I am dying, I've started appreciating the simple things in life: the beauty of the sky, the sound of leaves rustling in the breeze, the chirping of birds and steady chorus of insects buzzing contently as they navigate the air around me, not to mention the pleasure of sitting in the quiet and reading a good book. I touch my abdomen.

Wish more than anything that I could reach inside and extract the tumour that is steadily killing me. God, how I hate it, how angry I feel that this has happened to me. The pain has abated a touch; it comes and goes I find, is worse after food or anything acidic, of which I didn't have much this morning.

Just then, as I'm thinking about getting up, my phone vibrates on the table next to my glass of Limonata, signalling a text. I think that perhaps it's Marcus. I've not seen much of him all morning. Before I went to find Johnny in the gym, he'd said he was popping down the road to fetch some more bottled water which we seem to be getting through by the crateload. I'd failed to put it on the list I gave to Padma, and he said he didn't mind the short walk to the local supermarket. With the villa to ourselves, I had seen this as the perfect chance to speak to Johnny. No one about to hear us confess our sins.

I pick up my mobile, go to messages, and open the text. See that it's not from Marcus, but Nick.

Panic rises to my throat as I read it. Marcus thinks Johnny and I are having an affair? Is that what Nick looked so grumpy about when I watched him jog off? No, it can't be, that was much earlier, before I'd gone down to the gym, and he would have told me straight away, plus it's not like it affects him as such. Marcus mustn't have gone out after all, or perhaps he'd thought of something we might need and had come down to the basement to check with me, remembering I'd mentioned joining Johnny for a workout in the gym, but unaware that I had an ulterior motive for doing so. My chest feels tight as I try and think up some credible explanation for our mutual display of affection.

I can't tell Marcus what we were discussing just yet. I must wait until after tomorrow, clear it with Johnny first, it's only fair to him. But I have to tell him something. Nick made it clear Marcus intends to confront me, so I need to have my answer prepared.

I realise there's only one thing I can say to him to explain our intimacy. And for once, I'll be telling him the truth.

That I owe Johnny my life.

Chapter Thirty-Nine

Marcus

Sorrento, Italy, Tuesday, 6th August 2019

'You nearly drowned?'

Ness and I are sitting at a table in the garden where I found her fifteen minutes ago. I'd half expected to find Johnny there with her, the pair of them engaged in some secret romantic tryst professing their undying love for one another, my imagination running wild once again despite Nick's attempts to convince me otherwise. And based on what Ness has just told me, it seems that Nick was spot on while I've been a fool. Again. I should be relieved, and to a degree I am. But I'm also livid with the pair of them, Ness in particular, for keeping something so huge from me, especially after all I've shared with her over the years.

'We were eight at the time,' Ness elaborates. 'Visiting Johnny's parents' second home in Scotland. It was an unusually hot day, and the house was adjacent to a vast lake. As usual, we sought solace in each other's company. Horsing around beside the water, playing hide-and-seek, sword fighting with sticks, skimming stones, while the grown-ups were inside off their faces on Champagne and drugs. They'd given our nannies the weekend off, but as usual they couldn't give a damn what we were up to. Just told us to go off and not bother them. I don't think my parents even realised I couldn't swim properly. It was yet another thing they left to the nanny. It was hot, like I said, so we were in our swimming costumes, but Johnny knew I wasn't as capable a swimmer as him, and he warned me that we shouldn't go in the water because it could be dangerous with no grown-ups about. I said OK, but inside I remember feeling cross that he was treating me like a child. Which I was of course, but an eight-year-old doesn't see it quite that rationally. Plus, I'd always been a bit headstrong.'

I smile to myself, thinking not much has changed.

'We'd been playing for a while,' Ness continues, 'when Johnny said he needed the bathroom. He said he'd be back soon, and I said OK. But I soon got bored. I remember looking at the lake which seemed so inviting and I guess I wanted to prove to him that I could swim. Usually, I was the sensible one, but at that moment I felt so angry with my parents for bringing us to this beautiful place and yet wanting nothing to do with us. I got in, started doing the front crawl, determined to swim to the other side. But it was further than I thought, and I got tired midway. I remember flagging, wanting to put my feet down to rest but it was too deep and that's when I panicked. As a child, you don't really think about your own mortality, but I can still remember the fear motoring through me as I went under. I have this vague recollection of Johnny hauling me onto land, screaming at me to open my eyes, to wake up. Saying that he needed me. Needed his best friend. Later, he told me that he'd seen me go under, had yelled for help, but when our parents had ignored him, he dove into the lake, swam to me like his life depended on it. I'd been under ten to twenty seconds when Johnny somehow managed to pull me up. Fortunately, I regained consciousness shortly after he dragged me to shore.' She pauses. Then says, 'I wouldn't be here if it wasn't for Johnny. I mattered that much to him when my own flesh and blood couldn't give two hoots about me. I vowed to myself from that moment on that I would always look out for him.'

I'm stunned. 'And your parents? What did they say?'

'As usual, all they could think about was themselves, rather than be concerned that I might have died had it not been for Johnny. After giving us hell, they threatened us. Made us swear not to tell a soul about their neglect. About what they'd been up to.'

'Why on earth didn't you tell me?' I ask, searching her eyes, which look tired, like they've lost their sparkle. Is it the burden of carrying this secret for so long that's worn her down? And now, having finally unloaded it, the adrenaline she's been forced to maintain over the years to keep it buried has dropped like a dead weight, causing her to come crashing down with it? Or is there something else that's troubling her?

'Believe me, there were countless times when I knew you'd mistaken the unbreakable bond Johnny and I forged that day for something else, and I had been desperate to set you straight. But I also knew there was every chance you'd want to rip my parents to shreds for their neglect, and I couldn't take that risk.'

I feel myself blush, embarrassed by my childishness, by my unfounded jealousy. Then again, I wasn't to know, it never occurred to me that something like this could have happened.

'So you see, it was life-changing for us both,' Ness continues. 'Almost as if we became brother and sister at that moment, bound by something deeper than friendship. Do you understand?'

'Yes.' I nod. 'I do. You must have hated your parents?'

Ness sighs. 'Hate is a strong word for a child. But I guess I did, for a time. Now I just feel numb. On the bright side, it toughened me up, made me the woman I am today. Which is no bad thing. Johnny found it harder to forgive and forget. I think boys that age are more vulnerable than girls, emotionally I mean. They need a strong guiding hand. But Ed failed him in that regard. Both he and my father are of the same ilk, driven by money and power and their own quests for glory, something our mothers have milked off for years.' She laughs bitterly, but there's a melancholy in her eyes that makes my heart ache. I think to myself how lucky I was to have a mother who really cared. And a father who still does. Who always put me first. I feel certain it's something that's rubbed off on me, eased my decision to quit work and become a stay-at-home dad.

I can't even fathom Ness and Johnny's parents not watching over their children, placing them in danger. It angers me, while my heart breaks for Ness. 'If I were your father, I'd never have been able to forgive myself.'

'I know,' Ness says. 'That's why I love you. They said if we dared breathe a word to anyone, they'd make sure Johnny and I never saw each other again. A thought that terrified our eight-year-old brains. Which is exactly what they were banking on, of course. Ed was especially frightened of the press getting wind of it.'

As I sit here listening to my wife pour out her heart and soul to me, I'm both amazed and saddened by her story. It can't have been easy keeping a secret so huge to herself for so long. Not for Johnny either. Even so, I wish she'd felt able to trust me. If anything, it would have made me less suspicious of Johnny, while at the same time eased her burden. She reads the disappointment in my eyes. Reaches out and strokes the side of my face. 'It's OK, love, please don't be upset. I wanted to tell you. Badly. Please believe that.'

I do, and I can't be angry with her for long. Nothing she could ever say or do could make me love her less. And besides, I should be rejoicing. Relieved she's not having some steamy affair with the best-looking guy I know. It's not worth dwelling on. Life's too short and I tell her this. She looks both relieved and distressed by my comment, and I can't think why. Perhaps she wishes she'd told me sooner. Perhaps she assumes I'm thinking of my own mother, so different to hers.

'Johnny's like the little brother I always wanted,' Ness continues, 'even though there's only a year between us.'

'Well, he's certainly the more juvenile of the two of you,' I chuckle.

'I can't deny that,' Ness laughs back, her face lighting up, her eyes displaying that magical twinkle I know and love so well, more like the old Ness I fell in love with. But there's no mistaking the dark shadows that underlie them, the pasty hue of her cheeks. It's as if she's not slept well in days. 'I've felt obliged to look out for him all these years,' she goes on. 'No, not obliged, that's the wrong word because really, I've wanted to. Even though it hasn't always been an easy ride. Has brought its fair share of grief.'

'You mean when he and Padma broke up?'

'Yes,' she nods, 'that and other stuff.' Her face darkens as she says this, and I think she might be on the verge of saying more, but then appears to have a change of heart. She kisses me on the lips, pats the side of my face, and says, 'Come on, we'd better get going, the others will be wondering where we are.'

I look at my watch, see that it's gone 1.30 p.m., and realise she's probably right. But as Ness picks up her phone and empty glass and we start walking across the grass back to the villa, I realise, what with me being caught up in the revelation that Johnny saved her life, I never asked her the other thing that had torn at my soul when I saw them earlier in the gym.

What was it they'd been talking about?

Chapter Forty

Lana

Sorrento, Italy, Tuesday, 6th August 2019

'So, how was everyone's mornings?' I plonk myself down next to Johnny at the dining table, finally feeling a bit more human after arriving home hot and sweaty and seriously in need of air con. 'We had a fabulous time, didn't we, Padma?' I glance at Johnny. 'Spent a bit more than I'd intended though.'

It's 1.45 p.m. and the six of us have gathered for a salad-based lunch washed down with some chilled water and thirst-quenching beers. We decided to eat inside, all of us feeling somewhat overheated from our morning exertions. Although it was good to get out of the villa and spend some time alone with Padma, traipsing around town for two hours did rather take it out of me. Granted, we had stopped off for a refreshing lemon granita in a café situated on Via San Cesareo – the most famous of the many side streets running off Corso Italia according to my guidebook, and rather charmingly coined 'the Drain' because of its narrowness – and this had cooled us down considerably, but it was only a temporary fix and by the time we hauled ourselves into a cab, my pale cheeks were beetroot red. In contrast to Padma's, who looked like she'd barely broken a sweat.

Padma didn't mention the text all morning, which was something of a relief. I'd been scared stiff she'd put me on the spot and question whether I'd broken my promise to keep its contents a secret from Johnny. I'm not sure I could have lied convincingly if she had done. Perhaps she trusts me to keep quiet because she knows Johnny and I aren't on good terms. That and the fact that since the lizard episode she and I have become close again. Alternatively, perhaps she thinks I'll delight in having this secret knowledge all to myself. And she wouldn't be far wrong. But when Johnny confronted me last night, I'd been too frightened of what he might do if I didn't tell him. I saw the way he smashed that lizard's head. He's got a temper on him when pushed plus, like he said, and although I would never admit it to him, I'm no angel here and so we all need to stick together. Anyway, we had a nice morning, exploring the lanes, venturing in and out of shops, buying a few trinkets for home. But now, with the six of us back together under the same four walls, that sense of unease has returned. Nick, who's sitting opposite me next to Padma, looks particularly on edge, and it makes me wonder if something happened while we were away. I suppose it could be something to do with the text Padma received. Perhaps Padma told him last night what it said. Then again, he seemed cheery enough at breakfast. Perfectly pleasant towards Johnny. So maybe not.

Despite the grimace he's wearing, Nick's the first to respond to me asking about everyone's morning. 'Well, you lot were right. It was pretty foolish of me to go jogging, nearly frigging died out there.'

'Babe, you need to be more careful,' Padma nestles her head into his shoulder. 'Besides, we're on holiday, it's meant to be fun not torture.'

Nick doesn't respond. Neither to her comment or her gesture of affection. Nor does he look at her. That's odd. Very unlike him. And I can tell by Padma's perturbed expression that she finds it odd too.

'You OK?' she asks, cutting me a fretful look as if to say, *what the hell's up with him?*

'Fine,' he says, still failing to make eye contact. 'Just a bit worn out.'

I give Padma a faint smile, my gaze telling her not to worry, that it's probably just the heat getting to him, and she smiles gratefully back, seemingly soothed.

'So, I thought I might cook for us tonight,' Ness says, lightening the mood. 'Cosy night in under the stars. What do you say?'

'Sorry, Ness, but Padma and I are having a meal in town,' Nick says.

'We are?' She turns her head sharply to look at him. Clearly this is news to Padma.

Finally, Nick makes eye contact. 'Yes, I thought it would be nice for us to have a quiet one.' His gaze works the table before he adds more jovially, 'Before we all celebrate Ness's birthday in style tomorrow.'

Makes sense. Still, there's something not right. Something in Nick's tone that worries me. He's just not sounding like the Nick we all know.

'Sure,' Padma says calmly, though her eyes remain fretful. 'If that's OK with you, Ness?'

'Fine by me,' Ness says. 'You two need some time alone together. I know how hard you both work and you can't get anywhere more romantic than southern Italy, so make the most of it.' She beams at Marcus. 'I only wish I knew what was happening tomorrow, but I've been told not to ask.'

'It's a surprise,' Marcus says, before kissing her on the cheek. 'All you need to think about is pampering yourself. On your special day you're not to lift a finger.'

I notice Johnny's reaction to this display of affection. Normally he resents couples in love, but there was no mistaking the sadness in his eyes, and I can't help wondering why.

Everyone is suddenly acting so strange, so out of character, and it makes me anxious.

Makes me think that at some point someone's really going to lose it.

Chapter Forty-One

Padma

Sorrento, Italy, Tuesday, 6th August 2019

It's 6.30 p.m. and the taxi's just dropped Nick and I off in Piazza Tasso alongside a string of identical white Mercedes parked up behind Il Fauno, the most popular bar in town on account of its slick, ridiculously handsome waiters, eclectic cocktails and preeminent location for people watching. I should be looking forward to a romantic dinner with the man I love, but right now that's far from the case. Because I can tell that something's wrong. He barely said a word to me all afternoon, and in the taxi just now he spent the whole time looking out the window, his arms folded defensively instead of holding my hand like he normally does.

After what happened at Oxford I lost interest in clothes and dolling myself up. I couldn't bear to draw attention to myself, fearful that my looks and predilection for the finer things in life had attracted the wrong sort, perhaps the jealous type, who'd wanted to teach me a lesson. But tonight I've made a real effort for Nick, because more than anything I want to please him, to make him feel lucky to have me, as I feel fortunate to have him.

I'm wearing a strappy cerise dress that shows off my olive skin to perfection, and have arranged my hair up, a few loose tendrils framing my face, classic diamante drop earrings completing the look. But I might as well be wearing a bin bag, because he didn't even comment on my appearance when I came into the sitting room earlier having told him to go downstairs and wait for me. He's never behaved this coldly towards me. Not in all the years we've been together. As soon as we locked eyes when Lana and I got back from town I knew something was up. He didn't welcome my kiss or seem pleased to see me. In fact, it was like kissing a statue, and when I tried to hug him, he tensed, as if my touch repulsed him. I can't think what I've done to make him so mad. Everything was fine between us when Lana and I left this morning, so I'm baffled as to what I could have done to upset him between then and now.

The other thing I find slightly odd, irritating even, is that Nick's been acting perfectly normal around Johnny. I mean, I know I told him not to say anything about the text, but you'd have thought he'd have been a bit off with him, in view of what it said, but if anything, he's seemed more at ease around Johnny than he has been around me, not dissimilar to the way he was so quick to defend him last night when I showed him the message. And it makes me wonder – did Johnny say something to Nick while I was out? Something to wind him up? Either about when he and I used to date, or something that paints me in a bad light? I wouldn't put it past him. Whatever's going on, I intend to get to the bottom of it as soon as we sit down to dinner. I have enough to worry about without adding my husband giving me the silent treatment to my list of problems.

I'm about to ask Nick where he had in mind to eat when he jumps in before me. 'There's a restaurant a little way down along Corso Italia that's meant to be good. It's got a garden out the back. Thought we could try for a table there.'

I'm relieved he's finally given me more than a one-word answer, but there's still a snappishness to his voice that hurts, as does his failure to touch, or even look at me, for more than a few seconds. My insides are heaving as he leads the way to the restaurant. I negotiate the crowds in something of a daze, nearly knocking into people I feel so unsteady on my feet.

We reach the restaurant which, although looks small from the outside, extends into a sizeable garden area as Nick mentioned, with plenty of dining space. Piano music is playing softly in the background, while the entire area is lit up with pretty multi-coloured lights that lend it a fairy-tale feel. It's the perfect romantic spot. But right now, it feels wasted on us. We opt for a table in the far corner, and before long the waiter has brought us some sparkling mineral water, a basket of focaccia bread and the menus. I sip some water but don't touch the bread, my appetite spoiled by Nick's surly behaviour. He grabs the menu, appears to study it intently, but it's at this point that I can't stand it anymore.

I reach out my hand and pull down the menu he's holding up at eye level.

'What the hell?' Nick barks. I notice the couple on the adjacent table looking at us, and I tell him to keep it down.

'What's going on?' I question. 'Since Lana and I got back this morning, you've been so short with me. Treated me like crap for want of a better word. I thought, after showing you that text last night, you'd be at least a little curt with Johnny, but if anything, you've been nicer to him than you have to me. So what the hell's got into you? I deserve to know.'

Having said my piece, I'd expected a look of contrition to sweep across Nick's face. Expected him to realise what a complete arsehole he's been and beg for my forgiveness. But rather than apologise, he launches into a tirade of his own.

'You're accusing me of treating *you* like crap? How can you sit there and be so sanctimonious after all the years I've been there for you, supporting you, caring for you, when all along you've been lying to me?'

Bile creeps up my throat. He knows.

'You know.' It's all I can say as he continues to stare at me with a look of disgust I never thought I'd see in his eyes.

'Yeah, I know, Padma,' he says scathingly. 'All these years I thought it was the stress of what you've been through, but no, it was you, being selfish, LYING to me!'

Now more diners are glancing our way, and I feel my face redden, literally want the ground to swallow me up.

I beg him to calm down. To give me a chance to explain.

'Explain then. Explain why I found contraception in your suitcase. All this time we've been trying to make a baby, you've been taking the pill. Making me believe it wasn't meant to be for us. Why would you do that? Why wouldn't you want our baby?'

It's hard to know where to start; there's just so much stuff occupying my thoughts right now, making it hard for me to see the wood for the trees, to even make trying to explain things to my husband in a way he'll understand possible. Because the fact is there are bigger issues at play here than me taking the pill behind Nick's back. Other stuff that's been preying on my mind for the best part of six months that Nick has no idea about. Stuff that's consumed me like a disease, making me sicker by the day. I should tell him everything, there should be no more lies between us, but I can't bring myself to; not just yet; it's not the right moment. One thing at a time, I must deal with this first.

But even though I've rehearsed how I'd explain my deception to Nick countless times in my head, when I say it out loud, it doesn't come out right. Rather, it sounds pathetic, unimaginative. I tell him how being attacked changed me, made me fearful, afraid of little things that never bothered me before. How I lost confidence in myself, in the people around me, never knowing who it was who attacked me, always looking over my shoulder. All this he knows, it's not news to him, and he gives me a look as if to say so, as if my excuses don't wash with him because he's heard it all before. As if he's lost all respect for me. Something I can't bear to happen.

'Say something,' I say.

He shrugs his shoulders. 'What's to say? I've devoted my life to you, made it clear how much I want a baby with you, and yet you repay me with lies. Making me believe it might even be my fault. You should have been straight with me. How can I trust you again? What happened eighteen years ago is no excuse for your lies, I'm sorry but it isn't.'

I want to lash out at him for saying this, but I can't. I have no right. He's not angry with me for feeling too afraid to bring children into this world, he's angry that I never had the guts to tell him this.

'I'm sorry,' I whisper, blinking back tears, aware that even the waiters are watching us intently now. One of those situations where you know you should look away, but you just can't bring yourself to because it's too enthralling. 'The job didn't help either.'

Nick frowns. 'How do you mean?'

'I deal with family problems all day every day: abused and neglected children, domestic violence. I guess it put me off having children. Put me off bringing an innocent child into this shitty world.'

Another unimpressed look. 'It just sounds like a cop out to me. Millions of social workers have their own kids. It's still no excuse for lying to me.' He gets up.

'Where are you going?' I ask in alarm. Hoping he'll say the men's room, but instinct telling me otherwise.

'I'm sorry but I just can't be around you right now. I'm going for a walk to clear my head.' He opens his wallet, takes out 100 euros, passes it to me. 'Here, have a nice dinner, I'll see you back at the villa.'

Before I can say another word, Nick walks away. I will him to look back, have a change of heart and return to the table. But he doesn't. Leaving me alone and humiliated.

Left to wonder if my marriage is over.

Chapter Forty-Two

Nick

Sorrento, Italy, Tuesday, 6th August 2019

I know I'm a hypocrite for accusing Padma of lying to me when that's exactly what I've been doing to her all these years, but I couldn't help myself. I guess the difference is, I never thought her capable of it. Not only that, I've kept the truth from her for her own benefit. Because I want her to be happy, to move on from that dark time. We've been so content together, I didn't want the truth to cause her further grief, to burst our bubble of happiness. That's the excuse I give myself anyway.

But what excuse does she have for lying to me? She should have trusted me enough to let me into her doubts about bringing another life into this world – our baby, the product of her and me, of our love. And I tell myself it's different to the lie I've kept from her because it only affects us, not Ness, not Johnny, nor anyone else for that matter.

Of course, my tolerance levels aren't helped by the text Padma received. Not knowing how much the sender knows. Not knowing their identity. Something I've not yet had the chance to discuss with Johnny. They could in fact know very little, in which case we have nothing to fear. On the flip side they could know every last detail and my best bet would be to run for the hills. So maybe Padma's deception is my out. Perhaps I should leave her while I have the moral high ground. As much as it would kill me to do so. Just because I live and breathe for her.

I'm looking out across the ocean, my arms resting over the handrail of the main viewing point in town, a long-walled stretch and one of the best spots to marvel at mighty Mount Vesuvius and the Bay of Naples. The volcano is just about visible in the distance, a magnificent gemstone necklace of glimmering lights that is Naples at its foot. Right now, it looks like a magical land, rather than the grubby, dangerous Mafia-dominated city it's famed for. Looking around me I see all sorts: starstruck lovers walking hand in hand, seemingly more captivated by each other than the view; families enjoying the freedom to roam in the cooler evening air – toddlers riding on their daddies' backs or running up and down in carefree abandonment; older couples partaking in a more leisurely stroll, who have perhaps been coming here year after year, and therefore take comfort from the familiarity of a place which has become like a second home to them. I envy all of them – the contented looks on their faces, the fact that they appear so free and unburdened in contrast to the cage of guilt and anger I find myself trapped in, making me feel like I can't breathe. I lean over the side and inhale the clean sea air, as if the act alone will cleanse me of the demons that stalk my mind.

Tomorrow is supposed to be a happy occasion, celebrating Ness's big birthday, but how can any of us relax with the threat of our secret being exposed hanging over our heads? I wonder about Lana too. Johnny's always maintained she knows nothing, but I'm not so sure. There's something in her eyes that tells me she knows more than she's letting on. She must do, to have kept Johnny on a leash all these years. Marcus is the only one who's oblivious to it all. But very soon, that may not be the case.

I continue to breathe in large chunks of air as all these thoughts compete for attention inside my mind, the faint sound of music, along with muffled chatter and laughter, in the distance behind me, both overpowered by the steady drone of insects penetrating the night air. It's the perfect setting to take Padma in my arms, to tell her how completely and utterly in love with her I am, but instead I am all alone and for the first time in our marriage I feel like we're drifting apart. And then, just as I'm thinking about heading back to the villa, I get a text. From Johnny.

> Mate, we need to talk. I've been getting threatening messages, presumably from the person who texted Padma, although I can't be sure. You, me and Ness, tomorrow morning, 6 a.m., bottom of the garden, near the statue of Apollo. Make sure Padma doesn't hear you. It's vital you slip away quietly.

Fuck, now I'm really getting scared.

And I wonder how on earth Ness is going to be able to save us this time?

Chapter Forty-Three

Vanessa

Before
Oxford, England, mid-October 2001

I'm dead to the world when my phone rings. Last night was a heavy one. I'm visiting an old boarding school friend up in Durham and we went a bit mad in the college bar which was offering all night two-for-one cocktails. I'm normally quite sensible with booze, but I was feeling the need to let loose after an argument with my mother before driving up here, and kind of let myself get swept up in the moment. My head is banging as I reach for my phone, still half asleep. Luckily, I'm on my own in the living room of the flat Nadine shares with another girl, sleeping on their sofa bed, so hopefully no one's been disturbed by Johnny's call.

Which is just as well because when I listen to what he has to say, I'm suddenly wide awake and have to muster up all the will in the world not to yell at him from the top of my lungs.

'What the fuck were you idiots thinking, organising something so vile?' I hiss. 'You total morons! You only have yourselves to blame!'

He's right, this is bad. It would be bad enough word getting out of the existence of a deeply chauvinistic male drinking society at Oxford, a university often criticised for its elitism and students who believe themselves to be superior, but news of a female fresher found dead next to one of its members the night after some depraved hunt orchestrated by the society's co-head, none other than Johnny Harker, son of scandalised Tory MP Ed Harker, now that would be on a whole other scale of catastrophe. Bringing the Harker name into disrepute. I know Johnny, he wouldn't survive the aftermath. I can't let him hang. Not after he saved my life. I wouldn't be here if it wasn't for him, for Christ's sake. And then there's poor Nick to think of. He only got involved to please Johnny who, in turn, was looking to impress his mates and live up to Ed's reputation from his days at Oxford. How could the idiot have supplied dodgy coke to Nick? If Nick loses his scholarship, he'll be done for. At least Johnny and I have rich families behind us. Connections. Nick doesn't have that cushion.

'We have to help Nick,' Johnny says anxiously. 'He's really freaking out. I think he's in danger of losing it, possibly doing something stupid. This can't come out, you know that.'

'Shut up, let me think.'

Johnny is silent as I lay down my phone temporarily and rest my throbbing head in my hands, hoping to be hit with divine inspiration. But as I sit here, racking my brain, there's only one solution I can think of. It's not a pretty one, but I can't see that we have a choice. We don't have time to procrastinate. Not if we want to keep this nightmare well and truly buried.

I pick up the phone, take a deep breath, then whisper, 'There's only one viable option that I can see. We have to get rid of the body. I don't want to drive home without saying goodbye to Nadine, it'll look suspicious, plus I'm not quite sober yet. But I'll be home by lunchtime. In the meantime, tell Nick not to leave the house or do anything dumb. And whatever you do, don't tell Padma. She's too good a person and she will never agree to keep this quiet. No matter how much she loves you. You need to hear my words, Johnny – she can never know.'

Chapter Forty-Four

Johnny

Sorrento, Italy, Wednesday, 6th August 2019

> I saw you that night. Loading a suitcase into the back of your friend's car. I know you killed that fresher. And so will the whole world very soon. Do the right thing before I do it for you.

I watch Nick's face fall as he reads the text message I received just after 8 p.m. last night, having shown him and Ness the two previous texts. All from the same unknown number.

I'd been sitting with Lana, Ness and Marcus at the table by the pool when this latest message had come through and had swiftly excused myself to the bathroom to read it. We'd had a simple dinner of spinach and ricotta ravioli followed by a tangy orange sorbet and were washing it down with a second bottle of wine. I was trying to be cheerful, for Ness's benefit mostly, and because I'd promised her I wouldn't say or do anything to alert Marcus to the fact that something might be up. But the deep sense of wretchedness that's been gnawing at my insides since

Ness told me she's not long for this world was hard to repress. When I came back from the loo, clearly looking preoccupied, Marcus asked me if I was feeling OK, and I fobbed him off, saying I was just a bit tired. That the heat had drained me. He seemed to believe me, poor sod. Of all people, he's the least deserving of the devastating news that's coming his way, a double whammy I'm not sure he'll ever recover from. Ness is still insistent we own up, and with this latest text, I fear we have no choice.

We've gathered at the far edge of the villa's gardens, accessed via a long, narrow concrete pathway where hopefully no one will think to look for us should they wake up and wonder where we are. I made sure Lana was out for the count when I slipped out of our bedroom, leaving a note to say I couldn't sleep and had gone for a run while it was still cool, in case she stirred early.

Nick's face is ashen. I think he might collapse so I urge him to sit on a nearby bench next to the statue of Apollo. He doesn't argue, allows me to help ease him onto it. It's 6.05 a.m. and there's a slight chill in the air, unusual for August. Apparently, there are storms sweeping across northern Europe, and they may reach us sometime tomorrow.

'What are you going to do?' Nick asks, his face still wan. I know what he's thinking. He's wondering if the person who's been texting me knows about his part in the whole affair. An accident that none of us could have foreseen. But there's something else bothering him too. And I think I know what it is.

'You're worried about the phone call, aren't you?' I say.

'Yes. I mean what if it's the same person Carys called? The one we presumed was her sister. What if she told her who she was with?'

239

'If she had done, don't you think the police would have knocked on your door by now?'

'True, I guess,' Nick says, looking mildly placated.

'And besides, it's not you this person has been messaging. It's me. They've told Padma not to trust *me*.'

'Yes, I suppose. Even so, like I said, what in God's name are you going to do?'

Ness rests a hand on Nick's shoulder. 'We have to own up, Nick, it's our only option. It's obvious Johnny and I were being watched that night. Whoever it is, they mean business; it's only a matter of time before they tell the authorities. I'd already planned on doing so after my birthday's been and gone. It's partly why I arranged this week. So we could all come together and tell the truth.'

Nick looks horror-struck. 'What? Why? Why would you do that? Are you mad? After all this time we've kept it under wraps? Why would you want to jeopardise our freedom, our lives? How can you do that to me, to Padma? It will break her knowing I've been lying to her all these years, knowing I played a part in that girl's death.'

I look at Ness and she gives me a faint nod, as if to signal it's OK to proceed.

'Nick, Ness is dying.' I can barely get the words out, they're so excruciating to say.

Slowly, Nick looks from me to Ness, then back to me again, disbelief engulfing his face. 'What?'

'It's true, Nick, I've got stage four bowel cancer and I probably won't see out the year.'

'Oh, Ness,' Nick murmurs. 'I – I don't know what to say. I'm so sorry. Can't they do anything? Surely, they can?'

Ness explains her reasons for not receiving treatment, and once again I have to fight the urge to try and convince her to at least give it a shot. I know I'm doing it for me as much as for her, because I can't bear the thought of life without my best friend, but I can't help it.

'And you've not told Marcus I take it?' Nick says. 'He seems too happy.'

'No, I haven't,' Ness says guiltily, before explaining why.

There's a moment of quiet, before Nick says, 'I'm so sorry, Ness, I really am. I can't quite believe it if I'm being honest, and I understand your need to unburden yourself before the worst happens, but what about the rest of us you'll leave behind? My marriage is rocky enough right now – I found out Padma's been taking the pill behind my back – and this will most certainly end it if she knows I had a hand in that girl's death. That I've been keeping something so massive from her all this time.'

Poor Nick, that explains things. He and Padma came back separately last night, Padma briefly popping her head through the terrace doors to tell us she was going to bed, while we didn't even see Nick. None of us had any idea what they'd clearly argued about, and ordinarily I'd have been intrigued to know. But having just received another text, their marital problems were the least of my worries. To think that a few days ago I'd have rejoiced at his fight with Padma. Would have told myself it proved how they were never meant to be together. That she didn't love him enough to want his children. But in my heart, I think I know why she's put off having kids. It's because she's haunted by that night. Too afraid to bring a child into this world. Scared she won't be able to protect them. And it's all my fault. I watch Nick bury his face in his hands. Can only imagine the turmoil he's in. I bet he sometimes wishes he never made friends with me at uni. Despite ending up with Padma, who he clearly loves more than life itself.

Ness sits down beside Nick, takes his hand in hers, and I realise what she's about to say. Something she and I discussed long and hard before Nick arrived. 'Look, don't worry, we won't mention you had any part in this.'

For a moment Nick looks at Ness like he doesn't believe her. So I step in and try to reassure him.

'Ness isn't joking, mate. I've never got over the guilt for supplying you with that coke. For organising that stupid hunt and making you a part of it. If I hadn't done any of it, you'd never have slept with her, never have offered her drugs, and in all likelihood she'd still be alive. None of this is your fault. And I'm guessing this person who's been making threats believes the same, because they don't even mention you. You're in the clear, but Ness and I aren't. We need to make sure we come clean to Padma, Lana and Marcus before this person goes public.'

Relief washes over Nick's face, the colour returning to it. Of course, Lana isn't entirely innocent in all this for reasons only Ness and I are aware of. But I don't want to complicate matters. It's not important for Nick to know that.

'But what will you say exactly?'

I tell Nick the plan, and again he looks both relieved and humbled by our sacrifice.

'And the other secret we've kept from her? Will you tell her that too?' Nick swallows hard, clearly fearful of my response, despite the reassurances I've just given him.

'Yes, I will, I have to. But I won't tell her you knew. As much as I've tried to push the memory to the back of my mind all these years, it's always been there, a curse I can never lift. And if I tell her about my part in Carys's disappearance, I might as well tell her what happened between us that Monday.'

A detail I know Lana has been too afraid to question me about, even though I'm certain it crossed her mind the moment she saw me standing over Padma's bed in the hospital. In fact, she's probably thought about it every day since.

I briefly think back to that night, when we'd rowed, and she'd made threats. I was already rattled from what Ness and I had done, from the fear of being found out, but then she'd started asking questions, and I had done something that I'd never thought myself capable of; something that had made me feel sick to my stomach in the hours, days, months that followed. And then I had run. Run to Ness and Nick's, told them what had happened. Confused, upset, hysterical. And that's when Nick had offered to go check on her, found Jacob crouched over her comatose body, calling for an ambulance.

'So,' Ness says, looking at Nick, 'we get today out of the way, try our best to act like nothing's wrong and enjoy it. And then tomorrow, Johnny and I will tell the others everything. But first, there's something else you should know. And for that, I suggest you remain seated.'

Chapter Forty-Five

Nick

Before
Oxford, England, mid-October 2001

I don't know how I let Johnny talk me into being a part of this thing.

It's gross, demeaning, represents everything I hate about Oxford, and yet here I am agreeing to be an active participant in it. He always manages to coax me into stuff; says it's just a bit of harmless fun, all part of being a student, that I need to lighten up. That life will be tedious enough once we start working in the real world. And so I guess I don't have the heart, or maybe the balls, to say no, just because he's always been such a good friend to me. I was known as a bit of a geek at school, a bit of a loner. Too busy burying my head in books to be bothered about being popular, doing fun stuff. But I guess, by the time I reached Oxford, away from home and its creature comforts, I felt the need to make friends. And Johnny had this magnetism about him, coming from a world I'd only ever read about in newspapers and in books, and I suppose I was flattered he wanted to be mates with me. Granted, he probably felt he owed me after I helped him out with a maths assignment in the early days of our degree. I'd already earned the reputation of being the college dork, and he knew sidling up to me would be a safe bet. Then again, he could have ditched me after I helped him. But he didn't, and we became firm friends, and slowly but surely, I got sucked into his world, became part of the cool crowd. It felt good to show my dad that I was finally popular, no longer an outsider. As for Johnny, I think he liked being friends with someone 'normal', someone who at least tried to put him in touch with reality.

I wonder what Padma would say if she knew what the male drinking society he forced me to sign up to in our first year, and which Johnny now helps run (just like his father before), really gets up to. To be fair, they've never organised anything quite this misogynistic. A secret event he and Richard, the other club leader, have planned and which, to our knowledge, those that run this place know nothing about. Richard's a pretentious wanker, who I really can't stand, but I bite my lip because he and Johnny are friends. I know Johnny feels the need to live up to his dad's expectations, to do risky stuff like he used to, just to maintain the 'hip' image he's got going for him – Ed Harker's son, the coolest kid in town who everyone worships, who always does one better than the rest. But I wish he wouldn't. He's got a beautiful girlfriend, he's smart and he's loaded. And yet it's never enough. What I wouldn't give to be him. To have what he has.

I'll be amazed if they manage to keep it a secret. I mean, Baron College may be one of over thirty in Oxford but even so, the city's a small place and if a bunch of us go running about town chasing down female students dressed as foxes, word's bound to get out. Even if it is taking place at night. I don't know why Johnny thinks it's a good idea to do this in our final year. It's hard to imagine Ness being

OK with it, but perhaps that's precisely why he's organised it the weekend she's away.

Us blokes are to select female freshers at our college whom we consider to be the 'hottest'. We're then expected to hunt down the girls through Oxford's streets. I've seen the invitations, printed in fancy lettering with gold-embossed edges. God knows they must have cost a fortune. They were sent out a few nights ago by Johnny and Richard, challenging the girls to evade their capture before eventually being seized by us, the 'huntsmen'. Meaning they effectively have no choice but to succumb, like defenceless prey, or rather, the 'weaker sex.' Doesn't exactly say much for the feminist movement, does it? I can't think what the left-wing press would make of it should word get out. I'm almost tempted to leak it myself, but I can't do that to Johnny. Just because deep down I think he's a good guy. Plus, like I said, he took me under his wing when I initially felt so out of place.

I can pretty much predict how things will go. Once the girls get caught, there'll be copious amounts of drinking, a fair share of drug-taking and then a number of them will end up having sex with the blokes. Not Johnny, though. He won't cheat on Padma, won't risk losing her. He loves her too much.

Johnny says I need to find a girl, get laid. He's probably right, I could do with a shag, just to get it out of my system. He's noticed the way this one fresher at our college seems to have the hots for me. I've noticed it too. She seems sweet, is quite pretty, with a nice smile, and I guess it's flattering to know she has a crush on me. Normally it's Johnny boasting about this girl or that pining after him, so it's rather a turn up for the books that a fit girl appears to prefer me over him. I've seen her in formal hall, and in the library. She blushes, looks away when I smile back, so seems quite shy. But then again, you can never tell with these girls. Sometimes they act all coy, like butter wouldn't melt, but underneath, they're vixens.

I guess I'll find out later.

Chapter Forty-Six

Lana

Sorrento, Italy, Wednesday, 7th August 2019

I hear the lock turn as I lie here motionless, my back facing the bedroom door, the duvet pulled up to my neck as if I am sleeping deeply, when in fact I am wide awake. My heart is beating erratically, my back saturated with sweat having not long returned to my bed in a frantic hurry to get back before Johnny suspects anything.

I'd been awake for some time before he slipped out of the room at 5.50 a.m. I never sleep well after too much wine. That, on top of worrying about the text Padma received, had ensured sleep proved elusive. And then there was the disturbed look on Johnny's face last night when he'd rejoined Marcus, Ness and me by the pool, having excused himself to use the bathroom. It had made me wonder if whoever had texted Padma had perhaps messaged him too? After retiring to our room, I'd questioned Johnny on this very subject, but he had refused to talk about it; snapped at me, in fact, said he was shattered and needed sleep. I didn't push it, there was no point, and we had gone to bed without uttering another word to each other.

I had lain there quiet, still, but unable to sleep, before hearing Johnny steal out of bed, dress then leave the room, closing the door gently behind him. There was no way I was going to let him disappear at such an unearthly hour without finding out what he was up to. Despite the note he'd left by my bedside professing to have gone for a run. Something I knew he'd never do with a gym onsite. And so, the minute I'd read the note, I had jumped out of bed, thrown on some clothes, softly opened the door and peeped out. And just at that moment, I saw Ness creeping down the stairs, and knew this couldn't be a coincidence. I followed her at a reasonable distance to the far end of the garden, accessed via a long pathway, suspecting she and Johnny had arranged some clandestine meeting, and that whatever they were meeting about had something to do with what happened that week at Oxford. It had to.

And now, having heard every word of what they discussed, I know that my suspicions were right. But I've also discovered several other shocking truths. Including that Nick was involved too.

I couldn't believe my eyes when he'd turned up. Had thanked my lucky stars that I'd been quick to hide myself. I thought perhaps he couldn't sleep either, had gone for a stroll and had stumbled upon them by chance. But then, when they'd started talking, I realised that this was no mistake. That Nick was involved far deeper than I could ever have imagined. The realisation horrified me. Set all sorts of alarm bells ringing. And between them, they had discussed details that had shocked me to my core.

I have only ever known the bare bones of what happened that night, enough to enable me to blackmail Johnny into marrying me. But now I know the ins and outs of it – that Carys was with Nick when she died, that my suspicions about what Johnny did were correct, along with another ghastly revelation made by Ness – my mind is in turmoil. For so many reasons. Reasons that send all sorts of questions racing through my head and feed the guilt in me.

Chapter Forty-Seven

Vanessa

Sorrento, Italy, Wednesday, 7th August 2019

'To Ness, *saluti!*'

I do my best to smile, to put on a brave face and appear like I'm enjoying myself as the others all toast me with a glass of my favourite Champagne, served in elegant crystal flutes, having sung me happy birthday. It's 9.30 a.m. and we're having breakfast by the pool. It's the cloudiest it's been since we arrived, with a nip in the air forcing me to wear a shawl. There's also a light wind causing a ripple effect in the pool, fallen leaves and twigs scattered on the water, swimming from end to end. Ordinarily I'd be disappointed the weather's failed me on my special day – being an August baby I'm generally used to blue skies and sunshine – but my mind is preoccupied with bigger things than the disappointing climate. Besides, the ominous weather seems apt.

I keep thinking about the look on Nick's face after we hit him with a third truth. He'd looked from me to Johnny as if my revelation required further clarification. As if my illness had perhaps sent me mad and that I was delusional. But on seeing Johnny's grim expression he'd realised I wasn't making things up. That this was for real.

And now, as I sit here, pretending to be cheerful, I can see that Nick is struggling too. He's barely touched his Champagne or the bread and fruit on his plate. It's not his fault, he wasn't to know, none of us were, but it doesn't make the guilt any easier to bear.

Two rather handsome waiters, wearing crisp white jackets and black bow ties, circle the table with chilled bottles of Bollinger. Trays of the ripest sweetest fruit and divine-smelling freshly baked bread, smoked salmon and scrambled eggs, along with any other cooked foods our hearts might desire, are on offer from the kitchen. That's what Matteo, the chef Marcus hired, said when he came out to introduce himself just after we'd all sat down. A larger-than-life character with a thunderous voice and cheery disposition, whose renditions of 'O Sole Mio' and 'Funiculì Funiculà' we could hear all the way from the kitchen. He doesn't know that food is the last thing I desire or am able to stomach, but I thanked him all the same and will do my best to keep something down, if only for Marcus's sake.

There's a gold number forty balloon tied to a corner of the table, which is covered in a cream lace tablecloth and strewn with heart-shaped gold and silver confetti. There are party poppers by each place setting, while the cutlery is real silver, the crockery equally fancy. Marcus has outdone himself surprising me this morning, and I couldn't help but cry when I realised how much trouble he'd gone to. I'm so lucky, but it's a bittersweet feeling, and it only serves to accentuate my feelings of shame.

'Thanks all,' I smile, looking at everyone in turn, before resting my gaze on my husband, who gives me a look of love that is almost too much to bear. Having sneaked back into the room around 6.40 a.m., I was relieved to find him fast asleep. I'd put my nightie back on and slunk under the duvet, then must have drifted off, because when I woke around 8.30 there was a note from him on my bedside table wishing me a happy birthday, telling me how much he loved me and giving me strict instructions not to leave the room before 9 a.m. This had brought a smile to my face because I realised he was downstairs planning something special, and not for the first time I felt grateful but also unworthy to have married such a wonderful man. But most of all, appalled by the way I have deceived him. I don't deserve all this love and special attention. And my heart aches knowing that very soon the man I adore is going to wish he'd never set eyes on me.

'So, how does it feel to be forty, Ness?' Padma asks, sipping her Champagne. 'I still can't believe you insisted on no presents. It doesn't feel right not giving you something on such a milestone birthday.'

'Forty? I feel about a hundred!' I say this in a tongue-in-cheek way, but it's not far from the truth, and as I look around and catch Johnny's and Nick's eyes, it's clear they know it too. It should be a time to reflect, to reassess my life, think about doing all the things I've not yet managed to accomplish but long to tick off my bucket list. A new chapter, my best years to come, even. But sadly, that can never be. 'And don't worry about gifts, I have everything I need right here.' I let my gaze rest on Marcus once again as I say this. 'I don't need more material things. I've come to realise in my old age that love and friendship are all that matter in this mortal life we lead. Stuff is one thing I've never lacked. I've been fortunate in that way.'

'That's very magnanimous of you, Ness,' Padma says. 'And I applaud you for it.'

'We all do,' Johnny says with a tender smile, his eyes filled with love. But also a pain only I and Nick can see.

More Champagne is served, and I struggle through the salmon and eggs laid out before me, telling Marcus I'm saving myself for later. 'I'm assuming there'll be more food on offer, that is?' I smile.

'Oh yes.' He grins. 'I have quite the food-and-drink-packed day planned. Only…'

'Only what, darling?'

His face becomes downcast. 'Only, with the weather looking so dodgy, I fear my grand plans might be scuppered.'

'And what do your grand plans involve exactly?'

He proceeds to tell me about the boat trip he's organised for the six of us, stopping off at Capri for a spot of shopping, lunch and people watching, before heading back home for more drinks and dinner, either at the villa or a nearby restaurant. It sounds like the perfect day, and I will myself to enjoy it before the darkness descends tomorrow.

'That sounds amazing, darling,' I say, looking around the table at the others. They all smile and nod their heads in approval. Even Nick does his best to look enthusiastic, while Lana and Padma seem positively thrilled with the idea. Despite Lana having seemed a touch withdrawn until now, causing me to wonder if she and Johnny have argued again.

'It doesn't matter about the weather,' Padma reassures Marcus, 'I'm sure this cloud will pass before long. It's not England. Here, you get a thunderstorm and the next minute it breaks out into glorious hot sunshine.'

Marcus's face brightens at this comment and I'm so grateful to Padma for lifting his spirits. She's such a kind person, it's why we could never tell her the truth, and it strengthens my resolve to finally be honest with her this week. She deserves to be put out of her misery, even though I know it will devastate her. In time, though, with Nick's help, she'll get over the pain and the shock. I'm so glad she found him. He was never at fault here; he asked for our help, and we gave it willingly.

And that's why she doesn't need to know about his involvement.

It's why my conscience is OK with keeping his part in Marcus's sister's death a secret.

Chapter Forty-Eight

Marcus

Before
Wimbledon, England, June 2015

'Ness, there's something you need to know. Something I should have told you a long time ago.'

My stomach is doing somersaults as I say this while looking into my wife's eyes, which are suddenly anxious. The children have been in bed for an hour, and we've just this minute finished dinner. My famous meatball ragu which the kids also enjoy, although Ness is never home early enough for us to eat together as a family. We're sitting at our kitchen table, a bottle of red wine resting in the centre, from which I've just poured myself a second large glass in a bid to work up the courage to say what I've been wanting to tell her since we became serious five years ago.

'What is it?' she asks. No doubt all manner of possibilities are raiding her mind. That I'm having an affair, leading a double life, have a secret love child, a dark past, am a closet homosexual. But it's none of those things. I take her hands in mine, lean across the table, say softly, 'I'm not an only child, like you always believed me to be. Like I told you when we first started dating.'

She cocks her head. 'You're not?'

'No, I had a sister. Well, a half-sister to be more precise. Two years after I went to live with John and Mum in Glasgow, Mum fell pregnant.'

'Had? What happened to her?'

'She died. Well, we assume she died.'

Her face falls. She clasps my hands tightly, then tenderly caresses the side of my face. 'Oh, love, I'm so sorry, is that why you've never mentioned her, because it's too painful?'

I nod. 'Yes, that's a large part of it. Despite being half-brother and sister, and me not having much time for John, who treated me more like a live-in lodger than a son, she and I were close, and we loved each other very much. She was four years younger than me. We all loved her. She and Mum were inseparable, in fact.'

I see Ness twig. 'Is that why your mum suffered so badly from depression? Because of your sister's death? Is that why she killed herself?'

'Yes,' I say, my throat constricting. I reach for my wine, sip it gently to calm myself.

'Why did you never mention your sister to me? And why do you only assume she died? I'm not quite following.'

'Because it's complicated. And because of everything that happened after she disappeared. It was too upsetting, and I didn't want the memories resurfacing. Didn't want to be reminded of that time or bring you into my pain. I know you always wanted to be with someone strong and uncomplicated, and I was so in love with you I didn't want to put you off.'

'Oh, sweetheart, I feel like a real hard-hearted cow now,' Ness says, her face aghast. 'I'm sorry if I made you feel that you couldn't confide in me. You know you can tell me anything.'

I hate to think I've upset Ness, and so I reassure her she's not to blame. 'No, really, I was happy not to talk about her. When Mum died, I promised myself I'd bury that part of my life, because I didn't want my sadness casting a shadow over my work, over any future relationship I might have that became serious.'

She shakes her head. 'Even so, I can't bear to think you've been suffering in silence all these years.'

I smile, grateful for this selfless woman I found and who agreed to marry me at a point in my life when I'd been suffering from bouts of depression, just like my mother. My sister's face would appear in my dreams like some ghostly apparition, the not knowing what became of her, what she might have suffered, whether her last moments in life were filled with terror and pain, almost unbearable. Because that's the thing – none of us know what happened to her. When my parents had first got the call, we'd tried not to worry, thought maybe she'd gone to visit a friend. But then, as the days turned to weeks and then months, with not a word, not a single sighting apart from the usual bogus calls, we knew that something terrible must have happened. And not being able to lay her to rest after all that time had tipped my mother over the edge. Every day was a living torture for her. And she simply couldn't bear it.

'The thing is,' I say to Ness, 'she never returned to her halls in Oxford after some party she went to one night. She hadn't even been there a month. This was back in 2001. You would have just started your third year, so it's highly unlikely you would have come across her. Although, as it happens, she was at the same college as Johnny and Nick. When you first introduced me to them shortly after we started dating and I discovered they'd been at Baron

College, a part of me had been tempted to tell all and ask if they'd ever come across Carys. But what with Baron having over 600 students at the time, and Johnny and Nick being in their final years, I figured the chances of them having met her were slim. Especially with you all living off campus. Plus, like I said, I'd tried to put the past behind me, and I wanted to shield you from my pain.'

I watch the colour drain from my wife's face. Clearly, she's in shock, upset for me and what I've been through. Just as I would be heartbroken for her. I'm touched by Ness's concern, relieved she's not angry with me for keeping something so huge from her all these years.

'You might remember the case, though? I expect the police questioned a lot of students who were there at the time. Particularly those who attended the party my sister had gone to. I say party, but there was talk of it being a somewhat distasteful affair, that only certain girls, i.e., the prettiest, had been invited, and that it was actually some kind of female fresher "hunt" organised by a group of male students. John was angry as he suspected some kind of cover-up by the Oxford bigwigs because they never actually named names and it was conveniently glossed over in the papers. He even accused the police of being corrupt and in their pockets because the officer leading the investigation was a friend of the College Master and an Oxford graduate. Who knows, that might have been true. Whatever the case, it didn't exactly endear him to them.'

Ness still hasn't said a word, so I press on. 'I was in Australia travelling when she went missing. It was John who visited the grounds and went on TV to make an appeal. My mother couldn't face it and he forbade me from getting involved, even though I flew back after three weeks when it became clear something bad must have happened to her. I wanted to help, but he wasn't the easiest of men, was adamant I stay out of it and I didn't want to upset Mum any more by arguing. It was at this point that I went to live with Dad down in Cornwall. Before starting my training contract in London.'

I stop talking. 'Ness, say something. Do you remember the case? You must have done, it made the news. A lot of students were interviewed.'

Finally, Ness says, so quietly I can barely hear her, 'I do have a vague recollection of it, yes. Obviously, at the time we were all a bit consumed by Padma having been attacked, which I think must have coincided with your sister's disappearance.'

I nod. Explain this as being another reason why I didn't bring it up. I knew how stressful those few months had been for Ness, and hadn't wanted to rehash memories of a time she'd also tried to forget.

'What was her name?' Ness tentatively asks after a pause.

'Carys,' I say. 'Although she was Leia to me. And I was Luke to her. When we were kids we'd watch Star Wars all the time. We wanted to be like Luke and Leia, an unstoppable brother and sister team who had each other's backs come hell or high water. I showed the police the last letter she sent to me, in which she talked about hoping to meet some guy she had a crush on at a party some of the freshers had been invited to. I'm guessing it was the same party or hunt I just spoke of, but obviously she was sworn to secrecy so didn't tell me the details. She also probably knew I'd have been appalled at the idea. She texted me about it on the day itself, said she'd speak to me soon, but of course, that never happened. The police allegedly questioned everyone who went, but because she didn't mention the name of the guy she liked in her letter, they had no way of knowing who he was. I wish I knew though. Whether it was him who harmed her, even though I realise that's a bit of an unfair assumption to make.'

'Yes, I mean, it could have been anyone, couldn't it?' Ness says.

'Yes, it could. I guess I'm just desperate to know the truth, to have some sort of closure. I felt like I let her down even though I know there's nothing I could have done, short of stopping her from going to uni. The thing is, when she was sixteen, she was attacked coming home from school. She got away, but the whole experience left her wary of men. But her last letter reassured me she was starting to feel like her old self. Growing in confidence. She was a passionate sort, always hankered after affection, perhaps because John, although he loved her, wasn't the most tactile of fathers. She said she'd be fine, that we'd see each other soon, and that she had something important to tell me. A secret she'd promised never to divulge, but which she didn't feel she could keep from me any longer. But, of course, that time never came. And so I never found out what it was she was so desperate to tell me.'

The tears are falling fast and furiously now as I think back to our childhood, those happy-go-lucky days when we'd play fight with our toy lightsabers. When Mum would gaze at us with smiling eyes, relieved that Carys and I had bonded even though John never took to me. I never felt jealous of Carys. Right from the moment she was born I wanted to protect my little sister.

'Having the kids, me telling them the other night how important it is for us not to keep secrets from the ones we love, I felt like a bit of a hypocrite, and realised I couldn't keep my sister's existence from you anymore,' I explain to Ness. 'And with today being Carys's birthday, it seemed like the ideal time to tell you.'

Ness looks at me with the same stunned expression.

'You OK?' I ask.

'I'm sorry, I'm not feeling so well,' she apologises. 'Give me a minute.'

I watch her get up, a little unsteady on her feet, before disappearing from the kitchen.

It's a lot to take in. I'm not surprised she feels unwell, and I feel bad for dropping this on her. For not being honest from the start of our relationship, or at least once we became serious. But it's also a relief to get it off my chest. And that she hasn't flown into a rage over my dishonesty.

It tells me I did the right thing in telling the one person I trust above everyone else the secret that still haunts me every minute of every hour of every day.

If only I knew where my sister's body lay so I could bring her home to rest.

Every day I pray that those behind her disappearance are found. Although I fear I won't be responsible for my actions when that happens.

Chapter Forty-Nine

Johnny

Sorrento, Italy, Wednesday, 7th August 2019

There are three ways to access the main port in Sorrento nestled at the bottom of the cliff-face. One is to bus or cab it down via a sprawling zigzag cobbled pathway, the second is to walk the same path at your own risk. The final option is to take the zillion steps from Piazza Tasso – safer than walking the path – but by the time you reach the bottom this has your legs twitching involuntarily. That's what we've just done. I'm not sure why Marcus thought it was a good idea. I think perhaps it was to work off the breakfast we recently consumed, and ordinarily I wouldn't have minded, I'm such an exercise freak, but I couldn't help feeling concerned for Ness who, by the time we reached the final step, looked done in. Marcus wasn't to know, of course, and Ness hadn't helped herself by insisting she'd be fine despite the sceptical look I'd given her. Even now, when she's so sick, she remains as stubborn as a mule. She's always been a fighter, never liked showing any sign of weakness. And, as ever, I am in awe of her courage in the face of such adversity.

Despite its name, Marina Piccolo is the larger of the two ports in Sorrento. With it still being the height of summer and the tourist season, the area is crammed with visitors from every corner of the globe, either queuing for tickets at the various booking kiosks or following the oversized umbrellas of eager tour guides, ready to embark on their over-priced day trips. The numerous hydrofoils or ferries that frequent the port several times a day will take them to various island hotspots – Positano, Capri, Salerno and Ischia being the most popular.

The sun is trying to break through, and it's muggy to the point of being oppressive. That, along with the smell of diesel and pervading sense of unease fermenting inside me, is making me feel slightly nauseous. I tell myself I'll feel better once we're out on the ocean, inhaling the sea air. For just a few hours I'm going to try and enjoy myself, enjoy Ness's last birthday. I owe it to her to be strong and make the day as special as possible for her.

'There's our man!'

Marcus points to where an assortment of smaller boats are moored. We start making our way down the harbour's edge towards them, past various boarding points swarming with hot and bothered tourists queuing impatiently in a haphazard fashion until I see a portly-looking man sporting a seaman's cap, who's maybe in his late fifties, waving at us. As we approach, I notice he has a rather leathery complexion, suggestive of someone who's spent hours on the water and in the sun. He's wearing a sea-green Lacoste polo shirt and white trousers, a cigarette hanging from his mouth. He grins broadly at us, gives a friendly 'ciao' and introduces himself as Luigi before ushering everyone onboard via a plank that stretches between the dock and the boat. He offers his hand to the ladies first, then Marcus, Nick and I hop on, causing the boat to sway a little more vigorously than it had done with the ladies' lighter step.

'Oh, Marcus, this is fabulous!' Ness says, her eyes lighting up. It's wonderful to see her looking so happy, to witness the pleasure Marcus takes from this. Any fool can see how much he loves her, but to think that this time tomorrow he'll most likely curse the day he ever met her. Every time I see him, I am filled with shame and remorse for the suffering we caused him. So much so it's a struggle to look him in the eye. I can't imagine how Ness has managed it for the past four years. It's hardly surprising she's buried herself in work.

'It is,' Nick agrees. 'Must have set you back a pretty penny.'

'She's totally worth it,' Marcus says, kissing Ness softly on the lips. 'Besides, you don't turn forty every day, and I knew I had to pull out the stops. At least I'll have a decade to think up something bigger and better for the next milestone!' He grins, and I can tell it's taking all the courage in the world for Ness not to burst into floods of tears.

'Come on, then,' I say cheerily, hoping to distract Ness from her melancholy, 'let's get ourselves settled, so the day can properly commence!'

The white and blue trimmed boat, named *Lady of Capri* is a fourteen-metre motorised yacht cruiser to be precise. I'm glad it's motorised so that we can all sit back and relax, or at least try to. Luigi instructs us to make ourselves comfortable on the plush beige leather horseshoe-shaped sofa at the stern, while he starts the engine up at the helm. We do as he says, Lana and Padma giggling like teenage girls, excited for the day ahead. It's strange seeing them so at ease in each other's company. I want to be happy for them, but I can't. Because, like me, Lana hasn't been honest with Padma, and it bugs me that she feels able to pretend they're best friends again, as if the secret she's kept is no big deal. I also find Padma's behaviour slightly odd. I mean, for years she's been so introverted, barely engaging in conversation. But here her manner has blown hot and cold. One moment she rushes off to the Ladies' having received a sinister text accusing me of lying to her about that night, the next she's all smiles and laughter. It's weird.

Perhaps, like me, she's putting on a good show for Ness's sake, wanting to make the day as relaxed and memorable as possible before we all revert to the darkness of our pasts tomorrow.

D–Day.

Chapter Fifty

Johnny

Before
Oxford, England, mid-October 2001

Last night was surreal, and a part of me thinks, or rather wishes, that I was delusional, high on some hallucinogenic drug that's had me in its grip these last forty-eight hours but will soon wear off. Alternatively, that I'm locked in a nightmare from which, before long, I'll wake up and Padma will be at my side telling me it's OK, that it was just a very bad dream. And that no, last night I didn't drive nearly two hundred miles to Yorkshire with Ness, a dead body lying in a trolley suitcase in the back of her car, which we weighed down with bricks and dumped in The Strid. Better known as 'England's killer creek' – a narrow body of water on the River Wharfe that appears as safe as any shallow river but has a dangerous combination of vast and deadly undercurrents that move at aggressive speeds, making it one of the most treacherous rivers in the world with parts that go sixty-five metres deep. Ness remembered it from a trip she took up there with school to visit Bolton Abbey, and where she and her friends had been warned not to venture on account of its ability to swallow victims up within seconds. Unsurprisingly, no one had been about when we arrived; it's dangerous enough in daylight hours so you'd be insane to go there in the dark. But that's precisely why Ness had chosen it, opting for a spot close to one of the river's deepest points, hoping and praying that the suitcase would be carried away and sink to the bottom, never to be found. Our secret intact.

It was like being in a scene from a horror film, helping Ness fold Carys's body into a foetal position inside Ness's large trolley suitcase. Thank God she'd been a petite girl, and that rigor mortis had subsided by then, her muscles having regained their flexibility.

Despite me wishing otherwise, what we did last night was not a dream or figment of my imagination. It was a real, living, breathing nightmare that right now I see no end to. After disposing of the body, we drove for an hour in silence, my hands shaking so badly I had no choice but to let Ness do the driving, before we slept overnight in a cheap hotel. I told Padma in my note that I wouldn't be back until late Monday afternoon because Ness had a family emergency, having called me in a state in the middle of the night, begging me to accompany her.

All the way back, I couldn't stop checking my side mirror, my heart pounding, terrified that we'd been found out, that the police had been trailing us since we left Bolton and as soon as we pulled up in Oxford, we'd be arrested and my life as I knew it, my future with Padma, would be over.

Why the fuck did I have to force those drugs on Nick? If I hadn't, Carys wouldn't have taken them, and she would still be alive. I'm such a screwup.

I also feel like a total shit for lying to Padma, who had been sleeping like a baby when I crept out of our bed.

For three hours, I had lain there wide awake, feeling like I wanted to throw up, terrified about what I was about to do, before sneaking out quietly, throwing on the clothes I'd left out under the bed in preparation, leaving her the note and stealing away like a thief in the night. I hope she believes what I wrote even though it seemed a bit dicey to me because Ness never gets that emotional when it comes to family. But it was the best excuse Ness could think of to explain us both leaving so abruptly. How we'll swing things should Padma see Ness's parents any time soon and enquire how they and the family are doing, I'm not sure, but Ness said we would deal with that when the time comes. I'm sure she'll think of something, she always does.

It's now 6.45 p.m. on Monday as Ness pulls up in front of the student house I share with Padma. We both look and feel like crap. Luckily, Monday's my free day so at least I don't have to concoct some excuse to explain my absence to my tutors.

'I'm scared, Ness,' I say. 'How will we be able to carry on living our lives, act normally, knowing what we've done?'

'We have to,' she says, squeezing my hand. 'There's too much to lose. You need to stay strong. There'll be an initial investigation when they realise the girl is missing, and they may even question some of us, but then it'll all die down.'

'What if the college finds out about the hunt?'

'Then you admit to it. But you also tell the Master that you went home long before she was seen leaving the bar. Which is true, let's not forget that. And with Ed being who he is and having contributed a lot of money to this place, I am certain they'll put a lid on it.'

Guilt consumes me as she says this. Knowing I am part of the 'establishment' – a rotten cliché – able to use my wealth and status to help me get away with my crimes unscathed. Nick wouldn't have access to such connections, and that's why I'm helping him. He doesn't stand a chance without my help. But that only brings me to something else that's been playing on my mind.

'And what about Nick? He caught her in the hunt, he was chatting to her in the bar. Everyone knows that.'

'Again, so what?' Ness says. 'Sure, they might talk to him. But he has an alibi – you. He followed you out twenty minutes before she left the bar alone. So as long as no one saw them together, he'll be fine. And, like I said, if Ed talks to the Master, he can make sure no specific names are mentioned. Yes, for a while it'll be a tense time for all of us, wondering if anyone did see them, but we just have to wait it out. We have no choice, Johnny.'

'I keep thinking about her family,' I say. 'Her parents, possibly a sibling she's close to, the way you and I are. If I lost you, I'd be in so much pain, Ness, I'd feel like dying myself.'

I look at Ness and can tell she's trying her hardest to hold back the tears as I say this. She gently rubs my shoulder. 'I know, and I've thought about it too. But we need to condition ourselves to blank all that out; we can't get emotional. Else we'll never be able to move on. Fact is, we'll never cross paths with her family, and that will make the guilt easier to bear. You need to focus on Padma and your future together. That will give you the strength to survive.'

Chapter Fifty-One

Johnny

Capri, Italy, Wednesday, 7th August 2019

I'm trying my best to enjoy myself, but it's tough beyond belief. Knowing I'm so close to revealing the truth, now that Ness, Nick and I have made a definitive plan. The tension inside me is almost too much to contain. It sits at the top of my gullet, making every intake of breath an effort. As we cruised around the islands, the sun peeking through the clouds, I'd tried to engage in general conversation – the stunning scenery, the natural beauty of the area, what we might have for lunch, the dent Lana will undoubtedly make in my credit card when we stop off at Capri and she raids its many boutiques – but it was always there, this growing sense of unease, knowing that this time tomorrow our secret will be out and Marcus might very well try to murder me after he hears I've known exactly where his sister's corpse has been lying these past eighteen years.

'*Ecco qua!*' Luigi sings from the helm. He turns off the engine and it's amazing how quiet it suddenly is as the boat is moored up to the dock.

'Jesus, I wish I'd tied my hair up like you, Padma,' Lana comments, 'I must look like a bloody scarecrow.'

She fiddles with her windswept hair, and I resist the urge to make a cutting comment. To be fair, I'm not in the mood for taunting her like I normally do. With Ness's illness, the texts, knowing everything will be out in the open tomorrow, having a pop at her seems pointless. I just don't have the energy or inclination for it.

'You look fine,' Padma says kindly. Her raven tresses are fastened in a neat bun, not a strand out of place. She's wearing minimal make-up, but still looks beautiful. She could have made so much more of herself, been anything she wanted to be. Set for a first at Oxford, for a celebrated career in magazines. She would have been perfect for it, would have thrived. But I killed her confidence, killed her dreams. Too chicken to own up, to do the right thing, and now it's too late to reverse the damage my actions have caused.

Before long, we've boarded a funicular up to the main town and bustling shopping area. The entire place oozes chic – sophisticated bars, cool cafés, high-end boutiques, not to mention tempting *gelaterias* everywhere you turn, tourists and locals ambling from store to store, soaking up the atmosphere of one of the world's most glamourous islands. I keep my eye on Ness, am relieved to see she seems to have recovered from the arduous trek down to the marina earlier, Marcus barely letting go of her hand. It's clear things still aren't right between Padma and Nick, though. They scarcely exchanged a word on the boat. I'm hoping they'll get through it, that Nick will find it in himself to forgive her for lying to him. Because after Padma hears the truth, she's going to need him all the more. Plus, let's face it, her lies are nothing compared to ours. He must see that, surely? He can't be that pig-headed.

After an hour or so spent roaming the streets we decide on a restaurant in the main piazza, great for watching the world go by and with a menu that suits the six of us. We sit down and order, the girls plumping for Diet Cokes, us blokes a round of beers.

'What shall we do after this?' Lana says.

'We could go up to Anacapri, check out Tiberius's villa,' Marcus suggests. 'It's less commercial than here, lots of interesting sights. Unless that doesn't appeal?' He searches our faces. 'Ness and I have visited here before as you know, but we thought you guys might like to explore? I mean, you don't come here every day.'

'Sure.' I nod. We've come this far, and if there's a chance I'll be going to prison after we confess tomorrow, I might as well see the island properly. This could be the last holiday I'll go on for a very long time.

'Great,' Ness sighs wearily.

'You, OK, darling?' Marcus says with a concerned look. 'Didn't you sleep well last night? You look shattered.'

Ness and I share a fleeting glance. It's clear she's flagging again. 'She was too excited about today I suspect,' I chip in.

Ness nods. 'Yes, that's exactly it.'

'Plus, it's been a busy morning,' Nick adds like the top friend he is. 'I'm done in too.' He stretches out his arms, gives a yawn.

'Nick's right.' Ness smiles. 'You know what, I've seen Anacapri before, like you mentioned, Marcus. Why don't you go up with everyone, show them around? I'll be fine to potter in and out of shops. I regret not buying a necklace I saw in one of the first stores we went in. I might go back and get it.'

Marcus frowns. 'We can't all bugger off and leave the birthday girl, I'll stay with you.'

'No,' Lana cuts in. 'I'll stay, you give Padma, Nick and Johnny the guided tour. I'm happy to keep Ness company. Dusty old villas aren't really my thing.'

She laughs and we all laugh too, although I'm surprised. Ness has never exactly been Lana's cup of tea, and I know for a fact that the feeling is mutual. Truth is, I'm not sure they've spent more than half an hour alone together since university. Making me wonder what's brought on this uncharacteristic show of charity from my darling wife. Whether she has some ulterior motive. From the look on Ness's face, along with her next comment, it's evident she's thinking the same. 'On second thoughts, I'll come. We should all be together, and I can always pop to that shop again on the way down.'

I watch Lana's face fall as Ness says this. It's as if she was desperate to get Ness alone, but why? What is it she wanted to speak to her about? The text Padma received? My behaviour at dinner by the pool last night? Is she worried I'm going to spill the beans? Or does she know something we don't? I need to warn Ness to be on her guard with my meddlesome wife.

We all need to be, because I'm sure she's hiding something from me. Although I can't think what.

Chapter Fifty-Two

Marcus

Capri, Italy, Wednesday, 7th August 2019

I'm pleased that Ness changed her mind and decided to come up to Anacapri with the rest of us. Still, I can tell that something's not right with her. I'm confident it's nothing I've done. I think I'd know if I had. Plus, since she told me about her traumatic experience as a child, it feels like we've become closer. It's also obvious how blown away she is over the trouble I've gone to make this day special for her. Even so, there's a weariness in her step, a haggardness about her face, that makes me suspect she's hiding something from me. I've also noticed she's not been eating much. I've noticed it for a while now. She keeps putting it down to being overtired, overworked, or having overeaten the previous night, or the climate not agreeing with her system, but such excuses have never been a problem for Ness before. And as we hike up to Anacapri, my insides feel knotted with worry over the possibility that my darling wife isn't well. I won't say anything today, I don't want to spoil her fun. But tomorrow I'm going to ask her outright if, God forbid, my fears are warranted.

Anacapri is a world away from the main part of the island. More rural, less commercialised, with fewer shops and a more traditional rustic feel to it, it remains equally beautiful, if not more so. The paths are dustier, the scenery wilder, but there's something of a natural charm about it, a feeling of being transported to the past, like a scene from *Captain Corelli's Mandolin*. In terms of history, there's a lot to see, but there's no way we're going to manage it all and we don't want to exhaust ourselves – it's not that kind of holiday – so we settle for exploring the centre, wandering around the lovely lanes and piazzas and historic churches and monuments before taking a chairlift to the highest point of the island, to the top of Monte Solaro. The fabulous chair journey starts in Piazza Vittoria and takes about twelve minutes to reach the most breath-taking spot in Capri. Each chair is made for two, we three couples riding one behind the other.

It's a shame the sun has never really broken through to make the most of the view, but it's still worth the trek up. As we stand there admiring the scenery, Ness turns to us all. 'Guys, I just wanted to say thank you for making the trip out here. It means a lot, it really does. It's been so special, and I want you all to know that, to never forget it, no matter what happens.'

No matter what happens? What does she mean by that?

'It's not over yet,' Lana says, voicing what I'm thinking. 'You make it sound like this is our last day. We still have tomorrow and Friday.'

I'm about to suggest we head back down, find a café for a quick drink before venturing back to the marina, when my mobile rings. I fish it out from my pocket, see that it's a UK number. For a moment I worry something bad's happened to the kids, and it's clear the same thought occurs to Ness seeing the anxious look on my face. 'What's wrong, love?' she asks.

I don't reply, too consumed with fear, while the others are all wearing similarly concerned expressions as I swipe to answer, then say, 'Hello.'

The caller introduces themselves and when I hear what he has to say, I drop the phone to the ground in shock.

Chapter Fifty-Three

Nick

Capri, Italy, Wednesday, 7th August 2019

We're back on the boat now, homeward bound. No one's saying much, all of us feeling alarmed by Marcus's rapid change in mood. His face had turned pale as he listened to whatever the caller had to say, and then he slowly lowered the phone to his side and let it fall to the ground. Ness was instantly at his side, asking him what was wrong, but he'd quickly retrieved the phone, excused himself and walked off, presumably to ring back whoever had called because he appeared deep in conversation for the next twenty minutes.

We asked Ness if she had any idea who it could be, but she was just as confused as us. It could have been about his father, I suppose, but then again, surely Marcus would have told us? When he returned and we enquired if he was OK, he simply nodded, apologised for his behaviour but asked if we wouldn't mind skipping the café and heading back to the villa.

It's greyer now, and I fear that before the night is over the storm that's been battering northern Europe will descend on us. It seems timely, in view of the tempest Ness and Johnny's confession is sure to unleash. If, that is, they follow through with their plan, based on Marcus's obvious distress. I'm thinking Ness will want to get to the bottom of that before she deals another blow that will surely break him.

I push down the guilt I've felt since Ness and Johnny offered to take the rap and leave me out of it, a guilt made more acute knowing it's Marcus's sister who died that night, something I still can't quite get my head around. It's not even been twelve hours since I learned the truth and it's been nothing short of torture having to look Marcus in the eye all day, knowing he remains oblivious to our deception.

And now, seeing him look so distraught, I fear what he might do when he learns the truth about Carys. It makes me wonder if it would be better for him and Padma to be told on home soil, rather than here in a foreign land, all of us stuck together under the same roof until our flight home on Saturday. I don't know why Ness is so insistent on telling him here. All I can think is that she wants to be away from home and the children when she comes clean. Neutral ground where she can think straight with no distractions. Where she can't be swayed by the sight of her children's innocent faces.

I turn to Padma and smile. I've decided to forgive her. When she finds out what Johnny did, how he and Ness have been lying to her all these years, she'll need me more than ever, and so, for the time being at least, I must push aside my anger with her. She's too special to lose. She always has been. And then, when I am there for her once again, it'll convince her to have a child with me. Knowing that, when the world around her is going haywire, I remain the one constant in her life.

Devoted to her and only her.

Chapter Fifty-Four

Johnny

Sorrento, Italy, Wednesday, 7th August 2019

The atmosphere is tense in the six-seater cab we hailed at the marina to take us back up to the villa. I've never been good with silence. I normally have to say something for the sake of it. But my usual way with words seems to have escaped me and I just have this bad feeling about whatever it was that Marcus learned on the phone.

Looking at Ness sitting opposite me, I sense she's thinking the same. Hopefully she can ascertain what's wrong once we're back. I'm guessing Marcus didn't want to say anything in front of us, and that whatever it is that's upset him is for his wife's ears only.

'What's up with Marcus, do you think?' Lana whispers in my ear as the taxi winds its way up the hill. It's gently spitting now, but hopefully we'll be safely inside the villa when the heavens fully open.

Marcus is up front with the cab driver so I can safely whisper back, 'No idea, but clearly it's hit him hard.'

Just then, my phone pings. Jesus, not another text. I feel my body tense, dreading another message. But it's not a text. It's my Instagram. Which I've not checked all day. I sigh with relief, then look to my right, see that

Lana has turned her attention to Padma and I hear them discuss what they might rustle up for dinner now that the weather's turned iffy and we've all agreed it's best we stay in. We're nearly home but I decide to see what the Instagram notification was about. Perhaps someone's commented on my latest post, a photo of us all lazing around the pool yesterday with the headline: 'Best friends chilling.' There are a few comments, including this latest one: 'Jealous!', but one stands out from the rest. Simply because it puts the fear of God into me.

> You are a fraud. And so is your 'best' friend. Come
> clean tonight before I do it for you.

Shit. I feel like throwing up. Fuck knows how many of my followers will have seen it. My bloody mother follows me on Instagram, but she can't have spotted it yet, else she would have texted me straight away. My boss follows me too, and some of my clients. Everyone's on social media apart from Marcus and Padma. I don't know why I'm getting so worked up, for Christ's sake the whole world might well know my secret before the week is through if Padma and Marcus decide to go to the police, which I'm betting they will, and so really, this person is just triggering the inevitable. But there's something about seeing it on my social media before I've had a chance to get in there first and explain myself, that makes me feel vulnerable. Like a sitting duck. No one's replied to the comment, but that's almost worse because neither has anyone stepped in to defend me. It feels like an invasion of privacy, like this person is out to expose me in the most public and humiliating way possible. I memorise the account username, before swiping and deleting the message which thankfully, as the creator of the post I'm able to do, then search for the ID, glancing again to my right at Lana and Padma who are still nattering away. Marcus is still noticeably quiet, Nick's on his phone like me, making me wonder what he's up to. Surely it can't be him? Can it? Payback for my digs over the years?

I think of the genuine shock I saw on his face when I showed him the texts and this tells me that it can't be, that I'm reading too much into things. I find the user ID, click on it, but damn, see that it's set to private. Why am I surprised? Of course the holder knew I'd try to look them up.

I stare at the name:

Oxford2001

They couldn't be more brazen about it, citing the year when life at university became a nightmare for us all.

This has to end. I feel like I'm going insane, which is probably the sender's aim.

I don't care that Marcus may have received upsetting news. We have to tell him and Padma tonight. No matter the consequences.

Chapter Fifty-Five

Vanessa

Sorrento, Italy, Wednesday, 7th August 2019

We all scramble out of the taxi, the rain getting heavier, the wind picking up. Johnny offers to pay while Marcus opens the front door, all of us getting drenched in the short time he fiddles with the lock. He didn't utter a word the whole ride and so my mind is in turmoil wondering what he'd learned on the phone in Capri. Whatever it is, it can't be good, but I'm going to do my level best to find out the truth as soon as we're in the privacy of our bedroom.

We rush inside, Johnny slamming the door behind him, before bolting up. We're all wet through, my feet making a squidgy sound in my sandals. I feel exhausted, and I'd like nothing more than to be able to lie down. But first things first, I need to get Marcus alone upstairs.

But just as I'm thinking this, for the first time in almost an hour, Marcus speaks. 'Listen, guys, sorry for the radio silence, but I received some rather distressing news.'

Padma's face creases with alarm. She goes up to Marcus, puts her hand on his shoulder. 'I'm so sorry, Marcus, what is it? Can we help?'

He shakes his head. 'No, not really, but that's kind of you. I need to speak to Ness alone.' He looks at me, his eyes harried. 'Ness, let's go upstairs.'

I'm full of trepidation wondering what it is he's going to tell me. And looking at the others' faces, it's clear they're feeling the same way. 'Of course, darling.'

'Sorry to have put such a dampener on the day,' Marcus apologises to everyone.

'Don't worry, mate,' Nick says. 'It's been a great day. We're just sorry you've had bad news. We're here if you need us.'

Everyone nods, and it's at this point that I wonder if I'm doing the right thing in owning up. In throwing the lives of my friends into chaos once our secrets are exposed. But then I think about the person who's been messaging Johnny and Padma. What if they mean business, get in there first? It's so hard to know what's best and my mind is swirling with all sorts of ifs and buts making me incapable of rational thought.

'Well, we all need a warm shower anyway,' Johnny says. 'Let's touch base later, shall we?'

He gives me a lingering look as if to say *good luck and let me know what the story is* before breaking eye contact.

Everyone agrees to Johnny's suggestion before I follow Marcus upstairs, speculating what fresh hell awaits me.

Chapter Fifty-Six

Lana

Sorrento, Italy, Wednesday, 7th August 2019

Johnny opens our bedroom door and I follow him inside, my nerves on edge. Hearing his private conversation with Nick and Ness this morning and now witnessing Marcus's disturbing behaviour, compounded by the inclement weather — it all sits ill with me, and I fear what might happen next. It's as if fate has turned against us all, reeling us in for punishment.

I'm also frustrated I didn't get Ness alone today. I was going to tell her I'd overheard them in the garden, beg her not to go through with her plan. On the boat ride over to Capri, I had noticed how weary she looked and was suddenly overcome with shame for having wicked thoughts earlier about how I'd stop her from revealing the truth. Despite knowing she's dying. Thoughts not helped by what else I know about that night. Details Ness has no clue about. I had wondered how she could have been so cold about the whole thing, disposing of Carys's body with little thought to her parents or the loved ones she'd left behind. But then, having admitted to myself that I wasn't an innocent in all this, that I too had prioritised my own selfish interests to secure the future I desired so badly, I'd had a change of heart, convinced myself I could reason with her, woman to woman, apologise to her for blackmailing Johnny, but citing the damage what she was proposing would cause, even though I know Marcus deserves to hear the truth. I was sure she'd see sense if I put it to her like that. And not just for the sake of our children, but for Padma's sake too. She took long enough to get over what happened to her, to get her life back on track with Nick, with her job. To throw everything in turmoil now would break her. Even if they do keep Nick's part in all this a secret. Something that still troubles me.

'I'm guessing you still have no idea what's up with Marcus?' I say to Johnny as he closes the door behind us.

He looks at me, his eyes sincere, and says, 'No, I honestly don't, but it worries me all the same.'

I take a deep breath, trying to pluck up the courage to say what's been on my mind all day. All I want is for Johnny to be truthful with me, to confide in me the way a husband should be able to confide in his wife. To tell me off his own back what I already inadvertently discovered. 'Johnny, what did you and Ness do that night? You've always kept the truth from me because you said it was for my own protection. But I want to know. I need to know. Particularly given the text Padma received. I know it had something to do with that girl – Carys – who disappeared. But I don't think you're a killer, I think it was some stupid accident, and that you got scared; that you may even be covering for a friend. I just need you to be honest with me, to stop lying to me, stop bending the truth.'

I'm hoping he won't twig and realise I was there in the garden this morning, that I know that Marcus's baby sister died in Nick's bed, and that they helped him cover it up.

What I still don't know is what they did with her body. I need to know for my own sanity. Can't bear to be kept in the dark anymore because the not knowing is driving me crazy. It's clear Johnny is dubious of my motives, though, his eyes suspicious.

'Is it you who's been sending me threatening texts? That Insta message?'

'What Insta message?' I say.

He ignores me. Continues, 'Who messaged Padma? Are you fishing for information so you can send more twisted messages to me and to her?'

Is he serious? 'What? No! That's ridiculous! I asked you before if the same person who texted Padma had messaged you and you bit my head off!'

He comes up closer, so I can feel his breath on my face, his eyes fiery. 'Whoever sent those messages said they know what I did that night, that I've been lying, keeping the truth from Padma. You may not know the ins and outs, but you know enough, and you hate me because I've made your life a living hell since we got married. How do I know you've not been sending them out of spite to torment me, drive me crazy, make me confess and then I'll be put away and you'll be free of me, able to take the kids and live off the alimony you'll get from our divorce? How do I know you're not trying to get the truth out of me so you can deliver the information to the police? Or is that something you've done already?'

I can't believe he's even thinking this. It's like he's gone mad. I also can't believe he wouldn't think to tell me, his own wife, about the messages, notwithstanding our differences. After all, this could affect me and our children. Any bad blood between us is ancillary. And as much as I resent him for the way he's treated me over the years, I could never want him behind bars. Jesus, since this morning I've been racking my brain trying to work out how to stop him from digging his own grave.

'It's not me, I swear it on our children's lives.' I keep my gaze firm, wanting him to believe me. And then, somewhat apprehensively, I touch his face. 'I hate you, Johnny Harker, but I will always love you. But you never gave me a chance.'

He recoils from my touch. 'You blackmailed me, what do you expect!'

'Because I knew you wouldn't want me otherwise. You made that clear. Believe me, if I could turn back time, I would never have forced you into marrying me. And I would never have kept the truth from Padma. I should have told her about our conversation that night, when she rang me in distress, but I didn't. Because I wanted to make you mine more than I wanted to be a friend to her. And I thought that by protecting you, you'd learn to love me, appreciate the sacrifices I'd made for you. But you were right not to love me, to disrespect me for betraying my friend the way I did, even though it helped save your skin. Because really, what kind of friend does that? It's what I deserved. And that's something that's torn at my conscience all these years. Making me bitter and resentful of everyone and everything, but even more so, of myself.'

And for other reasons too, reasons I can't possibly begin to explain to the others.

'But we've come too far now,' I go on. 'We can't confess, it's too late for that.'

I look at Johnny, willing him to believe me, to hear what I'm saying. I'm not expecting him to take me in his arms and tell me it's OK, to be bowled over by my speech, to suddenly fall in love with me, but I expected some sort of reaction. Rather than the blank one he's giving me right now, almost like he's looking right through me and hasn't heard a word of what I've just said. It irritates me, having poured out my heart and soul to him. So typical of him not to listen to anyone but his own voice.

'Did you hear any of what I just said?' I yell.

Still the same vacant expression.

'What, Johnny?' I say. 'What the hell's wrong? Tell me for Christ's sake!'

He opens his mouth, like he's about to tell me, when his phone receives a text.

'Leave that,' I say. 'Answer me for once, God damn you.'

He glances at his phone. 'I can't, it's Ness.'

I watch him check the message and then, before I can say anything, he's making for the door. 'Johnny, you're still soaked!' I say. 'Can't it wait until you've had a shower?'

'No, it can't, I have to go. Stay here.' He pauses at the door, his back to me, then spins round, notes the wounded look on my face. He comes back over, rests his hands on my shoulders. 'Look, I did hear you just now, and I appreciate what you said. That your intentions were good. But Ness said it's urgent and I must see what's up. I'm guessing it's to do with the phone call Marcus received, so let me go find out. Have a shower and I'll be back. OK?'

I'm not sure he's spoken to me that kindly since the births of our children. And because of this, I agree to do as he says.

For one, I'm not sure I can face any of the others right now. Every time I look at Padma all I feel is shame and regret.

For reasons that involve Nick, but not in the way Johnny and Ness might assume.

Chapter Fifty-Seven

Nick

I'm quite pissed. I know this because my words are starting to come out slurred, while my vision is increasingly distorted, the room on a tilt that wasn't there an hour ago. I must have had three pints and four shots of sambuca. Not unusual for a night out with Johnny's drinking club, but somehow, it's gone to my head quicker than usual. I'm still alert enough to acknowledge my inebriation and yet I'm also getting to the stage when I'm beginning to lose all sense of reason, the ability to press the off switch where the booze is concerned. I know I should stop right now, but I'm in a self-destructive mood, largely because earlier this afternoon Johnny announced that he's going to propose to Padma on graduation day. He said he couldn't imagine being with anyone else for the rest of his life, that he wanted to prove to her how much she means to him, and that popping the question was the best way to do that. Inside I had felt crushed. I mean, it's not as if I didn't know this day would come. I just hadn't expected it to come around so soon. I asked him whether he was perhaps being a bit rash – *you're both so young, shouldn't you wait, see if you feel the same way once you leave uni, start working?* It wasn't an unreasonable query – after all, here at Oxford we live in a make-believe world, it's not real life – and I think he sort of got where I was coming from, didn't get angry with me for not immediately congratulating him and wishing him the best. He patted me on the back, said he appreciated my concern, called me a real mate, but assured me he knew exactly what he was doing, Padma being the best thing that had ever happened to him, and that he couldn't imagine life without her. So, I let it be, and instead threw myself into tonight, wanting to blot out my feelings for his soon-to-be fiancée with booze and drugs and something wild and depraved.

And in the end, I rather enjoyed the hunt, although I'm sure the sober me would be ashamed to admit it, and the guilt will undoubtedly follow tomorrow. Not only did it help me forget about Padma, there was also something rather empowering about the whole thing. Plus, I knew there was at least one girl taking part who wanted me, even if she wasn't the girl I dream about every waking hour of every day. I'd taken a line of coke before with the rest of the guys – it wasn't really optional and I thought, what the hell, it can't do me any harm even though I'm not really into drugs – so I felt quite hyped-up before we set off, and when we were all gathered on the lawn, Johnny and Richard giving us our instructions to follow a specific route around the City, I guess I got wrapped up in the adrenaline rush of the moment. Like I said, I knew who I was aiming to catch. And I'd told the others to leave her to me. To be fair, we'd all chosen which girls we liked the look of from the photos Johnny and Richard had shown us, so there was already this implicit understanding between us as to which girl we'd each be aiming for.

Johnny came round town with us, but of course he didn't catch a girl, even though most of them would have done anything to be caught by the hottest guy amongst us. He was just there to ensure the whole thing went off without a hitch, and even now, with Padma away for the weekend, he's still here in the bar, drinking with Giles and Tom and two female freshers who are completely hammered and all over their captors.

I found my 'fox' hiding in an alleyway running parallel to the Botanical Gardens. She wasn't really hiding, though, she was standing there, waiting to be caught because she knew that's what was expected of her. I saw her eyes light up when she realised who her captor was, and that was a huge boost to my ego. She looked quite cute with her fox ears, a bushy tail pinned to her bottom. The girls had been instructed to collect their 'props' first thing from a secret location. Again, I'm sure the sober me would be disgusted with myself for being OK with this, but not today. Today, I'm someone different, and my morals have taken a backseat.

'Found you,' I'd grinned, and she grinned back. I could see her boobs heaving, her heart beating double time, but there was also a slight fear in her eyes, and I had fleetingly wondered whether she was regretting her decision, perhaps a sense of degradation setting in. 'Don't worry,' I'd assured her, 'I'm not going to bite. Fancy a drink?'

She'd relaxed a little then, and I took her hand and together we walked back to the college bar, which is where we are now, a few others having joined us. It's hot and heaving, and I'm starting to feel the need for some air. She's wearing a strappy white tank top with jeans, her slim belly slightly exposed, her nipples just visible making it clear she's not wearing a bra. I've learnt a bit about her. That her name is Carys, and she's studying history, with a particular fascination for ancient Rome, hopes to study for an MA after she graduates here, before finding a job working as a curator in a major museum, either in London or abroad. She's not Padma, but she's certainly not boring, and I'm quite enjoying myself, wondering about asking her back to the house, just because I know Ness is away overnight, back tomorrow afternoon. It's obvious she's plastered too, having been drinking vodka and lemonade all night, along with some shots, and really the gentlemanly thing to do would be to escort her back to her halls. But I'm not feeling very gentlemanly, and her come-to-bed eyes are too much of a turn on. I find myself wanting to have sex with her, and feel sure the sentiment is mutual. In fact, a part of me thinks she's a little infatuated the way her eyes hang on my every word. But I brush it off. After all it's not uncommon for girls her age to have crushes on slightly older guys, and I should be flattered, feasting on the attention from a member of the opposite sex for once.

I'm about to suggest we get out of here when Johnny walks over. 'Mate, can I have a word outside?' I'm slightly irritated and think about saying no, just because I don't want my 'fox' to get the hump, but I can tell from Johnny's grave expression that it could be important, so I quickly apologise, say I'll be back ASAP. She doesn't seem upset, assures me she'll be waiting right here. Starts joining in a conversation with the others in our group.

I follow Johnny out of the basement bar, stumbling up the stairs into the chilly evening air. It's 11 p.m. so deathly dark, and although the weather has been unseasonably mild in the day, at this late hour the temperature feels true to the time of year. I shiver on the spot, although the crisp, cold air is quite refreshing after the sweaty atmosphere of the bar.

'What's up, mate?' I ask.

'It's Padma.'

My heart stops, and for a minute I think something bad might have happened to her, seeing Johnny's fretful look. But I can't go overboard with my concern. Instead, I ask in a measured yet sympathetic tone, 'What? Has something happened?'

Johnny rumples his hair. 'She's back in Oxford, having found out about tonight. Caught a fast train home.'

Inside I breathe a sigh of relief. I also can't help feeling a trace of satisfaction in Johnny's distress. Knowing he's in his gorgeous girlfriend's bad books.

'Well, I can't say I didn't warn you.' I'm drunk so the words just fall out. He won't thank me for my bluntness, but I can't help myself. Plus, I *did* tell him. Did warn him she's bound to find out, but as usual he was so sure of himself.

He glares at me. 'Thanks, mate, really helpful.'

'Look, I'm sorry, I just wish you'd listen to me some- times. How did she find out?'

'One of the freshers leaked it to someone at Raziel and they called her at Lana's. Padma just phoned me. Asked how the hell I could have orchestrated something so demeaning, and that I had better come home now if I didn't want to find my stuff flung out on the street.'

I suppress a grin. Can't quite decide if I've made a good job of it, because I'm still too bloody pissed.

'Will you let me tell her it was your idea?'

This sobers me up. 'What? No! Fuck off. You must be joking.'

Johnny grimaces. 'Worth a try. Well, what do you suggest?'

'I dunno, just tell her it was all Richard's doing, that you're both nearly at the end of your tenure as the club's leaders, and he wanted to end it with a bang. Tell her you thought it was a sick idea, but he made you go along with it.' I pause, shrug my shoulders. 'It's the best I can come up with. Plus, I know how charming you can be. I'm sure you can win her over.'

Johnny grins. 'Thanks, mate, that's not a bad plan, you're the best. Let's hope so, I can't lose her. And you're right, I was dumb to go along with this. But Richard was so up for it, and I guess I didn't have the balls to say no. Couldn't chance word getting back to Dad, and him calling me a sissy. Even though I hate him, I can't help craving his approval.'

I roll my eyes. 'But you're rich, handsome and popular. Most of all, you're dating a beautiful woman who adores you. Why do you need his approval when you have all that? Why do you give a shit about what he says?'

Johnny sighs. 'You're right. I'm bloody stupid. But it's force of nature, I guess. Despite always doing everything he asks of me, it never feels like enough for Dad, and so I'm forever seeking his approval, wanting to make him proud, even though I realise what we did tonight isn't something to be proud of. But he's old school, stuck in the past and his Oxford traditions.'

I sigh. Still unable to fathom the twisted mentality of Johnny's family. In many ways I feel sorry for him, but on the flip side I wish he'd stop wallowing in his well of self-pity and for once stand up to his father.

'I'd better go,' Johnny says. But just then he grins, having spotted something over my shoulder. 'At least it looks like tonight's working out well for you, mate, even if I'm in the doghouse.'

Puzzled, I turn around to see Carys standing there. 'I thought you'd abandoned me,' she purrs.

'I'll leave you to it,' Johnny says with another grin. He's about to walk off, but then stops short, pulls something out from his trouser pocket, slips it into my hand. A small plastic pouch. I realise it's cocaine. I try to protest, tell him I don't need it, but he insists. 'Just in case. I know how shy you can be. Offer her some, it'll help break the ice.' I don't argue this time. Tuck the stash into my jeans pocket. Watch Johnny walk off.

I'm finally alone with Carys. No one else from the bar has emerged since we've been out here. 'Abandoned you?' I say in response to her comment. 'Never.'

I reach for her hand and lead her away, in my mind thinking how, with Ness up in Durham, we may not even make it to my bedroom.

Chapter Fifty-Eight

Johnny

Sorrento, Italy, Wednesday, 7th August 2019

I gently knock on Ness and Marcus's bedroom door, not wanting to alert Padma or Nick to our secret meeting, my heart in my mouth, my brain still flipping over what just occurred to me as Lana was talking – something which makes total sense and should have crossed my mind before – but which at the same time seems too incredible to believe.

Before long, the door opens, and I see Marcus standing there, Ness over his shoulder, perched on the edge of their bed. She glances up at me, her face pale, but there's also a flash of anger in her eyes that frightens me. I wonder if I've done something to upset her, but can't think what it could be. She knows all my secrets. Good and bad. I've never kept anything from her. Not since we were kids.

I go inside, close the door behind me. 'What is it?' I ask, looking at both in turn. 'I'm presuming it's something to do with the phone call you received, Marcus?'

'Yes,' he nods gravely. 'It was my stepfather. John.'

'Your stepfather? But you haven't spoken to him in years,' I say, genuinely amazed.

'Yes, that's correct.'

'So, why did he call you now?'

Marcus gives a laboured sigh. 'I'll come to that in a second, but there's something you need to know first, something I told Ness about a while ago, but which I kept from you, and the others. Just because it's not something I like to share. I still don't, but the truth is going to come out before long and, having heard what you did for Ness as kids, I wanted to do you the courtesy of hearing it from me first.'

My pulse quickens, just because I know exactly what he's about to tell me. But why does he think the truth is going to come out before long? That's what scares me.

I glance at Ness and she gives a vague nod. As if to say let him speak. And so I do, all the while wondering where this is going.

I sit down beside Ness on the bed while he recounts his story: Carys, the half-sister he adored, who disappeared one night from Oxford eighteen years ago while he'd been travelling in Australia, the ensuing grief and everlasting agony of not knowing what became of her, the fact that it destroyed his mother and led her to take her own life and caused him and his stepfather to fall out for good. The fact that they haven't spoken since his mother's funeral. And all the while he's talking, I almost feel like I'm going to burst with guilt, like I'm suffocating on it, drowning in the weight of my lies. Marcus sees the anguish on my face, and it's clear from his expression that he mistakes it for sympathy, and perhaps astonishment at the secret he's been keeping all this time. He has no clue that my shame and repulsion for what I did to his sister is at the core of my torment.

Finally, he stops talking, and I tell him how sorry I am, at the same time feeling like the biggest charlatan. All the while, the rain seems to be getting worse, lashing at the French doors, flashes of lightning piercing the shutters.

'So, why are you telling me this now, Marcus?' I almost can't bear to ask the question because I think I might already know what his answer will be. 'What did John say?'

Before he can respond, Ness turns to face me, her eyes wide and starry, almost as if she's in a state of disbelief. 'Over the weekend, two scuba divers alerted the police to a suitcase they found at the bottom of the River Wharfe where they'd been daring to go deeper. The local coast-guards helped to bring it ashore, and when the police opened the case they found a skeleton buried amongst a number of bricks.'

My insides are churning now, and I'm starting to sweat, my pulse racing.

'Forensics performed an initial post-mortem at the scene, not wanting to risk cross-contamination by moving it,' Marcus explains.

An excruciating pause.

'And?' I say.

'And they identified my sister from dental records.'

Now there's a lump in my throat I can't seem to dislodge, no matter how hard I swallow. It's like my wind-pipe is plugged with cement.

'Marcus, that's horrific, I'm so sorry.' I feel like such a fake for saying this, because of course this isn't news to me. Ness and I are the ones who fucking put her there! But, at the same time, how can I not empathise with the poor man based on what he's just told me. It would look odd not to. 'Do they know how she died?' I say, almost inaudibly. In my mind I wonder if it's possible to tell from a skeleton whether the deceased had taken drugs before they died. I glance at Ness. Still with that furious look in her eye.

'John said she'd suffered multiple fractures. There was also evidence of blunt force trauma to the back of her skull which will undoubtedly have caused internal bleeding.'

What the fuck? That can't be right. My legs feel anesthetised as I contemplate the implications of what he's just said. 'What exactly are you saying?'

'I'm saying the police believe my sister was brutally attacked before she was put into that case.'

Chapter Fifty-Nine

Vanessa

Sorrento, Italy, Wednesday, 7th August 2019

All this time I've felt sorry for Nick. Sorry that he was dragged into Johnny's stupid drinking society. Sorry that my reckless best friend thrust dodgy drugs on him; drugs that supposedly killed the innocent girl he'd slept with. Marcus's half-sister, Carys. Johnny and I risked everything for him, but he lied to us, allowed us to suffer, to take control of a situation that was entirely of his own making.

Every day since has been marred by the tragedy of that night. Eighteen years spent feeling guilty, Johnny losing Padma, the love of his life, being forced to hide the truth from her, to lie to her.

Toxicology reports resulting from bone marrow samples taken from Carys's skeleton confirmed there were no drugs involved. Marcus told me this after I asked him if he knew whether illegal drugs may have contributed to her death. It wasn't an unreasonable question to ask, based on her last being seen alive at a university party. So he wasn't in the least bit suspicious.

To think that Nick had been prepared to let us take the rap, to let Johnny and I go to prison, to let our families bear the shame of a police investigation, while he got off scot-free. If I had the strength, I'd kill him myself, and make it as slow and painful a death as possible. And looking at Johnny's expression right now, I'm guessing he'd like to do the same. In fact, he looks like a ticking timebomb ready to detonate, and I'm not quite sure how he's managing to hold it together in front of Marcus.

Nick murdered Carys. There can be no other explanation. But how to prove it when all that remains of her is a skeleton? DNA will have been lost years ago. Nothing to prove that she and Nick had sex, that he attacked her the same night before calling us for help.

I think back to when Nick first showed me her body, lying cold and naked in his bed. There was no blood, no suspicious bruising as far as I could tell. Just the usual evidence of rigor mortis setting in. There was no reason to doubt his explanation as to how she died. And the same is true when we shifted her body into the case; something we did gently, carefully, before filling the gaps with bricks I'd purchased from a local hardware store. It makes me wonder how the injuries came to be internal and therefore not apparent from the corpse I saw?

I think of Padma, the shock of learning she's been married to a killer all these years. Someone who wormed his way into her affections, keeping the truth from her, pretending he's this goody-two-shoes who saved her from falling into a black hole from which she'd never return, after her shallow self-absorbed boyfriend, Johnny, abandoned her in her time of need. And then there's the other secret we've kept from her. A secret we'd been planning to reveal along with Carys's 'accidental' death, tomorrow. A secret that's haunted Johnny day and night since it happened. She'll never survive the trauma, it will finish her. I almost feel like my head is going to explode as these thoughts swim around in it, not knowing what the best course of action is now that the truth has come to light. I still want to admit to what we did, but there's no way I'm doing that without Nick confessing his part too. But I also realise it's imperative we move quickly, because what if the person who's been sending Johnny messages gets in there first? Clearly, he or she has no idea about Nick's involvement because there's been no mention of him.

'I'm sorry, but we'll need to catch an earlier flight back to London, my love,' Marcus says, bringing me back to the here and now. 'I hope you don't mind, but now that Carys's body has been found, I need to be back on English soil. Which unfortunately means having to see John for the first time in sixteen years. To think he was so adamant I keep out of the investigation, insisting that he handle everything. But I guess now that he's older he's not such a tough guy and needs my help.'

'I'm so sorry, darling,' I say. 'And of course, there's no question we'll fly back early.'

Johnny simply nods, incredulity swathing his handsome face.

'But there's no reason why you, Lana, Nick and Padma shouldn't stay on, Johnny,' Marcus says. 'There's nothing you can do, so you may as well make the most of the last day or two.'

I'm guessing the last thing Johnny wants is to spend more time with Nick. 'That's kind of you, Marcus,' Johnny says, 'but I think we'll head home too. This week was about Ness, not us.'

'But—' Marcus begins, a guilty look on his face.

'Marcus, really, it's fine, there's some urgent work stuff that's come up anyway.'

'OK,' Marcus relents, his features relaxing slightly. 'If you're sure.'

'You should go have a shower, Johnny, your clothes are still damp,' I say, holding his gaze as Marcus fleetingly checks his phone. 'We'll chat more later.'

Johnny appears to read my thoughts as I say this. He nods then leaves the room. I tell Marcus to go take a shower himself, then pick up my mobile and text Johnny:

> Don't do anything foolish. I know you want to kill him, as do I, but he's not worth it. We need to talk first, make a proper plan.

Chapter Sixty

Carys

Before
Oxford, England, mid-October 2001

I dial her number as I creep up the stairs, and after two rings she answers.

'It's me,' I say. 'I'm at the hot guy's house. Couldn't wait until tomorrow to phone you. Just so excited to tell you what happened.'

'And? What did happen?'

'We had sex and it was amazing.'

'I'm glad for you, but shouldn't you have waited until you got back to your halls to tell me? Where is he now?'

'Sorry, I was too excited, like I said. I want us to be able to confide in each other, it's important to me. He's in the bathroom. I've just come upstairs to find something to wear.'

'You're butt naked? That I really didn't need to know.'

I giggle. 'Sorry to put that image into your head. Really, I wanted to see his bedroom, was hoping he and I might snuggle up together under the covers. His flatmate's away for the weekend.' As I say this, I spot a t-shirt lying on the floor. I pick it up, fling it on. Hear him come out of the bathroom, then his footsteps trotting down the stairs.

Obviously, he has no idea I've come up here. I feel a bit bad being in his room without his permission, and really, I should go back down. But like I just explained, a part of me hopes him finding me in here will lead us both into his bed.

'Is that wise? You don't know him that well. Shouldn't you just go back to your halls?'

'It's fine, he's such a lovely guy, and I get the feeling he really likes me too.'

'Well, you'd better get off the phone or you might put him off. Call me later?' Just as she says this, I notice a brown manilla envelope lying on the bed, several photos spilling out of it.

'Wonder what this is all about?' I say out loud, more to myself than to her. It's wrong of me, I know, to be so nosey but I've always been an inquisitive sort and can't resist. I put my mobile on speaker, pick up the photos, start leafing through them, and before long am filled with horror.

'Wonder what what's about?' she asks.

'I just came across a stash of photos,' I say in alarm, nausea taking hold of me. At the same time I hear footsteps coming up the stairs, the sound of a nearby door being opened. 'They're of some girl. Of her undressing, touching herself. What the hell!'

'He sounds like a perv, you'd better get out of there. Call me when you're back in halls.'

'Will do. Shit, I think he's coming. Maybe there's some innocent explanation.'

'Don't be dumb, leave now.'

'Sorry, gotta go, bye Sis, speak soon.'

'Bye Carys.'

I wait with my heart in my mouth as the bedroom door opens and I see my crush standing there, his face cloaked in darkness.

What monster have I unleashed?

Chapter Sixty-One

Nick

Before
Oxford, England, mid-October 2001

It's 1 p.m. and Ness has just walked through the door of our student house following a four-and-a-half-hour drive from Durham. She looks dead on her feet, dark shadows beneath her eyes, a beleaguered expression etched across her face. It's no wonder, given what's been thrust upon her. I can barely look her in the eye, knowing I've been lying through my teeth, to both her and to Johnny. But I'm too full of shame to tell them the truth. Too afraid that if I confess to what really happened, they'll ask me why I did what I did and then I'll have no choice but to tell them about the photos she came across. And that would be crazy. Hell, keeping the truth from Johnny was the whole reason I did it. Should he and Ness discover that her death had nothing to do with his drinking society, or the drugs, but because I was trying to keep my infatuation with his girlfriend a secret, they'll want nothing more to do with me. Christ, Johnny might even kill me.

And who could blame him? Because the fact is, Padma's special, one in a million, and once you find a girl like that, it's like your entire life revolves around her and you'd sooner die than let anyone harm or take her from you. No one knows that I've been in love with her since the day Johnny introduced us. I hide my feelings well; even Ness, who's the most intuitive of our circle, doesn't know, I'm sure of it. She's not shy about speaking her mind, so I'm certain she would have pulled me up on it by now, plus we live together so there'd be no avoiding the interrogation. We're good friends, we'd have to be to share a house, but I don't for one second believe she'd choose me over Johnny when push comes to shove. There's also no way she'd be able to stop herself from saying anything to him if she suspected I was in love with his girlfriend.

I've always been good at keeping my head down, hiding my feelings. Pretending. Even as a child. Too shy to approach the girls, picked on by the cool boys, who considered me a bit of a nerd. Ness and Johnny even thought I was gay when we first met, perhaps because, given the chance, I prefer romcoms and cocktails to playing rugby and downing pints of beer the way so many of the blokes here do.

It's been agony living with the feelings I have for Padma. To be honest I can't wait for mid-June, when I'll be out of here and won't have to see her every day. Won't have to witness her and Johnny fawning all over each other, a sight that's sometimes almost too much to bear. I expect they'll get married fairly soon, have babies, meaning I'll have to endure the torture of their wedding, christenings and so on. Having said that, maybe once we've graduated, Johnny and I will grow apart. He'll get sucked into his corporate world, a world that's not for me, and then he won't have time for his very average friend.

At least I'll have memories of her stored on my laptop to look back on, even though I know I'm only prolonging my agony by doing so. Being a bit of a geek, it was a piece of cake installing the tiny spy camera I got off the internet in their bedroom. My dad works in security, so I've also learned a trick or two from him over the years.

It's something at least, to be able to watch her undress, gaze at her beautiful face and body whenever I like. Naturally, it's torture watching them have sex, but at the same time it's fascinating. Like I'm receiving a private tutorial in what she likes, in the vague hope that one day some miracle will happen to make them split up, at which point I can swan in and fulfil her needs the way Johnny does. OK, so that's never going to happen, but can't a guy dream? When I turn off the light, I think about those videos, imagine it's me doing all those things to her. I'm not obsessed, I'm just in love, and love can do the craziest things to people. That's what I tell myself at any rate. But like I said, no one can ever know that I've been watching them all this time, and that's why I must lie to Johnny and Ness, make them believe it was the drugs that killed Carys, as selfish as that may be.

Ness drops her overnight bag to the floor, then starts to walk over to where I am standing. For a moment I think she might slap me across the face. But she doesn't. She reaches out and takes me in her arms. Hugs me tight to her chest, tells me she's here for me, that it's all going to be OK. And at this point I have never felt more grateful to have her as my friend. As much as the guilt is eating me up inside. I sob into her jumper, tell her I'm sorry for causing all this trouble. Which is true, I am. And this appeases my conscience ever so slightly. She strokes my hair, tells me not to blame myself, that this was something I cannot have foreseen, that she blames Johnny who should never have got me involved. Again, I swallow my shame but at the same time feel relieved, and then she asks me to show her the body.

After speaking to Johnny, I'd shifted Carys onto my bed. It's amazing how much heavier someone is when they're dead. Or perhaps that's just me imagining things. The weight of my own self-reproach having made every step an effort. First, I stripped off her clothes and tossed them haphazardly on the floor, indicative of our frenzied love making. Then, I lifted her legs, which were slowly adopting a purple hue around the ankles, thighs and back and therefore hopefully covering up any evidence of the injuries she may have suffered – although I'm guessing they're mainly internal, it's not as if I struck her, plus her death was swift, clean – before placing them under the duvet which I then pulled up to her collarbone. I gazed down at her face for a few seconds, pale and cold to the touch, appalled by my senseless crime and wishing to God I'd never brought her back here. A life wasted. A mother and father soon to have their hearts crushed. A possible sibling now an only child. *Stop it, don't go there, you can't think like that.* I kept telling myself this, over and over. I still am. It's the only way to stay sane.

'Jesus Christ.' Ness puts her hand over her mouth on seeing Carys lying there. She knew what to expect, but surely nothing can ever prepare a person for seeing a dead body in the flesh. I linger there nervously, praying that she doesn't suspect foul play, and again thank God that Carys didn't cut her head when it happened.

Ness asks me to run over the events of last night once more and I repeat the lies I told Johnny. 'Perhaps it was an allergic reaction to the coke,' Ness says. 'I'm not a doctor, and I haven't a clue if this is possible, I'm only speculating. Do you know where she's from?'

'Glasgow, originally, I think. That's what she said. Why do you want to know?'

'I'm trying to think of places to avoid.'

'Places to avoid for what?'

'For getting rid of her body.'

I don't know why I'm surprised, why I find myself ingesting oxygen like it's in short supply, the air in my bedroom having suddenly got thinner. What other choices are there? The police can never find her body because it won't take forensics five minutes to determine it wasn't the drugs that killed her.

'It's the only way,' Ness goes on. 'Thankfully, she's small. And by tomorrow, the stiffness will have started to disperse. We put her body in a massive trolley suitcase, fill it with bricks, then drive it somewhere remote, and dump it underwater.'

She studies my face. 'Don't get me wrong, it horrifies me that her parents will never have peace,' she says, clearly thinking I'm in shock at her suggestion rather than bathing in the guilt of my own sick secret, 'but it's our only option. If we don't, they'll find out you and she had sex in no time at all and then everything will come out.'

She doesn't know the half of it. I remind myself again that it won't take a pathologist worth half his salt any time at all to figure out what really happened here, and then Johnny and Ness will know I've lied to them. Like Ness said, this is our only option. Still, I'd rather they handle it than me.

'I – I suppose you're right,' I make a point of stammering. 'What do you need me to do? I'm worried my nerves will get the better of me.'

'Just stay put, act normal. Leave the rest to us. You may not have been spotted leaving with her, but some, if not all, of the others who took part in the hunt will remember that you were the one to catch her. And when the college realises she's missing, they'll bring the police in and the first thing they'll want to find out is who she was with last night and where, not to mention the last people to have seen her.'

My insides flip on hearing this, and the worry must show on my face because immediately Ness rests her hand on my shoulder. 'You need to stay calm. Until the college discovers otherwise, all they need to know for now was that she was at a party last night. You admit you were with her in the bar but explain that you left with Johnny. Which is true, after all. I've talked to Johnny and he's going to tell Ed in confidence that this girl was a participant in a hunt he helped organise, but that you and he obviously had nothing to do with her disappearance. Hopefully he'll have a word with the College Master should it come to that, and this whole hunt business can be swept under the carpet.'

'But what if someone saw me leave with her after she came outside, and then they tell the police? I'll be their prime suspect, not just because I left with her but because I lied.'

'I know, and it's a risk. But really, what choice do you have? You didn't see anyone about at the time, and so we must hope and pray no one was watching. What about her phone? Did you destroy it like Johnny told you to?'

I did, and I tell her this. When Johnny had asked me if I knew whether she'd had a phone on her, I had pretended not to know. All part of my blithering, flustered act. In truth, I knew full well she'd had one with her, not only that, that she'd been speaking to someone called Sis – presumably her sister – while I'd been in the bathroom, and after I'd gone downstairs to find her. Having gone back upstairs, not knowing where the hell she was, I'd heard her voice coming from my bedroom, and wasted no time in confronting her. I just pray her sister doesn't know my name or what Carys found in my bedroom. That's the other thing that could ruin everything, because once people realise Carys is missing, her sister may come forward and tell the police what Carys told her on their call, quite possibly leading them to me and exposing my lies. *Stop it*, I scold myself. I can't think like that, I must take things one step at a time and hope for the best. But also, be proactive and, like I did with Carys's phone, dispose of any evidence that implicates me, including my laptop and the spy camera. The first is easy to deal with, the second not so much, because it means getting access to Padma and Johnny's bedroom. Luckily, I have the photos stored on a memory stick I'll make sure the police never find.

'In the early hours of the morning,' Ness goes on, 'Johnny and I will drive the body somewhere remote, get rid of it, then come back later. I'll say I had a family emergency or something.'

'And then?'

'And then we pray the truth never comes out.'

Chapter Sixty-Two

Johnny

Sorrento, Italy, Wednesday, 7th August 2019

I want to kill Nick, my body on fire with a rage I'm not sure I'll be able to contain the minute I see him. Right now, I want to put my hand through the wall I've propped myself up against outside Ness and Marcus's bedroom, imagining it's Nick's face I'm smashing. All this time he's lied to me and Ness, led us to believe it was the coke that killed Carys, when in fact all the evidence points to him being responsible for her death.

I have loved him like a brother, treated him as such. My sensible, reliable, honest friend who, aside from Ness, knows me better than anyone, calms me down whenever I have a problem. Certainly, that was the case at Oxford. He'd put me on the straight and narrow, always ready to knock some sense into me when I said or did anything dumb. Like that ill-fated night, when I told him Padma was furious with me for organising the hunt and he said to blame it all on Richard. But now I'm wondering if he was secretly praying for us to break up, so he could muscle his way into her affections, even though he never showed any romantic interest in her before. After all, he encouraged me to distance myself from Padma after that night, told me he'd keep an eye on her, let me know if she'd started to remember anything. But was he really looking out for me, or his own interests?

But why kill Carys? That I don't understand. What did she say or do to provoke such a response in him? Was it some kind of sex game gone wrong? I can't imagine Nick being into that sort of thing, but then again, I'm starting to think I don't know him at all. Or maybe it was her idea? She seemed quite wild. I wish I could ask Marcus, but the last thing I want is for him to take offence. I mean, he's just received confirmation his sister was murdered for Christ's sake.

It's bad enough knowing Nick killed an innocent girl, but the double shock of learning she was Marcus's sister is nigh on unbearable. How can we not tell Marcus what really happened that night? But then again how will he survive such devastating news?

And then there's Padma. I'm not sure she'll ever recover from learning the truth about her husband. Which brings me to another thought, a thought triggered by my discussion with Lana earlier, but which I'd parked at the back of my mind since discovering Carys's death wasn't accidental. Not for the first time I tell myself it can't be true, but I wonder if that's just me feeling too frightened to accept what's been staring me in the face?

There'll be an inquiry. The police will want to re-interview everyone who knew Carys at Oxford, including those of us involved in the hunt and who might have spoken to her in the bar that night. There's no way I'm going to keep quiet about Nick now, but how on earth am I going to prove he's responsible for her death after all this time?

I don't want Padma to suffer anymore, but neither can I allow Nick to get away with what he's done. I pull out my phone and respond to Ness's text warning me not to do anything foolish.

> We need to tell Padma everything before this thing goes public. She needs to know the truth about Nick. As does Marcus.

Chapter Sixty-Three

Nick

Sorrento, Italy, Wednesday, 7th August 2019

Padma is in the shower, and I'm sitting on the bed, listening to the wind howl and rage outside, still wondering what the phone call Marcus received was all about. It's weird Marcus hasn't told us. If it was something to do with his father or work, I'm certain he would have done. And this worries me. A sixth sense telling me it might have something to do with Carys's death, even though that seems impossible after all these years. I mean, granted, you do hear stories of missing people being found decades later. But it's rare, and that's the hope I'm clinging to.

It's not like I set out to kill Carys, but after she worked out the photos were of Padma and threatened to tell her, I couldn't allow that to happen. Even so, every day since I've worried about the phone call she made to someone called 'Sis' before I walked in on her snooping. At the time, Johnny, Ness and I had presumed it to be her sister, but as the weeks, months passed, there was never any mention of a sister in the press, only a brother whose face we never saw, but who I now know to be Marcus. I suppose it could have been a close girlfriend, someone who was like a sister to Carys. Whatever the case, I can't help wondering if it's the same person who's been messaging Johnny and Padma this week. I tell myself that it can't be because the texts have all placed the blame squarely on Johnny's shoulders, no reference to the sodding photos which I'm presuming Carys mentioned in her frantic phone call. I mean, I can't think she would have kept quiet about them; she'd certainly had a guilty look on her face when I'd walked in on her. Then again, if Carys did mention the photos to this 'Sis' person, why didn't she speak up at the time, knowing the police were investigating Carys's disappearance? To this day I have no idea if Carys revealed my name to her. I can't think that she could have done, because surely whoever this 'Sis' is would have told the police? It bothered me that I never got access to Padma and Johnny's bedroom to remove the spy camera before it became a crime scene. All I could do was live in hope that destroying my laptop would be enough to remove any possible link to me.

There was certainly no mention in the press of the police having spoken to anyone who'd received a call from Carys the night she went missing. God knows I scoured every newspaper going about everything and anything to do with her disappearance in the months that followed so I'm certain I would have known.

The whole thing is a mystery, but one I hope never to solve.

Anyway, like I said, I've made my peace with Johnny taking the hit for me. He's led a charmed life, and I don't feel sorry for him despite all his sob story antics about what a shit father and mother he had. Fact is, he went to the best school, had the best five-star holidays as a kid, got into Oxford without having to work his arse off like me, went out with the most beautiful girl in our year, and yet he was never content, ever the attention seeker. And arrogant enough to believe he could get away with something as depraved and reckless as that hunt. All a product of his own narcissism. And so, when I realised Carys was dead, I knew what I had to do to survive. Unlike me, Johnny had money and influence behind him. And Ness was equally privileged. If the truth came out, they'd be able to survive, whereas my life would have been over. That's what I tell myself every day. It's how I'm able to look at myself in the mirror, how I'm able to face Padma.

And, whatever else I might have done, I've never laid a finger on my wife, so in that regard my conscience is clear.

Unlike someone I know.

Chapter Sixty-Four

Padma

Sorrento, Italy, Wednesday, 7th August 2019

It's still blowing a gale out there, hailstones falling in bucket-loads as if we're in the throes of an Indian monsoon, the intermittent rumble of thunder and crack of lightning making me jump in fright every so often. I've never liked thunder, it scares the hell out of me, and I just wish this storm would pass. I don't like the feeling of being trapped inside the villa, even though I'm meant to be with my closest friends. The ones I should feel safest with. The fact is, there's only one person here I really trust, and that's my husband.

It's 7.30 p.m. Johnny hasn't appeared yet, but the rest of us are assembled in the sitting room at Marcus's request. No one's eaten anything, none of us have an appetite, but we've all helped ourselves to a stiff drink from the bar. Mine a double vodka and tonic. Indicative of my nerves. We're nearly at the end of our trip away together and I'm starting to feel restless, having allowed myself a few days to try and forget things, to momentarily believe that I'm here to relax, recuperate and have fun. Like a normal person. But my row with Nick, and now Marcus's abrupt shift in mood, has unsettled me. Hence the vodka. And the

Valium I took after taking a long, hot shower. I don't take pills every day, not like I used to, but I keep them handy in case of particularly stressful moments like the one I'm facing now.

I notice Ness looks unnaturally pale; it's clear that something serious is occupying her thoughts. She's hardly said a word, barely glanced in my and Nick's direction, almost as if she can't bear to look at us. It's weird, and I'm almost certain it has something to do with the phone call Marcus received. Lana joined us five minutes ago, saying Johnny was just finishing up in the shower, and would follow shortly. The room is thick with tension, and so I get up and put the sound system on, find some soothing jazz to break the stifling silence.

'Hope you don't mind.' I look at Marcus when I say this, chiefly because he's the one who's called us here.

'No,' he shakes his head, 'it's fine.'

At last, Johnny enters the room. 'Sorry,' he says, helping himself to a neat glass of whisky, then plonking himself on a sofa next to Ness. Like Ness, he deliberately avoids eye contact with me and Nick. *What's that about?* Has Marcus confided something in him too?

'So,' Nick says, his expression solemn, 'why have you gathered us here, Marcus?'

I notice Johnny and Ness keep their eyes focussed on the floor as Nick asks the question. And now I'm convinced they know what it is he's about to tell us.

Marcus takes a large gulp of his whisky, then looks at each of us in turn. 'There's something I've kept from you all. Something that's haunted me every day of my life for the past eighteen years. And it's the reason my mother killed herself.'

My heart flutters. Eighteen years? Surely that's a coincidence. I glance at Nick, who looks as tense as I feel, while I notice Lana shift in her seat.

'I had a sister. She was at Oxford, funnily enough, around the same time as you all, bar Lana of course; the same college as Nick and Johnny, in fact, although you all would have been in your final year, while she joined in October 2001.'

No, it can't be.

'She disappeared three weeks into her first term, and was never seen again.' Marcus looks directly at me. 'And judging by the look on your face, Padma, I think you know who I'm talking about.'

'Carys,' I murmur. 'The girl who went missing two nights before I was attacked.'

'Yes,' Marcus nods, 'that's correct. You won't have known she was my sister. For one, we were half-brother and sister on my mother's side. And two, my stepfather, John, didn't want me involved in the investigation. Didn't want me anywhere near it, in fact, even after I returned home from Australia where I'd been travelling with a mate. He wouldn't allow me to visit Oxford to help the police with their enquiries, banned them and the press from putting my photo in the papers. He was a controlling sort and we never gelled. It was painful for me, but my mother was fragile, and when she urged me to do as he said, I relented. Went down to Cornwall to live with Dad. As much as it killed me not to try and help find Carys.'

I look at the others. All transfixed by Marcus and what he is saying. And with his next sentence, I almost gasp out loud in shock.

'Last weekend they found her body. It had been lying at the bottom of the River Wharfe in Yorkshire and was discovered quite randomly by a couple of daredevil scuba divers. I know this because John, who I hadn't spoken to since Mum's funeral, called me earlier while we were in Capri to tell me so.'

At this, Nick appears to choke on his whisky. I don't blame him; I'm knocked for six myself. Still trying to process the fact that Carys is Marcus's little sister. I can't quite fathom it. I look at Ness and Johnny whose eyes still haven't left the floor. Did they know? If so, since when? I don't have to wait long for my answer in Ness's case.

'I told Ness about Carys when Owen was two. It was killing me keeping something so huge from her. She'd given me two beautiful children, and there could be no more secrets between us, as much as I was worried about scaring her off with my complicated past.' I watch the tears stream down Ness's cheeks. 'It felt wrong keeping it from the rest of you, particularly since you three – Johnny, Nick and Padma – had been at Oxford with Ness at the time this all went on.' Marcus glances at Johnny, then Nick. 'And, of course, I was aware you'd both attended the same college as Carys. But, as I explained to Ness at the time, I also knew there were hundreds of students at Baron, and so the odds of either of you having ever come across her were low. I mean, she'd barely been there a few weeks, plus you lived off-site. There seemed little point in raising it, and I guess it was easier to keep it between Ness and I.' A pause, then, 'Padma, I feel like I've wronged you the most and I hope you'll forgive me. I know you've often wondered if your attacker was the same person responsible for Carys going missing. But there's nothing I could have said or done to help answer that question. Please believe that, and say you'll forgive me.'

I look at Marcus, my heart bleeding for him, but I'm also full of anger and resentment at those responsible for his sister's death. And it means that I can barely get my response out. 'Oh, Marcus, of course, there's nothing to forgive.' I go up to him, put my arm around his neck. 'There's no need to apologise, I can't imagine what it's been like for you. I just can't believe it. Can't believe Carys was your sister.'

'It's a lot to take in, I realise that,' Marcus says.

It is. And once again, I feel furious. Furious at the injustice of it all. I glance at Lana, see the uneasy look on her face. What's she thinking, I wonder. And is this as much of a shock to her as it is to me?

'Do they know how she died?' Nick suddenly asks, his eyes flitting around the room, presumably wondering if the same question is running through our minds. It certainly is mine.

At this, Johnny and Ness finally look up, as if anxious for Marcus's response.

'No,' he says. 'They're still investigating.' I notice Johnny breathe an almost imperceptible sigh of relief, while Ness lowers her gaze once more to the floor. 'But it does mean Ness and I will have to fly back tomorrow. I need to help the police with their enquiries.'

'What can Nick and I do to help?' I ask, glancing at my husband, who's poured himself another large whisky.

'It's kind of you to ask, but nothing, really. Just being here, for me and for Ness, is enough. I only pray they find whoever did this to her. I won't have peace until that happens.'

Chapter Sixty-Five

Lana

Sorrento, Italy, Wednesday, 7th August 2019

'What aren't you telling me, Johnny? I know you're hiding something. Tell me, for Christ's sake!'

The rain is starting to die down, just a faint drizzle falling, while the wind is almost non-existent. Eerily calm, in fact. But it feels like the storm isn't over yet. That it's having a rest before unleashing round two. I've followed Johnny outside to the soaked pool area, after he said he needed some air. No one questioned it given what just happened inside. It was a lot to digest. Nick also left, giving the excuse that he needed to make a phone call, while Padma stayed put consoling Marcus, Ness silently looking on.

I'm still in shock on hearing that they've found Carys after all this time, something I'm certain Johnny had already learned from Marcus when he'd gone to his and Ness's room earlier. Marcus presumably requested he keep quiet about it, having wanted to break the news to the rest of us himself. And now that I know the truth, I fear what this might mean for the rest of us. Marcus said the police don't know how she died, but I saw the fleeting eye contact between him, Johnny and Ness when Nick asked the question – it was as if they were privy to some secret information they didn't want us to be in on. And it makes me wonder – what is it they know that's so bad they've deliberately chosen to keep it from the rest of us? A part of me fears that I may already know the answer to my question. My fears in part confirmed by the fact that Nick bothered to raise the point in the first place. I mean, if he believed she'd died from a drug overdose, as I heard them all discuss this morning, what other explanation might he have been expecting Marcus to give?

As ever, I feel left out, having only been given part of the story, despite being Johnny's wife. Despite knowing something the others don't.

Eventually Johnny turns to face me. 'Marcus knows how his sister died. He just didn't want to tell the rest of you yet.'

As I suspected. 'Why?'

'Because Ness convinced him not to. Told him to hang on until the police have more definitive answers.'

'But why?' I ask again. 'Wasn't it something to do with the drugs Carys took?' In my mind I pray this is the case. If only for my own selfish reasons. Even though there's something about that theory that feels off to me.

His eyes narrow. 'How would you know that?'

I feel my face flush at being caught out. Realise I can't lie anymore. Not when I'm asking him to be honest with me. So, I tell him about overhearing his conversation with Ness and Nick in the garden. Learning that Nick slept with Marcus's sister, of her alleged fatal reaction to the coke and him and Ness helping Nick to dispose of the body because they were all too scared to face the consequences of her death. Also, that Ness has cancer, something I know must break Johnny's heart. There's another glaring issue I don't address. But that ship has sailed, and telling him now won't change the past, even though I am filled with remorse for keeping silent.

I wait for him to explode having learned I was eavesdropping on their conversation, but he doesn't. It's like he's past shouting at me, has bigger things to worry about than my snooping.

'So,' I say, 'if she died after suffering a reaction to the drugs, why would you want Marcus to keep quiet about that? Is it because you supplied them and I'm presuming he has no idea?'

'No,' Johnny says firmly. He pauses, and my heart is in my mouth as I wait for him to continue. 'It had nothing to do with the drugs she took. She didn't take any. Carys was murdered. And it was Nick who killed her. He lied to us all, and hell will freeze over before I go down for his crime.'

Chapter Sixty-Six

Nick

Sorrento, Italy, Thursday, 8th August 2019

It's the middle of the night and I wake with a start, having taken several hours to drift off, tossing and turning, my mind full of crazy thoughts. After I'd excused myself from the sitting room, pretending I had a phone call to make, I'd gone for a walk in the garden before the storm started up again as if to deliver a grand finale, trying to clear my head. But it had done no good. How could it?

Now that Carys's remains have been found, I can't help wondering why Johnny and Ness haven't told Marcus the truth. I mean, I know it's a shock — it shocked the hell out of me — but on the flip side, this should have given them even more of an impetus to proceed with their plan. Unless, that is, they're hiding something from me, something the police uncovered, but haven't yet made public. Something I'd hoped and prayed would never come out, but now, with her body having been discovered, along with the wonders of modern science, is perhaps a real possibility.

My anxiety isn't helped by the way they reacted when I asked Marcus if the police knew how Carys died. It was as if they were on tenterhooks waiting for his answer, sighing with relief when he revealed there'd been no conclusive findings as yet. If they still believed Carys had reacted to the drugs, why would they appear so afraid of his response? Call me paranoid, but something's not right, I can feel it in my bones.

It's so dark in our room, owing to the thick black-out curtains blocking any natural light, I can't even make out the silhouette of my wife lying next to me. I shuffle up closer to her side of the bed, yearning to feel the warmth of the woman I'd do anything for, who I've lied to all these years because it's the only way I've felt able to hold onto her. But I can't hear a sound, can't even detect her presence, the sound or movement of her breathing. And then, when I put my hand out to touch her, to my alarm all I find is an empty space. I feel all around for her, my hands tracing every inch of the mattress. I call out her name, but there's no answer. Quickly, I switch on the light, my worst fears confirmed when I find myself alone in our room. And neither, when I get up to check, do I find her in the bathroom.

Where on earth can she be at four in the morning?

Chapter Sixty-Seven

Johnny

Sorrento, Italy, Thursday, 8th August 2019

I pray to God that Lana didn't hear me creep out of bed fifteen minutes ago. Particularly now that I know she followed me to the garden yesterday morning. As I had listened intently to her breathing, she'd seemed to be flat out, no doubt exhausted by everything that's transpired these last twenty-four hours. As am I. Now that she knows the truth about how Carys died, I think she may have had a change of heart and come to terms with Ness and I telling Marcus about our part in his sister's disappearance. Something we plan on doing after breakfast. Along with, and more importantly, revealing Nick's part. I had reassured her that Ness and I will impress upon the police and Marcus that she had nothing to do with it. Which is the truth. Even though some might say she's guilty of perverting the course of justice based on the little she did know at the time. I'll always resent her for blackmailing me into marriage, but I have to prioritise our kids. Fact is, she's a good mother, and our children need one parent they can depend on in their lives. It'll be ugly for a while, but we cannot continue to live this lie.

Ness and I will tell Marcus and the police that Nick deceived us, that we had genuinely believed the drugs I'd supplied had caused her death, a tragic accident, and that we'd never have disposed of her body had we known any different. It still doesn't excuse our actions, but I'm hoping it might go some way to explaining what we did and why we did it. As much as I want to strangle Nick with my own bare hands, I know it won't do me, Lana or the kids any good. I cannot come down to his level, and I cannot have my children suffer the stigma of their father being a murderer as well as a liar.

And then, after that, we'll tell Padma everything. Not just about Carys, but the truth behind what happened to her that Monday night. A prospect I'm almost frightened of more, knowing the heartache it will cause her. Why she's asked me to meet her now in the middle of the night at the villa's prime viewing spot just beyond the pool area I have no idea. It makes me nervous. Makes me wonder if I'll have no choice but to tell her the truth now, before Ness and I speak to Marcus. We've not spoken alone once the entire time we've been here, and so her text caught me off guard. I'm usually the last person she cares to spend time with. My best guess is that she wants to confront me about the text she received, having told Nick and Lana she intended to wait until Ness's birthday was over. And no doubt she's chosen this remote location in the early hours of the morning to make certain we're not overheard.

I rest my elbows on the damp balustrade built into the cliff-face, looking out into the blackness, feel a faint spit in the air, and then hear a noise, the sound of light footsteps approaching from behind me. I turn around, my back against the railing, and before long she appears. Dressed in jeans and a half-sleeve t-shirt, her hair tied in a low ponytail. She comes up close, so close I can make out the sound of her breathing. The underlying friction between us is almost unbearable.

'Padma, what's wrong, why have you called me here at ten past four in the morning?'

She raises her hand, and I instinctively gasp out loud, having realised she's holding a knife, the blade glimmering in the moonlight. 'Because I want the truth.'

'Jesus, Padma, what the hell are you doing, put the knife down.' I take a deep breath, then say, 'Is it the text?'

'Forget the text. What I want to know is how you could have sat there listening to Marcus talking about his sister's body being found and said nothing. Nothing about what you and Ness did that night. You need to answer me, because if you don't, the way I'm feeling right now there's no telling what I might do.'

Chapter Sixty-Eight

Padma

Before
Oxford, England, mid-October 2001

It's Sunday evening and Johnny has been acting strange all day. We've just had dinner – my dad's signature chicken biryani, one of his favourites – and now I'm washing the dishes while he dries up. Normally he'll be chatting away about this and that, but he's so quiet and that's how I know something's wrong. While we were eating he had this faraway look in his eyes, like something weighty was preoccupying him. Normally he wolfs down anything I make, but it was as if he had no appetite, pushing the rice around his plate as if it was a struggle to force it into his mouth.

'Don't you like it?' I asked, unable to watch him play with the food I'd lovingly prepared a second longer. At this he had looked up, startled, having been lost in his thoughts, then flashed that gorgeous smile of his, reassured me that of course he loved my food, but actually, his stomach wasn't quite right, and he was feeling a bit off colour. Hearing this, although it pained me that he was feeling unwell, I also felt relieved that his distant behaviour wasn't anything to do with me or the food I'd made, but presumably down to a bout of gastroenteritis he'd picked up earlier. Or perhaps the result of too much booze the night before, although I had bitten my tongue in this regard, not wanting to agitate him further. But now, as we move to the sitting room to watch telly, something tells me there's more to his low mood than a dodgy tummy.

Is it me after all? Did I come on too strong last night, was I too overbearing? Giving him that ultimatum, reprimanding him for organising the hunt, telling him if he ever again orchestrated such a loathsome event he could kiss our future together goodbye. It's possible, I guess. I wasn't in the best mood, and perhaps I overreacted slightly in cutting short my stay with Lana. But in truth, and although I didn't tell Johnny this until after we made up, I wasn't exactly upset to leave Lana's early. She'd been in such a foul mood from the moment I got there on Friday night – nothing I did or said was right – when I told her I was heading back to Oxford, not saying why, just that neither of us seemed to be having a good time, she didn't stop me. And I've not heard from her since. To be fair, I haven't tried calling her either. I guess we're both as stubborn as each other.

Anyway, after I'd lost it with Johnny when he returned to our flat around 11.30 last night, there was no mistaking the genuine remorse in his eyes, and I believed him when he promised never to do such a thing again. Soon after that we had sex and I could feel how deeply he loved me, as I love him with all my heart. Which is why I remain puzzled by his distant behaviour as we sit beside each other on the sofa in silence in front of some police drama neither of us is taking in.

It gets to 10 p.m. and Johnny announces that he's off to bed. I can't even remember the last time, if ever, Johnny's gone to bed that early.

'Really?' I turn to face him. 'That's early for you. Still feeling under par?'

'Yeah, I am a bit,' he sighs. 'Aside from my stomach feeling iffy, I didn't sleep great last night.'

That's out of character too. Usually, after Johnny and I make love, he sleeps like a baby. What's troubling him? Still, I keep my concerns to myself. 'OK, I'm sorry to hear that, babe. You go ahead, I'll probably be another half hour. Don't worry about locking up, I'll see to that.'

'No rush,' he smiles, then kisses my forehead tenderly. I feel reassured by this sweet show of affection, but even so the worry is there, chafing at my insides.

What isn't he telling me?

After watching a bit more telly, then locking up, switching off the lights, going to the bathroom, it's gone 11.15 by the time I tuck myself under the duvet. Johnny appears to be fast asleep. Hopefully, I was overthinking things earlier, and all he needs is rest. But later, around 2 a.m., I wake with a start. Perhaps it's my subconscious worrying about Johnny that's causing my sleep to be light, fretful. As I think on this, I turn to face his side of the bed, wanting to see how he's doing, but he's not there. Alarmed, I get up, go to the door which – to my surprise – is shut. I always leave it slightly ajar in case either of us needs the loo and so as not to disturb the other by opening and closing it. Gingerly, I open it, creep out onto the landing and spy Johnny downstairs in the hallway. He's on the phone and I hear him say, 'Ness, Padma's asleep. I'm coming now.' There's a pause, presumably as he listens to whatever Ness is saying, then he whispers, 'Yeah, I've left a note on the kitchen table in case she wakes up like you said. I only hope she buys it.'

My heart kicks. What the hell is Johnny hoping I'll buy? What in God's name are him and Ness playing at? Surely, they're not having an affair? I mean, I know they're close, but I've never suspected anything sexual in their relationship.

I watch him slink out the front door, and then, my instinct telling me there's no time to lose, I rush back to the bedroom and slip on some pants, joggers, and a sweatshirt before scrambling downstairs, throwing on my trainers and exiting the front door. I meant to go and check the note Johnny referred to, but in my haste, it escaped my mind, too curious to find out what he and Ness are up to. I'll read it when I get back.

I take a punt on Johnny being headed for Ness and Nick's place and start walking in that direction. A part of me wonders whether they're planning a surprise for me, hence all the secrecy. But why meet at 3 a.m.? Surely there's no need for that. My gut is swirling with anxiety, as I wonder if their covert meeting could be linked to Johnny's weird behaviour yesterday.

Ness and Nick's house is around a seven-minute walk away. Johnny's a fast walker and a little over six foot in contrast to my five-six frame and so there's no way I'll catch up with him before he gets there. I plough on all the same, determined to find out what he's up to. Despite it having been unusually warm for October lately, the night air is biting; it cuts through me as I stride along so I start jogging in a bid to keep warm. Also to get me there faster. I scan my surroundings as I do, alert to any sign of danger, any weirdos hanging about. And then, finally, I reach Ness and Nick's. There's no sign of Nick, but I do see Johnny and Ness standing by Ness's car, the BMW her father bought her. A massive trolley suitcase rests on the ground by the boot. I watch Ness pop the trunk, and then Johnny mumbles, 'One, two, three, lift.' With every ounce of effort, they haul the suitcase up and into the boot before Ness shuts it as quietly as she can.

I'm tempted to shout out, 'What the hell are you guys doing?' but I guess I'm too stunned, not to mention creeped out, to do so. And then, before I know it, they've both got into the car, Ness in the driver's seat even though I know Johnny is insured to drive the BMW. I hear the rev of the ignition, see the headlights come on, then watch the car pull away and drive off. To where I don't know. I'm tempted to go knock on the door, ask Nick if he knows what they're up to, but I can see that all the lights are turned off, and so I'm assuming he's fast asleep.

Clueless as to the one burning question that keeps turning over in my mind.

What the hell was in that suitcase?

Chapter Sixty-Nine

Padma

Sorrento, Italy, Thursday, 8th August 2019

'I remember everything, Johnny. The whole of that missing week came back to me with crystal clear clarity six months ago during a session with a new therapist. Shortly before Ness posed the idea of this trip.'

Johnny says nothing, just looks at me vacantly, calmer than I had anticipated, given what I've just told him. I had expected shock to envelop his face, but he doesn't look that surprised. It throws me a little, but I carry on all the same, clutching the knife at my side.

'I know it was you who attacked me, who knocked me out cold. Left me to die.'

I glare at him, my entire body bristling with anger and hurt, gripping the knife tighter as I let it all pour out. It's not like I plan on stabbing him, but I know Johnny is dangerous – I mean look at the way he smashed that lizard's skull – and so I need to protect myself. All these years he's lied to me. Acted like he knew nothing. But now I know different. I'd nearly fainted on the spot when images of that week flashed through my brain. I told the therapist I wasn't feeling well, but I'm not sure she believed me. I'd excused myself all the same, aimlessly wandered the streets for an hour or so, nearly getting run over in the process, before hailing a cab back home and locking myself in the bedroom. Thankfully Nick was working late, so I had time to gather my thoughts. To make a plan of action. Thereafter I spent more time at work, not wanting Nick to guess that something was wrong. I knew he'd be livid, would be round at Johnny's in a shot, possibly do something he'd regret. But I didn't want Johnny to find out that way. That would have been too easy. I wanted to make him suffer, for his mind to be in turmoil the way mine has been all these years. And it just so happens that Ness's invitation provided me with the perfect set-up to do that.

'It's you who's been sending me those messages, who left that comment on my Instagram, isn't it?' Johnny says. 'It dawned on me on Wednesday night that it had to be you. You also sent yourself that text, didn't you? Using the same burner phone. Pretending to look shocked over dinner on Monday night. But then appearing to move on, giggling with Lana as if you were best buddies again. That felt off to me. As did the way you've been dressing more provocatively. Why, Padma? To tease me, torment me, push me to the limit and leave me with no choice but to own up?'

I don't bother responding. He can see it in my eyes. The look of triumph. Of satisfaction in seeing him suffer. Although I have to say I'm disappointed he'd already cottoned on. Clearly realising that the only person who he knew for sure had seen him and Ness put that case into her boot was me. It had been staring him in the face since that first text I sent him from the burner phone I bought last week, just before we took off at Gatwick, but until now he hadn't twigged because he believed my memory of that time was lost forever. And who could blame him after eighteen years?

After I'd watched Johnny and Ness drive off that night at Oxford, I ran home, read Johnny's note. His explanation for leaving in such haste – that Ness had a family emergency – didn't hold up for me, just because Ness has never been that close to her family. It also made no sense that Johnny wouldn't have woken me to tell me what was wrong. And then there was the suitcase, which had blatantly been a struggle to lift and not in keeping with an overnight stay. The one glaringly obvious factor that sent alarm bells ringing in my head. I'd frantically paced our house, the note clasped in my hand, knowing sleep would prove impossible. I was desperate to talk to someone. But there was no way I was going to ring my parents – they would only worry and tell me they'd been right about Johnny all along. And of course, Aunt Rani, the woman I had loved like a second mother, was no longer around to confide in. As for my brother, I couldn't risk it, knowing he was bound to call Mum and Dad the minute we'd finished speaking. So, I'd rung the only other person I could think of who I was close to: Lana. Despite our argument, she was still my best friend, the one who'd had my back since primary school. Or so I'd thought. It was 5 a.m., and she'd been half asleep when I called, still sounding cross with me. But when I'd told her what I had witnessed less than an hour before she was suddenly very much awake.

'God only knows what they were up to, Lana,' I said, 'but it didn't look good. I watched them hauling that case into the back of Ness's car. It was a real struggle, like something super heavy was inside. And Johnny's been acting strange all day, so quiet and distant, I know something's wrong.'

'And you say Ness only recently got back from visiting a friend in Durham?' she asked.

'Yes. On Sunday afternoon. Johnny's note claimed that she had a family emergency and needed him to accompany her, but why the massive suitcase? Why the secrecy? If there was nothing dodgy going on I'm sure Johnny would have woken me, told me Ness needed his help. Christ, he might even have asked if I wanted to go with him. It smells bad to me, Lana. Plus, I heard rumours this afternoon that a female fresher's gone missing. They say it's early days, but it makes me wonder if she was at the hunt Johnny organised. What if something happened to her, and they were getting rid of the evidence? I mean, I know it sounds crazy, but even so.'

At that point Lana had told me I was letting my imagination run wild. That it was probably just a coincidence. Nevertheless, she had urged me to confront Johnny when he got home, ask him what he'd been up to. She said it would fester inside me if I didn't, even though he'd realise I'd been spying on him. I think she was right about that, it would have driven me crazy, but now that my memory's returned, and I remember the call I made to her, I know that she's also been lying to me all along, keeping our conversation from me. Lana, my supposed best friend, has known all these years what I spotted Johnny and Ness doing, and yet she kept quiet about it. Perhaps wanting to spark a row between me and Johnny in urging me to challenge him. Because of this, I'm also betting she blackmailed Johnny into being with her, after telling him what I had told her over the phone. That's how she convinced him to marry her, even after her miscarriage. She wouldn't let it go, and he couldn't trust her not to tell me, not to tell the world. It is his penance for the crime he committed and covered up. I say all this to Johnny and the guilt is written all over his face.

'You texted me around 10 a.m. on the Monday to say you were still with Ness at her parents' place,' I continue. 'That you wouldn't be back until late afternoon, but that I shouldn't worry. I knew something wasn't right then. There's no way you wouldn't have called me if you'd been telling the truth. You'd have wanted to hear my voice. Fact is, it was easier for you to text because you were too chicken to speak to me.'

The nearby garden lights, designed to detect movement, have illuminated Johnny's face, and I can see that it's gone very pale. He's leaning back further over the railing now. Dangerously so as I veer closer, still clenching the knife in my hand. One almighty push from me, that's all it would take. 'Look, Padma—' he starts, but I cut him off. Closer still.

'Shut up, let me speak.'

He raises his palms. 'OK, OK, yes, speak. I realise it's a lot to get off your chest.'

'How gracious of you,' I scowl. 'As it happens, you didn't walk through the door until nearly 7 p.m. Looking deadbeat, as if you'd hardly slept. You asked me if I had eaten dinner and I told you I wasn't hungry. And then I asked you what had happened with Ness's family, and, after a bit of dithering making me certain you were lying, you claimed her uncle had had a stroke. Like that would have caused her to go dashing off in the middle of the night.'

'Padma, I—'

'I saw you and her hauling that case into the boot of Ness's car. I didn't know what was in it then, but now I'm certain it was Marcus's sister based on what he told us last night. And I'm guessing you and Ness drove to Yorkshire and threw it in the River Wharfe hoping she'd never be found. I'm not sure what happened – maybe you lied to me and slept with her and she'd threatened to talk so you killed her? It wouldn't surprise me, now that I know what a liar you are. Point is, your sick secret was safe for eighteen years, but now it's all going to come out. Soon the world will know what you did.'

'Padma, I never slept with her. Listen, you—'

'Stop talking,' I growl.

I don't know what garbage he plans on spouting to get himself out of this one, but it won't wash with me. I keep going. 'I told you I had seen you, and I demanded the truth. You told me not to ask questions, that it was for the best, and that you didn't want to bring me into this. I said I didn't want a relationship based on lies and that people don't go driving off in the night with heavy suitcases in the boot for no good reason.

'"Tell me what was in the case, Johnny," I said. "Tell me now or I'll go to the Master, tell him what I saw you and Ness doing. You know a fresher's gone missing. Just yesterday, the day after your 'hunt'." I remember my words clearly. But also your eyes. They were rabid, like you'd been possessed. Not the Johnny I knew and loved. You sprang forward, grabbed my forearms, so tight it made me wince. Your eyes still brandishing a madness that scared me. And then I knew for sure that you and Ness had done something bad.'

'It's not what you think. You don't know the full story.'

More lies. Even though his eyes appear sincere. I'd like to believe he's telling the truth, but he's kept his cruel deceit from me for far too long, and I can't trust anything that comes out of his mouth.

'I begged you to let go of me, told you that we were finished, that I couldn't be with someone who wasn't honest with me, and that's when you'd started to shake me, as if you wanted to make me forget what I had seen. Shake the truth out of me. Make me take back my words. I struggled, yelled again for you to let go, and that's when you pushed me hard, and I stumbled backwards, struck my head against the back of the coffee table.' I pause as Johnny hangs his head in shame. 'And you left me. Not knowing how badly I was hurt. I could have died from bleeding in the brain had Jacob not found me in time. But you didn't care. All you cared about was covering up the crime you had committed.'

Johnny moves closer. 'Of course I cared. I loved you with all my heart. I still do.'

'You don't leave the person you love when they're hurt. You don't lie to them for nearly two decades.'

'You don't understand, it's not what you think. It's not even what I thought it was, but now I know better, although if I tell you the truth, I think it might break you.'

'I'm already broken, you bastard! You killed her, didn't you? Maybe it was an accident, or perhaps she overdosed, but something you did caused her death and when you realised she was dead you panicked because you knew it would bring shame on your family, fuck up your future. So you called the only person you could trust: Ness. And she came running to your aid as usual. Helped you get rid of the body. You left me because you knew I was onto something, and you were hoping I was dead too!'

'It's not true, Padma. I was scared, confused, I didn't know what to do. And then later, after you were taken to hospital and we learned that you had amnesia…'

'You were relieved,' I finish his sentence for him. 'No doubt you hoped my memory would never return. As did Ness. And Lana. But then, when I started to remember stuff, you must have been shit-scared. And that's why you couldn't be around me. Couldn't even look me in the eye. You were too ashamed, terrified that being around me 24/7 in the house that we shared would trigger something, and that before long I'd remember what happened between us that night. How lucky for you that all these years that one memory has eluded me. Probably because it crushed me, physically and mentally. Allowing you to walk free, live your life. Although how you were able to do that is beyond me. That takes a certain callousness, don't you think? Now I know why you ditched me, why you avoided Nick and me for so many years. But I'm betting that as the years went by and it became clear I was never going to recall that night, you grew more comfortable being in my company, believing yourself and your sordid little secret to be safe. But you're not safe anymore. Because I'm telling Marcus what happened, and soon you'll be behind bars where you belong.'

I stop talking. Exhausted. For years I had longed to remember what happened that night. To know who attacked me and why. I had thought that getting some answers would bring me peace. But peace is the last thing I've found. Every day since I remembered has been torture. Keeping quiet, keeping the truth from Nick, communicating with Ness, Johnny and Lana as if nothing's happened, as if we're still friends. I've no idea if Lana knows that Johnny attacked me that night; I mean she must suspect something, after all it was her who urged me to confront him. But even if she doesn't know the full story, she still betrayed me. She knew what I had seen, and she had used my pain for her gain. To get her claws into Johnny. And that's why I put that lizard in her drawer the first day we arrived, having told Nick I'd gone in search of hangers. I was going to wait, but her snide comment about me becoming a social worker rather than editor of *Vogue* had maddened me. How dare she make such a spiteful remark when, had she told me what I'd said to her on the phone that night, the course of my life could have been so different. The others were still outside drinking on the terrace, and so I'd taken the opportunity to scoop one of the several geckos I'd seen slithering across our balcony into one of my plastic shoe boxes while Nick was in the bathroom, before slipping into Johnny and Lana's room which they'd thankfully left unlocked. I did it because I was angry, and I wanted to unsettle her, because that's what she deserved. But also, to bring us closer. Make her think I was her friend again, only to throw her to the lions when I tell the police her husband is a murderer. That he and Ness put Marcus's sister in that suitcase and dumped her in the river. I knew she'd tell Johnny what the text said. I was banking on it. Because I also knew that when she did, he'd tell Ness, and then the both of them would be running scared.

Closer still, and a part of me feels that pushing Johnny off this cliff will help make things right. I'll have my revenge for years of suffering, but also for the young woman who lost her life because of some sick chauvinistic game.

'Padma, listen, it's not what you think, there's so much more to it than that.'

'It's true, Padma, there is more to it than that.'

I spin around to see Marcus standing there, Ness just behind him. I quickly move to the side, raising the knife, not wanting to give Johnny the chance to escape with my back being turned to him for too long.

'Marcus, what are you saying? Please, don't listen to them. They're liars, both of them. They killed your sister for Christ's sake! They're the ones who dumped her body in the river.'

I hate the fact that I am breaking such horrifying news to Marcus in this way, but I can't stop myself. It's been agony hiding the truth from Nick all these months, the strain of my deceit eating away at me like acid. But not as excruciating as having to keep control of my emotions this week. And that was before I learned Carys was Marcus's sister. Until last night I thought she was just some girl with no connection to any of us. But seeing the anguish on Marcus's face as he broke the news to us, knowing he's spent the best part of two decades wondering what happened to her, me now knowing that his wife was responsible for her disappearance and kept quiet about it, it's just too much to bear.

I raise the knife higher, edge nearer to Johnny once more, so tempted to murder him on the spot, to have my revenge for the years of lies and deceit and pain of not knowing what happened that night.

'Padma, don't do anything stupid,' Ness says.

I glare at her, amazed at her hypocrisy. 'How dare you preach to me when you helped cover up your minion's crime. Because I'm certain that's what happened here – after all, you were away, and so you can't have had a hand in Carys's death. But what I'm betting is that he called on you for help, like he always does, and you took charge, the way you always handle his messes for him. Tell me, how could you do it, Ness? You wanted to be a lawyer even then. How could you take such a risk?'

'Because I owed Johnny my life.'

I stop short at this unexpected eye-opener. Feel the wind taken out of my sails. Listen in stunned silence as Ness explains. I guess I shouldn't be surprised, there was always something curious about their relationship. Still, to cover up the death of an innocent young woman at Johnny's hands like that? She doesn't get off the hook that easily because she felt indebted to him for something he did when they were kids. I tell her this.

'Put down the knife,' Marcus says.

I look at him, my eyes squinting. 'Don't you get it? Johnny killed your sister and Ness helped him get rid of the body. And when I confronted him, he tried to kill me too. They lied to you all these years. Even after you told Ness about Carys, she said nothing.' I look at Ness, then Johnny, eyeing them with disgust. 'Fuck, it must have been hell for you waking up every day not knowing if I was going to remember. I'm not sure how you managed to live like that. Lana too, based on what I told her. But then again, you three always look so miserable so maybe it has been torture. The one saving grace.'

'You're right,' Marcus says, 'they did lie to us, Ness told me everything last night when we went up for bed. And I wanted to murder the pair of them. My heart is broken and I'm not sure I'll ever recover.' He looks at Ness, a pain in his eyes that would melt the hardest heart. 'But they didn't murder my sister, Padma. Nick did.'

Nick? *My* Nick? What is he saying? For a moment, I think that maybe this isn't happening. That I'm actually having a nightmare, my worst fears playing out inside my head. I slyly pinch my side, like I'm trying to wake myself up, but nothing happens, and I realise this is real, and from the look on Marcus's face he means what he says. But it can't be true, it can't. Clearly, they've brainwashed him.

'What the hell are you talking about? You're lying! Have you gone mad? Why are you trying to blame this on Nick? I saw them with my own two eyes, don't you get it! How can you be OK with that?'

Marcus takes a step closer. 'I'm not OK with it, believe me.' He gives Ness another cold stare. 'I feel crushed. To think that Ness never said a word when I told her about Carys, to think that they disposed of my sister's body, with no thought given to the family who mourned her, who needed answers…'

'Marcus, I told you I—' Ness begins, her eyes flooding with tears.

'Shut up!' Marcus barks. 'I don't want to hear it. I bared my soul to you, and you kept silent. There is no excuse, and as much as it tears me apart that you have cancer, I can't forgive you for that.'

Cancer? I frown. Look at Ness. 'You have cancer?'

'Yes, it's why I wanted us all here. To have one last birthday with the people I love. And to confess what we did all those years ago.'

It's all too much to take in. There's a part of me that wants to console Ness, despite everything, but I'm too angry with her. Angry at her deceit. Angry at them all for trying to blame this on Nick.

'My sister suffered blunt force trauma to her skull, along with multiple fractures to her body,' Marcus explains. 'It was Nick who Carys went home with that night. Now that your memory has returned, you must know yourself that Johnny came home to you as soon as you told him to. Nick and Carys had sex, but for some reason that still escapes us he killed her. He rang Johnny in a panic, blamed it on the drugs Johnny had given him.'

'I felt I owed it to Nick to help him,' Johnny adds. 'That it was my fault he got caught up in this mess. That it was my drugs that killed her.'

'But there were no drugs found in the bone marrow forensics extracted from my sister's skeleton,' Marcus says. 'She was clean.'

My legs are suddenly like jelly. Marcus's point about Johnny coming back to me that night is a good one, but that doesn't necessarily mean nothing happened between him and Carys earlier. And yet, Marcus seems so sure that Nick is behind her murder. I still can't believe it's true, but all three of them are looking at me so earnestly, they can't all be wrong, can they? Why would Marcus relay such a tale if he didn't believe it? And now, as I think about it, look back, I can't help wondering about all the times Nick took Johnny's jibes on the chin. Why? Because Johnny helped him cover up Carys's death and he felt that he owed him? Because he was afraid of Johnny telling me what happened that night?

It doesn't excuse what Johnny did, but it explains why he broke up with me, why he felt he couldn't face me. Why he resents Nick so much for being with me.

'Let's say I believe you,' I say, another thought occurring to me, 'did Lana know?'

'She didn't,' Johnny says. 'Not until this week. All she knew was what you told her that night – that you saw me and Ness putting a case into Ness's boot. She had no idea what was in it, and she never openly asked me although I'm guessing she had her suspicions based on your conversation. I told her it was best for her not to know. I thought I was protecting Nick.' He turns to Ness. 'We both did.'

'It's true,' Ness says, 'Lana knew none of the details. Including what happened between you and Johnny that Monday night, even though, again, she may have suspected. But Nick did.'

I say nothing, still struggling to believe that my husband is the villain in all this. I can't bear for it to be true because I'm not sure I'm strong enough to survive more heartache. He's the one person I thought I could count on. 'How do you know it's Nick who inflicted those injuries on Carys?' I ask.

'Because I saw her lying dead in his bedroom with my own two eyes,' Ness says. 'Who else could have been responsible when he's the one she went home with?'

All she says makes sense, and now I feel faint, like I'm suddenly seeing stars, the full horror of the situation becoming clear in my head.

Chapter Seventy

Lana

Sorrento, Italy, Thursday, 8th August 2019

My sleep is disturbed, and I wake up in a cold sweat to find Johnny's side of the bed empty. Panic consumes me. Perhaps he and Ness have confessed everything to Marcus, or maybe Johnny couldn't take it anymore and has gone to confront Nick. Something I can't exactly blame him for; it's been a struggle not to have it out with him myself. I just hope he doesn't go too far and do something he'll regret. I can't hear any noise or shouting so perhaps I'm wrong. Maybe he's just gone downstairs for a glass of water. Even so, I tell myself I'd better go and investigate.

I fling off the duvet, grab some knickers, leggings, a sweater and trainers, slink out the door, not wanting to wake anyone, then tiptoe down the marble stairs. It's dark, unsurprisingly, not a sound to be heard aside from the natural creaks and moans of the villa which are made more pronounced in the still slumber of night. I first try the kitchen, but even before I enter the room, I can see that the light isn't on, telling me Johnny can't be inside.

Still, I flip the switch, just to check I'm right. Which I am. Instinct tells me to grab the carving knife I see lying in the dishrack. Only because, if I don't find Johnny in the villa I intend to explore outside, in case he's gone for a walk to clear his head. The dark scares me – you never know who might be lying in wait – so I need something to protect myself. But then I notice the block on the worktop is missing two knives. I'm holding one of them, but what of the other? A chill runs through me at the thought.

Having left the kitchen, I go and investigate the other ground floor rooms, my movements guarded, my senses on high alert, but find each one encased in darkness. In the main living room, I unlock the latch fastening the sliding doors leading out onto the terrace, pull them across, feel the early morning air in my face. It's still cool in comparison to the temperatures we had the first two mornings, with a sprinkling of rain, and I'm glad for my sweater. I cautiously step outside onto the terrace, leaving the doors slightly open to allow myself easy access back inside, take a left down the steps leading to the pool area, still wet and strewn with leaves and other debris that have been dislodged in the storm. Not that it matters. We'll be leaving later today – Johnny amended our flight home late last night – the holiday well and truly over.

No sign of him here either and now I'm really getting worried. The only other places I've not explored are the villa's vast gardens surrounding the pool, along with the main viewing point beyond it built into the cliff-face. I suddenly get a sinking feeling, fearful Johnny may have gone and done something stupid after all. But then I hear a noise, a rustling that seems to be coming from the palm trees standing like soldiers on guard the other side of the pool. I keep the knife low at my side, primed and ready for danger. Hopefully it's Johnny, but you can never know. And then I hear panting, movement, more rustling and before long a figure appears. I squint, recognise the face.

It's Nick. My heart stops, fear gripping me. Where's he been? What's he been up to?

He's the other side of the pool, but starts to walk around it, heading my way. I grip the knife tighter, my pulse accelerating.

'What are you doing out here at this hour?' he asks. He doesn't raise his voice, but there's a definite edge to it that frightens me.

In my mind, I see a face. A face I barely knew. I shrug the image away, tell myself to focus.

'I could ask the same thing.'

'I needed some air. You?'

'I was looking for Johnny, he wasn't in bed when I woke up. Thought he might have gone for a stroll. Don't suppose you've seen him?'

'No, sorry, I haven't.'

He's lying, I can hear it in his voice. See it on his face. Anger boils up in me. How I despise him for manipulating Johnny and Ness, for lying to them and to Padma, for pretending to be this decent guy, when all along he was far from that.

Closer now, so he's my side of the pool. Maybe thirty feet away.

I can't resist, can't hold back any longer. 'You need to come clean, Nick.'

'Come clean about what?'

'Please don't lie anymore, we all know. And very soon Padma will know too.'

Silence. And then he laughs. A low, disturbing laugh that terrifies me. 'Actually, she already does.'

I flinch. 'How do you know?'

'Because I've just heard Ness, Marcus and Johnny telling her.' He says this through clenched teeth, edges closer. 'Like you, I found Padma's side of the bed empty, so I came outside to find her. Heard them talking, telling her I killed that girl.'

'Marcus's sister you mean – she had a name! Carys. Just like she had a mother and a father who never knew what happened to their daughter. A mother who took her own life because the not knowing made her feel like she might as well be dead herself. You need to own up. You can't let Ness and Johnny take the rap for something that had nothing to do with the drugs Johnny gave you. You are to blame and you alone. Because you killed her in cold blood.'

'You don't know that, and you can't prove it. The DNA will be long gone by now. All that's left is a skeleton. The fact is, Padma saw Johnny and Ness put the suitcase holding her body into the boot of Ness's car. The suitcase which the police have now found. Padma remembers everything, it all came back to her six months ago during one of her therapy sessions, I heard her say as much.'

Fuck, that means she knows I kept our phone conversation the night before she lost her memory from her. Telling me what she'd seen Johnny and Ness get up to.

'She will tell the police what she saw,' Nick goes on, 'I'll make sure of it. And I'll convince her when she comes back to our room that they're just using me as a scapegoat. Making up some bullshit story because the police have found a body and they know their days are numbered.'

'What the hell are you talking about?' I say. 'Part of the reason Ness came here was to confess; she had every intention of telling Padma, of covering for you yet again, before the police discovered Carys suffered multiple fractures and blunt force trauma to her skull.'

'Again, it's just hearsay, Ness's word against Padma's. They can't even prove Carys was with me exclusively that night. And after Ness and Johnny have spent eighteen years lying to her, not to mention Padma remembering it was Johnny who knocked her out cold, who do you suppose she'll believe?'

God, how he sickens me. Still hanging on, clutching at straws, trying to manipulate the situation to his advantage. No way am I letting this piece of shit win.

'Not when I tell the police what I know,' I say. 'Something I should have done a long time ago. Only, like you, I was too selfish. Wanting someone I had no right to make mine because they were in love with someone else.'

I notice his eyes harden as he comes closer. 'What the fuck are you on about?'

'I think I know why you killed Carys. I think it's because she found something you were terrified of becoming public, and you couldn't take a chance she wouldn't talk. Isn't that the truth? Tell me, you bastard!'

Closer still and then he grabs me by my shoulders, so hard I start to scream, the knife still in my hand although it's an effort to hang on to it. I try to wriggle free, manage to angle the blade so as to plunge it into the side of his thigh. He yelps in agony, and I seize my chance to turn and run, but then he grabs my ankle and I fall, dropping the knife to the ground, banging my face on the tiled floor. It draws blood from my brow and bottom lip. I spit it out, my teeth throbbing, a searing pain shooting through my head. And then I hear voices. I glance up to my right, my chest aflame with fear, wondering if today is the day I will die, and see Padma, Johnny and Ness standing the other side of the pool.

'Stop it, Nick, let go of her!' Padma yells.

Nick pulls me up roughly, puts the knife to my throat.

Fear like nothing I've felt before stifles me. My children's faces flash before my eyes. This can't happen. I need to be around for them. They'll have no one if I die. I act on impulse, just as I spy Johnny racing around the edge of the pool. I swing my knee up, then kick Nick with my right foot deep in his groin with all the force I can rally. Distracted by Johnny running towards us, the kick catches Nick by surprise and he loosens his grip, giving me time to make my getaway. Praying to God I don't slip, I race around the pool to where Ness, Padma and Marcus are looking on in alarm, only to see Johnny launching himself at Nick.

I glance at the others, their faces aghast, all of them screaming at Nick and Johnny to stop wrestling, Nick still holding the knife. Locked in a tussle, their bodies are almost touching now.

'It's over, you can't get away with it,' Johnny says, 'we know you killed her. You fucking let us think it was the drugs when it was you who murdered her. You ruined my life, you bastard! I thought you were my best friend.'

Nick scowls. 'Do you expect me to feel sorry for you? The rich, handsome, privileged boy who got the girl, the money, the fancy lifestyle. I had nothing to fall back on.'

'Why kill her in the first place?' Marcus screams, tears in his eyes. 'What the hell had my baby sister done to you? You barely knew her for Christ's sake.'

'You lied to me, made me believe you were good and honest and true,' Padma starts walking towards Nick and Johnny now.

'Don't do anything stupid, Padma,' I mutter under my breath. 'He's not worth it. He's a slimeball, the lowest of the low, but he fooled us all.'

'But really, you are the worst of them,' she goes on, ignoring me. 'Selfish, cruel, manipulative and weak. You disgust me, Nick, and I thank God we never had children. Thank God I took those birth control pills. You belong in prison, but don't expect me to ever visit you. You are dead to me, do you hear! Dead!'

For a fleeting moment, both Johnny and Nick pause in their brawl, seemingly transfixed by the words of the woman they both love. And it's at this point that I catch Nick's eye, and in that split second he knows that I have the truth at my fingertips and won't hesitate to make it known to the world. Seeing his resigned expression, I think he might relent, admit what he did. But then, before anyone has time to think, he kicks Johnny in the stomach, before putting the knife to his own throat. It's as if Padma's words and my unspoken message have taken the fight out of him. As if he sees no point in living.

'I did it for you, Padma. It was always about you.'

'No, Nick,' I hear her cry. But it's too late. Everyone looks on in horror as he slices the blade across his throat before toppling sideways into the pool.

Chapter Seventy-One

Nick

Before
Oxford, England, mid-October 2001

Fuck me. She's more of a wildcat than I expected. Perhaps it's the booze we've both consumed, but no sooner have I unlocked the front door, Carys is pushing me inside, up against the wall, no longer the meek, bashful girl I cornered in the alleyway. I wonder to myself if it was all just an act, whether she was luring me in with her damsel-in-distress persona. Whatever the case, I don't care, I'm way too horny, and all I can think about is tearing off her clothes and fucking her. It's been so long, I need this. There's only so much jerking off to photos of Padma I can do. Right now, I need to be inside a woman, need to touch her in all those delicious places, feel her hand slide over my dick as I cup her breasts and make her scream with ecstasy. That's what I've seen Johnny doing to Padma, even though it kills me to see the pleasure he gives her. Especially when he goes down on her and she moans like he's taken her to heaven and beyond. Carys kisses me long and hard, and I feel myself becoming more and more aroused as our tongues explore one another. I slide my hand up the back of her top, delight in the touch of her soft feminine skin, and then her own hand wanders down to my crotch and begins to undo the buttons running down my fly, and I'm suddenly so hard I might burst. I ask her if she's on the pill and feel relieved when she confirms that she is – it saves the hassle and mood kill of going to find a condom. Before long, we're on the floor in the living room, naked. I push the coffee table aside with a strength that can only stem from wanton desire, then she moans as I penetrate her. She grabs the back of my head as I do, clasping chunks of my hair, and I randomly suck her erect nipples as I continue to thrust, imagining it's Padma I'm inside as I do. And then, after maybe a couple of minutes, I cannot contain myself any longer and find myself climaxing. She cries out too. I don't think she's pretending, she seems genuinely turned on, but you can never tell with girls. I'm breathing hard as I rest my chin against the side of her neck, and she lets out a sigh. It's always such a turn on having sex anywhere but in the bedroom, but I realise it can't have been comfortable for her with her spine drilling into the wooden floor. I raise myself up slightly, ask her if she's OK. 'Never better,' she grins, bringing my mouth back down to hers and kissing it hungrily.

I realise I'm still inside her. I pull away and slide myself out, then head upstairs to the bathroom to clean myself and pee. Having peed, I run the water for a while until it is cold, then splash my face, rinse my mouth, before jogging back downstairs to the living room.

But she's not there. 'Carys,' I call out, pulling on my boxers as I do. I notice her clothes are still on the floor. She's not in the kitchen either. 'Carys,' I repeat again. The house is small, and aside from the bathroom upstairs and the downstairs loo there're only two other places she could be – either Ness's or my bedroom upstairs. So

I trudge back up. Check in the bathroom again. Then Ness's room. But she's not in either, which leaves one remaining option. Just then, I'm sure I hear her voice. Is she talking to herself? It seems to be coming from my bedroom. I push open my bedroom door and find her sitting on the bed, a stack of photos meant for my eyes only lying beside her, along with her mobile phone. Had she been talking to someone on it? But why would she have brought her phone upstairs with her? I normally keep the photos hidden away in a brown manila envelope underneath my bed, but I realise to my dismay that, with Ness being away for the weekend, I must have left them out on my bed when I'd been leafing through them earlier. Forgetting that I might be bringing someone back here tonight.

'What the fuck are you doing?'

She looks up, startled. Guilt clouds her face. It's clear she's looked at the photos. Still images of Padma taken from my video footage: close-ups of her lovely face, of her undressing, checking herself in the mirror, brushing her hair. Touching herself. It's not the same as watching a video, but I wanted something I could print from my laptop and look at whenever I desired. I'm suddenly furious. What the hell gave Carys the right to snoop around my personal stuff? Like some stalker. I think she's a bit obsessed.

'How dare you poke around my things, you had no right!'

My voice is angry, mirroring the rage boiling up inside me. What if she says something to someone? What if she tells Johnny, assuming she recognises who Padma is?

'I wasn't sure at first, but isn't this Johnny's girlfriend? The guy who organised the hunt. Your friend who we were chatting to earlier.'

And there's my answer.

I feel sick, my culpability doubtless written all over my face.

'Look,' I say, 'it's…'

'It's not what I think?' She laughs. But it's more of a cackle, steeped with contempt and perhaps a tinge of bitterness. As if she feels wounded, betrayed. I see the tears filling her eyes, and it tells me she perhaps thought something more permanent might happen between us, that I might even be falling in love with her. It's an expression I recognise. Only because it's the look I see in the mirror everyday: the look of unrequited love.

'These photos are pretty sick, you know that?' she says. 'How the hell did you get hold of them? Are you spying on her? Do you have a camera hidden in her bedroom?' She motions to the laptop lying on my desk. 'Is it linked to that? Is that how you got them?'

I dart over to her. 'This is my room and you're trespassing, it's none of your business. I barely know you for Christ's sake!'

She gets up from the bed, her eyes full of hurt, but also a touch of contrition as the tears start to flow. She flings her arms around my neck. 'Oh, but I do know you, Nick. I think you're amazing. That we could be good together if you just give us a chance.'

I grab her arms and push her away more forcefully than I intended, causing her to stumble backwards. 'This was a one-time thing only. We aren't a couple. I'm in my last year and you've only just started. This will never work. Once I leave here, we'll never see each other again.'

Despite all I say, she persists. 'But just now, when we made love, I could feel how into me you were. I know you have feelings for me, as I have for you. Don't tell me you didn't feel a connection when we were chatting in the bar. After all, you picked me. Why would you do that if you didn't have feelings for me? We can make this work. Or I can quit my course, follow you wherever you like. I'll get a job, help with rent.'

'What the—?!' I say. There's an almost psychotic look in her eyes. Telling me that this is more than just a crush. She's infatuated, the way I am with Padma, only I manage to keep a check on my emotions. It's how I've been able to fool Ness all this time.

'I just want to be with you. You don't need these photos. Not when you can have me in the flesh. I'd do anything for you. Anything to make you happy, just say the word.'

I try a gentler tack. 'Look, Carys, I'm flattered. You're a beautiful girl, and tonight was fun, but like I said, it was a one-off. I'm just not interested. I'll be out of here in a few months, and you need to forget about me, find someone in your own year.'

Anger sweeps across her face. It's as if she's gone all *Fatal Attraction* on me. I realise I need to tread carefully, but I'm worried about those damn photos. How could I have left them out? Better still, I shouldn't have developed them, period. But I never expected anyone to go sneaking around my bedroom. Christ, I've not had a girl in my room in months.

'How can you live with yourself?' Her voice is suddenly hard. 'I saw the way you and Johnny were chatting outside the bar. He's your best mate, he trusts you, respects you, and this is how you repay him. Perving all over his girlfriend. Spying on her in secret. You have got a camera installed in their bedroom, haven't you?' I say nothing, but I feel myself redden, clench a fist at my side. 'It's sick, you know that don't you?' she carries on. 'What do you think he'd say if he knew what you've been up to? As for the lovely Padma, she'd be well within her rights to press criminal charges, I would have thought.'

'Stop talking,' I say. 'You need to promise me you'll say nothing. Not to Padma, not to Johnny, not to anyone.'

She pushes past me. 'I'm not promising anything. I thought you were different. Nice, kind, normal. But it seems I was wrong.'

Hearing her say this, I get the feeling something bad happened to her in the past. Involving a man.

I grab her arm as she marches past. 'Did something happen to you? Really, I'm not like that, let's talk, I'm a good listener.'

She cuts me a wary look. 'Yeah, that's what all the creeps say.' Still, I don't let her go.

'Get off me, I need to get out of here.'

'Promise me you won't say anything.'

She doesn't answer and this freaks me out. My head is reeling with a whole host of thoughts. What if she does tell Johnny? Or worse, Padma, my tutor group leader, or the College Master? And then, if she does, soon the whole college will know, and before long the entire university. And then I might not even graduate, I'll be jobless, may even go to prison. It'll be in the papers and my parents will be distraught, they'll disown me. My entire life ruined.

I try one last time.

'I'm not a bad person, and I'm sorry if this brought back awful memories for you. But you need to promise me you won't talk. A lot of innocent people could get hurt.'

She's discarded my shirt now, cast it aside like she's repulsed by it. She runs down the stairs, naked. I follow. Watch her start putting her own clothes back on. I scratch the back of my head in something of a frenzy, my head spinning, unable to think straight or decide what to do. All I know is that this can't get out.

'Shit, my mobile,' she says. Before I can stop her, she's raced back up the stairs to my bedroom and grabbed her phone, me chasing after her.

As I stand in the doorway, she makes to get past me, but I grab her arm. 'Get off me!' she shrieks. I can't bear to do this, but neither can I risk my secret coming out. I push her to the floor, pin her down with my left arm pressed hard into her chest. She's kicking and screaming now, writhing around like a wild animal. 'Get off me you maniac!'

I reach out and grab one of my jumpers lying on the floor from earlier, press it hard against her face. Her legs continue to thrash around under my weight, and I think I'm almost there, but she's stronger than I imagined, somehow breaks free, scrambles to her feet, makes it to the open door. I tell her to stop, to let me explain, but she's calling me a psychopath. She pauses at the top of the stairs, looks at me with a hatred that gives me chills.

'You're crazy, sick. People like you need to be locked up and I'm going to make sure that happens.'

I don't even hesitate in making my next move when she says this. It was dumb of her to pause. She should have carried on running. 'I don't think so,' I say with a calmness that surprises me. And then I do something I know is going to haunt me forever, but at the same time it is the only choice I have. There is no going back.

In one swift motion I place my hands on her chest and push her. Hard. In that fraction of a second, I watch her eyes become wild with surprise and fear as she trips backwards on the top stair and tumbles in one fell swoop to the bottom, hitting her head violently on the floor. And then she is still. My heart is racing as I stand there immobilised for a second or two. Then I rush down, check for a pulse. There is none, and neither, when I look at the back of her skull, is there any bleeding. Not to any part of her head nor, when I examine the rest of her, her body. That's good; it means it's all internal, less easy for anyone to pinpoint how she died. Also, less mess for me to clean up. I thank God the stairs and hallway are carpeted, no sharp edges to cut herself on. But just then, a wave of nausea overcomes me, knowing that this girl, this daughter, possibly someone's sister, is dead.

But I also feel relief. That my secret is safe. It's the thought I cling to, to stop insanity from kicking in. Even though I fear I've already passed that point.

But one question races through my mind like a speeding bullet: *how the fuck do I get rid of the body?*

I think quick. Realise my best option is to call Johnny. But he can never know the truth: that tonight I became a murderer. I must make him believe it was an accident. A cruel twist of fate of his own making.

Chapter Seventy-Two

Lana

Dorset, England, December 2019

I've moved myself and the children out of London. Close to Jess and Tim in Dorset. Away from Johnny's family, and the violent intrusion of the media.

We were all in shock after Nick killed himself. Padma had collapsed to her knees, screaming and shaking, all the trauma of the last eighteen years having come to the most horrifying crescendo, and in a way she could never have imagined. She'd allowed me to console her as Ness called the police, but I knew even then that she'd never forgive me for lying to her, even though she's agreed to keep my part in what went on a secret. For the kids' sake. It's more than I deserve. I don't blame her for sending those messages to Johnny. I can't imagine the shock she had when it all came back to her. It's understandable her wanting to torment him, to force him to come clean in the most twisted way possible; it's only natural to be drawn to the darker side of human nature when you discover the people who were supposed to have your back have been living in darkness for years.

The fact is, if I'd told her after she'd lost her memory what she'd said to me that night – about seeing Johnny and Ness putting a suitcase into the boot of Ness's car — all this could have been avoided. She and I could have gone to the police, forced Johnny and Ness to admit the truth, and Nick's crime would doubtless have been unearthed by forensics before he'd had the chance to manoeuvre his way into her life. Granted, it would have destroyed Johnny and Ness's immediate futures, damaged their families' reputations, but the point is, they didn't kill anyone, and in time, they would have got out of prison, recovered, made something of a life, if not the lavish ones they've led these past eighteen years, rather than be allowed to perpetuate their lie until it ate them up. Marcus, too, would have found peace. And perhaps his mother would never have committed suicide, knowing that her daughter had been brought home to her, that they could bury her, say goodbye properly. But I kept quiet. Partly because I saw Padma's amnesia, along with what she had seen that night, as a gateway into Johnny's life.

But also because of something else. Another reason I had no idea at the time would end up having grave consequences for us all.

Chapter Seventy-Three

Lana

Before
Reading, England, September 2001

'You're my sister?'

I stare in disbelief at the petite blonde girl sitting across from me in a café on Reading High Street, a ten-minute walk from my mum's house. She had somehow got hold of my email address – I suppose it's pretty easy to do these days – and sent me a message saying she knew my father and wondered if we might be able to meet up and have a chat.

My mother hasn't mentioned my father's name more than twice in twenty-odd years. He abandoned us before I was born, and so I can't entirely blame her for not wanting me to have anything to do with him. Over the years she's fobbed off any questions I've had about him, claiming she has no idea where he is or what he's up to, even though I secretly think she knows more than she's letting on. I despise my dad for wanting nothing to do with his child. All the same, curiosity has got the better of me over time and I've secretly tried to find out what became of him. I have one photo taken when he was young. I found it in Mum's dressing table drawer, and had a duplicate made on the sly. Obviously, he must look very different now, but as I don't even know his surname – it's my mother's maiden name on the birth certificate – my efforts to locate him have been pretty much a non-starter. I've often wondered how he could have deserted his own child, whether he regrets it. I guess, if he did, he'd have tried to contact me, and so because of this I've told myself repeatedly that I am probably better off without him. Even though, when I look at my friends, Padma especially whose father dotes on her, it's tough not to resent what they have. And it hurts deep inside. It hurts like hell.

So when this girl sitting across from me – Carys – emailed saying she knew where he was, although I had thought perhaps it was some kind of scam, or she wasn't quite right in the head, I couldn't resist hearing what she had to say. And I agreed to meet her in Reading, where I live, during my last week of the holidays, before I go back up to Leeds for my final year.

When we'd first sat down with our coffees, she'd told me she lived in Glasgow with her mother and father and was off to Oxford Uni next month. She also said she had a half-brother who was currently travelling in Oz but would be starting a training contract as a lawyer when he got back to the UK. I was tempted to tell her about my best friend who's studying at Oxford and who I visit quite regularly, but something held me back; the fact that I didn't know this girl I suppose, and was cautious about giving her too much information on my comings and goings or my friends', for that matter, just in case she was some kind of crackpot. She'd proceeded to explain how her mother had been previously married to her half-brother's father who lives down in Cornwall, and that she and her brother were very close. She'd also known for a while that her father too had been married before, a long time ago, but that he never spoke about his first wife. She said although she loved her father, he was a hard man, prone to hiding his feelings. The total opposite to her. One day, she'd overheard a conversation between her parents in which they had discussed the unborn child he had abandoned. She said she'd been shocked to hear this, but with her father not being the most approachable of men, she didn't dare question him about it. But one day she had plucked up the courage to ask her mother instead. Apparently, they're exceptionally close – the opposite of me and my mother, I couldn't help thinking to myself – and so her mother didn't feel she could keep the truth from her daughter given what she'd overheard. She told Carys all about the tempestuous relationship her father had had with Kathy Davis, my mother, Carys's father's first wife, and that things had come to a head three months into her pregnancy. He knew he couldn't be with her anymore, and so he had walked out, sometimes regretting abandoning the daughter – me – he never knew, but telling himself I had been better off not suffering the effects of their toxic relationship.

'My mother is a good, kind woman,' Carys assures me as I continue to stare at her across the table, 'and unbeknown to our father, she's kept tabs on you, tracked your progress, made sure you're OK. She showed me your photo, told me where you live. Gave me her blessing to find you. But she made me swear never to tell Dad.'

I'm in total and utter shock. How can I not be? But how do I know she's not lying? I ask her this very question and she pulls out a photo from her handbag. Of her and her father. Taken last year. Naturally he looks older, but there's no mistaking it's the same man I know from the single photo I have of him.

'As much as I love my brother, I always wanted a sister,' Carys goes on. 'To talk about girlie stuff – boys, periods, weddings and so on. And now, it seems I have one. I know it's a lot to take in, but please say you'll give us a go? Please don't resent me for having grown up with the father you never knew. I want us to be friends.'

Part of me wants to tell this girl I've only just met to fuck off. She comes across as such a goody-goody and that gets on my nerves. As does the fact she's had the father I always wanted to herself these past eighteen years. The father who didn't give a toss about me. But the fact is, I don't have anyone else. My mother is a shit mum, and my best friend is so wrapped up in her boyfriend, the guy I secretly adore, I worry I'll be left with no one. So how can I ignore this girl, my sister, so desperate to be friends with me?

So I find myself saying, 'Sure, let's swap numbers, keep in touch while we're at uni and perhaps we can visit each other during term time or hook up in the holidays?'

She beams at me when I say this, like it's the best thing that's happened to her, promises me she'll write, tell me how she's getting on at Oxford. Now's when I should tell her about Padma, my friend who's also there. But I hold off. The last thing I want is her meeting Padma and being overawed by her the way people tend to be. Right now, I'm the new and special person in her world, and that makes me feel important, like I'm number one in someone's life for once, and I want to hold onto that feeling for as long as possible.

We say our goodbyes, sharing a somewhat awkward hug, just because it's weird hugging someone you've only just met, and I walk her to the train station. She gets onboard but turns back to wave before the doors close. Says, 'I'm going to tell my brother about you when he gets home. I'm sure he'd love to meet you. He's the best.'

'Are you certain you can trust him not to tell our father?' I ask.

'Oh, yes,' she replies with an impish grin. 'Between us, he can't stand Dad. They've never seen eye-to-eye.'

Sounds like my kind of guy, I think to myself. 'What's his name?'

'Marcus,' she shouts back as the guard blows his whistle, signalling that the train is about to move. 'His name is Marcus.'

Chapter Seventy-Four

Lana

Dorset, England, December 2019

Johnny is out on bail, waiting to be sentenced. Naturally, the kids are devastated, and it's another reason, besides all the media intrusion, I left London. Josh is at that vulnerable age, and I worry that remaining in the big city, with all its various temptations, might send him off the rails, and to a dark place from which he'll never return. As for George and Erin, I feel sure they'll find comfort being around Jess, Tim and the kids. Me too, I guess.

Ness only has a few weeks to live and is receiving palliative care at home. In the end the courts ruled that it's not in her or her children's best interests to be punished at this juncture. I wouldn't have blamed Marcus for leaving her to die alone, but for the children's sakes, he's remained at her side. He's a good man, the best of human nature, putting the rest of us to shame.

I kept quiet, as I said, partly because, like Nick, I was blinded by love, by my desire for Johnny. A desire that knew no bounds. I saw Padma's vulnerability as my chance to get what I wanted, with no thought to the consequences. Even when I suspected he might have attacked her, having encouraged her myself to confront him. And at that stage, although I'd been horrified to hear from Padma on the phone, and then later on the news, about a fresher called Carys – the sister I had not long realised I had – having gone missing, I had no idea that Nick had anything to do with her death because she never mentioned the name of the guy she'd slept with when she called me that night. Plus, the photos she came across could have been of any female student. There was no reason to think they were of Padma. Despite the police later finding a spy camera in Padma and Johnny's room, I simply never made the connection, because Carys had only ever referred to finding naked photos of some girl. No specifics. And even though Padma had mentioned watching Johnny and Ness drive off with a suitcase, I couldn't be certain it had anything to do with Carys. I mean, why should it have done? Yes, she went to that hunt, but that didn't mean they'd killed her. Ness wasn't even around that weekend by Padma's own admission. Even though, I suppose, the fact that Johnny allowed himself to be blackmailed by me, on account of my phone conversation with Padma, should have told me he'd done something bad he couldn't risk coming out. But, like I said, I was set on making Johnny mine and I wasn't going to do anything to jeopardise his freedom or any chance of having a future with him. It wasn't until I overheard Nick, Johnny and Ness discussing Carys's supposed reaction to the drugs Johnny had supplied and which Nick said he had given her that I realised Nick was the one she had been with that night, and whose photos of Padma she had therefore found in his bedroom. This had horrified me, learning what a creep Nick had been, realising he had been infatuated with Padma long before they got together. It also hadn't quite rung true with me that Carys had died from a reaction to the drugs, just because she'd sounded perfectly fine on the phone. And it was something I almost told Johnny about before we'd all set off for Capri, but in the end decided against, for one, because I feared what Johnny might do, and two, because I couldn't bear for Padma to get hurt again, for our relationship to be tarnished, having only just reconnected with her. All this despite having been shocked to learn that Carys was Marcus's half-sister. The Marcus she had fleetingly mentioned when we'd met in Reading, but who I had never seen in any press coverage because my father had made sure he stayed out of it. It was only my father's face I'd seen on the news, and which I'd realised had got Mum so upset, even though, like the hard-hearted cow she is, she never told me the cause of her distress. Never mentioned that I was looking at my father.

Furthermore, Carys never showed me a photo of Marcus that day we met, and so I didn't think twice about Ness's new boyfriend having the same name when she first introduced me and Johnny to him. Eight or so years had passed, and there are lots of Marcus's in this world. Plus, he'd always professed to being an only child.

Before learning how Carys really died, and having overheard Johnny, Vanessa and Nick talking in the garden, I had appeased my conscience by telling myself that just because she'd chanced upon photos of Padma in Nick's bedroom, it didn't mean Nick had killed her. I'd tried to convince myself that he may never have known she'd found the photos, that she might have hidden them in time before he'd appeared, and so it could just as easily have been a reaction to the drugs as I had heard them discuss, even though, as I said, I'd found this explanation a little odd. But, of course, when Marcus had gathered us in the sitting room that Wednesday night and told us that Carys's body had been found, I'd panicked. Knowing I had concealed information from the police that could have prevented this kind and decent man from suffering eighteen years of heartache. And then, when Johnny told me the results of the post–mortem, I got even more of a shock. Realising that Nick must have found her with the photos after all, and killed her, later getting rid of her phone knowing she'd made a call to someone called 'Sis', me, which is how she'd programmed me into her phone when we'd exchanged numbers.

I should have told the police back then about the phone call I received from her that night. It's something I did do when we got back to the UK from Italy, via an anonymous note I am certain can't be traced back to me, and which has finally given Marcus and my father peace and the answers they crave. If I had spoken up, so much anguish could have been avoided. Padma would never have ended up with Nick and her life could have been so different. But when I saw my father's face on TV, full of sorrow for the daughter he'd wanted, acknowledged, helped raise, as opposed to me, the one he'd abandoned without a second's thought, it had stirred a cruel kind of pleasure in me. I had enjoyed seeing him suffer after all the years I had suffered without a father, and I had wanted him to be in pain until he went to his grave.

It's been the story of my life. The girl who only ever wanted love from the two men from whom she craved it the most. But Marcus can never know the truth. No one can.

That's one secret that's going with me to *my* grave.

A Letter from Alex

Dear Reader, I hope you are keeping well. Firstly, I just wanted to say a huge thank you for reading my novel. After all the months of hard work and editing, it really means the world.

This is my third psychological thriller with the fabulous Hera Books, following the publication of *She's Mine* and *The Loyal Friend* and I'm so thrilled to be publishing with Hera again. I started writing *The Final Party* in April 2022, two months before *The Loyal Friend was* published, and finished the first draft in August of the same year. I always love writing my books – it's why I'm an author (!) – but having been fortunate enough to have visited Sorrento and the Amalfi Coast on numerous occasions, I especially loved writing this one and immersing myself in the stunning setting, despite the darkness my characters manage to bring to such a beautiful part of the world!

I first visited Sorrento with my parents aged nine. They instantly fell in love with the area – everything from the culture, the history, the people and their relaxed way of life, not to mention its breath-taking beauty, while we also made some great Italian friends over the years, two of whom came to my wedding. It ended up becoming a home-from-home, I guess. So much so, it's where my husband and I got married in front of fifty friends and family back in 2007 in an outside venue close to one of the prime viewing spots I mention in the book. This in turn has enabled me to write authentically about the area, almost as if I can close my eyes and inhale the sights and sounds, visualise every nook and cranny of Sorrento's many cobbled streets, while bringing back many happy childhood memories.

It took me four months to write the book, and then another four months of editing to make it as perfect as possible with the help of my wonderful editors, Keshini Naidoo and Jennie Ayres. In the book it was my aim to explore and vividly portray the group dynamics, the interplay of class and privilege, the fact that everyone has light and shade to them and, more importantly, how holding onto secrets and guilt can almost destroy a person and have a knock-on effect on so many lives. Guilt, betrayal, revenge, lust – these are all darker traits of human nature none of us are immune to and which fester inside my characters, notwithstanding their false pleasantries and the seemingly idyllic holiday scenario they find themselves in, and for this reason I hope you found it a fast-paced, twisty and compelling read that kept you guessing until the end.

If you enjoyed *The Final Party*, I would be absolutely thrilled to hear your thoughts via a review, and which I hope might also encourage other readers to read it. It's so heartening seeing positive reader reviews; they are hugely inspiring and greatly appreciated in that they give me the encouragement to keep writing, as well as perfecting and improving my craft. Incidentally, if you enjoyed this book and haven't yet read my other books with Hera, *She's Mine*, published in August 2021, and *The Loyal Friend*, published in June 2022, I'd love for you to look them up. They're available at Amazon, Waterstones and all good online book retailers.

Again, thank you for your support on my writing journey and I hope you'll continue to follow me as I work on new releases.

You can get in touch on my social media pages: Twitter, Facebook. Instagram, LinkedIn and TikTok. Also, please visit my website for further information on my books, and latest news/blog posts. I'd love to hear from you if you'd like to talk about *The Final Party*, *The Loyal Friend* or *She's Mine*, or anything else for that matter. Without readers' support, we authors would be adrift; it keeps us going, drives sales and helps grow our readerships and so I hope you know how much I appreciate your time and trouble.

Warmest wishes and happy reading!

Many thanks,

Alex x

Facebook:
https://www.facebook.com/AAChaudhuri/

Twitter:
https://twitter.com/AAChaudhuri/

Instagram:
https://www.instagram.com/A.A.Chaudhuri/

TikTok Handle:
@alexchaudhuri0923

Linkedin:
https://www.linkedin.com/in/
a-a-chaudhuri-55a83524/

Website:
http://aachaudhuri.com/

Acknowledgments

I started writing this book in April 2022, two months before my second thriller with Hera Books, *The Loyal Friend, was* published, and finished the first draft in August of the same year. I loved every minute of writing *The Final Party*. Not simply because I adore writing psychological thrillers, but because the Sorrentine peninsula is an area I am very familiar with, and therefore it was a joy to transport myself back there via the magic of writing.

Writing is my passion, something I love to do more than anything else. But it's also hard work, and as with all my books, I've spent hours trying to make it the best version of itself and a book I can be proud of, and that will bring my readers joy. Having said that, this book would not have been possible without the help and support of the following:

My brilliant editors – Keshini Naidoo (Hera co-founder) and Jennie Ayres – two of the loveliest people I could ever have hoped to work with, and whose boundless enthusiasm for the book from the outset was so inspiring. I am so grateful for all your advice, insight and commitment to getting the book into the best shape possible, with no query of mine being too much trouble, and I feel very fortunate to have had the benefit of your guidance and expertise. You and the whole Hera/Canelo team have continued to be such a fantastically kind and supportive group of people to work with and a special thanks must also go to Canelo/Hera Managing Director Iain Millar, for your support, encouragement and faith in my books, along with Kate Shepherd, Francesca Riccardi, Thanhmai Bui-Van and Dan O'Brien for all your help on the publicity and marketing/production side of things, and for being such lovely people!

The copy editor, Phil Williams, for your incredibly helpful comments and eagle eye (!) and the proof-reader, Rachel Sargeant, for helping to make it as error-free as possible. I'm also very grateful to you both for saying such lovely things about it! Thank you also to Chris Shamwana at Ghost Design for creating such a stunning cover. I love all my covers with Hera, but this has to be my hands-down favourite. I'm so grateful for the time and effort invested by you and everyone involved – it was certainly worth it!

My wonderful agent, Annette Crossland of A for Authors agency, for reading the first draft in super quick time and, more importantly, for loving it!! You have been such a massive help through all stages of the book, as well as a constant source of support, friendship and encouragement. Thank you for taking me on eight years ago, for believing in my books, and never giving up on me. I will always be grateful for your kindness and faith in me.

Kirstie Long and Caroline Raeburn of A for Authors for reading *The Final Party* in its infancy, and for your selfless support, encouragement, and friendship. It means the world.

Danielle Price for reading an early copy of the book, for all your help, infectious enthusiasm and creativity on the promotion side (you are so super talented and I hope you know that!) and for being the kindest, most fabulous friend and supporter of my books over the years.

Sabine Edwards for your incredible work ethic, creativity and brilliance in organising my book launch event, and for generally being such a kind, lovely and supportive friend over the last four years.

Awais Khan for being such a wonderful, kind and supportive friend. You are always there to offer me such good advice, while boosting my spirits and making me laugh when all I want to do is cry! I am eternally grateful.

All the lovely and talented authors who read an early copy of *The Final Party*. I so appreciate you taking time out to read the book and for saying such nice things about it. Also a general thanks to all my writer friends – it's been so great to meet some of you in the flesh at festivals this past year, and I hope to meet more of you going forward!

The amazing book blogger and reading community on Twitter, Facebook and Instagram. I wish I had the space to list out all your names (!) but I hope you know how grateful I am for your selfless support with my books. With a special mention to The Squad Pod ladies, everyone on the *She's Mine* and *The Loyal Friend* book tours, Stu Cummins, Melissa Allen, Molly and Kim and everyone at Bookscape Books, Kelly Lacey, Simon Berwick, Shay Griffiths and Surjit Parekh. The same goes for friends and family who've supported me and my books over the last few years. It's such a tough, competitive industry, so I can't begin to express how much I appreciate you sharing my posts, buying and reading my books and spreading the word.

Dr Jacky Collins (Dr Noir) for all your help, advice and selfless support with my books. You are truly one of the kindest people in the industry and we authors are so lucky to have you in our corner!

Ayo Onatade for your incredible support, guidance and friendship over the last four years. Again, you really are one of the kindest people in the writing community, and I'm so grateful for all the help you've given me.

The CWA, Newcastle Noir and Capital Crime for your fantastic support over the last few years and for giving me such brilliant opportunities to promote my books and help them to reach wider audiences.

My two very special girlfriends – Chika Ripley and Priya Pillai – for always supporting me and my books, and for always being there to listen and raise my spirits when I feel low. I hope you know how wonderful you both are, the sisters I never had!

My husband, Chris, for being so patient, and for giving me space and time to write, and my gorgeous boys, Adam and Henry, who make me proud every single day. Love you all so much.

Finally, thanks to my parents, Mukul and Diane. I'm so grateful for your love and support with my writing. Dad, I'm not sure this novel would have been possible if you hadn't taken your colleague's advice and booked that first holiday to Sorrento all those years ago. Our holidays there formed some of the happiest memories of my childhood, and I will never forget them. xx